DAVID AXTON is the pseudonym of a journalist on the night editing team of the *Financial Times* in London.

His earliest interest in aviation was aroused at age three when living under the approach to RAF Manston, Kent, in the Cold War days, and catching the whiff of kerosene as USAF F84s and B47s landed.

The interest now manifests itself in occasional articles for the *FT* on business aviation and in flying training on Cessna singles.

A linguist, Axton is widely travelled in Europe and the US. Given the time, he enjoys walking, cooking and listening to Dire Straits. He is married with a teenage daughter and lives in west Kent.

Also by David Axton

STOLEN THUNDER

and published by Bantam

DRAGON JET

David Axton

BANTAM BOOKS
TORONTO • NEW YORK • LONDON • SYDNEY • AUCKLAND

DRAGON JET

A BANTAM BOOK : 0 553 40617 5

First publication in Great Britain

PRINTING HISTORY
Bantam edition published 1994

Set in Linotype Sabon 10/11pt by
Hewer Text Composition Services, Edinburgh

Bantam Books are published by Transworld Publishers Ltd,
61–63 Uxbridge Road, Ealing, London W5 5SA,
in Australia by Transworld Publishers (Australia) Pty Ltd,
15–25 Helles Avenue, Moorebank, NSW 2170,
and in New Zealand by Transworld Publishers (NZ) Ltd,
3 William Pickering Drive, Albany, Auckland.

Reproduced, printed and bound in Great Britain by
Cox & Wyman Ltd, Reading, Berks.

Special thanks are due to: Trevor King of Magec Aviation; Rich Rhodes, Mike Gray and Jim Butchard of FR Aviation; numerous people at British Aerospace Corporate Jets, but in particular Alan Piper, Mike Brown and John Horscroft; Graham Wilmshurst of Civilair, Biggin Hill, for a graphic demonstration of VOR navigation and the air traffic procedural approach; Ian of Chelsfield Motor Works for advice on electrical engineering; and Shari Daneshkhu of the *Financial Times* for her invaluable linguistic pointers.

This one is for Christine

AUTHOR'S NOTES

Naming aircraft

While this book was in preparation, British Aerospace sold its Corporate Jets division, which builds the 800-series and 1000-series models of what had been the BAe 125 (and which had started life in 1962 as the de Havilland 125) to Raytheon of the US, which owns Beechcraft, a Wichita-based leading producer of executive turboprops and small jets. Raytheon has renamed the two current production models the Hawker 800 and Hawker 1000, the name harking back to the British builder of the Second World War Hurricane fighter. I have chosen, in referring to the aircraft here, to stick to the older designations, BAe 125-800 and BAe 1000.

Foreign language spellings

Turkish spellings have not been rendered entirely faithfully. I have chosen to use diacritical marks where they are likely to be familiar to the Western reader – for instance, *ü* and *ç* – but, in the interests of minimizing confusion, have not attempted to use the soft g or dotless i.

In spelling Iranian place names, I have followed the style of *The Times Atlas* – hence *Elburz* instead of *Alborz* – except where an older spelling is likely to be more familiar – hence *Isfahan* instead of *The Times*'s *Esfahan*.

My apologies to purists.

PROLOGUE

Night wind muttered low on the bare Anatolian steppe and Darvish Aksoy knew his position was badly exposed to the soldiers hunting him.

He could handle this, though. Three weeks now he'd been on the run and he'd always kept at least one step ahead of the forces that were determined to destroy his movement; determined the way Darvish Aksoy was to overthrow the forces that opposed the will of God and His instruments; instruments like Darvish.

Darvish's picture was on every newspaper front page now. They said he was the most wanted man in Turkey. They called him a terrorist; they ignored the true terrorists, the men like Kemal Koz, head of operations of Merkezi Istihbarat Teskilati − MIT − the country's central intelligence organization.

Rana Tezcan was awaiting trial even now in Evin jail, Tehran; the girl Darvish was going to marry had been betrayed to the godless pragmatists of the Iranian government by Koz's henchmen in MIT. The bitterness of anger fuelled the hatred in Darvish's soul, and the will in his mind to overcome.

An owl called in the distance. The bleak landscape lay silent, but the soldiers weren't far away.

They would have traced him, Darvish knew, by the minibus.

He'd merged easily enough with the travellers on the big bus that had brought him to the town of Aykurt, but on the minibus to the village that had placed him within what he knew was walking distance of Ankara airport, he'd known he would stand out. Any stranger would. Aykurt was full of soldiers, full of Koz's brutal minions, and by now they would have questioned every driver of every minibus that had left the main bus station late that night. After that, it would be a case of questioning the villagers, and they'd have had no compunction about betraying a stranger. They'd had no means of knowing that this stranger was there for *their* good, to free them from the yoke of a misguided, secular, anti-Islamic state.

Imanin Yolu was the name Darvish and his followers had picked for their movement, the Way of Faith. For short, simply *Yol*, the Way.

There wasn't cover for a rabbit on this barren steppe and first light couldn't be far off. Darvish moved stealthily towards the glow in the sky to the south that he knew came from the airport.

Despite the cool of the summer night he was sweating in his brown lightweight suit and the shirt he wore with no tie. Ties were a Western invention; wearing one symbolized a fawning imitation of the opponents of God. Darvish wasn't a big man, five eight and skinny, light on his feet after a succession of childhood illnesses, and the bushy black moustache he wore looked like compensation for a frail physique.

It wasn't. Darvish Aksoy could be tough when occasion demanded, and physically more powerful than his build suggested.

Pale moonlight showed a domed structure half hidden amid wild pomegranate trees. A countryside well. Darvish was thirsty.

He kept the shadow of the low rise behind him. As he moved softly towards the well, his foot snagged in some unseen thorny growth. Darvish froze.

Two soldiers came out from behind the dome of the well, one with a rifle, one with an ancient British Sten sub-machine-gun. They were looking all round in the darkness. The breath stopped in Darvish's throat. A third soldier with a rifle came out from behind the well. He was the one with the radio backpack.

Darvish snatched out the gun from his waistband and squeezed his eyes to slits. If they used a torch . . .

The soldiers hadn't seen him. They began moving near-silently across his front, left to right. Darvish had both hands on the gun. It was a Beretta 70, chambered for 7.65mm, fully loaded, and Darvish knew at this range, hardly five metres, he could knock all three of them down but he couldn't do it silently.

Half of him wished they would give him the excuse.

His other half reasoned that where these three men were, there would be others by the score, and he couldn't take on a whole regiment. Even if he had that Sten in his hands he would have to run.

He couldn't believe it. They hadn't seen him, they were moving off. Lucky. All his life Darvish had been lucky, since the day he'd been born the youngest, only boy in a family of five kids, a rich Istanbul upbringing, school in Germany, language school in America. He stayed where he was, as if frozen. It was movement that would get him spotted. He waited while the soldiers merged slowly with the shadows. They'd moved round to his right, on to the shallow slope of the rise that hid the village, moving north, leaving him only the south as an option.

Well, that suited Darvish. The airport was to the south and that was what he wanted.

Stealthy again, Darvish crept to the well. He had the Beretta in his right hand, cocked and ready in case they'd left someone on guard. No, they wouldn't have boobytrapped the well. Any of the local farmers might be wanting it when morning came.

Inside, the darkness was like something solid. Darvish brushed his left shoulder against the rough stone wall – it was all there was to guide him.

He found the retaining wall, a single hewn stone's height above the ground. He put the gun away and knelt and then scooped blindly for the water. He drank.

When he emerged, the stars were fading. He hadn't much time now.

The road would be the next danger point.

Ten minutes of cautious movement and Darvish was there. He crouched on the edge of the road, listening, straining his eyes.

The sky shaded slowly to the charcoal colour of first light. Wind whispered in the scratchy grass at Darvish's back and no owl or animal called. The dawn air was chilly, dry like everything else deep in the centre of this miniature continent of Anatolia.

No cars came, no light showed. No sound came to warn Darvish of the soldiers; only, very distant from over the lonely hill, the faint, metallic wailing of the muezzin – the Muslim call to prayer – in the village that he'd used for his jumping-off point.

He crossed the road fast in a crouching run, one hand cupped over the pistol ready for a rapid draw.

In the shadows of the long grass south of the road Darvish crouched, eyes wide, breath shallow. Sweat prickled on his neck and forehead but his hand, close by the gun, was steady. Darvish was a man who had never in his life doubted the rightness of what he did.

Nothing.

He straightened and looked carefully all round. From the airport now he could see a flashing light that he knew must be on the top of the control tower, the highest building. To his right as he faced the airport – west of him – the gaunt cylinders of the cement plant silos stood silhouetted against the sky like some godless parody of minarets. East of him, hardly three hundred metres to his left, wooden scaffolding marked the skeleton of an unbuilt factory. There were lights here and there at the cement plant. None at the unbuilt factory.

Darvish began moving east.

He should have been feeling tired, he reflected, and the fact that he wasn't lent him a moment's jubilation. *I am not as other men are.* He was in hard condition, fit, yet that wouldn't have been enough by itself. It was the nervous intensity that drove him on; the conviction of his mission; the hatred for Koz and all his despicable servants, the drive for vengeance over Rana's plight. Willpower alone could drive Darvish Aksoy.

Light seeped into the sky. He was picking his way now into the edge of the building site. Piles of sand, heaps of aggregate for cement, stacks of breeze blocks, stacks of piping. A cabin stood, over by the road, with no visible light. Darvish relaxed a fraction. Over by the cabin he could see two Toyota pickups and a dump truck.

Either of the Toyotas would do.

Darvish scanned the airport. He could see right across it from here. In fact, he realized, this construction site wasn't even fenced off from the airport. No aircraft was moving yet, but Darvish could see the tiny headlamps of the servicing and loading vehicles as they moved slowly around the ramp. He could see the aircraft all right. On the righthand side, viewed from here, there were DC10s and Airbus A300s of Turkish Airlines' fleet, and, even bigger, the 747s of a couple of foreign airlines. Centre left, there were four or five Canadian-built de Havilland Dash 7s, the four-turboprop type that Turkish Airlines used on regional routes where the destination airfields were short or the runways were rough. Left of the Dash 7s were the light ones. Darvish couldn't tell the types precisely – they looked too small at this distance – but he could tell there were one or two single-prop or twin-prop types, aircraft that didn't interest him; and, among them, the ones that did. Even in this light he could make out the swept tail of at least one executive jet. Not the Lear 35 like his father's shipping company owned, but it didn't matter. The Lear wasn't the only exec jet Darvish knew well.

Still no sound anywhere on this site. Darvish turned and made his way quietly to where the two pickups and the dump truck stood beside the cabin, where the rutted little track from the road broadened into a sandy-muddy vehicle park.

He tried the door on the first Toyota pickup. Open.

Darvish peered inside in the darkness to see if the keys were in the ignition. Yes.

A puzzled voice at his shoulder said: '*Merhaba*'.

Darvish whipped round.

The man was a touch taller than him, solidly built, in a battered suit and light woollen sweater; evidently some sort of foreman; alone; his round, honest, Turkish face unsuspicious, uncertain. Dawn light gleamed on his eyes.

No need for the gun with this one. Darvish smiled, '*Merhaba*,' showing the expensively treated teeth in his gaunt, hollow face, and stepped closer to the foreman. With a practised thrust he drove a big knife up to the hilt in the foreman's ribs.

The foreman grunted and doubled over, astonishment on his face. Darvish ripped the knife out. The foreman made a gurgling noise, terrified, still on his feet but staggering, and Darvish rammed the knife into him again, suddenly scared that this man might be too tough for him. Still the man wasn't down: he was grappling for Darvish, his head bent over, the choking sound in his throat, and Darvish wrenched the knife out of the man's body and drove it back into him. This time as Darvish hauled on the knife it wouldn't come out, and he sprang back into the dim shadows, grabbing now for his gun.

The foreman dropped on to all fours with an amazing sound coming out of him. The knife hilt stuck down out of his body. Darvish dragged the Beretta out of his waistband and cocked it in a practised thumb movement.

The foreman rolled over on to his side. It took Darvish a couple of seconds to realize he was really dead.

He put the gun on safety and shoved it back. His hands were steady again as he crouched and grabbed the foreman by the shoulders. He shifted him roughly one pace. The man must have weighed a hundred kilos; Darvish weighed less than seventy. Crouching on one knee, he swung round.

The site workers would be here very soon now.

Darvish dashed to the dump truck. Speed mattered more than silence now. He swung into the saddle and started up. The motor caught with a roar that echoed off the stack of breeze blocks in the still morning.

If the soldiers heard that, they would simply think someone was starting work early. Darvish rolled the dump truck forward, leaning round it to see where he was going. He stopped just short of the foreman's body. He tilted the hopper. Then he rolled the dump truck carefully forward until the rim of the hopper nudged just under the dead man's shoulders.

There was a lot of blood. Darvish could see the dark stain as the dawn light grew. There was blood on the foreman's face as it ran from his open mouth. It didn't bother Darvish. He'd killed before and he would kill again if he had to; his way was *right*, and anyone who obstructed it was by definition a servant of Satan and had to be eliminated.

He tilted the hopper back upright, and the foreman's body slumped inside it. For a moment Darvish wondered about trying to get his knife back, but it had felt very firmly stuck that last time and he wasn't optimistic. He would get another knife, and meanwhile he still had the gun. He rolled the dump truck with its unsilenced motor bellowing right around the stack of breeze blocks and up to the pile of aggregate.

He up-ended the hopper. The dead man tumbled out like a rolled-up rug. Darvish reversed, lips tight, then swung the big, flat wheel to go forward again. This time he dug the hopper forcefully into the pile of aggregate; a full load. This would clear up any blood that had got on the hopper, but that wasn't the main reason he was doing this.

He backed off again. He went forward, up to where the dead foreman lay inert. Up-ending the hopper, he poured the whole load of aggregate over the body.

That would gain him time, that was all. But time was the main thing Darvish needed right now.

He drove the dump truck back bouncing over the uneven ground and parked it exactly where he'd stolen it from. He turned off the engine and went openly to the two pickup trucks. He looked inside both, turning on the batteries each time, and then got in to the one that had more petrol in it.

It fired up after two turns of the starter. Darvish put on the headlights and drove carefully through the building site, weaving amid the obstructions until he was clear of the site and inside the airport perimeter fence. He turned left and switched down to sidelights and drove about a thousand metres, far enough away from the building site to be inconspicuous. Then he cut the lights and engine.

Nothing was moving yet over by the terminal, but the approach was lit and the runway lighting stretched far out across the emptiness, little points of amber. Darvish settled down to wait for his moment as the sky grew colourless and the light flowed into the landscape.

He was good at waiting; he was good at judging his moment.

CHAPTER 1

Ankara, Thursday, 11 June, 0840 local

Working for a woman boss was one thing, Keith Cross thought, but the last thing he'd expected when he joined Dragon Jet Charter was to find himself flying alongside a woman captain.

Keith didn't rate himself as prejudiced, no more than anyone else from a grammar school background in the North of England; he just hadn't expected it. Dragon Jet's boss – known throughout the company as the Dragon Lady – was a lean, iron-grey-haired, fiftyish dynamo who ran three miles every day (well, almost every day) and signed herself Felix Wyer, which wasn't quite the way she'd been christened; and although her hands-on flying was restricted to piston singles on a Private Pilot's Licence, she knew a thing or two about how to market an expensive – if not necessarily luxurious – service in the middle of a recession. Keith's day-to-day boss in the cockpit of the British Aerospace 125 business jet that bore the fleet name *Dragon Rapide* was Captain Tamasin Masterson, a rather curvy lady from an old Cornish aristocratic lineage, whose combative nature made her look bigger than her five foot five. With only the hint of a grudge, Keith admitted Tamasin knew her way around executive charter flying.

Kerosene fumes hung in the clear morning air – a DC10 was running up its engines shrilly eight hundred metres away – and what little cloud there was was the scraps of summer cumulus twenty thousand feet over Ankara airport. Keith sauntered on his long legs beside Tamasin Masterson who, with her uniform cap at a rakish tilt on her short, dark hair, prowled through the dry heat

1

radiating off the white concrete. From the operations block to the executive aircraft park was a long walk, and even at twenty to nine Keith was noticing the heat. The square, black flight briefcases they each carried felt heavy in the weather.

Dragon Rapide stood where they'd parked it last evening. It was at the end of a small row of jets: a couple of Lears, a Cessna Citation II, *Rapide*'s sister aircraft *Dragon Spitfire*. Tamasin stood, briefcase in hand, as Keith reached to unlock the handle on the airstair door. She always got Keith to do that, as she almost always got him to do the pre-flight walk-round checks: Keith was a solidly built six foot one and he could reach where she couldn't.

'God!' Tamasin said, and stepped up inside the cabin with the agile grace of a panther. 'Didn't think it would've got this hot, this quickly.'

They weren't carrying passengers for today's forty-minute hop to Antalya, on the Turkish Mediterranean coast. Tamasin shoved her briefcase into the bottom of the rack, peeled off her uniform jacket, and hung it up. She took Keith's briefcase and stowed it for him. His eyes met hers as she reached for his jacket, three gold rings against her four, and she gave him that wide, snub-nosed smile of hers. Not for the first time, he wondered how she could make those big, dark eyes beautiful and desirable one minute, and then all cold efficiency the next.

She hung his jacket next to hers. Her white shirt had the four bars on the shoulder boards, matching her jacket cuff. It also had a neat little pocket on the upper left sleeve that today contained a couple of ballpoint pens and two screwdrivers, one straight, one crosshead.

'May I leave you to do the honours?'

'Sure,' Keith said.

He left Tamasin in the airless confines of the cabin. As he went back down the airstairs the DC10 was taxying out, distant, for its take-off.

Keith was twenty-three and counted himself highly

2

lucky to be sharing a jet cockpit with anyone, even this dauntingly competent woman – thirtyish, that bit older than him – with her American-based, Learjet-flying history and the rumours that sometimes surfaced about her, about some even wilder flying escapade in a bomber. Twelve months before, Keith had been creaking around the sky in a twin-prop Piper Aztec older than him; it was the Dragon Lady who'd given him the chance to fly jets.

Even in that Aztec, though, Keith knew he'd been a source of immense pride to his parents in the dull brick house on the edge of Scarborough that they'd bought when the council put the houses up for sale. His dad was just an ordinary plumbing and heating engineer, but Keith was proud of him.

Keith brushed the back of his hand through the sheen of sweat on his forehead and looked up at *Rapide*. Simple colour scheme: keel, unpainted, natural metal; red cheatline; white upper surfaces, including wing and horizontal and vertical tail; and the small dragon logo on the vertical tail, red in a red-bordered square. The aircraft name was lettered in red immediately to the right – aft – of the airstair door.

Rapide had been here in Ankara as a relief aircraft. Three weeks earlier, *Spitfire* had had an encounter with a four-kilo white stork that had left its righthand Garrett TFE731 turbofan too upset to be interested in propelling British Aerospace engineering any further through the atmosphere, and the jet had been grounded while Garrett sent a spare engine over from the States. *Rapide* had dashed to the rescue from Dragon Jet's base at Biggin Hill, on the south-east rim of London, and taken over *Spitfire*'s contracts while the latter recuperated. You see lots of white storks in the sky over Ankara, but Keith never looked at them the same way any more.

Keith fleetingly thought of Felix Wyer. She'd started the company with two early-series 125s and now Dragon Jet had four on its own strength and two that it operated on behalf of other corporate owners.

It also had four Dassault Falcon 20s, a rather different sort of executive jet, but that was another story.

The first thing that had happened to the two original 125s was that they'd been christened: *Dragon Rapide* and *Dragonfly*. It was a harmless enough fad on the part of the Dragon Lady that she didn't like soulless numbers on her aircraft, she preferred a name. She'd been delighted when she discovered that de Havilland – which had designed and built the jet at Hatfield, north of London, and first flown it in 1962 – had originally dubbed it the Jet Dragon, a name that evoked the twin-prop biplane Dragon and Dragon Rapide of the 1930s. The romance enthralled her. She even had the cabins decorated in a style that conjured up the more leisured pace of life in the years before the Second World War.

Or the way she thought it had been, Keith thought sourly as he started the walk-round.

Since then, *Dragonfly* had been flown to the end of its useful life and been taken off register, and *Rapide* was the only one left of the first two Dragon jets.

Only two things on *Dragon Rapide* told you this was anything other than an ordinary early-series BAe 125.

The cigar-shaped blister on the top of the fin was the one that stood out. It took sharper-than-average eyes to spot the way the keel fairing – the bulge under the fuselage that carried the wing spar slung underneath so as not to bark the passengers' shins in the cabin gangway – extended aft further than on a normal 125.

The blister on the fin housed the antenna for a radar warning receiver. The extended keel fairing was home to a chaff launcher, to hide the aircraft from radar, and a flare dispenser, to deceive infra-red-guided missiles. *Rapide* was a quick-change, dual-purpose aircraft.

Jerry Yeaver was the man who'd built those mods and got them past the sceptical eye of Britain's Civil Aviation Authority. *Yeaver*, to rhyme with *favour*. Jerry Yeaver was an ex-US Air Force captain and his degree was in aeronautical engineering. He'd done the British Aerospace course and these days he worked as Felix Wyer's chief engineer. Ex-B52 bomber aircrew, so the rumours said.

Down the flight line, *Spitfire*'s pilots were going through the cockpit checks. This was an 800-series aircraft, much more modern than *Rapide*. Today *Spitfire* was off to Cairo.

Methodically Keith went round the old 125's nose. Panels undamaged. Pitots clear.

Turbine noise whined through the air as the first of *Spitfire*'s Garretts spooled up. In the lefthand seat in the cockpit, Tamasin got on with the most important action of the flight, hooking Buster by the collar over the peg behind the seat that was really meant for hanging the headset on. Buster was a white fluffy toy rabbit, a present from a school friend on her seventeenth birthday – the day she'd flown her first solo – and he'd been with her on every flight she'd made since.

She glanced back towards the electronic warfare operator's station, behind in the cabin and on the right. Dials and triggers and the big spectrum analyser screen. She could just imagine the fun Jerry Yeaver had had, putting that lot together.

The spectrum analyser screen read off signals from the RWR atop the tail so that you could tell the wavelength of the radar pulse painting you. Jerry hadn't managed to lay his hands on the sort of computer he was used to from his B52 days, one that would tell you straight away whose the pulse was. Instead, you had to do it manually; but, to help, Jerry had taped a list beside the screen giving you the likeliest suspects.

The knobs were for playing sneaky tricks with the return radar wave. The triggers were for the chaff and flares. Rather him than me, Tamasin thought as she watched Keith carry on round the nose to the starboard leading edge.

Spitfire started taxiing.

Tamasin put the one-million Aerad ME1 navigation chart on the clipboard and started working out her headings with the computer. This flight was going to be a milk run, 211 nautical miles down airway VW77D, with nothing but a bit of cumulus at 20,000 and a surface wind of six knots at 295 degrees.

Spitfire was at the holding point for zero three left, the new runway they'd added recently, parallel with the old one.

Tamasin was testing generators, beacons, flap drives. She broke off now as *Spitfire* started its roll. It went against pilot nature not to watch a colleague flying a take-off. The jet accelerated, small on the expanse of the airfield, and its nose came up. It lifted cleanly into its element.

Tamasin went back to her checking.

A pickup truck came in sight, over by the construction site. Dust drifted as it approached at speed, and Tamasin gave it a glance, lashes drooping critically over her eyes. She'd been listening to the background radio chat and she hadn't heard anyone clear it to cross the runways. She thought: typical sloppy Turks. Yet the thought was unfair to a generally pretty efficient bunch. She started the batteries. Satisfied, she ran up the auxiliary power unit. The APU was a miniature jet engine and they used it to start the turbines on the main engines.

Keith came up the airstairs with his checklist and ducked stooping into the cabin. 'No need to keep this thing on, is there, if we're just going to the Falcons?' He tugged at his tie, an encumbrance in the warmth.

Tamasin pulled a face. She'd been brought up on the idea of executive jet crew looking efficient as well as acting efficient. 'Well, it isn't going to look very good . . .'

Keith looked put out, but he wasn't going to argue with his captain. Suddenly Tamasin sensed male unhappiness over a woman captain, and for an instant her eyes flashed. Then she contained her anger. You had to be able to contain your anger, to fly any aircraft safely.

Keith turned back to close the airstairs door. The APU whined thinly.

The pickup from across the airfield swung close around

Dragon Rapide's nose. It swerved towards the wingtip and halted just clear of it, three yards from where Keith was stooped in the cabin doorway. Keith stared.

A man threw open the pickup door. He was a skinny five foot eight and he wore a brown suit of what looked like a Turkish cut, and no tie. It was a popular dress style, but the suit was looking battered, mud on one knee, some dark spatters on the lapel. He grinned up at Keith from a thin, hollow-cheeked face with a big black moustache and a lot of dark stubble.

'Hello,' Keith said uncertainly.

The skinny man walked unhurriedly to the foot of the airstairs. He had a sickly look about him. The only thing about him that suggested anything but plain insignificance was the strength of purpose visible in his stride.

He smiled. He said in English: 'Take me on board.'

Tamasin couldn't hear him. The APU was working, and she turned, impatient, wondering where Keith had got to.

'Sorry, pal,' Keith said. He was a toughly-built man and for a moment it crossed his mind to get physical; but he didn't think he'd need to. 'We're going to Antalya.' He didn't yet know what to make of this.

The skinny man stepped on to the airstairs. 'I am not asking you,' he said evenly, just loudly enough to be heard. 'I'm telling you.'

Unhurriedly he pulled a Beretta 70 single-action automatic out of his waistband. He cocked it and pointed it at Keith.

CHAPTER 2

Near Biggin Hill, Thursday, 11 June, 0600 local
To anybody burgling Rob Pilgrim's first-floor flat in
Bromley, south London, the only obvious clues to his present and past lives would have been the jacket on the coat
rack with the co-pilot's three gold rings and the painting
on the living room wall, above the gas log fire. It showed
an RAF Vulcan delta-wing bomber, painted in camouflage
colours for low-level intrusion, against a stormy sky.

It was six. Rob rolled out of bed. His mornings followed
a routine because it was efficient on time that way; his
checks at every stage of a flight in one of Dragon Jet's
executive aircraft followed routines, too.

Drizzle fell thinly. Not bad vis for the take-off, Rob
thought, and above cloud it would be nice in the sun.

The radio prattled away as he started shaving. He
looked at the face that looked back at him. You'd think
anyone could walk all over the owner of that face, until
you saw the character in that quietly determined wedge of
jaw. Unruly dark brown hair, not too much grey through
it – not when you knew he'd be fifty in a couple of years –
and the hairline receding a bit; wind-reddened cheeks, a bit
hollow; calm, dark eyes, still clear now that he'd cut right
back on alcohol; and without much fatigue bagging, even
after stopping up late over a letter to a fellow ex-RAF pilot,
in the Gulf now. It was still a point of pride to Rob Pilgrim
that he had perfect eyesight, even for close work.

He slung his raincoat onto his shoulders, jammed his
cap on his head, picked up the flight briefcase that always
stood by the door, and went down the bare stairs to the
hallway with its post boxes.

Rob got a bank statement, a mailshot, a TV licence

reminder and a postcard from Kate in Bali. Nothing from Azra Tabrizi, but by then Rob knew he wouldn't be getting anything from her; he just never stopped hoping. Kate was Rob's ex-wife. They'd divorced when he'd still been on Vulcans and now she was married to a man who'd made Air Commodore at a sickeningly young age and was destined for greater things yet; and whenever they went somewhere exotic on holiday or she went with him to some high-ranking conference she would send Rob a card to remind him of what he hadn't succeeded in doing for her.

The flats resembled a modern brick cube with all the charm and atmosphere of an empty bean can. The old MG Midget was red, the right colour for an irresponsible small sports car. It was practically Rob's sole concession to bachelor living and it made a neat fit for his wiry-tough, slightly built five foot nine.

He backed out. Whenever he got in this car it reminded him of the Midget that Azra Tabrizi had owned before she went back to Iran. That car of Azra's had been a real old wreck, and the only time Rob had attempted to help Azra make it go, he'd discovered that she'd had so much practice at mending duff bits of ancient MG, she knew more about it than he did. But she'd accepted it as normal that a man should want to help a young woman with her looks.

He hadn't so much as kept a picture of her. They hadn't been lovers – they'd never been to bed together – they'd just enjoyed one another's company. Rob had had affairs in the years since Kate, and they'd always been with women much closer to his own age; with Azra he kept his meetings strictly platonic, really because of the age thing. He liked her a lot but she was far too young for him; he didn't want to mess up a promising young woman's life.

Rob shoehorned the Midget into a gap in the traffic.

He would always have that mental picture of Azra Tabrizi, though. Five eight, almost his own height, slim and curvy with the olive tan and the long dark hair framing

9

her classical oval face with the big, gorgeous eyes. Brainy and talented, too; like her sister Bibi – the one Rob had got back in touch with – who worked as a junior doctor at Lewisham Hospital.

And now Azra was out there and out of touch, and all her English possessions sold off and gone.

The first thing Rob had done when they bumped him up from Flight Lieutenant and ushered him out of the air force on a Squadron Leader's pension was to get a job as a salesman. He'd hated it. After a bit he found himself managing a riding stable, and one day a very beautiful young company solicitor had turned up and hired a horse. Rob had taken her for Indian. Her impeccable English in the very county delivery, so confident it was almost high-handed, simply added confusion. She'd turned up again the day Rob put in his notice after getting a job as a co-pilot with Dragon Jet; he'd flown Dominies, the RAF's adaptation of the BAe 125 executive, after coming off Vulcans. Rob had half-jokingly suggested a meal out to celebrate; he almost fell through the floor when she accepted like a shot.

Rob drove down by the college entrance for the road to Biggin Hill.

Getting Azra to talk about herself hadn't been difficult.

'My cousin in Iran flies jets,' she'd said one day.

'Oh, yes?' Rob had prompted.

'Moussa Rezania. They say he's one of the best F14 pilots they've got.'

Once, imperial Iran had had eighty F14s, the high-tech, highly capable US-built swing-wing dogfighter. Only a handful were still flying, no-one in the West knew for sure how many.

'I was in Iran once in the Shah's days.' Rob narrowed his eyes. 'What age is this cousin of yours?'

'Thirty-seven.'

His memory was immediate: the exercise they'd flown with the Iranians, old Vulcans against newer F4s, F14s, and the wily British had sneaked in on their targets at terrain-hugging, bone-shaking height, and for Rob's bomber it had been touch and go against an aggressive young Iranian, confident of his F14 even though he hadn't finished his type conversion training on it. He'd met Moussa afterwards at the formal dress dinner, 20 years old in 1977 with fire in his eyes.

'What happened to him when Khomeini came in?'

What had happened to many of the Shah's expert pilots was that they'd been stood against a wall. Partly that accounted for the Iranians' dismal performance against Iraq after 1980.

'Oh, he was always a very committed Muslim.'

So that was the source of the fire in those eyes.

Azra's father, dead now of leukaemia, had been a wealthy man; an arms adviser to the late Shah. Wealthy in Iran in the Shah's days had been seriously wealthy, and at first Rob had been inclined to take some of the tales with a pinch of salt.

Then after some months Azra had taken him to a family reunion at her mother's place in Redhill, the beech and maple downland of Surrey. That was when he'd met Bibi, and their mother, Mansoureh Tabrizi, a beautiful and quietly sad widow whose English wasn't up to her daughters' standards, and bits of the family history started coming out. It added up.

The traffic light on the roadworks was turning red but Rob nipped through.

The wealth was there all right. Much of it, anyway; there was muttering about property and heirlooms still in Iran. Old Tabrizi had seen the writing on the wall before the Shah had. By January 1979, when the Shah finally flew out of Tehran, Tabrizi had much of his wealth tucked away in Swiss bank accounts, and he and his family had been safely out of the country. Rich families that didn't have such forethought had suffered badly.

But you can't move houses abroad, you can't move estates. Some of it was still nominally in the family; but to get possession they would have to go through the courts in Iran. No-one had seen fit to start that process yet.

The drizzle wouldn't turn into rain but wouldn't stop splattering on the windscreen, either.

Then there'd been recession in the UK.

*   *   *

As recession took hold, most of Azra Tabrizi's company were made redundant, including Azra. Moving in with her mother in the big house amid the beeches, she found Mansoureh pining for her homeland.

Traffic was speeding now, over the brow and down into the dip and up to the green. Rob Pilgrim glimpsed the weathered white clapboard of The King's Arms and glanced at his wrist-watch. Not quite late yet.

Things in Iran weren't the same any more. Back in the early '80s it had been horror and bloodbaths, and Mansoureh knew families whose 14-year-old kids had been arrested in the afternoon in a demo and shot at dawn next day, and the first the parents knew about it was when the regime rang them up to fetch the bodies. These days in Tehran, common sense seemed to prevail.

Rob turned left and drove into the executive section. At the gate he showed his pass, then drove along the ramp past the two Cessna Citation jets and the King Air and Cheyenne twin-turboprops standing rain-glossy on the wet tarmac, up to where his own jet stood outside the Dragon hangar. *Dragon Tempest* was a 125-800, one of two current production models.

His captain was there. Melvin Trail was from Los Angeles and had flown F105s in Vietnam, F4s in Laos in the early '70s and Boeing 747s across the globe. With his clear, wily eyes and the white in his beard giving him the air of some old-time master mariner, he always got the passengers eating out of his hand; none of them ever guessed he was the most disreputable old crook in the company.

'Hi, Rob,' Trail grinned, looking up from his charts and his weather faxes. 'If you think that's rough out there, take a look at what it's like over Belgium.'

'I can guess.' Today was a company flight, Antwerp, then Cologne, then Mannheim, and back.

'You wanna go check the plane?'

Trail was filling out the flight plan form as Rob went back down the stairs in his raincoat.

The plan Mansoureh and Azra had brewed up was to sell up in England and move back to Iran, to the Rezania family town of Roudabad, some hundreds of kilometres east of Tehran. The simple life, that was what Mansoureh needed.

The head of the town of Roudabad these days was Mansoureh's brother – Azra's uncle – Ardeshir. He was a *hojatoleslam*, a senior cleric, and a mullah who, like Khomeini himself, traced his lineage back to the Prophet Muhammad.

The airstair door up to *Dragon Tempest*'s cabin was the sort that doesn't quite reach the tarmac when you pull it down. Rob hunched his shoulders and climbed in, unscrewed the control lock and tested the battery master. Then he climbed back out and started the inspection.

Drizzle touched cold fingertips to Rob's neck. He remembered the shock he'd had when Azra told him.

He hadn't mentioned her looks. What he'd pointed out was that with her talents and training and ambition, and particularly with her Western upbringing, the last thing she needed was life in a country that locked up its womenfolk and hid them under chadors when it let them out for a run.

That wouldn't happen, Azra had answered with a hard smile in her big, glittery eyes. She would go to Tehran and study Islamic law and meanwhile she would use family money to hire a lawyer and go to court to get possession of the house and land in fashionable north Tehran that she'd inherited from her father. To Rob she'd sounded really convincing.

13

Wingtip, security. The metal was wet. Starboard navigation light, security, check colour: green. Aileron, full and free movement.

Of *course* I'll write, she'd said, *silly*! Rob promised to write, too. If there was one thing Rob was good at, alone in that flat, it was writing letters. It puzzled him when the weeks became months and there was nothing.

Maybe he'd taken the address down wrongly, he'd thought, and that was when he'd phoned Bibi to check. Dr Bibi Tabrizi hadn't gone to Iran; she'd poured any amount of derision on that idea.

Port leading edge slats.

The address checked. She's been complaining, Bibi grinned down the phone to Rob, she says you must be lazier than she thought if you haven't written her a single word yet.

Rob said, *she what*?

Port rear fuselage, panels undamaged. Wing root, security. Flap tracks, undamaged. Movement distracted Rob, and he glanced over as Trail walked through the rain from the hangar mouth and exercised captain's privilege by hopping up promptly into the cabin. Anne, the stewardess, was with him, wearing lots of make-up, and smart in her crisp blouse and skirt. Then the Ford Granada was there with their passengers.

They were crossing the few paces from the car to the airstairs as Rob finished the checks, four engineer-salesmen in smart suits with briefcases. Rob followed the passengers up the airstairs.

It was pretty obvious what was going on. It made Rob's blood boil, the idea of religious fundamentalists thinking they had a right to intercept people's post.

It's nothing to do with religious fundamentalists, Bibi had told him wryly, it's a hillbilly priest with a bee in his bonnet and too much local power; real Islam doesn't treat its cats like that, never mind its womenfolk. All the same, she agreed with Rob. It was

14

desperately worrying to think of Azra in this sort of fix.

Then between the two of them, Bibi and Azra cooked up a code, a letter within a letter that the self-appointed censor of Roudabad wouldn't spot.

Rob hung up his cap and raincoat and jacket and climbed past the throttle quadrant into the co-pilot's seat. He turned a page in the checklist and read off the items while Trail ran his fingertips over the instrument panel. Trail's fingertips were faintly yellow but the nicotine had been mixed lightly with high-grade hash. Rob had never caught him smoking on a flying day, which was some relief.

Trail twisted round and set the auxiliary power unit running.

The first coded message Bibi had received from Azra said she'd had enough and she wanted out. There were two main snags. A woman in Roudabad needed a male relative's permission to travel, and anyway Hojatoleslam Ardeshir Rezania had Azra's passport.

'Ten minutes to our air traffic slot,' Trail said in his lazy Los Angeles drawl. 'We'll roll in five.'

Rob twisted and grinned up at Anne. He could see the reason for the make-up. Anne was looking tired. She'd been married almost four months to a lusty young Spaniard who mended Saab cars at a nearby garage. 'Want me to do the safety briefing?'

'You're an angel.'

Rob swung up and ducked through the cockpit door. So much more space on a thing like this than you got in a Vulcan. He pushed past the curtain and smiled at the passengers, his three gold bands on his shoulders.

'Good morning! Have you been on this type before?'

Two of them had, two of them hadn't.

The other, more worrying, thing in Azra's coded message was that she suspected there was trouble coming. Big trouble.

'Well, you'll find it's much like an airliner in miniature.

15

Here's the emergency exit, over the wing on the starboard side. If we lose pressure, there'll be oxygen masks drop from the ceiling like so. Life jackets . . .' It had never been like this on Vulcans.

CHAPTER 3

Ankara, Thursday, 11 June, 0902 local

Craning forward, Tamasin Masterson could see the pickup parked just off the port wingtip. They could clear it if they wanted, but it was damned annoying and she wanted Keith to shoo off whichever bonehead had parked it there. She twisted the other way, poking her head into the cockpit doorway.

'Keith!'

Keith backed into the cockpit and bumped his head in the doorway. Surprise widened Tamasin's dark eyes as she realized the man from the pickup was aboard the aircraft.

'What's going on?'

Keith said in sober Yorkshire, 'Look, this guy's got a gun!'

Tamasin wrenched around.

*　　*　　*

The skinny man was standing confidently at the top of the airstairs as if he'd spent most of his life aboard executive jets. His smile became a little laugh that suggested nerves. Tamasin couldn't believe what she was seeing.

'Right, now you will close the door and not talk on the radio and then we'll take off.'

Her lips parted, Tamasin didn't move.

The skinny man knew both the pilots would be paralysed with shock. He took the advantage.

'If you use your radio, I will kill your co-pilot.' He hadn't expected a woman in here any more than most of them did, but he knew enough to tell which one was the captain.

17

Anger more than fear sparked in Tamasin's eyes. 'But I'll *have* to use radio! I haven't got my clearance!' The tan over that fine, aristocratic bone structure was a legacy of her years in the US South-west, but now she was pale under it.

'Then wait. Use your radio when your co-pilot finishes closing the door. See, I will go into the cabin.' He backed off but he kept the Beretta levelled.

Helpless, Keith turned to Tamasin. His bulk jammed the cockpit doorway.

'Do as he says,' Tamasin said grudgingly. Maybe while these two got on with things she might think up some way of getting out of this.

Keith lumbered forward. He latched the door. He hadn't expected to find his hands shaking this way. In the corner of his eye, the skinny man scrutinized him while remaining aware of what Tamasin was doing in the cockpit.

'Good,' he nodded. 'Now you sit down.'

Unhappily, Keith turned his back on the gun. He scraped his knee on the edge of the instrument panel as he levered himself into the righthand seat. The gunman paced forward smoothly. He looked from one to the other of them.

'Now you take off.'

Angrily, Tamasin said: 'I'm not going anywhere until you put that gun back on safety!' Too much could happen that might jog a hand.

The skinny man looked sulky. He set the safety but he didn't put the gun away. Tamasin didn't still really doubt that she could handle this. Good pilots deal in confidence, not self-doubt.

Keith was pretty sure they were dealing with a lunatic. He swapped a glance with Tamasin as he fastened his harness. Her dark eyes held a dangerous look.

'We better take off,' Keith muttered. 'He'll not shoot us once we're in the air.'

'Suppose you're right,' Tamasin said grudgingly. She

18

looked around at the gunman. 'Listen, I'm going to call the tower and get runway and wind details and then get my airways clearance to Antalya. Then we're going to finish the cockpit checks, then start the engines, then taxi out. Your English seems to be pretty good. Just listen carefully to what I say on the radio, because I'm not going to try any clever tricks and I don't want you thinking either of us is up to something when we're not. All right?'

Sunlight made the cockpit bright, catching the tiny unevennesses in the grip of the ram's-horn yoke that always reminded Tamasin of bicycle handlebars. She glanced at Buster, but he wasn't bringing them much luck this flight.

With the skinny gunman poised in the doorway the cockpit felt small and crowded. Keith couldn't believe the man would actually shoot, but still he felt scared.

'All right,' the gunman said, and gave his little nervous laugh again. His brown suit had torn threads in it.

Lips pursed with that understated make-up on, Tamasin reached right to reset the radio frequency, the tuner tiny between her fingertips. She listened out on the tower frequency for a gap in the chat to call in and get her clearance.

*   *   *

She taxied *Rapide* briskly. The tower hadn't realized; there'd been no way to slip a coded message through. Maybe when they got airborne she could set the transponder code for hijack.

On the taxiway the jet rolled with an undulating motion. With the engines at the back, the cockpit and cabin were quiet.

At the holding point, Tamasin set the parking brake. 'Ankara, *Dragon Rapide* holding for zero three.'

'*Dragon Rapide*, Ankara, you are cleared for immediate take-off.' The controller's voice reached them over the cockpit speakers, distorted through the fizz and splutter.

No more bright ideas. Tamasin released the brakes.

She steered around on to the end of the runway. Black streaks smeared the threshold bars. '*Dragon Rapide*, rolling.' No need to run the engines against the brakes, on this size of runway. She steered on to the centreline and pushed the throttles fully forward.

At the edge of her eye, the gunman had his pistol loosely at his side. The jets wound up to a soft screech behind them and the deep roar filled the cockpit as *Rapide* accelerated.

With gentle back pressure on the yoke, the nose came up. V2, take-off speed. They were off the ground and they still had no idea what the hijacker wanted.

*   *   *

Keith held the throttles against the stops. Tamasin trimmed for the climb and then rolled into a climbing turn left to pick up her southerly heading for Antalya.

She knew now in creeping fear that she'd miscalculated. The time to have tried something *had* been when they were on the ground.

Tamasin had the scars on her body where she'd been shot with a pistol. She still had nightmares about that.

The skinny man said amiably: 'What is your name?'

Tamasin glanced at him, surprised. She rolled the wings level on the new heading, still climbing for the Victor Whisky airway. He was lounging in the doorway, his pistol loose in his hand, smiling.

'I'm Tamasin – this is Keith.' Keith was looking puzzled, his ginger hair sticking up at the back. Sun fell dazzlingly into the cockpit and Tamasin stuck her dark glasses onto her short nose. 'What's *your* name?'

'I am Darvish.'

Tamasin shot Keith a look. Keith went on looking blank. 'Darvish Aksoy?' she said.

'Yes.'

'Are you anything to do with that lot, *Yol*?'

'The Way of Faith.' He said it in English, proudly. 'Yes.'

They had the most wanted man in Turkey aboard their jet.

* * *

Their assigned altitude was 28,000 feet and they reached it at 0914 and levelled out. Struggling to hide her tension, Tamasin throttled back. She didn't know whether to set the autopilot. She didn't know what Darvish Aksoy wanted. Maybe after all he did want to go to Antalya and after that someone else could take the worry of all this. *Walter Becker*, she thought. Walter Becker captained one of the Falcons at Antalya, a barrel-chested ex-MiG 29 fighter pilot, commonly known as the Oberleutnant because that was the rank he'd held in what had then been the East German air force. The Oberleutnant would know what to do in a case like this. She was hand-flying *Rapide* but the aircraft was trimmed out, in balance, happy to fly itself. She had slightly over half tanks.

Now when she stole a glance at Darvish, he was checking his watch. He had a plan all right.

She glanced at Keith. Keith said nothing but he wasn't happy. He wasn't helping, either; he was leaving it all to the captain. Well, that was her job . . .

Darvish nudged her arm, indicating with his free left hand. 'Now you will descend. We must go under radar.'

That puffy cumulus was at 20,000 feet – they had nothing at their height. Fear haunted Tamasin, this time the new fear of breaking the rules of flight safety.

'I'll have to let Ankara know!'

'No radio! We go under radar!'

She twisted against the shoulder harness. 'Listen, we don't know what other traffic's around! Do you want to get us into a mid-air collision? I *have* to know that!'

'It's clear,' Darvish said relentlessly. 'There won't be collision.'

'This is an emergency – I've got to declare an emergency.'

Anger darkened Darvish's face, his impatience growing. 'No radio. No emergency. I told you. Descend!'

It had been worth a try. 'All right,' Tamasin said, an almost frantic note in her voice, 'then I'll have to change the radio frequency so as to listen to any transmissions between Ankara and any aircraft they're controlling.' She was on the Antalya frequency, the way Ankara Radar had told her as they signed her off.

'All right, but no radio by you!'

'Fine,' Tamasin said, reaching to the centre panel. 'Let's just stay alive!'

She spun the frequency button. She got Ankara. She turned up the volume on the cockpit speakers and the fizz and crackle filled the air. Then without looking at Darvish she reached to the transponder tuner, in the full knowledge that if Darvish knew what she was doing he would probably shoot her.

The transponder works on radio and will identify an aircraft on secondary radar. If you set transponder code 7700, the signal to the controller is the same as calling Mayday on the radio. Set 7500 and they know you've been hijacked.

Angrily, Darvish shouted: 'Descend! I told you, descend!' He hadn't noticed.

Tight-lipped, Tamasin eased back the throttles and let the jet sink. Keith craned forward, keeping what lookout he could; but they both knew nothing would show them an aircraft underneath. They were straining their ears for the radio, listening for anything leaving Ankara for the south, anything approaching from that Med coast.

Tamasin trimmed into the descent. She was watching the VSI – vertical speed indicator – alert in case she needed the dive brake. 'Keith, how are we for high ground?'

He reached for the visual flight chart, perched precariously atop the panel coaming. It was in half-million scale and it gave the heights. 'Doesn't look too bad,'

Keith said with a trace of tension. 'That steppe country seems to average about 4,900 AMSL.' Feet above mean sea level, Tamasin understood. 'There's that mountain chain, though, before we hit the coast.'

The little white needle on the VSI was flickering around 5,000 feet a minute. The altimeter unwound through 22,000 feet. They were descending straight ahead, nicely in balance.

'OK,' Tamasin said, 'MSA 5,900.' Minimum safe altitude. She reached across to set the radar altimeter.

'What you do now?' Darvish asked sharply. His knuckles were white where he held the Beretta.

'This is the radar altimeter.' Tamasin fought to sound patient, hiding her tension behind the dark glasses. 'It sends a wave down to the ground and times the return wave – that way, it can determine what our height is above ground. *This* altimeter' – she tapped the pressure altimeter, the needles moving now past 19,000 feet, down to 18,900 – 'takes its reading off air pressure, so all it can tell you is height above sea level.'

On a conventional altimeter you can set QNH, the pressure in millibars for sea level, or QFE, pressure at the altitude of the airfield where you're landing. What Tamasin had was standard setting, 1013.2 millibars, the convention all aircraft use when they fly the 'flight levels' of the airways.

They passed through the belt of scrappy cloud. They went through 15,000 feet, still coming down straight ahead. Tamasin was keeping the descent rate steady at 5,000 feet a minute but she was growing uneasy.

'Darvish, what do you want us to do?'

'You go under radar.'

Keith turned his ginger head. 'Damn it, Tamasin, we're probably under radar now! They've got next to nothing out this way.'

Eleven thousand feet. Tamasin flicked a glance at the transponder. Still on 7500. Keith was probably right, no-one had even noticed their signal. Seven thousand

23

five. Now they were less than 2,000 feet above the bleak terrain of pale grey earth and every detail of the landscape showed: hardly a tree, hardly a road, hardly a habitation.

'Darvish!' She tapped an index at the panel. She'd raised the nose now, slowing the descent. 'I am going to level out at 6,000 feet, and that's as low as I'm going. There's no radar getting us. Now will you bloody well tell us what we're supposed to do?'

'We go to Iran.'

*   *   *

Tautly she rolled out heading due east. She neutralized the elevator trim. They were still at 6,000 feet on the pressure altimeter but the radar reading was bobbing about between 1,100 and 450.

'We haven't got charts for Iran,' Tamasin said. The Aerad ME1 went as far as Tehran but they needed VFR charts. 'How the hell are we supposed to navigate?'

She'd cut the transponder. It hadn't done them any good. Keith wasn't helping, wasn't saying a word, just shuffling what charts they had and frowning at them. *The loneliness of the long-distance captain.* This low over the steppe, they were catching turbulence and the wing rocked; the jet dropped and bounced. Tamasin hoped they wouldn't catch a bird like *Spitfire* had done.

'Is all right,' Darvish said. He'd lost his nervousness enough to park his pistol back into his waistband, but his knuckles were still white, this time where they gripped the door frame. 'You pick up Tehran on radio, then I guide you rest of the way.'

Tamasin jerked round. 'What rest of the way?' She didn't know what the distances were, but Tehran was far enough away from Ankara to be an hour and a half ahead in time zone.

'I tell you when the time comes.'

Her voice went shrill. 'And how about I tell you when

we run out of fuel and crash? You've got to give me *some* idea!'

They hadn't even had full tanks when they'd taken off – hadn't needed to – for Antalya. Now the tanks were down to under half.

'We got enough fuel,' Darvish said. 'I know this jet. Long-range jet.'

Tamasin flicked him a venomous look. He really did know business jets, curse him; she wondered how. She tried another shot. 'Why Iran, anyway?'

She looked at him out of the corner of her eye and saw the sudden rage on his face. 'Rana Tezcan is there.'

'Rana Tezcan?'

'Rana is my bride – my fiancée. She was betrayed two days ago by the forces of the Devil in Ankara to the godless backsliders in Tehran and now she is in prison.'

Keith was frowning at his charts again. 'If we're going to Tehran, we've some thumping big hills to climb.'

* * *

'Look at it.' He was on the ME1, taking them east of the Turkey–Iran border. They had their heads down now, craning over the navigation. 'The route is this place Malatya, then Van, then, what? Tabriz, I suppose, and on to Tehran. And get a load of these spot heights!'

Around the town of Malatya the peaks went up to 6,700 feet; they were still only at 6,000 themselves. On towards Van and the border they went to 13,000 feet, getting on for the height of Mont Blanc. Her big eyes wide, Tamasin turned to Darvish.

'Listen, we're going to *have* to climb! Do you want to splatter yourself into a mountain?' She gestured. Heights showing on the radar altimeter were getting lower as the ground rose up to meet their flying altitude. Through the cockpit windscreen they could see the great, gaunt mountains, rising brown and black ahead of them. 'For God's sake, we're nowhere near any radar!'

Darvish sucked his lips. 'All right, you climb to 8,000.'

'We're going to need more than that before we cross the border.' But already in thankful relief she was pushing the throttle levers forward, lifting the nose.

'We can climb later.'

Overhead the cloud had thickened up, solid. It was reaching down towards them.

*　　*　　*

Gusts were getting them and *Dragon Rapide* was feeling lively, rolling, bouncing. Darvish wasn't having an easy time, holding on. Tamasin switched on the autopilot and set Turb mode. She knew of old that the autopilot would manage this sort of flying better than most humans could. Up here, there were better chances of showing on someone's radar and Tamasin was still hoping they'd be challenged. It was ten. Good. Their ETA at Antalya had been 0950, so already they'd have been missed.

Smugly, Darvish said: 'I tell you where we go.'

The pilots glanced up. 'OK, where?' Tamasin said.

'Zedasht.'

'Where the hell's that?'

He was still looking thoroughly self-satisfied. 'Air force base. East of Tehran, south of Shahrud. Old Iranian air force base. They don't use it for flying any more.'

'What d'you mean, they don't use it for flying?' Horror marked Tamasin's eyes. 'Has it got a runway?'

'Oh, it got runway. Is all right.'

Shahrud wasn't a town she'd heard of. Darvish hadn't given them a clue about the distance. 'What sort of runway?' Tamasin persisted. 'What sort of base was it, what sort of aircraft?'

The heights on the radar altimeter were getting shorter again. The cockpit grew dark as they bored eastwards under the heavy cloud.

'C130s,' Darvish said.

Air forces all round the world use the US-built C130 Hercules four-turboprop transport. The USAF and RAF have them as well as the Iranians.

'Oh, for God's sake!' Tamasin exploded. 'Don't you know *anything* about this aircraft?' She waved her right hand under his nose. 'The C130 is a military plane built for short, rough strips. This here is an executive jet and it needs twice the length of runway a C130 needs. Now let's have an end to this nonsense! If you want to get down in Iran, let's go into Tabriz or Tehran – they've got grown-up-sized runways there.'

Darvish was immovable. Keith looked immovable, too, monitoring the instruments as Tamasin argued, minding the autopilot, minding the nav, watching for high ground.

'Zedasht,' Darvish said. 'We go into Zedasht.'

'I'm not putting my aircraft into a runway if I'm going to run off the end of it and wipe my undercarriage off. *You'll* get hurt, too, if that happens!'

'You can land at Zedasht.'

And now they *had* shown on someone's radar. It must have been getting up over those peaks. A new voice boomed through the cockpit speakers. It was Turkish, it was angry, and it was an obvious challenge.

*   *   *

Scared now, Tamasin blinked at Darvish. 'Jesus. What's he saying?'

She looked at Keith. He'd reset the radio frequency, it was on 121.5 megahertz, the international emergency channel. A wise move.

Darvish hesitated. The voice paused, then came on in thickly accented English. 'Diyarbakir Military Control calling unidentified aircraft crossing Ayvali prohibited area, course zero nine eight, speed three two zero knots, identify yourself, identify yourself!'

With terrifying clarity Tamasin saw what *Rapide*'s size and speed would look like on a military radar.

'Shit,' she muttered. Automatically she pressed the transmit button on the yoke handle. 'Roger, Diyarbakir, *Dragon* . . .'

The back of Darvish's hand slammed across her face and the impact smashed her back and aside in her seat. She cried out in pain, her hands released the yoke.

Keith twisted sharply left. '*Hey! You bastard!*'

'No radio!' Darvish shouted, furious. 'No reply!' He yanked the Beretta out of his waistband. He held it muzzle down but he cocked it in a practised flick of the wrist.

This was a man who'd killed many times over.

Tamasin turned haggardly. She was breathing heavily, she had tears at her eyes from the blow that already was starting to show in a bruise across her right cheekbone. She took the yoke in her left hand but she left the transmit button alone. The autopilot carried on with the flying.

'What the hell are we doing in prohibited airspace?'

'There's no prohibited area on my chart,' Keith said, blankly.

There was, but he was gambling on Darvish not seeing it. He'd shuffled the relevant chart resting on his knees underneath the next one east.

Tamasin blinked, but her eyes were still watering. She appealed to Darvish. 'We've *got* to reply to that! They'll put fighters up! Christ, we'll even *look* like a fighter on their radar!'

She didn't know how, but she sensed that all along Keith had been taking more of a crafty initiative than she'd given him credit for.

'No radio!' Darvish shouted angrily above the jet roar in the cockpit as the gusts rocked them and the cloud clawed down and the hills rose up.

'Darvish . . .' Her voice was a wail.

'No!' He was still seething and he raised the Beretta. In the cockpit doorway he half-turned towards Tamasin.

Decisive suddenly, Keith twisted round. 'That's enough

of that, Darvish, we're taking enough chances with the flying as it is!'

Darvish tossed him a contemptuous glance, then turned, gun raised as if to attack Tamasin. Keith wrenched around in his seat. He flung his right arm across him, defending Tamasin instinctively, grabbing without thought for the gun.

Darvish swung back around and the gun went off. The bullet hit Keith.

CHAPTER 4

Southern Turkey, Thursday, 11 June, 0700 local
For the first time for days you could see round Antalya
Bay to where the mountains dropped slaty blue to the
sea. Warm breeze had shifted the sticky swelter and from
the airport you could see out to the jagged brown peaks
of the Taurus range that barred off the littoral from the
desert and steppe of the interior.

Five was a crowd in one of Dragon Jet's Dassault Falcon
20s but there were five people striding out now in the
bright morning to the aircraft, not in the white-and-red
livery that the 125s wore but in the sort of low-visibility
pale grey that the Royal Air Force uses to paint its Tornado
long-range interceptors. Only the red name lettering by the
door and the dragon in the red-bordered square on the tail
marked them as contract aircraft.

On their target-towing or radar-training missions for
the Turkish navy the Falcons carried a pilot, co-pilot,
electronic warfare operator – EWO – and a local naval
officer as observer; but today they had two observers,
neither from the navy. The one in the olive flying suit with
the air force colonel's badges on his shoulder boards was a
gifted 38-year-old called Mahmut Barka who commanded
a wing of F16 fighters at Diyarbakir, in the restive
south-east of Turkey. The F16s were US-designed but had
been built in Turkey and the young colonel was as proud
of the aircraft as he was of the men who flew them.

The other observer, the one in the cotton slacks and
lightweight zip denim cowboy jacket, grey so that oil or
hydraulic stains wouldn't show, was the Dragon Lady
herself.

Felix Wyer didn't often get out of the office at Biggin

Hill but she liked to see every now and then what her employees and aircraft were getting up to. She enjoyed flying. On this trip to Turkey her main business had been in Ankara but she could always find an excuse to get down to Antalya for a flight. Under her cowboy jacket she wore a black blouse open at the neck, and she wore sensible glasses and shoes, her iron-grey-hair styled efficiently – if not quite as short as Tamasin Masterson liked to wear hers.

Felix and Mahmut walked a pace behind the other three.

The first three all wore flying suits. On the left was the co-pilot, Chris Norton, a lanky six foot two, ex-Royal Navy lieutenant; most of his flying so far had been on helicopters, Lynx and Sea King. On the right was the EWO, Ron Harper, stocky, balding, a veteran of many foreign postings. In the middle was the Oberleutnant.

At five ten, Walter Becker wasn't tall, but he made up for it with his broad shoulders, hairy chest and powerful limbs. Felix knew she wasn't the only woman who found Walter sexy. His ginger moustache bristled from a face with square-jawed good looks and an air of confidence that belied a sneaking German *Angst* over any threat of chaos; posed by *Yol*, for instance. He had an un-Germanic distaste for uniform, maybe because he associated a uniform with totalitarian regimes. He'd lived under one. He'd hated it, but that hadn't prevented him from calculatedly joining the *Sozialistische Einheitspartei Deutschlands*, since without the Party card they'd never have let him loose on the MiG 29s that he'd lusted after. One of the benefits of SED membership – he'd told Felix once – was very short branch meetings. You didn't – heaven forbid! – *debate* policy, you just agreed with what the Party secretary said.

To get in they used a wooden box. Chris Norton did the walk-round. Walter, wearing his summer garb of Bermuda shorts and a flying overall, took the captain's seat.

'You'd better take the jumpseat, Mahmut,' Felix smiled,

and followed Ron Harper aft. The Falcon 20 was much smaller inside than the 125s and at five ten, Walter's height, Felix had to stoop.

'Thank you,' Mahmut said gravely. He was at Antalya at the invitation of one of the Turkish navy officers who commonly flew observer with Walter, and Walter had invited him along on this flight before he'd known Felix was coming down.

But the more contacts you made, the better, Walter thought as he set things running on the jet.

Four Dragon Fleet Falcons stood on the flight line but *Falcon Firecrest* was the only one with its intake covers off. In christening these aircraft Felix had gone mainly on alliteration; there weren't the 1930s associations that had prompted the naming of *Dragon Rapide*, or her mother's memories that had given her *Dragon Spitfire* and *Dragon Tempest*. Gail, Felix's mother, was these days a doughty old lady, and in the Second World War she'd worked as a ferry pilot, delivering aircraft from the factories to the squadrons on the airfields. She'd flown Spitfires and Tempests. She'd also bequeathed her daughter a lifetime's fascination for flying in all its forms.

Gail was a fighter, a breaker of ground. Felix was a fighter herself. So, Felix reflected, was Tamasin Masterson.

Chris Norton latched the door. Ron Harper was testing systems on his EWO console; Felix had taken the seat opposite Ron, aft of the door, while Mahmut Barka sat in the cockpit doorway. At one time the aircraft had been in French service, and it amused Felix to see the placard left in place by her seat referring to *la ceinture Mae West*.

Falcon Firecrest rolled.

The pilots liked this aircraft, Felix reflected, but to her it had nothing of the romance of the Jet Dragon. There was style in that name. The original Dragon Rapide had first flown in 1934 and de Havilland hadn't stopped building them until 1945. On its twin prop engines and its multi-strutted, wire-braced biplane wings it had carried six to eight passengers over a 580-mile range at a cruise of 132mph. A far cry, Felix thought, from her *Dragon Tempest* and *Dragon Spitfire*: eight to twelve passengers, range 3,300 miles, cruise 525mph.

The Jet Dragon – Felix always used that title – had been designed from the outset as a business aircraft. Dassault, conversely, had started with the wing they'd designed earlier for an interceptor and ground attack fighter called the *Mystère* and simply bolted an executive-jet fuselage on to it. The wing still had its old bomb and rocket hard-points. On the Falcon they used them to mount a target winch or an electronic warfare pod – much easier than the adaptations Jerry Yeaver had had to make to *Rapide*.

Walter belted down the runway and stood on the tail. Three thousand feet came up on the altimeter and he stood on a wingtip. Chris Norton glanced back at Mahmut Barka as the beaches wheeled into sight below.

'Walter misses those MiGs.'

'Almost made life worth living in the DDR, did those MiGs.' Walter rolled out crisply on the new heading. Actually he'd had a terrific battle with his conscience before joining the SED; he'd always nurtured a healthy scepticism about Honecker and his regime; and the old East German leader's successors. In the end, though, the drive to fly had almost quelled his doubts. Then, as now, it had been a function as basic as breathing.

Off the shore, Walter started losing height. Felix glanced across at Ron Harper.

'What's our target?'

'Destroyer,' Harper said, relaxed at his console with no work yet to do. 'Ex-US Navy. They've put a lot more up-to-date stuff on her in the last refit.' He nodded outside. 'This'll be primary entry control point for the run in.'

Firecrest was out of sight of land, down to 100 feet over the wave tops. Gentle swell, no white horses. Felix resettled her headset and tightened her seatbelt. Glancing out, she got an almost frightening sensation of speed.

On the intercom Harper said: 'Got him yet?'

'Negatiff,' Walter said. He was searching for the destroyer on the nose radar. 'Why, he got us yet?'

'I'm picking up search pulses,' Harper said through the slipstream and engine noise.

Walter said something Felix couldn't begin to catch and then Chris Norton said, 'Walter, you really are going to get yourself into trouble in the air one day, with that accent.'

'*Ach, was!* I like to see you do so good with your second foreign language. Russian I learn first in the school. Ron, what you say you got?'

'Bloody pilots,' Harper groaned. 'All right, Walter, I know you're the guy who thought pulse repetition frequency was what happened when you'd been eating lentils. Search pulses, Walter – he's not tracking us yet. He's at, ah . . . four zero.' He meant forty nautical miles.

'Ah, we be all right. We spoil his morning coffee.' Walter rolled in for the final run and let down to 50 feet above the gentle crests.

Steely sea streaked past below. Walter had the speed at 410 knots, almost seven nautical miles a minute. If the destroyer was at 40 sea miles' range, they would reach it in under six minutes.

'Why this height?' Mahmut said on the intercom. He spoke better English than Walter did.

'We're really an Exocet.'

Harper said: 'Tracking. He'll have lock-on any moment.'

In real life, lock-on would be the cue for the destroyer's defensive armament to open up.

'Range?' Walter said.

'Three zero.'

'Got him on the nose radar,' Norton said from the co-pilot's seat. 'He's broadside to us.'

Felix watched Harper. He looked content, relaxed, his fingers adept as they fined the tuner. 'Spot noise,' he mused, more for Felix's benefit than anyone else's. 'This should upset him.' Spot noise was the simplest form of jamming: radar energy on the same frequency as the transmitter.

'Are we over the visual horizon?' Felix asked.

'Only just.'

Harper said: 'Range two zero. We're in burn-through range.'

A ground or shipborne radar transmitter will usually have greater power than an airborne one. You can outjam the jammer aircraft – 'burn through' its transmissions – by, in effect, turning up the volume on your own.

'Range one five,' Harper said.

'I can't see him,' Walter complained. 'It's all spray up here.'

Salt spray was the bugbear of this sort of operation. Hardly anything rotted an airframe so fast.

'He's burnt through,' Harper said nonchalantly, 'he's locked us in. I'll have his range gate.' He turned the knob on the console that said RGPO, range gate pull-off. The destroyer's radar had *Firecrest* locked into a range gate; it was shutting out in between known time intervals of picking up *Firecrest* on the scan. What Harper did was to turn up the volume of *Firecrest*'s return so that the radar on the destroyer tuned down to compensate. Then he delayed the return so the destroyer thought that *Firecrest* was somewhere else.

'Got him?' Walter said gruffly, eager for the next bit of fun.

'Affirmative, pulled him off.'

'Rog.'

Walter stood *Firecrest* on its port wingtip. Felix grabbed her harness; for a moment she thought she might need *la ceinture Mae West*. Holding the height reassuringly well, Walter rolled level.

'He's lost us all right,' Harper confirmed.

'Rog,' Walter said. 'Initial point for the run in, stand by.' He rolled *Firecrest* sharply again, over to the right. They were 10 nautical miles off the destroyer's stern quarter.

'Do you always go in this low?' Felix asked.

'*Ja*,' Walter said. 'If we really would have been a hostile with an Exocet, we would launch 25, 30 seconds ago.'

They closed fast with the Turkish ship.

The destroyer's radar caught them at five nautical miles, locked on at three, and lost them at two as Harper dealt it another wallop of spot noise. Walter pulled back the yoke and Felix caught a breath to see how close the destroyer's masts were under them as they scorched over the ship.

Walter let the height build back up to 3,000 feet and rolled uncharacteristically gently on to his heading for Antalya. Harper slid Felix a knowing look.

'Enjoy yourself?'

She grinned. For a woman who was fifty-one and never made a secret of it, she was fit and on form, and she hadn't expected to find her heart rate going like this.

*   *   *

Prickly pear and barren brown earth slid below as Walter caressed *Firecrest* down the approach.

'Should see *Rapide* there when we land.' *Should see Rapide's captain, too*, he was thinking.

Mahmut said: 'Does *Rapide* carry the same electronics suite as this one?'

'Just chaff and flares, really,' Felix said. 'And some basic ECM.' She was craning a bit over Mahmut's shoulders but he was too far away and her view through the front was too restricted. She was very keen to see *Rapide* again. Given its history, it was her favourite aircraft of the whole fleet.

The wheels thumped on; the Oberleutnant's landings were apt to be firm.

Then as they taxied to the Falcon flight line Felix knew what was missing.

*   *   *

Felix ducked through the low cabin to unlatch the door. Mahmut Barka stepped back to let Walter clamber over the throttles and through the cockpit doorway. Walter's face, with its bristling moustache, was blank; Felix realized he was worried.

'Chris can tidy up in here,' Walter muttered. 'Let's get over to ops. Probably they just took off late.' He hopped down, grasped Felix's hand, and steadied her down. Mahmut followed mutely.

'Don't forget the water!' Walter shouted over his shoulder. They had the Falcons hosed down with fresh water after every Med flight.

In the ops room the Turkish despatcher wasn't happy. 'I'm sorry, Mrs Wyer, we can't raise *Dragon Rapide* on radio. She's fifteen minutes, almost sixteen minutes overdue.'

The fear that seized Felix was deep and dark and overwhelming. She'd never lost an aircraft in the entire history of the company, never lost a crew, never – she dreaded the thought – passengers. And it had to be *Rapide* this happened to.

With alarm, Felix saw that this could mean the end of her company. Yet it wasn't Dragon Jet that was uppermost in her mind.

She caught Walter's eye. The lurking *Angst* was there for Tamasin.

Mahmut murmured, 'May I?' and picked up the phone. He dialled Ankara Radar. He started talking in crisp, hard Turkish.

In the ops room the despatcher was behind a long, wooden counter and Walter strode round behind it, still in his flying suit. They had radio there to talk to the aircrews and Walter keyed the company frequency. Nothing. He reset the frequency for Antalya Control, waited for a gap, then called *Dragon Rapide*. Still nothing. He dialled the international emergency frequency. No-one was transmitting. No-one answered when he called *Rapide*.

In his mind's eye Walter could see Tamasin's face as

if she'd been standing there. Something was hurting inside him.

Mahmut hung up from talking to Ankara and rang up Antalya instead. Another rattle of Turkish. Mahmut hung up again. 'It's all negative,' he told Felix, his face solemn. '*Rapide* signed off from Ankara normally but it's not showing anywhere on radar now.' He shook his head. Ankara to Antalya was such a short flight.

Felix turned to Walter. 'What does it look like?'

Walter poked out his lower lip. He thought of those dark eyes, the snub nose, the pent up energy in that agile figure. It wasn't just a sexy body that made the challenge, though. It was competence and flying skills and sheer will power to match his own.

'Not very good,' Walter muttered.

Neither said it but the same thought was in everyone's mind.

Felix turned to the despatcher. 'Have we got an aircraft out there that's not needed this morning for operations?'

The young Turk blinked his dark eyes. '*Falcon Fang*.'

She turned to Walter. 'Do we know what Tamasin's flight plan was? If you could get hold of Chris, we could retrace her route.'

*   *   *

Shortly before eleven, Walter set *Falcon Fang*'s wheels down on 21 Right at Ankara with a bit less panache than he'd shown landing at Antalya. They'd flown the whole way following VW77D north-eastwards at 2,000 feet above ground and there'd been nothing; and no word in the interim. Felix, in increasing misery, followed Chris Norton and Walter over the hot concrete ramp to the ops wing.

'She was at 28,000 feet,' Felix fretted. 'How come she didn't even have time to put out a Mayday?'

Walter held his peace grumpily.

'Well . . . ' Felix gestured. 'It's only if you get a

38

bomb on board, or something really disastrous like a sudden structural failure, that you don't have time for a Mayday.'

Norton glanced at Walter but still Walter said nothing. Usually Felix found Walter's presence reassuring, but not today.

'Those aircraft are phenomenally strongly built,' Felix said. 'They just don't *have* structural failures.'

'*Gott*, Felix,' Walter said, 'it's no good asking me!' In his concern his accent had gone thicker than ever.

* * *

When ops at Ankara airport couldn't help her Felix took a taxi into town. She left Walter stumping back to *Falcon Fang* for the return to Antalya.

She'd liked Tamasin, that was the thing. Walter was more fond of Tamasin, too, than he cared to let on. Tamasin was such a good pilot.

Both Felix's kids had been boys. Recently in her talks with Tamasin she'd found herself starting to cast Dragon Jet's only woman captain as the daughter she, Felix, had never had.

The long, straight road south could have been on some uninhabited planet. Hardly a tree, hardly a bush; just greyish, undulating steppe. Felix chewed her lip and wound her bag strap round her hand.

At last the blacktop curved down into a canyon of barren brown hill and Felix saw the first rooftops of Ankara. The houses were red cubes of bare brick with no streets between them, and, from the looks of it, no utilities. Felix watched a thin girl of maybe fourteen, in a headscarf, struggling uphill with two plastic water containers slung from a yoke across her shoulders.

The air was drier here than in Antalya, the atmosphere lighter; Ankara lay high – and paid for it in hard winters. Erol Ersin was Dragon Jet's Turkish director. In return for giving Felix the naval training contract, the Turkish government had wanted a mutually agreed Turkish national on the company board. Ersin had directorships in several big Turkish companies and he spoke faultless English. Felix liked him.

The pedestrian zone could have been anywhere in Continental Europe. Felix slung her overnight bag on her shoulder and took the lift to the second floor. She went into Ersin's outer office without knocking, as usual, and Ersin's secretary recognized her and smiled. Twenty-two, dyed blonde, her manner unfailingly helpful, her English disastrous. Felix communicated with her in a mixture of slow English, slower German, and Felix's few phrases of Turkish.

Ersin appeared without having to be summoned. 'Felix, my dear! Back so soon?'

He was younger than her, six foot three with little sign yet of paunch, and today dressed imposingly in a cream-coloured suit and blue tie; his dark hair was always scraped back the way the founder of the modern Turkish state, Atatürk's, was in all his pictures – but Felix always thought that, given a war bonnet, that hook nose and the tanned, impassive features, his features could have belonged to a Red Indian chief.

Very controlled, Felix said: 'I'm going to need a phone to call England.' Then she told him what it was about.

*   *   *

The craggy face with the bushy eyebrows was intent. 'So no emergency radio message, no radar trace, no signs of wreckage, no reports from anyone on the ground.' Ersin had a think. 'Maybe I should call some people I know.'

That was at least half Ersin's value to Dragon Jet: the number of people he knew.

'Keith's parents in Scarborough,' Felix said, fighting to keep her voice steady. 'It's only fair that they should hear it from me.'

Ersin gestured. The dyed-blonde had a bank of phones

next to her and had understood enough of the conversation to look worried. 'Are you happy to use the phones here?' he said.

'Yes, of course . . . thanks, Erol . . .'

Thoughtfully, Erol Ersin walked back into his office. The man whose number he dialled was one of the most powerful, yet one of the least known, in the country.

CHAPTER 5

Overhead eastern Turkey, Thursday, 11 June, 1016 local
The Beretta was chambered for 7.65mm. A 9mm round
would have done far greater damage. As it was, the
bullet punched through Keith Cross's forearm, broke
both bones, then slammed into the instrument panel
between the airspeed indicator and the altimeter on the
co-pilot's side. It hit the inner surface of the nose bulkhead
– the one that supported the radar antenna – ricocheted
off, and smashed into one of the oxygen bottles stored
immediately forward of the instrument panel. That was
another of the mods on *Dragon Rapide* – along with the
Garrett turbofans that replaced the earlier, much noisier
Viper engines – normally the 400-series aircraft carried
the oxygen in the tailcone.

Oxygen streamed out and fed through the bullethole
in the panel with a thin, keening noise over the ragged
damage petals.

Keith yelled aloud in pain and fear and doubled over
the yoke, grabbing his right wrist with his left hand. Bright
blood ran through his fingers.

'*Keith!*' Tamasin cried out.

The sharp nitrocellulose smell filled the cockpit. Darvish
Aksoy was looking pleased with himself.

Moaning, Keith rocked slowly, face pale, eyes squeezed
shut. He was struggling to fight it but he was in agony.
Tamasin could see it and there was nothing she could do.
She twisted around.

'Get the first-aid kit! It's just back there, in the
galley!'

'And what do you do if I go back there?' Darvish's
hollow face was impenetrable.

42

Keith's breath came out in shudders, knuckles white where he gripped his arm. 'What d'you *think* we'll do?' Tamasin protested. 'There's nothing we can do!' She had tears in her eyes.

'I watch you here.' The blank look in his fanatical, black eyes was infuriating.

Close to despair, Tamasin realized she wasn't going to get her way. 'All right, then, at least put that gun away and let me get on with flying this jet safely!'

Darvish didn't have a quibble with that.

*   *   *

It was 1020. The nav chart had spatters of blood on it as Tamasin took it from Keith. Below them the land lay flatter for a spell. She looked in anguish at Keith. That ashen face, the blood still flooding. It was bad.

'Where the hell are we? Must be abeam Diyarbakir.' She'd heard of this place, a town with a big military presence, on the edge of what the Turkish government refused to call Kurdistan. 'One way to find out.'

According to Aerad, Diyarbakir had a VOR navigation aid – a VHF Omnidirectional Range station. Tamasin dialled in the frequency on to her receiver, 110.0 megahertz. The line on the dial moved. They were past the VOR, the arrow showing in the *From* instead of the *To* window. She was picking up the station's signals at a bearing of 115 degrees.

She kept glancing at Keith, her mind anguished. He was trying to fight the pain, moaning a little, still rocking, but she wasn't convinced he was fully conscious all the time. So much blood, soaking dark into his trousers, dripping bright through his fingers, starting to pool in the footwell.

Last time she'd seen blood like that, the man had died.

Over her shoulder she told Darvish piercingly: 'Listen, we're really exposed to fighters here. If they intercept us I'm going with them, 'cos if I don't they'll shoot us down and we'll all be dead anyway.'

She had a nasty suspicion that the Turkish air force might not give them the option. She didn't want to be here, doing this. This was no time to get killed.

Last time she'd seen blood like that in the footwell, she'd had to stick her boots into it and fly a B52 bomber herself.

Reaching to her right, in the middle, she switched the radio output on to the cockpit speakers. She told Darvish: 'Just listen to what comes off this and let me know what it is. I can't follow Turkish.' Maybe Darvish wouldn't be able to, either, depending on how clearly any radio message came across. 'OK?'

'OK.' He seemed dubious but he couldn't see where the trap might be.

In the rising turbulence the jet was kicking about. Tamasin had it trimmed into a gentle climb as the rocky land under them rose.

She set the radio tuner to 243.0. It was Guard, the international military emergency channel. Any message aimed at them would almost certainly come off that. She wondered briefly whether to set the transponder to hijack again but she didn't know whether Diyarbakir had a secondary radar to read transponders, and anyway, with no co-pilot she was too busy.

What Diyarbakir *did* have was a NATO airfield with a damn great wing of F16s. Colonel Barka's unit. She'd heard his name mentioned.

The F16 was an oldish aircraft now, first flown back in 1974, but none the less a damn good dogfighter. Against an F16, *Dragon Rapide* would be a sitting duck.

Turkish came through angrily on Guard.

Darvish said hesitantly, 'I think he wants . . .'

'*Shut up!*' Military control was repeating the message in English.

'. . . having violated Ayvali prohibited area, stand by for fighter intercept, stand by for fighter intercept. Follow orders from your fighter intercept. I say again . . .'

Anxiously, Tamasin glanced over at Keith again, too

worried to be greatly concerned about any consequences if she failed to answer the controller's message.

A rain shower. The droplets streamed off the screen but it was chilly in the cockpit. Close above them the cloudbase grew darker and ahead Tamasin could see peaks vanishing into the murk. She was throttled back to 320 knots and it seemed a hell of a speed, this close to the ground.

When she'd been this low before, at this speed, she'd been navigating and she hadn't had a direct view out. She'd hated that as much as she hated this.

Height check, 250 feet above ground. Sweat stood cold on her neck, stark fear in her eyes, and she was scarcely aware of Darvish, behind her to the right. Here and there, ahead of her, rain squalls reached to the ground, charcoal-coloured, angry smudges. The jet swayed and the wing rocked.

On the Guard channel, a crisp, shortish command. A fizz of static and another voice answered it. Then a second. Then two more. *The F16s.*

'Darvish, what was it?'

'I think there are fighters taking off.' For the first time, the strain showed in his voice.

'How many?'

'I think four.'

Tamasin thought so, too. She didn't know what their rules of engagement were, didn't know how trigger-happy they'd be. Down here *Rapide* was skirting the northern rim of the Kurdish region and there was an undeclared civil war going on. So far, the Kurds hadn't used jets, but whether a bunch of Turkish fighter pilots keen for the taste of blood would remember that was another issue.

His voice high and edgy, Darvish said: 'If you make me get caught inside Turkey, I will kill both of you!'

'For God's sake stop talking crap! We're all going to be killed together if we hit a mountainside or if those jets fire missiles!'

Ironically, Tamasin thought, this jet, alone of the

45

Dragon Fleet, carried radar warning and chaff and flare dispensers. But the controls for them were aft where neither of them could reach to operate them.

Fleetingly, Walter Becker crossed Tamasin's mind. Walter would have known what to do.

She flicked a glance aft. Darvish was looking scared for the first time. Serve the bastard right. As her eyes came forward she saw Keith again. It was horrible to see the agony on a person's face; horrible to see Keith still losing blood.

More voice off Guard.

Darvish said: 'Now he says they're climbing. That must be the fighters . . .'

They'd scrambled, then. A prompt response, Tamasin thought as the ground rose up ahead of her and she pressed back the yoke to rise with the terrain. Would the radar catch them? Or would the terrain mask them, down here?

She said: 'Darvish, get a scarf out of that coat rack.' It was just behind him, forward of the galley. 'Do something with that wound of Keith's.'

It seemed a lot more work, flying this thing with no co-pilot.

Darvish turned round from the cockpit doorway. It almost surprised Tamasin to find him doing as she'd said.

Her mouth was dry. The mountains rose in a great wall ahead of them with their tops vanishing into the rainy cloud. Darvish crouched and leaned forward over the throttle quadrant. It took him a couple of tries before he got Keith's attention.

Tamasin increased throttle. She couldn't see a way through. Get up over that range and she'd be in full radar view of everyone.

Darkness, a big jolt, and they slammed into a rain squall and for an instant Tamasin was blind. They came through and then the fright got her, the way she'd lost vision so suddenly. She twitched the jet back on to its south-easterly heading.

A valley opened, heading south of their track. A way through. She tilted the aircraft into the valley mouth.

The valley floor rose and Tamasin lifted the jet with it. Speed drained off, back to 280 knots. Plenty, even now. Darvish was winding the scarf tightly around Keith's arm but the movement was hurting Keith. He cried out. Tamasin wound on aft trim until the yoke relaxed in her hand, and headed them upwards towards the ragged, gloomy cloud. Another rain squall bounced the jet. Any moment now, Tamasin thought, any moment now those F16s are going to challenge us. Cloud reached down to them in clammy tendrils and the vision vanished for over a second. When they came clear again, Tamasin's spine was tingling.

All they needed was for that to happen just as they came up against a rock wall.

*   *   *

Voice again, off Guard. Tamasin couldn't understand the words, could barely distinguish one voice from the other. But this sounded like the F16 section leader asking fighter control for a vector on to target.

'*Bir dakka.*' One minute.

In the air they should have been speaking English, NATO forces' standard.

'*Tamam.*' OK.

It sounded like hesitation. Maybe ground radar had lost them after all.

The valley led them to a rocky saddle just under the cloudbase and Tamasin let them get close to the jagged outcrops to cross it; a better option than getting into the cloud. Darvish straightened back from Keith's side, then the cockpit floor sank under him and he clutched the door frame to brace himself. Tamasin started letting down cautiously, following the line of the valley where it picked up after the watershed. She hated this flying. All her instincts warned her not to gamble with lives.

Keith was still clasping his arm, his head lolling. The blood hadn't come through the scarf yet.

Guard fizzed open again in static and warbles and the voice that came through it was crisp. A longer message this time.

'Did you get that, Darvish?'

'I think . . . radar has lost us. But they have a computer projection of . . .' He broke off as another voice replied. Tamasin strained her ears in case they surprised her and used some English.

Darvish said tensely: 'The F16s . . . they are at 30,000 feet.' NATO standard, feet not metres. 'They are asking if ground radar can see us.'

Tamasin knew hiding down here in the terrain was their safest bet. What she didn't know was whether Diyarbakir had airborne radar. The radars on an E3 or E2 AWACS aircraft would pick this jet out easily amid the ground return.

The valley took a turn to the left, bringing them from mostly southerly back to south-easterly. Tamasin banked around the turn. More rain streamed on the windscreen. Speed, 280 knots. Dear God, please don't let there be electricity cables down here. She was sweating.

The valley bottomed out. Tamasin levelled the aircraft and kept the speed where it was.

At the edge of her vision, Darvish seemed to be fingering the gun in his waistband, his eyes wide, watching for trickery. Turbulence was getting them and now the aircraft pitched sharply up, only to drop sickeningly. Wind grabbed it by the nose and Tamasin fought the yaw.

They were going to get themselves in dire trouble down here. One of these jolts was going to have them scraping the ground. Tamasin trimmed back and let the speed tail off a few knots as she eased up towards the dark tatters of the cloudbase. She was risking radar, but she needed height in reserve and engine power in reserve.

Another voice on Guard, crisp, cut-off. *Fizz*. Another voice. *Crackle*. A different voice again.

'They're getting closer,' Darvish said. 'Can't you do something?'

'Yeah,' Tamasin snarled, 'I could get on the radio and surrender to them so they don't shoot!'

'If you fool with me, you get hurt!' He was rattled but his anger came through.

So many distractions down here. Tamasin's breath was shallow, her mouth parched with fear. Too many things to be done all at once, too hard to concentrate on which need was urgent *now*. Keith seemed to have passed out. Darvish was fretting about those F16s and so was Tamasin. She realized with a pang that she hadn't given a thought to the navigation since they got down here south of Diyarbakir. They might be heading into Syria instead of Iran. Then around them the valley walls rose toweringly and steepened.

No room to turn. In front of them, rising almost to the cloudbase, a razorback ridge blocked their path in a giant wall of rock.

*   *   *

Tamasin cried out incoherently. Terrified, she slammed both throttles forward to the stops and hauled the yoke all the way back. It jammed on the elevator stop. Noise flooded the cockpit and Darvish grabbed at the door frame. They weren't going to make it this time. The vision vanished as the nose blocked it from view but Tamasin craned over the high coaming where it rose jam full of instruments and switches. She glimpsed the rock wall coming closer. Speed tailed away. They were going to stall into the mountainside. A shudder went through the airframe and Tamasin had her right hand tensed on the throttles in case they vibrated loose. It was piston-engine-think but right then it seemed to help.

Dragon Rapide stood on its tail with the Garretts howling, open to full take-off thrust.

She was going to cook both the engines. Felix would

49

never forgive her. But there was nothing else for it, the alternative was death. Through his daze of pain and the slow sledgehammer at his temples Keith remembered what was happening.

'Hey, Tamasin . . .'

He struggled to help but the pain pounding in his wrist was too much.

The speed was down to 150 knots and falling fast and Tamasin couldn't remember what speed a 125 would stall at with this angle of attack. She craned over the nose.

The rocky, scrubby top of the razorback slashed away under them. It looked about six inches away. A shudder went through the airframe, the first hint that the wing was going to stall.

Tamasin rammed the nose fully forward and pulled back the throttles. The engines survived. At last she could see, and she saw room ahead for flying. As she let out her breath they went slap into a big rainy squall and the whole aircraft jolted.

Vision returned. Darvish was hanging onto the door frame, a bemused look on his stubbly face.

'I hope you're pleased, Darvish Aksoy!' Tamasin cried, eyes flashing. 'We very nearly all got killed, just then! This aircraft's going to be in no fit state to fly again by the time we get it down!'

This was a business tool they were flying, not a jet fighter. It amazed Tamasin that the aircraft had put up with the treatment she'd given it. Her calves were shaking, her palms slippery on the controls.

'You very good pilot,' Darvish said.

Tamasin couldn't believe it.

The valley was descending, opening out. Tamasin flicked a glance at the radar altimeter. Three hundred feet clearance. She settled the speed back at 280 knots and her breathing began to ease.

More voice off Guard – they'd been hearing it all through. Now Darvish could listen again.

'Fighters have lost us.' His voice seemed calm. Maybe he

just hadn't realized what had been happening back there. 'They're over Van – where are we?'

'Haven't a clue,' Tamasin snapped. They'd been flying south as much as east, she reckoned. Or maybe mostly eastish. Good morning, Baghdad. Or was it Damascus?

Then the mountains fell away and they came out over a huge body of water, gleaming dully under the heavy cloud, spreading away left and right of them as Tamasin brought the heading back on to due east.

'God,' she said, alarm piercing into her, 'it's Lake Van – we're right under those bloody fighters!'

Darvish paused. Keith stirred, moaning softly, grasping his arm. Blood was starting to show through the scarf. The whistle of air through the damaged panel was barely audible.

'No,' Darvish said thoughtfully, 'Lake Van is too fat for that.'

Tamasin glanced up uncomprehendingly. 'Fat?'

'We're flying east, no?' His voice was sharp.

Despite herself, Tamasin was impressed at the way he'd read the direction indicator, over her shoulder. 'Yes.'

'Lake Van is too fat, too far east-to-west. This one runs north and south. It's Lake Urmia.'

'Lake Urmia? What's that?'

Darvish started to sound excited. 'It's near Tabriz! We're in Iran!'

Almost immediately the new challenge came on the Guard frequency, this time given first in Farsi.

CHAPTER 6

IRIAF Tabriz Three, Thursday, 11 June, 1205 local
At the Islamic Revolutionary Iranian Air Force fighter station of Tabriz Three they'd hardly had a genuine combat scramble since the end of the Iran-Iraq war.

Groundcrew were running, ducking under wings and missile racks through the drizzle falling thinly from the purplish grey overcast as the eight flight-suited men, with their bone domes under their arms, raced to their aircraft.

Tabriz Three had a half-strength squadron of old American F4 Phantoms; a full-strength squadron of Shenyang F6 fighters, the Chinese derivative of the supersonic Russian-designed MiG 19; and a flight of six F14 Tomcats.

The US-built F14 was old, although not so old as the F4. It was a superb fighter. Back in the 1970s the Shah had bought eighty of them to counter overflights of Iran by Soviet MiG 25 reconnaissance fighters but with the shattering of relationships that accompanied Khomeini's Islamic revolution of 1979 the supply of spare parts to keep them flying had dried up. So had supplies of the formidable Phoenix air-to-air missile that the F14 carried.

The Chinese F6s had radar but nothing like as good as the Hughes AWG9 that the F14s carried. That AWG9 even now was probably the best airborne radar in Iran.

Major Moussa Rezania left Reza, his radar intercept officer, scrambling up into the rear cockpit to start his checks on radar and electronic systems, and went through the pre-flight walk-round at a run. Missiles on and secure. Arming pins out. Undercarriage condition.

This aircraft had been designed for the US Navy and its undercarriage had been built to withstand being slammed on to a pitching steel deck at 100-odd knots. The tyres were worn but the hydraulics weren't leaking. Wing underside, panels undamaged.

The wind was choppy, warm, mostly along the runway. Looking good for take-off, Moussa thought. He scrambled up the ladder.

For a man in his mid-thirties he was in hard condition and the run hadn't made him short of breath; only the adrenaline charge quickened his heart rate, and that was good. Moussa had the typical Rezania build: chunky body, powerful limbs, round, aggressive face and hardly any neck. He had big, capable hands, a mat of black hair on his chest, and a balding forehead. He was a thinker as well as a doer. Fire flickered in his piercing eyes.

'Reza, intercom check.'

'Copy, Moussa.' The voice was firm and strong on the phones inside his heavy bone dome as Moussa fastened the chin clip.

The groundcrewman at the top of the ladder was plugging in Moussa's oxygen.

'Systems?'

'Check.'

As he talked tensely, Moussa was running through his own cockpit drills, watching the gyro instruments spin up, adjusting the direction indicator to the compass reading, testing his own radar screen. This was an old fighter. Tough as it was, it lacked the digital cockpit of more recent models.

The groundcrewman scrambled down and the ladder vanished. On the radio the ground chief said: 'Clear to start engines.'

'Roger,' Moussa said. 'Clear hood!' He pushed the key and the big, power-operated hood came down, close over the bone domes. Moussa reached to the engine start panel.

No-one had been expecting a fighter scramble today.

No-one had a clue what the intruder might be. But if anything could catch it, it was Moussa Rezania's F14s.

'Eagle's Nest,' the disembodied voice said inside his bone dome, 'Tiger Three Three.' *Eagle's Nest* was today's callsign for fighter control. *Tiger Three* was Moussa's flight of four aircraft, *Three Three* was Moussa's own.

'Tiger Three Three copies.' Jet noise pierced through Moussa's bone dome and there were drizzle spots on the streamlined cockpit canopy.

'Tiger Three Section, report ready to scramble.'

Pushing his strong shoulders against the harness, Moussa peered to the right, along the short line of aircraft. 'Eagle's Nest, Tiger Three ready.'

'Tiger Three Section, scramble, scramble!'

Moussa stabbed forward with his toes and released the brakes. The Tomcat rolled forward.

At Tabriz Three, everyone held Moussa Rezania in awe. He was one of very few Iranian pilots who'd actually shot down Iraqi fighters in the course of the long, debilitating war of 1980–88, and he'd been critical from the outset of the Iranian command's tactics of using the F14s principally as radar platforms, finding Iraqi aircraft and vectoring other fighters to attack them.

Iraq's MiGs and Sukhois were good aircraft, and the new 29s were better than the 21s and 27s they'd been up against in those days, but Moussa knew F14s inside out and he insisted that they were a match for anything the Iraqis could put up, even now. Maybe even a match for Israel's F15s and F16s, depending on how you flew them. The radar, certainly, was far superior to the export-issue stuff on Iran's MiG 29s.

The taxiway ran right and Moussa steered around and set the pace of a gentle jog. The second F14 started moving – Ali's aircraft. Ali was another veteran of the Iraqi conflict, a thin man with a heavy black moustache and the same intensity of religious belief that Moussa had. He'd been flying with Youssef, his backseater, for years.

Both men had since their teens been powerfully influenced by the teachings of Hojatoleslam Ardeshir Rezania. Ardeshir was the priest of Roudabad and was Moussa's uncle.

Still there were checks to do and Moussa was running them on the roll. Flaps, full and part extension. Speedbrakes. Fuel. None of them had more than half tanks. The air force operated under a permanent fuel shortage.

'Tiger Three Three, this is Tiger Three Five!' In the headset the voice sounded alarmed and Moussa glanced over. He was just rolling past Tiger Three Six, the last jet in the line, and he craned back to see Three Five.

'Tiger Three Three, go ahead, Three Five.'

'Tiger Three Five, I can't get full and free on the rudders!'

Moussa Rezania was probably the Islamic Revolutionary Iranian Air Force's best F14 pilot, and his engineers were probably the best F14 engineers in the country, and Moussa made it a point of pride to keep his flight of fighters in the best state of readiness possible. For all that, serviceability could be patchy when you couldn't get the parts and you couldn't even make them. Mentally Moussa cursed. Maybe this trouble was the linkage, maybe something in the hinges, maybe a loose nut fouling somewhere. The F14 had two big fins-and-rudders, and if even one of them jammed, the jet wasn't flyable.

'Tiger Three Five, abort, abort.'

He'd just have to shut his engines down. Moussa thought grimly of all that good fuel gone to waste. Worse still, now he had at least one bogey aircraft to contend with, and only three fighters.

'Eagle's Nest,' fighter control reminded him. 'Tiger Three Section cleared to go.'

Moussa turned left to the holding point and glanced over his shoulder as he turned. Three Four and Three Six were on the taxiway, their massive jet nozzles blurring the view with their heat ripples.

'Tiger Three rolling,' Moussa said. He thought: this time let's see you do it properly. For two years now he'd been struggling with ground control to get the quality of the radar intercepts up to a level he could feel happy with. Maybe this time they'd surprise him and actually find the bogey aircraft.

With his left hand, Moussa shoved the throttles up to the stops. For a moment the F14 rolled slowly. This was a big aircraft; it took a lot of fuel to get it up where it belonged. Then he felt the satisfying shove in the back as full reheat punched in.

*   *   *

Blind in cloud, the Tomcat climbed almost vertically. The weather kicked Moussa about but he'd be through it very soon. The altimeter needle was a blur, going through 15,000 feet. Reza was warming up his radar, running the checks. Moussa couldn't see the other fighters.

'Tiger Three aircraft, condition check.'

'Tiger Three Four, all systems check, climbing.'

'Ti . . . ee . . . Six, all sys . . .'

'Tiger Three Three for Three Six, say again your condition.'

He got the call, clearly this time. The F14 felt solid around him, driving upwards through the cloud. Then all at once it broke out of the fog and into a blinding sunscape. Twenty-five thousand feet. Moussa levelled off.

'Eagle's Nest, Tiger Three section is at patrol height.'

'Roger, Tiger Three. Your bogey is a singleton, speed two eight zero knots, heading zero nine, sector Delta Four South and at 15,000 feet at this time. Signature suggests MiG Two Five. Report in radar contact with bogey.'

Odd, Moussa thought. Two eighty knots was a bit slow for a fighter like the big old MiG 25, the one the NATO air forces codenamed *Foxbat*. Fifteen thousand was a bit low for a fighter like that; the Russians and others had flown them up to 70,000.

'Tiger Three Three copies. Radar on. Tiger Three aircraft, check in.'

'Radar on,' Ali said. 'Tiger Three Four.'

Nothing from the third Tomcat. Angrily Moussa twisted right, glimpsed Ali's aircraft, wings fully swept, sliding dangerously through the atmosphere, then he twisted to look left.

Four hundred metres away, Tiger Three Six waggled its wings and then peeled off, wheeling away and back over the cloud. Complete radio failure, Moussa realized, and cursed inwardly.

Behind the angularity of the forward ejector seat, Reza was frowning, fiddling with the brightness control on his scope. 'Nothing for Delta Four South, Moussa – too much ground return.'

A MiG 25 could move very fast if it chose. 'Eagle's Nest,' Moussa radioed, growing impatient, 'Tiger Three Three. No trace yet for bogey – is it still on your radar?'

Experience in the Iraqi conflict had demonstrated the difficulties of an accurate fighter intercept. Hardly ever had the two sides exchanged shots or missiles as a result of a ground-controlled radar intercept.

On the radio, the pause fizzed softly. The cloud lay in heaps and every facet danced white with sunlight. What Moussa wanted was a kill.

'Tiger Three Three, Eagle's Nest. Bogey is sector Charlie Four South at this time.'

Moussa frowned. 'Eagle's Nest, Charlie sector is *west* of Delta sector. I thought you said this bogey was flying east.'

A pause. Typical, Moussa thought in mounting anger. Maybe the bogey aircraft had registered Tabriz Three's radar waves and thought better of it, and now they wouldn't catch the intruder at all. Maybe there never had been an intruder in the first place.

'Eagle's Nest copies.' No comment.

They were heading west, the turbines idling, hardly flying at more than 300 knots now. Ali kept formation a kilometre to starboard.

'Tiger Three Three standing by,' Moussa needled.

'Eagle's Nest,' the controller said, 'our original data may have been faulty. Confirm bogey is Charlie Four South and flying east.'

'Tiger Three Three copies. Say height information.'

Reza kept quiet.

'Eagle's Nest. Bogey is 12,000 feet. It's lost some height, over.'

Or maybe they'd had duff height info in the first place, Moussa thought.

Reza said: 'Overhead Charlie Four South now. Negative on bogey.'

In the slow speed the wings had swept forward.

'Eagle's Nest, Tiger Three aircraft,' the controller said suddenly. 'We have bogey Echo Four South, heading east on one zero, speed three two zero knots.'

Shit. Moussa cracked the throttles open and hauled the big fighter steeply round to the left, right round on himself. Ali was turning with him; he'd anticipated as soon as he heard Eagle's Nest's transmission.

'Tiger Three Three,' Moussa said coldly, 'confirm bogey Echo Four South.' The F14's instruments were calibrated in knots for airspeed and feet for height, and the controller had to convert from metres, another reason Moussa didn't trust what he was being told. 'What type? Are we still saying MiG Two Five?'

A pause.

'Eagle's Nest. We now think it's a bomber.'

Those morons. They hadn't the faintest idea.

*　　*　　*

Cloud lay in heaps, hiding the ruthless rock of the mountains. Moussa had the formation wings swept and barely subsonic, tearing eastwards now for Echo Four South. He glanced at the fuel. Enough so far, but not for long.

The idea of a bomber penetrating from the Turkish border didn't make sense. Moussa was going to have to find this bogey visually and identify it for himself.

'Here we are,' Reza said.

Moussa radioed: 'Eagle's Nest, Tiger Three section is overhead Echo Four South.'

He throttled right back. The speed came down to 300 knots and the wings eased forward.

'Eagle's Nest copies. Any radar contact yet?'

'Negative. Tiger Three Three.'

Heading: a little north of east now. That fuel wanted half an eye keeping on it; they'd burned a lot in that reheat climb.

'Contact!' Reza yelled. 'Ten o'clock low, he's crossing us, port to starboard. Turn starboard now!'

Back pressure on the chunky control stick with its trim control and gun buttons. Moussa stood the Tomcat on its starboard wingtip, aware of Ali doing the same. In a deliberate action, Moussa began switching his missiles to *armed*.

Each jet carried four infra-red-guided Sidewinders. Only one Phoenix, it was all the air force could spare. The Phoenix was a radar-guided rocket that could destroy an enemy well beyond the visual horizon and you couldn't get replacement rounds from the usual illicit arms dealers.

If all else failed, there was always the gun.

'Contact!' Reza called again from the aft cockpit. 'We're in his six, he's right low down. *Allah, Allah*. He's right down in among the peaks, I can hardly see him for the ground return.' The ground return looked like orange mould growing in patches all over the scope.

'Eagle's Nest,' Moussa radioed, 'Tiger Three Three. Contact one bogey ahead. We're going down. Tango Three section, dive!'

Then he throttled right back and put the nose down and the F14 was in cloud. Blind again.

*   *   *

'Reza,' Moussa said on the intercom, 'I'm relying on you to keep us clear of these mountains.' *Insh' Allah.* If God wills.

They were coming down steeply and there was nothing around them but whitish fog. It was bumpy and the F14 was dropping and lurching in the turbulence, trying to drop a wing. The long radar nose kept yawing off its course.

'I can still see him,' Reza said.

The altimeter unwound through 18,000 feet.

Reza said: 'He's extending now. He's got more forward speed than we have.'

Moussa flattened the dive slightly. They went through 16,500 feet. Fuel still adequate. Just.

'Tiger Three Four,' Ali said edgily in the headset. 'This is MSA we're going through.' Fifteen thousand: minimum safe altitude.

'Tiger Three Three copies.' It was eerie here with nothing surrounding them, *knowing* those peaks were there. Ali had closed the gap between the Tomcats. Fourteen thousand. Thirteen thousand. How far did this cloud go down?

'Clear ahead on this track,' Reza said reassuringly. 'Strong ground return now, we seem to be in a valley between peaks.'

Death lurked close in this innocent-looking white fog. Moussa Rezania didn't want to die. Yet if his dying was the will of God, then he must and would submit. 'Bogey still in contact?'

'Ah . . . negative.' Right now the bogey wasn't uppermost on Reza's mind.

Submission to God's will was like obeying a military order. You just did it. Yet the submission couldn't damp out the prickle of sweat on your neck, the tremble of your hand on the chunky stick with its levers and buttons.

Moussa Rezania had important things yet to do with his life.

They broke cloud. Under the base the world was grey and wet and not far away; a bleak, uninhabited landscape of cruel rock. Moussa looked to starboard for Ali's aircraft.

Hardly two hundred metres away, Ali broke cloud and the breath stopped in Moussa's throat, Ali was twenty metres above ground and still descending.

'*Allah, Allah!*'

As Moussa watched, Ali stood the Tomcat on its tail and banged in full reheat. He vanished immediately back into cloud, leaving scorch marks on the scrub.

'Tiger Three Four, breaking off.'

So that was enough for Ali. Well, maybe it wasn't such a bad idea, keeping his aircraft from hazard. 'Tiger Three Three,' Moussa acknowledged.

'We're in Foxtrot Four South,' Reza reported.

'Contact with bogey?'

'Negative.'

How on earth could they just lose it like that? Moussa's lips were tight behind the oxygen mask. He was at 10,000 feet and he levelled off, weaving amid the mountainsides at 300 knots.

Terrain obstructions. That was how they'd lost the bogey. This was going to be difficult.

Murky rain squalls trailed darkly from the cloudbase and the F14 rocked whenever they went through one. Static fizzed in his headset and his oxygen mask smelled of rubber.

Reza said: 'And now . . . Golf Four South. Where *is* he?'

A jagged peak loomed up and Moussa rolled starboard to weave around it.

Reza said: 'Fuel's getting low.' Many of the pilot's instruments were duplicated in the rear cockpit.

To Satan with this. 'Always supposing there was a bogey in the first place,' Moussa said angrily, and cracked the throttles open as he climbed the F14 steeply. 'Eagle's Nest, this is Tiger Three Three calling bingo fuel.' Just enough to get back to base. 'We're breaking off.'

They bored upwards into the cloud and once more the white murk enveloped them.

*   *   *

The ILS at Tabriz Three wasn't working. Reza got them over a patch of flat ground and Moussa let down in cautious spirals until he could see again. Silently he was seething.

Ali's aircraft was on the ground, parked, as Moussa brought his F14 over the fence with the wings swept forward and the flaps and gear down and the two big Pratt & Whitney TF30 turbofans running on fumes. A gust caught them over the runway and the landing was two hefty thumps.

Moussa raised the canopy as he taxied in. Thunder was rumbling in the hills. Tiger Three Five was there with a platform up to the tail and men working on it, but Tiger Three Six was missing. Moussa hoped they'd been able to divert successfully.

He shut down the engines and the systems and then started unfastening his harness, angrily, ready to climb down and give fighter control a piece of his mind.

CHAPTER 7

Somewhere south of Tabriz there'd been pursuit by Iranian fighters but now it had fizzled out. Tamasin Masterson was exhausted but still she kept looking over at Keith Cross, conscious, biting his lip as he fought to suppress his moans. She'd picked up the 205 degrees radial signal from Tehran's VOR on 115.3 and she'd used it to aim off, skirting south of the capital.

That was when they'd come clear of cloud and Darvish Aksoy had stooped forward over the throttle quadrant to start guiding them visually. Tamasin hadn't thought he would.

The road Darvish picked up ran east-west. From 2,000 feet above ground it looked busy with lorries and buses; but they were off the eastern end of the chart now and Tamasin had no idea where they were going. Darvish had somehow produced a road map of Iran. He didn't let Tamasin look at it. She still had the dashboard clock set to Turkish time, 1302. In Iran that made it 1432.

'How far is this place Zedasht?' Tension shivered in Tamasin's voice. She tapped the fuel gauges. 'We're going to be on reserves in a minute.'

She'd been involved in military flying years before as a pilot in her University Air Squadron, a reserve training corps for Britain's university students. Since then – except for just once – all her flying had been commercial. You didn't shave safety margins to the bone the way you would sometimes on a bomber or fighter; she was out of practice for this.

Left of them the mountains rose up in a solid blue-black wall: the Elburz. The sun gleamed golden on the Caspian beyond and made the cockpit warm. To the right Tamasin's view wasn't clear but there seemed to be a lot of desert. A glimpse of memory brought Tamasin suddenly back to one Sunday afternoon at Keith's flat, talking to his girlfriend. Most Iranians belong to the Shi'a sect, she'd said in her academic soprano, Turkish Muslims are mostly Sunni. The Sunni are the mainstream followers of the Prophet Muhammad, the Shi'a are a branch that broke away shortly after Muhammad's death. Tamasin remembered Keith's girlfriend. She was called Emma. She was built like a borzoi and had endless supplies of rare information.

'Not far now,' Darvish said. 'I think maybe five minutes.'

They were still cruising at 280 knots, taking it easy, the air much smoother here. Presently, at the foot of the hills to her left, Tamasin made out a small town.

Darvish saw it, too. 'Ah, now we go too far. Turn back. Turn to the right.'

Nothing on the radio, no telling whether there was other traffic out here. Tamasin craned forward unhappily over the coaming, peering out all around. Nothing. She held the speed and banked steeply to the right, pressing the yoke back.

The nose tracked round the desert horizon. She picked up the road again and rolled level.

'It's south of here,' Darvish said above the soft, steady roar in the cockpit.

Tamasin screwed up her eyes and peered out in the dazzle to the left. Nothing. 'How far to the south?' she asked.

'Six thousand metres from the road, not more.'

Again Tamasin pressed back the yoke to keep the nose on the horizon. This time she rolled left. The yellow-brown bleakness of the desert swung round with its dusty dark scrub. 'OK,' she said, 'I'll start searching.'

The sooner they got down, the sooner she could get

some help for Keith. But what would Darvish do when he didn't need them any more? Would he just shoot them both out of hand? She'd been afraid before, she'd faced death before; but mostly, when she thought back to those times, she knew she'd had a measure of control over how it would be.

Geometric shapes against the undulations of the desert scrub; half-glimpsed, the long, dusty scar of the runway. She'd never have seen it if she hadn't had years of practice looking from the air for runways.

'It's there, Darvish! Ten o'clock – out to the left.'

He craned to look past her. 'Yes, that's it.'

Clear ahead at this height. Eyes on the runway below, Tamasin reached right and pulled back the power levers. She came south of the airfield buildings and turned left; in a left turn, she could see everything she wanted. The speed came back to 130 knots and she lowered a notch of flap. Now that she could see where she was going, she knew she had enough fuel for the job.

'What are you going to do when we get down?' She was peering at the runway, trying to gauge its length.

'You don't need to know that,' Darvish said.

'Oh yes I bloody well do,' Tamasin blazed over her shoulder. 'If you're going to shoot me as soon as we come to a halt, it alters the way I might plan going about things.'

Darvish gave his shallow, nervous laugh again. 'I don't shoot you. Why should I shoot you?'

The runway was aligned at 04/31 – some way off east-west – any one strip of asphalt is actually two runways, a different one for each end you start from. This one looked long enough, just. 'I don't know why you should shoot anyone,' Tamasin said, eyes sullen. 'I don't know why you had to shoot Keith.' She was coming back to the north again, towards the road and the little town at the foot of the mountain. There was a railway, too, she saw now.

'I don't shoot you,' Darvish repeated. He rasped

a laugh. 'You give me one very good flight. I just go.'

But would he?

She was now down to 1,000 feet. With no QFE pressure reference from a ground controller, she was gauging her height by the radar altimeter. She turned, following the runway westwards again. As far as she could make out, the wind was more in the east than in the west. She lowered the undercarriage.

'OK, I'm going in there.'

More flap. The nose started forcing its way steeply down and Tamasin spun on the trim wheel as she rolled in on to final approach. Wind rocked *Dragon Rapide*'s wide, solid wing. Through the faint haze of desert dust Tamasin was straining her eyes for a sight of the threshold bars, but she realized they were almost eroded away. She aimed at where she thought they ought to be.

The wheels hit the spot with a single, satisfying *whump*.

* * *

She'd guessed 4,000 feet for the runway length but now as *Dragon Rapide* decelerated it was starting to look better, more like 4,500. The surface was terrible, potholed and patched and in places half-covered in orange sand, and the jolts as they careered down the old asphalt brought another cry of pain from Keith. As Tamasin stood on the brakes she was aware of buildings out to her right, an old control tower, no radar, a hangar beside the control tower, something more behind the hangar, she wasn't sure what. The jet shuddered and shivered and at last slowed down to walking pace.

Tamasin reached right and raised the flaps. Anything might be lying on this surface and if it got a chance to fly up and damage the jet, it would do. From the end of the runway a taxiway ran right and Tamasin steered around on to it.

Darvish yelled: 'Here! Stop here!'

His urgency alarmed Tamasin. She rammed down on the brakes. She didn't know what he wanted.

There was movement beside her. She twisted round. One last glimpse of the skinny figure in the brown suit, the thick black moustache and the stubble, then Darvish had gone. Over the noise in the cabin she heard the graunch and thump as the cabin door opened.

'Darvish, wait! Let me get these engines stopped!' But with a screech of turbine the engine noise came flooding in the cabin and Tamasin knew Darvish couldn't have heard her.

She turned quickly to the panel, and in the glimpse she saw Keith still ashen, the grip on his forearm weak now. High-pressure cocks, fully off both. The turbines whined down. Already as she reached for the electrical system switches she could feel outside air swirling into the cockpit, hot as a jet blast. At breakneck speed Tamasin finished the drills and set the parking brake.

'With you in a sec, Keith!' She threw off the harness and scrambled past the throttles, agile despite her stiffness.

Desert heat punched her as she stood in the airstair door in a silence that left her weak, dizzy. The desert came right up to the edges of the taxiway, gritty, yellow-brown. Darvish had vanished.

Maybe he's gone around the other side, Tamasin thought, the side where the buildings were. So let him go. She swung smoothly back to Keith.

She craned to him over the quadrant. He raised anguished eyes, still conscious.

She stroked his head for a second, then she swung aft again. At the galley she drew a beaker of water. She dug out the first-aid box and snatched it open, her skin beginning to sweat in the heat and tension. The strongest thing in there was a packet of Distalgesic tablets. That time in the B52 they'd had morphine syrettes. They'd needed them, the way Keith needed one now. The scarf

67

round his forearm was a sodden mess, dark with blood, and his wrist seemed articulated from his arm, his hand loose. His face was like blotting paper.

He was half-choking on the Distalgesic, struggling to swallow as Tamasin held the beaker to his lips, when a Suzuki field vehicle with two men in raced around the nose and skidded to a stop.

* * *

The floor swayed under Tamasin as the two men climbed on board. Over her shoulder she saw puzzled faces, military fatigues, no weapons.

She ignored them. She got Keith to swallow the second Distalgesic tablet.

The first of the men in fatigues was a tubby man with a full beard. The other man peered worriedly over his shoulder, six foot, thin and clean-shaven. The tubby one said something in Farsi.

Tamasin looked back, one hand on Keith's shoulder. Dark eyes hard with tension, she shook her short, charcoal hair. 'Either of you speak English?'

Keith shifted in his seat. The pain wouldn't go away.

Until she'd spoken, the two men hadn't seemed to realize she was a woman.

Tubby looked blank. Tall said: 'No Engleesh. *Français*.'

Better than nothing. Tamasin took a breath and tried to remember. '*Mon co-pilote est blessé. Il a besoin des drogues pour la douleur.*'

The worried look grew on Tall's face. Perhaps he didn't really speak French after all.

He managed: '*Venez avec nous. Nous avons des choses dans le bureau.*'

'*D'accord.*' She started unfastening Keith's harness.

* * *

A couple of times Keith knocked his arm as they got him out past the quadrant. His moans of pain were becoming quieter. Tubby, surprisingly strong, half-carried him down the steps. The heat didn't help. It was as much as Tamasin herself could do to withstand it.

She left the two Iranians half-lifting Keith into the back of the Suzuki and went back for the jackets and her bag. She hadn't expected to find her hosts this friendly; the thought almost started tears. She got in the back of the Suzuki and steadied Keith by the shoulders as Tall took the wheel and drove briskly back to the buildings.

The 'office' was on the ground floor of the deserted control tower. Tubby and Tamasin supported Keith out of the vehicle and into the office. There were flies trying to get into his wound.

The office was roomy, cluttered, but at least it had a couple of ceiling fans. Those and some shadow helped keep it cool. A camp bed stood propped against one wall and Tall set it up quickly. He was vanishing through a door opposite as Tubby and Tamasin got Keith on to the bed.

Tall rushed in, set down a first-aid kit, and rushed out again. Tubby opened the kit and started loading a syringe. Morphine; it had instructions in English and French as well as Farsi.

The way the tubby, bearded guard injected Keith, you could tell he knew what he was up to. Tall came back with warm water, towels, a blanket. He put the blanket over Keith.

Tamasin had to look away when they got the scarf off his wound. They washed it, they dressed it, but almost at once blood soaked through the dressing. They improvised a tourniquet. Keith wasn't reacting now, possibly relaxed by the morphine.

Tall vanished, then came back with water for Tamasin. She accepted it gratefully.

Tubby said something to Tall. Tall translated: '*Tous les deux os sont rompus.*' Both bones broken.

Tamasin slumped on to a chair. Both guards seemed a bit in awe of her now they'd discovered she was the captain. For a few moments she watched them working on Keith.

She said in French: 'Can I make a phone call?'

More startled looks, a quick gabble of Farsi. Tall said: '*Je regrette* – no telephoning.' Tamasin didn't know whether that meant they had no phone or that she wasn't allowed to use it.

Maybe this *was* going to be awkward after all.

Tubby vanished through the door. Tall peered at Keith, but Keith was half-conscious, his arm bound up tightly now with wound dressings, bandages, splints. Then Tamasin heard Tubby talking in Farsi and she realized they did have a phone.

Weariness washed over her in waves, now that it was over. An urge came over her to cry; but she never cried, it was too self-indulgent. She scarcely ever prayed, either, but now she was praying frantically for Keith. Biting her lip, she looked at her watch, still set to Turkish time. Quarter to two in the afternoon in Turkey: 1515 here, 1145 in the UK. She wondered what was happening back there. She wondered suddenly what had become of Darvish. No-one had said a word about him yet.

It occurred to her that, getting out the port side of the aircraft like that, he'd been screened from the buildings by the jet itself.

Tubby hung up and walked back in, looking worried. He looked at Keith, but Keith seemed to be sleeping. He glanced at Tamasin, then had a quick conversation in Farsi with Tall.

Tall turned to Tamasin. 'Our officer is coming,' he said in French.

'And the other man?' Tamasin said. 'The one who escaped?'

They just looked at her blankly.

Tall pulled up a wooden chair and lowered himself onto it six feet away from Tamasin. He smiled at her. 'You are American? English? You have lost your way in the air?' It was good-natured enough but there was no mistaking what it was: an interrogation.

* * *

Shortly after half past two local Tamasin heard the helicopter. It landed on the ramp twenty yards from where she sat; a Bell 214 Isfahan, the variant of the noisy old Vietnam-era Huey that the company had developed for the Shah in the mid-'70s. The pilot stayed put with his turbine idling and four other men got out. Two wore whites and carried a stretcher; one was a minder, a tall burly man with a dagger at his belt in a scabbard and something black rolled up under his arm; the fourth wore a major's badges.

He was the same height and skinny build as Darvish, hollow-cheeked and mean-looking, wearing thick glasses. His seamed, dark face had an oddly bluish tinge; Tamasin guessed his age as anywhere from fifty to sixty-five. He looked them over, with cold appraisal for Keith, eyelids flickering a little as he lay white-faced on the camp bed; then with something akin to horror at Tamasin.

The two with the stretcher were looking for Keith's vital signs. The major spoke in Farsi to Tubby, then turned disdainfully to Tamasin. He spoke English, well enough but with very rolled *r*s. 'You are the pilot of the plane outside?'

'The captain, yes.'

'Why do you land without permission on Iranian soil?'

There was something chilling in his reedy voice; it had something of the implacable self-confidence that Tamasin had recognized in Darvish. In the corner of the room they were getting Keith onto the stretcher.

'We were hijacked and my co-pilot was shot.'

The major didn't seem the least bit interested. 'You have landed without authorization in a prohibited place and you have illegally violated Iranian airspace. The authorities in Tehran will want to speak with you about this.'

Her eyes widened. The least she'd expected was to be believed. 'Look, *we're* the ones who've got a complaint! My co-pilot was shot by a man named Darvish Aksoy.' She gestured. 'Examine him if you don't believe me. Take a look at the aircraft – you'll see the damage from the bullet in the cockpit.'

'You will please come to Tehran immediately.' The major pointed to the door. They were carrying Keith through it, on the stretcher, out to the idling helicopter.

Fear prickled on Tamasin's neck. It came to her insistently that Walter Becker would have known what to do. She didn't. She'd been so suspicious of Walter when they first met; a MiG pilot, a regular Party member. Only latterly had she talked enough to him to discover the secret, forbidden thoughts he'd had, his scepticism for the one-party state, his contempt for the Honecker regime and its bankrupt morals.

The fans whirled, and flies buzzed about the room. Dazedly, Tamasin stood and pulled on her jacket.

The big thug with the knife on his belt unrolled the black thing he'd been carrying and held it out to her. A chador. Anger and disgust filled Tamasin. The big Iranian pushed the chador at her.

The whistle and boom of the helicopter turbine crowded Tamasin. She snatched the chador. Tight-lipped, she pulled it over her jacket. With the hood she rebelled.

Her eyes met the hollow-cheeked major's. He didn't need to say a word to remind her that she was in his power. Tamasin pulled the hood up over her short hair.

With a mutinous flash of her eye, she stooped. As she reached from under the chador for her flight briefcase she made damn sure the four gold rings showed.

CHAPTER 8

North of Ankara airport, Thursday, 11 June, 0530 local
Dawn wind moaned softly around the dark bulk of the
Mercedes van parked a bit away from the row of articulated trucks in the quiet lot. Down the wide dirt road to
the village of low, shabby houses the few people awake
wouldn't have heard the mutter of the van's diesel – not
powering the heater but the radios hidden in the back.

The man at the wheel was called Mehmet. It was his real
name, not a nickname, even though the Turks themselves
used a play on the name, *Mehmetçik*, to denote an
infantryman, much the equivalent of the English *Tommy
Atkins*. Mehmet really was a soldier: line regiment, then
special forces, and now attached to MIT, the Turkish
central intelligence organization. There was a good reason
for the Heckler & Koch HK53 collapsible-stock 5.56mm
sub-machine-gun Mehmet kept down between the seats.
Apart from driving the big van and mending any of the
radios that needed mending, Mehmet was here as minder
for the boss.

Kemal Koz was MIT's director of special operations.
It was a post he'd worked for years to attain. Now that
he'd attained it he meant to make a good job of it, and
so far it looked as if this operation was turning out as
successful as most of his other operations against *Imanin
Yolu*, the ones he saw as a bunch of religious crazies –
Yol, for short. He'd got Darvish Aksoy, *Yol*'s leader, on
the run.

And he'd done so rather neatly. Leaking the whisper
to those lunatics in the Iranian security service so that
they got their hands on Rana Tezcan, Aksoy's girlfriend,
and slapped her into Evin on some catch-all terrorist

conspiracy charge. Koz had known Aksoy wouldn't be able to resist.

Koz's officers who'd traced Aksoy's movements via the minibus had checked through the village, and confirmed that Aksoy had left on foot, walking through the night. Then he'd got what that trio from the countryside well had claimed was a definite sighting; they'd moved so as to drive Aksoy towards the northern rim of Ankara airport, Esenboga, just the way they'd been told. Always assuming it was Aksoy they'd seen, and always assuming they'd seen someone in the first place.

Since then, it had all gone a bit quiet.

Koz stretched, grunting. He was a big man, with a gut that reflected a non-Islamic liking for beer. He hadn't touched a drop tonight, though; his views on militant fundamentalists were those of a convinced atheist, but he wasn't anti-Turk and he took national security seriously. His tousled hair and straggly moustache had white in them these days, and his eyes had the same old challenging look as ever. He was wearing an oil-spattered blue overall with a dirty vest under it. It wasn't the least bit his style but if anyone saw him they would see a scruffy-looking trucker, not the country's foremost security agent. Mehmet was dressed better.

It was stuffy in the van. The night was mild and the wind was faint.

Had they but known it, their quarry was even then burying his latest victim under a pile of aggregate.

The light grew slowly. Presently a minibus trundled by on the dirt road and soon one of the lorries, then another, started its engine. On the lonely steppe the rumble echoed.

Mehmet took a watchful sweep, leaning over the big, flat wheel, then twisted round to look into the back. From a vacuum flask Koz poured tea, bitter and clear. Mehmet's flask of tea was long since empty.

'Well, sir? How long would you like to carry on waiting?'

Sullenly, Koz snapped his fingers for the cap of Mehmet's flask. Mehmet reached it. Koz took it, topped up the driver-bodyguard's cap, and passed it back. They sipped. The tea, clear and strong, was scalding.

Mehmet nodded thanks and lowered his flask cap. 'It's going to be good visibility now, all across that airfield.'

Koz grunted. His angry eyes ranged around the enclosed shadows of the van, crowded with equipment.

In the distance from the airport, a jet engine whined up shrilly.

'*Tamam*,' Koz muttered, 'OK. I'll give him one more hour, then let's get back into Ankara.'

* * *

It was ten when Mehmet drove the van into the compound with the armed guard on the gate and the barbed wire on top of the high walls. Koz rubbed his eyes as he went up in the lift. He was getting old for this sort of stunt and for losing a night's sleep. He trudged into the office. What he needed was a couple of beers, ten minutes with his saxophone, and about ten hours' sleep. He slumped into his office chair and phoned his wife. She was at work in her lawyer's practice, one of the 'new' breed of Turkish women; although she'd taken quite a long career break when the kids had been small.

'Hello, darling, how are you? Just to let you know — it's looking OK, I should be home pretty soon.'

As he hung up, his assistant walked in, wearing a snappy suit. He spoke fluent, American-accented English and was a Harvard MBA. Complacency oozed from him and Koz rated him as a spoiled brat.

'I thought you ought to see this police report, sir.'

Knowing him, the little smart-arse was probably right. 'Thanks,' Koz grunted ungratefully. Asprawl in his chair, stubble white-speckled on his cheeks, he took the report.

The assistant hovered, taut-limbed from the gym, half-hiding a smirk. Koz read the report through.

A foreman on a construction site on the ·north side of Ankara airport had been found buried in a pile of aggregate, dead with three stab wounds, the last so deep that the murderer hadn't been able to get the knife out again.

Koz groaned inwardly. Aksoy had killed several times over, and he'd used a knife more than once.

This wasn't the way it was supposed to have happened.

'Keep an eye on the police wires,' Koz said, dismissing his assistant. 'Let me know directly you hear anything.' As the young man walked out, he dialled his wife's number again. 'Ah, correction to that last . . .'

He had that airport terminal crawling with MIT agents watching for Darvish Aksoy, and not a peep out of them yet. He rang the team leader. They used coded language.

'Any trade?'

'*Yok,*' the team leader said, 'there's no sign of him. He hasn't boarded any flight that's left since operations started this morning.'

Koz hung up. Something had gone wrong all right. He forced his tired brain to try and work out what. This time when he called for his assistant it was to send downstairs for coffee.

Beyond the venetian blinds the day was colourless and the heat was dry. Traffic grumbled around the streets, truck horns blew. Koz felt his eyelids drooping.

His assistant came in twenty minutes later. Along with the coffee he had another police telex. Koz waited till the door shut again before reading it.

He frowned. He took a sip from the tiny cup and pulled a face. That buffoon downstairs had mixed it with sugar. Koz read the report again, still mystified; yet he knew this must mean *something*.

A Toyota pickup truck, seven years old with an out-of-date licence, had been found evidently abandoned on the part of the ramp at Ankara airport where they parked the general aviation: everything from two-seat prop trainers to Gulfstream intercontinental executive jets. The pickup was registered to the building company, one of whose foremen had just been offed; the bereaved colleagues had been too busy sorting out the repercussions to miss the pickup at first, but when the police mentioned it to them they agreed at once it was theirs.

If that little swine Aksoy had nicked the pickup, where the hell had he *gone*? Koz shifted his bulky body uncomfortably in his seat. He poured the coffee into a pot plant.

The phone rang.

Koz grabbed it. '*Evet?*' It was the insecure outside line, the one with the number he gave only to a handful of trusted sources. He didn't attempt to sound friendly.

The voice on the other end gave a codename Koz recognized as that of a businessman with international connections called Erol Ersin. Ersin wasn't a professional MIT agent but he was a man with useful contacts who wasn't averse to helping the state.

'I do you many favours,' Ersin said when he'd finished the initial pleasantries.

'Indeed you do,' Koz grunted. He wasn't in a mood for people calling in their debts.

'I wonder if perhaps now you might do me one in return.'

'Of course, my friend. Whatever you like, so long as it's in my power.'

'My English colleague Mrs Wyer is very worried. One of her jets is missing, with one man and one woman crew on board.' Ersin ran through it.

'Yes,' Koz said. 'Yes. Yes, I see.' He'd had a lot of practice keeping his feelings out of his voice. He had a sinking feeling in his stomach. Not many people knew that when under stress Kemal Koz sank his voice to a near-whisper and became excessively polite. 'No, I do most regret, I've heard nothing. Yes, of course. I'll have the reports checked at once. Very good of you to let me know. Of course, my friend, I'll let you know the moment I find anything out.'

Koz put down the phone. He ran a big palm over his lower jaw, his temples pulsing, his brain tired. Ersin and Wyer were thinking *crash*. That wasn't what Koz was thinking.

Not only had his carefully thought-out plan gone wildly wrong, now – they could virtually count on it – that son of Satan had stolen the one jet in the whole of Turkey that MIT couldn't afford to have stolen.

Koz knew Felix Wyer – by repute, not personally. He also knew that one of the main reasons that she'd got that naval contract down at Antalya – not that Koz objected to that: if the Turkish navy had tried setting up the operation Felix Wyer had set up for them, you could put a couple of noughts on the end of what they paid La Wyer – was that she was an old and close friend of the man who was Minister of the Interior and had hire and fire of senior MIT personnel. And if *that* man got one inkling of how far wrong Koz's plan had gone . . .

What that little polecat Aksoy was supposed to have done was to have gone into Ankara airport terminal and bought a ticket to Tehran. Somewhere in Iran there was a whole bunch of wanted *Yol* terrorists and MIT didn't know where they were but they knew damn well if they chased Aksoy out of Turkey he would go to Iran and join up with the rest of his crazies. MIT had three teams of two waiting at Tehran's Mehrabad airport ready to pick up Aksoy as he came through and tag him all the way to his cronies. And then what happened?

Koz saw one glimmer of hope. Executive jets carried transponders and if Dragon Jet's aircraft had been hijacked, the captain – the woman, Ersin had said – would have changed the transponder code accordingly. Ankara's radar room would have known immediately.

The man he rang at Esenboga wasn't the leader of the team he'd had watching for Aksoy coming through; it was a senior manager in administration.

'Has there been any interference with any aircraft taking off from Ankara today?' That was officialese for hijack.

The manager hesitated. 'Nothing whatever. It's been . . . well, a normal day, apart from a bit of an alarm over a positioning flight to Antalya.'

Positioning was when you flew from Airport A to Airport B with no payload, just crew, because your next payload was starting from Airport B.

Koz could feel a throbbing starting in his temples. 'So if an aircraft leaving you set the 7500 transponder code, you would have seen it?'

'Oh . . . well, no.' Again the manager hesitated. 'Our secondary surveillance radar has been down since yesterday for maintenance. We have no transponder information for the moment.'

'Thank you very much.' Koz hung up.

* * *

Jets flew high up, Koz thought; this one surely wouldn't get far without showing on radar.

The military. He grabbed for a reference book and then dialled the number for Incirlik. It was the big NATO base close to Adana; Adana was on the Med coast just west of where the coastline curved round to the south to meet the Syrian border; Incirlik had launched missions against Iraq in the Gulf war. Koz used the secure phone and went through to the intelligence office. The code he used ranked him as a military intelligence brigadier from the Ankara staff; yet the influence Koz wielded was far greater than that of any common brigadier.

'Has your radar shown any traces of a bogey aircraft flying east this morning? Or anything that suggested an executive jet heading east?'

'One moment, sir.'

Koz rubbed his eyes as he waited. The man at Incirlik came back.

'No, sir, there's been nothing unusual in our sector.'

Koz hung up. The next most obvious place would be Diyarbakir, which Koz regarded as a godforsaken dump in Kurdistan – Koz used the term, privately at least, even if it went against official policy. Diyarbakir was another big NATO base and a key Turkish air force headquarters.

Same code, same question.

'Yes, sir, our officers challenged a bogey aircraft today at 1006 hours. F16s were scrambled at 1018 hours when the bogey failed to reply to the challenge, but radar lost it in ground return when it opted to fly dangerously low amid mountain terrain. It was heading east. Flight profile and radar return suggested a returning fighter, maybe F4 class, maybe one of those Chinese ones the Iranians have.'

'Humph. Have the Iranians ever penetrated that far into Turkey before?'

'Not to our knowledge, sir.' It was a mystery, but the officer at Diyarbakir left that as an implication to be picked up.

'From its flight profile, could it have been an executive jet?'

'At *that* height?' Diyarbakir sounded at once incredulous and tickled at the thought of what high speed and low altitude would have done to the financial director's breakfast.

Koz thought for a moment. 'Have you got any airborne radar there that could "look" into Iran?'

'Not at present, sir. There are three based at Konya but they're on joint ops with the ones at Preveza, Greece, monitoring events in Bosnia.' Koz knew that. Konya was south-west of Ankara; ironically, as well as being a massive NATO combined forces station, the city was the Islamic cultural centre where Darvish Aksoy had acquired the particular religious bee in his bonnet. Diyarbakir added: 'We're expecting a deployment of E3 Sentry aircraft in a couple of days for the Iraqi operation, but there's nothing until that time.'

The Iraqi operation existed mainly to stop the country's dictator bombing the hell out of his Kurds while Turkey quietly bombed the hell out of its own – those in the guerrilla movement, anyway. The guerrillas had probably shot or blown up more fellow Kurds than they had Turks.

If Koz had his way they would let the Kurds have their Kurdistan – it wouldn't be mortal injury for Turkey to part with a modest chunk of rock and desert – so long as the other three nations involved, Syria, Iraq and Iran, chipped in their share as well. It would at least save all this present expensive hypocrisy.

He told Diyarbakir goodbye and hung up. The more it started to fall into place, the less he liked it. It was time to call on those three teams at Mehrabad; the poor sons of bitches must be bored out of their skulls by now.

This time the method wasn't straightforward. Koz placed a phone call to a haulage company out in Van, way in the mountains of eastern Turkey. The hauliers then made contact – *insh' Allah* – with a freight agency in a shed on the edge of Mehrabad. The person there then got in touch with the bloke in the terminal with the message suitably dressed up in code.

Koz got his call through to Van about 1220 Turkish time. It was almost 1500, Koz's stomach rumbling after an inadequate lunch, before his reply came back: there hadn't been an executive jet into Mehrabad all day.

That was it, then: that one of Felix Wyer's couldn't be still travelling now; it would have been long since out of fuel. Koz's plan hadn't gone wrong, it had gone disastrously wrong.

He wanted to go home, but first he *had* to have definite word on that jet. At this rate, Mrs Koz would get back from her second day at the office before Mr Koz got back from his first.

At 1600 his worst fear materialized. The minister came on the phone in person.

'Agent Koz, are you aware of the case of a British jet that has gone missing today from Ankara?'

'Yes, Minister, the case has been drawn to my attention.'

'Something very serious appears to have happened. We

have air traffic control looking everywhere for the plane. There is interest in this at the highest levels and this is a major embarrassment for the government. What can you tell me?'

'I have my best-placed assets at this moment investigating, Minister. There are leads' – *were there hell* – 'but at present it would be unwise to speculate without definite information. Rest assured that I'm devoting all my resources to finding the aircraft.' Actually, he was devoting all his resources to making sure that his present interlocutor didn't discover that if it hadn't been for Koz's plan screwing up, that jet would have been safely in Antalya.

'Let my office know as soon as you get word.' The minister hung up.

It was an hour later, roughly 1830 Tehran time, when word came through. It came via Van from the shed at Mehrabad, but this time the source was a sergeant in the Islamic Revolutionary Iranian Air Force. The sergeant was a secret communist sympathizer who had actually been a KGB source until the Soviet Union disintegrated into the CIS – Commonwealth of Independent States. A carefully worded approach by MIT had left the sergeant fondly imagining that all his reports now went straight to Peking, being almost the last place left for a true socialist.

What he reported was a woman – a Westerner – currently held at an IRIAF helicopter facility on the outskirts of Tehran. There was a man with her but he was dead.

This sounded as if it might be it.

CHAPTER 9

Overhead Thames Estuary, Thursday, 11 June, 1750 local
Cloudbase was higher on the return than it had been when
Rob Pilgrim and Melvin Trail had set out for Belgium and
Germany that morning. They were out of it at 2,900 feet
on the procedural approach, Thames Radar giving them
headings and heights to fly, and from eight miles out they
could see Biggin Hill's runway lighting like a neon sign
amid the tangle of street and house lights dotting the swirl
of charcoal and black below. Trail had done the landing at
Antwerp, Rob at Cologne, Trail at Mannheim, and now
Rob nursed *Dragon Tempest* down the glidepath and set
the wheels on to the big runway at home.

Inside five minutes of brakes-on, the engineer salesmen
were through customs and back in the waiting Granada:
another advantage of exec jet charter. He who got to fly
the landing also got to fill out the logs, so consequently
Trail, and Anne, the stewardess, were long gone by
the time Rob Pilgrim trudged up the stairs into the
ops room.

'Hi, Zafar.'

'Hi, Rob.'

Zafar Rahim was the despatcher, a studious Asian
man of about thirty who'd struck a chord with Felix
at the interview when she recognized that he had the
same lifelong fascination as her with aviation. Part of
his payment came in the form of flying training on Felix's
single-prop two-seater Chipmunk – another de Havilland
classic.

Zafar smiled shyly. Zafar was like Dr Bibi Tabrizi,
Azra's sister, Rob reflected: a moderate, common sense
Muslim. Today Zafar was behind the long counter that

the pilots used to rest their papers on when filling out flight plan forms. The noticeboard had Met faxes on, and a sketch weather map, and a bulldog clip with Notams – 'notices to airmen', a term that always got Tamasin wound up – with updates about royal flights and which airfields' radio aids weren't working. Behind Zafar the big white plastic locator board showed the names of the aircraft, their registrations, their crews, their status and where they were.

Against *Dragon Rapide* nothing was showing. But you wouldn't write *missing* on the board; you never knew when some visitor was going to happen by.

'Zafar, what's up with *Rapide*?'

* * *

It was always possible, Rob thought grimly as he lowered himself into the old Midget, that it wasn't a crash.

In his RAF days he'd been no stranger to crashes. Trail had flown in real combat, Rob never had, but both men had lost colleagues to the sort of risky flying that you got up to in an air force. This peace-time business left an even deeper shock. You flew with such huge safety margins – most of the time – you didn't really think of crashing as an immediate sort of danger, the sort that haunted an air force crew.

Rob started the Midget and got into gear.

He'd liked both of them. Tamasin had been a real professional, Keith had been just one of those natural pilots.

He stopped himself. They didn't know it was past tense yet.

The overcast lay black and Rob had his headlights on to drive across the wide darkness of the green, heading for Bromley. This immediate reversion to past-tense thinking was something else he remembered from his military days. Then, in the unexpected, clear vision of memory, he could see himself co-piloting the bomber again, the one real exploit of his career.

There'd been six Vulcans in the formation and the flight had become a legend. From Scotland they'd gone in right over the Arctic, right over Canada, and got through scot-free into US airspace at over 50,000 feet, right up where the radar should have been trampling all over them but wasn't. They'd 'bombed the hell out of' America.

Afterwards, the lead bomber pilot and his lead EWO had a considerable say in some of the gizmos the Americans put on their satellites to prevent anything like that happening again, particularly from quarters other than Scotland.

Rob didn't talk much about that. Also, he didn't talk about the Dominies they'd transferred him to when they started taking Vulcans out of service. The Dominie was the RAF's adaptation of the same BAe 125 he and Trail were flying now. He'd been a captain, his only captain's assignment ever, for just over a year before the day his aircraft ran off the end of a runway that had so much rain on it, it almost qualified as navy territory. The inquiry blamed Rob for the damage and Rob was back to being a co-pilot. Kate, his ex-wife, had laughed when she heard the story.

Traffic was queueing to the red light at the roadworks. Rob set the Midget's handbrake, still thinking about that missing aircraft. He didn't fret. He'd long since learned not to fret about things he had no control over.

He wondered now whether this was something Bibi could usefully know. But then, they hadn't anything definite yet to go on.

CHAPTER 10

IRIAF base east Tehran, Thursday, 11 June, 1540 local
Two ambulances were waiting by the landing pad as the
Bell 214 Isfahan settled on its skids. Tamasin Masterson
reached from under her chador and squeezed Keith Cross's
hand one last time as he lay on the stretcher. She couldn't
tell whether she got a response. He looks terrible, she
thought, his face greyish white, his eyes sunken, not quite
closed; evidently still losing blood.

Outside in the heavy heat the two waiting women
in chadors shepherded Tamasin towards the second
ambulance as the first sped away with Keith.

'But there's nothing wrong with me, I don't need an
ambulance!'

'Come, please.' The one who spoke English was at
least polite.

The doctor was a woman. She seemed to have been
brought in specially. She was friendly, efficient, thorough.
Her equipment was comprehensive; the surgery immaculate; Tamasin started to feel confident that Keith would
be in good hands.

'You are tired,' the doctor said with a smile. 'Other
than that, you seem fine.'

'Thank you.'

They took her to the women's quarters. By the time
they locked her up there, she was too exhausted to care
any more.

*   *   *

Exhausted or not, she slept little that night. Somewhere
close by there was a mosque, maybe on the base itself,

87

and the muezzin seemed to be wailing on all night long.

The next day was Friday, 12 June, and it dawned cloudless and dusty, the weather sweltering even before breakfast. Tamasin's room wasn't air-conditioned and the ceiling fans didn't make much impression on the heat.

At seven they gave her breakfast and after that they took her to a bare room where she fretted about Keith and kicked her heels for almost four hours with only a few Farsi newspapers for company.

It was gone eleven when they escorted her, still in the chador, to the office of someone senior. The two sullen women who formed her escort stood a pace behind the chair where Tamasin sat before the desk. Again the ceiling had fans, a couple of flies buzzing against the dust-speckled window.

The man had both passports in front of him, hers and Keith's. He studied her a moment, gravely. 'My name is Colonel Alijani.' His English was good, with little accent, but the slow delivery suggested that he had to think everything out first. 'I believe I have the honour of addressing Mrs Masterson. How are you, Mrs Masterson? Are you being treated well?'

'Bored out of my skull, thank you,' Tamasin said. 'Apart from that, fine. Can I get rid of this thing?' She tugged at her chador sleeve.

Alijani's face registered something approaching horror. 'I am very sorry, Mrs Masterson, that would not be proper. You and I are strangers.'

'How is Keith Cross – my co-pilot?'

A shadow passed across Alijani's politely serious face. 'Mrs Masterson, truly I am sorry to have to tell you – Keith Cross died yesterday about six.'

*   *   *

She wanted to cry but she couldn't. Crying seemed expected of her; and the anguish inside was quite enough to justify crying; yet instead she just felt numbed, overwhelmed. Part of her refused to believe it. Part of her knew it had been inevitable from the moment Darvish Aksoy had squeezed the trigger.

'Our doctors tried their best to save him.'

She was nodding, face half-hidden in the chador, eyes down. She knew the care here was good.

'He had lost too much blood. His circulation failed.'

'I understand.' The medical term was shock. Her voice was a near-whisper.

'Mrs Masterson, would you rather be alone?'

She was a tough jet captain; she'd seen death in combat before; her body bore the marks of her own battle scars. 'I'm OK.'

Still Alijani waited. At length Tamasin raised her eyes to his.

'It will be necessary to ask you certain questions, Mrs Masterson. But it is not necessary at this very moment. If you would rather . . .'

'Please go ahead.'

*　　*　　*

'How,' Alijani asked, 'have you come to land at an Islamic Revolutionary Iranian Air Force facility?'

Her eyes widened. 'We were hijacked at gunpoint in Ankara by the most wanted man in Turkey – Darvish Aksoy. He ran off as soon as we landed. Now who's out looking for *him*?'

What exactly had happened?

Tamasin told him. In the sultry heat with the faint currents of cool from the fans, she knew she wasn't getting through.

'Look, you've got my co-pilot out there on a slab!' The tears springing to her eyes came as much from desperation as from grief. 'Go and ask the pathologist what sort of wound he's got! D'you think I shot my own co-pilot and put a hole in my jet? It's bloody hard work, flying one of those single-handed, I can tell you. And what am I supposed to have done with the gun?'

If the gun had been thrown from the plane at cruise altitude, it could be anywhere.

She knocked away a tear. 'We wouldn't have been anywhere near Iran if it hadn't been for Darvish Aksoy. You check with Ankara and see where we were flight-planned to yesterday. Darvish Aksoy is the one you should be looking for.'

'There is a difficulty.' Alijani focused thoughtful eyes on her face. 'You say a man ran off. We have questioned both the guards on the airfield, and both say they saw no sign of a man running off.'

Of course, Tamasin realized. When she halted *Rapide*, it had had its starboard side facing the buildings, and the door was in the port side. And the air force was going to take its own men's word rather than an infidel's.

'You get the police out to that jet and go over it with fingerprint dust. You'll find five sets there – mine, Keith's, your two guys' and Aksoy's.'

'We may consider doing so, Mrs Masterson.'

Back in her room she gave in to the tears at last.

*　　*　　*

Early the next afternoon, Saturday, they led her to a different interview room. A venetian blind muted the sunlight and a squad was drilling outside, a lorry engine rumbling at idle. Colonel Alijani wasn't alone. In the middle chair at the desk another officer in air force uniform was sitting; an older man with a paunch – and so much gold braid he must be a general, Tamasin thought. At the general's other shoulder a younger officer was sitting uncomfortably, wearing scruffy denim overalls with blue shoulder boards. He wore a beard and his eyes were jumpy.

Once again Tamasin let her jacket cuff show just clear of the chador hem.

The general studied a report he held in both hands. He raised sour-looking eyes to Tamasin's face. 'Mrs Masterson.' His English didn't seem as confident as Alijani's. 'The Islamic Revolutionary Iranian Air Force has sent a technical specialist to inspect the jet you landed two days ago at Zedasht.' He half-glanced sideways at the bearded youngster. 'Mrs Masterson – what was the purpose of your flight into Iran?'

'I've been over that,' Tamasin protested. 'We were hijacked. We never had the least intention of flying into Iran.'

The general sniffed. He turned to the youngster. 'Lieutenant Kabir?'

The lieutenant spoke good English with only a trace of an accent. 'I found the following equipment aboard the British Aerospace 125-400 at Zedasht: a radar warning receiver mounted on the vertical fin; an electronic warfare control panel installed in the cabin; and a fairing under the fuselage concealing chaff and flare dispensers for use as an anti-missile defence.'

The general turned back. 'Mrs Masterson, do you deny that this equipment was on board your aircraft?'

'No,' Tamasin said, suddenly fearful. 'The company had it fitted specially . . .'

'What was the purpose of this equipment?' the general snapped.

'Training,' Tamasin said. 'Our company has a training contract with the Turkish navy – we were flying to Antalya to test the equipment.'

The old general's face was hard. His eyebrows were black and bushy and had traces of white in them. 'If your company has a contract with the Turkish navy, why should you need to test the equipment?'

'It's normally used on our Falcon 20s – that's really quite a different aircraft. On the 125 it's a new application.'

The general pursed his thin lips. 'I suggest,' he said, 'that your mission into Iran was for spying, that an accident took place in your cockpit, resulting in the death of your co-pilot, and that you landed because you were low on fuel and needed medical help. Your spying mission went wrong!' He paused. 'Tamasin Masterson, you are charged with espionage against the Islamic Republic of Iran.' He looked past her, his eyes meeting the guards'. 'You will be held in Evin jail pending your trial.'

CHAPTER 11

Roudabad, Iran, Thursday, 11 June, 1615 local

Jubilant blowing on the car horns told Azra Tabrizi that this time something different was happening. The shouts, echoing off the walled houses of Roudabad, might otherwise have been from a bunch of young boys herding goats.

Azra swapped looks with her cousin Miriam. This wasn't the first strange thing that had happened today. There'd been that jet they'd heard landing down in the desert, out of sight over the mountain ridge; and then the noisy helicopter that had flown in and then flown out again westwards, towards Tehran. Azra and Miriam were in the women's wing; Azra looking surprisingly docile, working on the washing with a flat-iron in a shadowy room with a big black kitchen range where they kept the fire burning summer as well as winter. Just the sort of thing you were suited for with an English solicitor's qualifications and no small experience at law.

'It's coming here,' Azra said, curious, 'whatever it is.'

Miriam went on fanning herself, her eyes round and blank, and didn't get up from the wooden chair where she was sitting slackly with her knees apart. She was overweight, hypochondriac, and, in Azra's view, man-starved.

'Wonder what it is.'

A fly buzzed and dived around the room. Azra plonked the iron on the hotplate to heat it through for the next lot of washing. She had the contours of her slim five foot eight body hidden under a loose blouse and an ankle-length full skirt, her long umber hair pinned back. She flipped her *hejab* veil over her face so that only her brown eyes peeped out, amused but purposeful, and

93

went smoothly to the window. Miriam lumbered over to join her.

An old Mercedes 230 roared up the slope and into the courtyard, packed with cheering people. Azra was surprised. Cars didn't often come right up into the courtyard, and when they did they had little space for manoeuvring. As far as she could see, there were three people in the front and four in the back, and she recognized only about half of them.

The driver was a Rezania, a young second-cousin of Azra's. Then she identified at least two faces belonging to the Turks who came up here sometimes from Shahrud – at the foot of the valley where the road and the railway ran – to hear Azra's uncle Ardeshir Rezania deliver Friday prayers. On an informal basis they were students – almost disciples – of Ardeshir.

As they watched, Akbar sauntered out into the sunlit courtyard and opened two doors on one side of the Mercedes. Akbar was an infantry veteran of the Iran–Iraq war; he'd been tough in the first place but his army experience had left him battle-hardened.

Someone reached out a hand to the man who'd been in the middle of the back seat.

The man clambered out of the big car and straightened up stiffly to look all around with a big grin. His eyes lighted on Azra and Miriam, in their veils, and lingered a moment. Had it not been for the man's air of assurance and authority, he might have been insignificant – a skinny five eight with a thick black moustache and a lot of beard stubble on his sunburned face, his movements stiff and tired; wearing a battered brown suit, shirt open at the neck.

The fanaticism in those dark eyes, though. It chilled Azra.

Men – no women – were crowding round, embracing the skinny man, shaking his hand. Small boys scampered in and out of the crowd to see the fun.

Azra's eyes met Miriam's.

'Whoever can that be?' Miriam asked.

The crowds began drifting out of sight inside the big, rambling house.

'No idea,' Azra murmured, and turned back, letting her veil fall as she reached for the iron, heated through now.

Miriam watched the men in the courtyard a moment longer, then turned to watch Azra, docile, pick up one of the men's shirts and resume ironing.

There were good reasons why Azra was being so conscientious about the washing and ironing, but Miriam didn't need to know that.

* * *

Hojatoleslam Ardeshir Rezania's house was the biggest in Roudabad and it was almost the highest up the mountain valley where the small town stood. It was built around the courtyard where the Mercedes had come in up the cobbled slope, and under where the rooms had been built over the archway entrance.

Miriam subsided onto her chair like a barrage balloon deflating and went on wondering who the new arrival might be. Azra spared a thought for Rob Pilgrim.

She'd liked Rob a lot from the moment they'd met. She wasn't sure whether she'd been in love with him – the age difference, and Rob's unconscious air of worldly wisdom, had always seemed daunting – but she prized him as a friend. He gave her a sense of being valued, a supportive friendship that she'd never had from lovers or even from women friends, and she respected him a lot for not crowding her. She missed him.

She kept thoroughly concealed how much it stuck in her throat, the way they vetted her letters; and the way, obviously, now that she'd compared notes on the phone with Bibi, they were intercepting Rob's to her. She hadn't been long in Roudabad when Mansoureh, her mother, had passed on a message from Ardeshir. Certain turns of phrase Azra had used were 'inappropriate' when writing to a strange man. Oh, and didn't she realize it was dangerous, getting involved in some liaison with a foreigner and unbeliever?

What a bloody phenomenal nerve.

Miriam said wistfully: 'It must be nearly supper time.'

* * *

In the big kitchen with its huge pots bubbling on its stoves, Mansoureh was with a bunch of female relatives fixing the men's evening meal. They always did it that way around: the men ate first and then the women. Miriam perked up, her energy back all of a sudden now that she wanted to take the dishes in to where the men waited to be served. Azra kept the grin off her face and let Miriam get on with it.

'Well?' she asked as Miriam came back from another inspection. Miriam seemed pleased that Azra hadn't gone out. Even with her veil on you could see Azra was better looking.

'I still can't find out what his name is,' Miriam said. 'But he's obviously popular – Ardeshir's all over him.'

That was good, Azra thought, at least Ardeshir was there. Ardeshir could sometimes be elusive. For a little while now she'd been wanting a word with her dear uncle.

* * *

The men had all vanished by the time the women got their chance to sit down and eat. Azra ate wordlessly and then went looking for Ardeshir.

Missing again. Annoyed, Azra tried the library –

Ardeshir's own collection of mostly Islamic works; then she tried each of the two living rooms, shadowy as evening turned to night. No sign. Azra sighed, reluctant to give up but becoming tempted.

Children's voices squealed with pleasure outside the door and a moment later Hojatoleslam Ardeshir Rezania sailed in with a smile across his dark, bearded face, and a little girl swinging on one arm and a little boy on the other. He was wearing the black turban that only those who can trace their descent back to the Prophet Muhammad are entitled to wear.

'Hello, Azra, they said you were looking for me!'

The smile contained nothing but benevolence. It was maddening when you knew how obstinate he could be. Bending to the kids, he tried cheerfully to disentangle his hands from theirs; he loosened the boy's grip but the girl clung tenaciously. With his free hand Ardeshir rummaged under his robe and came out with a handful of boiled sweets. The kids squealed again and pounced on the sweets. Laughing, Ardeshir turned to watch the youngsters as they ran outside. If Roudabad had nothing else going for it, at least it was a place where kids could have fun safely, in the street or anywhere else.

'What can I do for you, Azra, my dear?' Ardeshir smiled, turning back.

It was impossible to get angry with this man. The smile Azra gave him hid her impatience.

'You said we could have a talk about when I could go to Tehran to get the possession hearing under way.'

'Yes! Won't that be wonderful when you can get possession of your own house?' Enthusiasm glowed on Ardeshir's face. 'Soon, my dear! We must move when the time is right.'

Azra watched him, a little cheery man hardly over her own height in those clerical robes and turban. Carefully, she said: 'You've been saying "soon" practically ever since mother and I arrived here.'

'Indeed I have,' Ardeshir agreed readily, 'I've been watching developments in Tehran. This is not a matter to be rushed into. We shall move when the time is right. Trust me!'

'Very well.'

'Azra, my sweet!' He put a strong, friendly hand on her shoulder, and at once his confidence flowed into her. 'Don't be downcast – rest assured, the time *will* come. You'll see!'

The time for something would come all right, Azra reflected as she mooched off towards the women's wing. Whether it was what Ardeshir was expecting was another matter.

In the bedroom she and Miriam shared, Miriam was in bed already, muttering grumpily as Azra flopped onto the chair in exasperation. All her conversations with her uncle seemed to end like that. The more it went on, the more she was sure it was deliberate.

She couldn't see what was in it for Ardeshir. There was no conceivable way he was going to get his hands on her property, or any of the proceeds from selling it; he didn't even seem to want anything like that. Yet there had to be a reason for him always stalling her like this.

Crafty old Ardeshir was up to something. Azra knew it.

What she wanted was a damn good ten-mile run to work off her frustration. But heaven only knew where the nearest gym was, and you couldn't do much running in a chador.

Mansoureh had been perfectly content when Ardeshir took her passport – 'for safe keeping'. Azra had given hers up with terrible misgivings, but the pressure on her had been too much. For both her and Mansoureh, as women, travel within the country – even the short distance down the hill to Shahrud – depended on getting permission from Ardeshir.

There were moves to make, though, even if you

could make them only once. With her thoughts grim, Azra sat down to write to Bibi in the code they'd agreed. This time Azra would try and get a line in for Rob.

CHAPTER 12

North Tehran, Saturday, 13 June, 1520 local

From the back of the military police van Tamasin Masterson couldn't see more than a small wedge of dusty street between the shoulders of the air force driver and guard. Her escort was an Iranian woman in a chador, older than her and a lot bigger; they'd had to wait three quarters of an hour at the air force base before she'd turned up. Now Tamasin was handcuffed to the escort's wrist.

She was scared but she was too angry for tears. Nobody knew she was here and she hadn't a clue how she was going to get out. With Keith gone she felt horribly alone.

The van turned tightly and stopped, and ahead Tamasin saw a big metal gate slowly opening. This was it, then.

She had to moisten her lips.

There was a courtyard with high, blue-grey walls and a lot of shadow and a dazzling square of blue high up, but Tamasin didn't see much as they pushed her through it too fast. The big woman she was handcuffed to treated her roughly. She didn't understand when Tamasin complained in English.

Somehow Tamasin hadn't been ready for the extent of offices she had to go through. Paperwork, computer screens, half the ceiling fans not working, little glasses of religiously correct tea, and the place full of mullahs, here and there a man in yellow-brown desert combat fatigues and carrying a rifle. Tamasin saw as many American M16s as she saw old Russian Kalashnikovs. Irrelevantly, her mind flipped back to the mid-'80s: maybe those M16s had been part payment for some of the hostages who'd then been released in Lebanon.

They stopped her in front of one of the desks. A fat man with stains at the armpits of his shirt made a show of looking at his watch. It was almost four, they wanted to shut down here. Then he made a show of ignoring Tamasin and talking past her in Farsi.

In evident response, the guard who'd sat in the front of the van handed over Tamasin's square-ended black flight briefcase. The fat man scrabbled through it with distaste in his sneer.

Passport. He opened it glancing at the picture. Then for the first time he looked directly at Tamasin in her chador.

'Why you fly planes?' The sticky, throaty voice was thickly accented, but evidently he spoke better English than he liked to let on. 'Why you not stay home and care for your husband and family?'

She'd have dearly liked to ask him what that had to do with a defendant facing a spying charge. 'My husband is dead. He was murdered before we could start a family. By an Arab terrorist, actually.'

'Ha,' the fat man said. 'Arabs.' There was contempt in his tone, and Tamasin remembered, not for the first time, that Persians, like Turks, were a distinctly different people from the Arabs. 'Are there not men who fly planes so that they have to have women flying them?'

'Look, it's my job . . .'

He flapped a hand, waving her away without interest. As the escort tugged Tamasin away she saw the fat man slide her passport into a drawer. She hadn't even had a receipt for it. This place was chaos. She'd expected a body search, the full works, but they didn't even pat her down or look for the dollars she was carrying the way all Dragon Jet crew did.

She smelt the cells before she reached them down a long flight of damp stone stairs. It was a smell of stagnant, stuffy air, stale water and drains and accumulated human presence. There were no men here now, all the guards were women. They weren't very old, many of them younger

101

than Tamasin, and they had contempt and implacable superiority on their faces.

The cell door clashed as they unlocked it. They pushed Tamasin inside, carrying her briefcase. She stumbled in the shadows, aware of a crowd already there. And before she'd even got her balance they were shrieking at her in Farsi, waving angry hands, while the guards behind her relocked the door.

'OK, OK!' Tamasin raised a palm, trying to take stock.

The shrieking died down.

Now Tamasin could see better. The cell was crowded; it wasn't a very big cell in the first place, probably about the right size for two. There were six of them already there, none of them wearing chadors because this was an all-women gathering, with all of them squatting against the walls.

A youngish woman with long dark hair and classic high cheekbones spoke to her, looking up from her perch on the floor with her eyes heavy-lidded. The language wasn't Farsi but Tamasin wasn't quite sure what it was.

She shook her head. 'Sorry.' She glanced about to see where she could find a place to squat down.

The long-haired woman paused, looking. She was wearing a stylish pair of blue jeans with what looked like a professional pair of running shoes. Tentatively, she asked: 'You speak English?'

Tamasin stared. 'Yes. I am English.' She managed a cautious smile.

The woman pointed downwards with a slim finger. 'You must take off your shoes. You are standing on our prayer mat.'

'Oh, God . . . sorry . . .' At once she put down the briefcase, and crouched to undo her laces.

Even then she wasn't prepared for the way they shrank away from her when she found a place to sit down.

*　　*　　*

She caught the long-haired one's glance. They'd all been eyeing her and muttering. The long-haired one half-grinned, crookedly; wary.

'They are afraid of you.'

'Afraid?' Tamasin stared. 'Why?'

The woman trailed four fingers across her wrist, indicating the four rings on Tamasin's cuff. 'They think . . . maybe you love other women.'

'Oh, for God's sake!' For a moment she was angry; then she laughed. The cautious grin widened on the long-haired woman's beautiful face. Tamasin said: 'You speak pretty good English. Where did you learn it?'

'America – San Francisco. And the University of Istanbul.'

Already Tamasin was getting the sense of relief from having someone she could get through to. 'Are you Turkish?'

'Yes.' She said it as if challenging Tamasin to think the worse of her.

The other women had fallen silent, watching. The Turkish woman fired off a stream of Farsi; one or two of the others replied.

'Do any of you speak any English?' Tamasin looked the question around the cramped, shadowy cell. From somewhere close by came a strong smell of drains and there was no escape.

The blank looks told their own story.

'They speak only Farsi,' the Turkish woman said, and tossed her head defensively. 'Why are you here?'

She told them. She told them her name. She asked the Turkish woman: 'What's your name?'

The Turkish woman was still looking defiant, her chin raised. 'Rana Tezcan.'

Tamasin froze.

*   *   *

She didn't look like an Islamic fundamentalist terrorist. Tamasin wasn't sure what a terrorist should look like. She wouldn't have guessed it about Darvish. But the sheer reflex had stiffened her up and from the close way Rana Tezcan was watching her Tamasin knew she hadn't missed it.

'You . . . you know a man named Darvish Aksoy?'

Rana's eyes narrowed. 'He is my fiancé. I am going to marry him.'

The air was stuffy, heavy with that odour of drains. The floor under Tamasin was hard and cruel yet not as cold as she'd have thought.

Involuntarily, her lips had gone tight. 'He hijacked my aircraft and killed my co-pilot.'

Rana blinked. 'Then your co-pilot must have done something stupid.'

Anger rose inside Tamasin fit to burst out of her rib cage. She could feel her face burning against the hot, heavy air of the jail. She wasn't at the controls now, she *could* allow herself the luxury of a tantrum; and yet that wouldn't get her anywhere. If all these people thought she was lesbian already and she let fly at Rana . . .

Maybe if she did there'd be worse charges against her. For a start, it wouldn't escape the five Iranian women that Tamasin was the only non-Muslim in here.

Rana had her eyes steady on Tamasin's face.

Tamasin hissed: 'Aren't you even sorry?' She felt a pricking at her eyes; yet the tears she held back were those of utter fury.

'Why? If Darvish did anything to this man, then he must have attacked Darvish. Or obstructed him.'

'Darvish was hitting me! I was flying the aircraft – all my co-pilot did was to try and defend me.' Poor, brave, reckless Keith. She'd prayed so hard that he would pull through.

'Exactly.' Rana shrugged and wrapped her slim arms round her knees. With her violet eyes wide like that, her thin nose, her high, arched eyebrows, she was a more

104

beautiful woman than Tamasin. Not to say ten years younger. 'Darvish has a mission given by God. If a man obstructs him, then that man is a servant of the Devil and must be removed.'

Tamasin could hardly believe her ears. Yet this was exactly the level of fanaticism that she'd met in Darvish.

She'd thought it enough of a nightmare when they'd charged her. She couldn't have imagined that it could get this much worse.

'Rana, you *believe* that? You're an intelligent, highly educated person, you're . . .'

'Educated, yes, but not *corrupted*.' Rana's high voice had a sneer. 'It isn't your fault that you were born into a world enslaved and corrupted by the Great Satan, with the disadvantage of not having the right culture to lead you into the Way of Faith. But you should take care and listen, now that you're lucky enough to have this chance.'

'If you want to know who *is* behaving like a servant of the Devil, it's . . .'

'How *dare* you!' Rana's violet eyes blazed. 'You know *nothing, nothing* of the Way of Faith, you know *nothing* of our leader and the purity of our goals!'

The only one she could swap a single word with, and her mind belonged to a cult. Tears of chagrin started at Tamasin's eyes as she held down her rage. She couldn't let fly now; anything she said would produce another sermon.

Rana watched her, chin propped on her palm. Her heavy eyelids drooped. 'Darvish is coming here.' She said it with a zealot's conviction, as if it was as obvious as the law of gravity. 'Darvish will rescue me from this place. You'll see!'

Tamasin turned her face away. She didn't know how she was going to bear being cooped up in here with company like this.

*　　*　　*

105

In the evening they fed the prisoners lukewarm tomatoes with a sort of tan-coloured mush that Tamasin thought might have been a chickpea paste. She had reservations about the water and so she was getting pretty thirsty, and the tiny glasses of tea were better than nothing, but only just.

After the meal they let them out one by one to the loo down the corridor. It was a squat job and it was disgusting.

Overnight, Tamasin hardly slept. The guards tossed in a blanket for her and she used it to ease the hardness of the concrete floor, her jacket spread over her.

There were prayers but Tamasin didn't know the words or the rituals. Rana didn't help her.

Never in her life had she been so alone, not even in the immediate aftermath of Edward's death.

All day Sunday she kept herself to herself, unwilling to provoke another of Rana's sermons. Yet in the end it was impossible not to speak, just to break the tedium.

Rana replied patronizingly. If Tamasin had had that attitude from a man, she'd have turned him into hamburger.

*　　*　　*

On Tuesday in mid-morning the guard called Tamasin out and made her put on her chador. For a moment she was apprehensive; then, to her relief, she found herself facing a British embassy official. They sat with a table between them, guards lining the walls, stony-faced. The Tehran embassy had received an enquiry yesterday, the man said, from Mrs Wyer via his opposite numbers in Ankara; it had taken until today to get permission to visit. As she listened to him Tamasin could hear the street sounds; even the stink of the lorries' diesels had a savour of freedom.

'How are you?' The man was younger than her, smooth-faced, yet already he seemed impregnated with

106

the complacency of all bureaucrats. 'How are you being treated?'

'I'm well, just awfully bored. I'm not happy with the way they're treating me – this is a remand cell, not punishment, and it's terribly overcrowded.'

'All the cells here are overcrowded. I'm not sure that there's anything we can do about that. What about this espionage charge? This really is jolly serious, you know.'

'It's total bollocks,' Tamasin said hotly. She went over her story again.

'Well, we'll have to get you a lawyer,' the envoy said. 'We shall really need to tread very carefully on this matter. If not, they could very well charge you in connection with First Officer Cross's death.'

The thought of Keith had her fighting tears again. She gave the man a shopping list. After that it was back to the cell with its crowded bodies and its smell of drains.

*   *   *

The lawyer turned up on Wednesday afternoon, a quiet-spoken, heavy-eyed Iranian who looked about sixty and spoke confident English. He brought the things Tamasin had asked for from the embassy man – at least the ones they'd been able to find in the poorly supplied shops.

'If anyone asks you, these things are a gift from your family. It is illegal to bring gifts for a prisoner to whom one is not related, or to buy items on such a person's behalf.'

He listened impassively to her story. When she asked whether the charges might be dropped before it came to trial, he was non-committal, but Tamasin got the impression that he didn't rate the chances very highly.

Back in the cell, Rana was speaking to her occasionally now without being spoken to first. The tension hardly seemed less between them, but Rana knew that, as the only one who spoke English as well as Farsi, she was the one with the power to exclude Tamasin totally from the luckless group, and she relented; she would translate sometimes when the other women spoke, and often she relayed words of Tamasin's back to them. Grudgingly Tamasin felt gratitude, enough now and then to listen to Rana when she talked of her mission for *Yol*.

'What have they got you for?' Tamasin asked.

'Conspiracy to commit terrorist acts.' Rana shrugged. 'They can prove anything they like on a charge like that. It's a death penalty, of course.'

'You don't seem worried.'

An ironic smile twitched at the corners of Rana's wide mouth. Spoilt brat or not, Tamasin had to admit Rana was an attractive woman. 'I keep telling you,' Rana said, 'Darvish will come. Darvish or his men. You'll see!'

Tamasin thought: the things desperation can do to you.

* * *

Thunder was growling around the mountains on Thursday morning and the cell seemed more airless than ever. Something was stirring, though and the Iranian women muttered among themselves, shifting, pricking up their ears. Tamasin was still aware of the drains but she'd long since stopped noticing the human odours.

'What's up?' Tamasin asked Rana.

'We're waiting to see how the demo goes.'

'What demo?'

'The march by the *Shohada*, the martyrs. They are demonstrating for an end to the government's consorting with the Satans of America and Russia and France.'

More fanaticism, Tamasin thought gloomily. 'Who are the *Shohada*?'

'They are our friends. They are Iranian but they support the Way of Faith.'

Tamasin didn't bother asking any more.

She knew all the daily routines of the prison now: she

knew the times when the others bent down to pray, the times when the meals could be expected, the times when they let the prisoners out to the toilet. They were the big events of any day, and between them all that happened was that bored and anxious people got fractious with one another.

Rain was falling faintly outside during the afternoon and a couple of the Iranian women were having a spat that Tamasin couldn't begin to follow. She was drowsing, almost asleep, aware no more than marginally that Rana had her head cocked, alert, and the sudden, dull rumble outside wasn't a thing that had relevance for her, maybe more distant thunder.

Then she saw that Rana was on her feet, grabbing the bars of the cell door, and the fight between the two Iranian women had stopped. Even then Tamasin hadn't realised this was anything to do with her.

It took the quick, wooden rapping of the automatic rifles to jolt her out of it.

CHAPTER 13

Ankara, Thursday, 11 June, 1700 local

Character, in one of the plentiful family-run local hotels, was really another way of saying 'lousy plumbing', Felix Wyer thought as she picked up the phone. There were advantages of sorts in the soullessness of the international chains. She dialled room service.

'A pot of coffee, please – French.'

She could take just so much of the Turkish stuff, tiny cups that never quenched your thirst, and all those gritty grounds if you drank too far down.

Whichever way you looked at it, her company was in danger.

It was no idle boast to say that Dragon Jet was Felix Wyer's own success story. Gerald had been dead a long time now, yet the central idea had been his; even so, it was Felix who'd driven the idea into reality, as much as anything to take her mind off her loss. She still missed Gerald.

Tamasin Masterson was a widow, too, Felix reflected. Tamasin, the daughter she'd never had.

A knock at the door. Room service, with the coffee. Felix tipped in US dollars and was popular with the waiters. The man set it down on the low table and left.

She'd sunk no end of her own capital into it, never mind the frightening amounts she'd borrowed from the banks. And the way she'd begun – it still thrilled her today. The two 125s stored at Las Vegas with their ex-owner bankrupt. Flying them across the Atlantic. The whole, exciting business of getting started. And then *actually* making a profit, *actually* being able to go back to the bank man and say: listen, the business is there – we could use *another* jet!

Felix poured herself coffee. Added cream. Fiddled with the sugar sachet that she didn't want. Listened for the phone but it didn't ring.

Recession, paradoxically, had helped. So many companies turned out to have shareholders who took a dim view of having what looked like an expensive luxury on the books, and so, suddenly, there were a lot of redundant executive jets around.

For Felix Wyer's Dragon Jet Charter, that had cut two ways, both advantageously.

She sipped. Too hot yet. She glanced at the phone. Erol Ersin was supposed to be calling her back.

She'd snapped up two 800-series 125s – one a replacement for *Dragonfly*, which they'd had to retire – making four Dragon Jets in the fleet. That had given her a pretty profitable stable when all the companies that had sold their aircraft discovered that they still had roughly the same number of key personnel, with roughly the same places as before to get them to, and that if they *didn't* charter, then the contracts would go to the competition.

Well, if it kept their shareholders happy . . .

This time the coffee was just cool enough. At the back of Felix's mind niggled the thought of who Ersin's mysterious contact might be.

Not all the deals had been straight sell-offs. Felix had deals with two industrial companies in which Company A owned the jet; Felix operated it; and what kept Company A's shareholders happy was the lease income that Felix paid, together with a percentage of what the aircraft earned her.

Her latest acquisition was the BAe 1000, the pride of the little fleet despite the monumental debt they'd taken on for it. The 1000 would do Biggin to New York non-stop.

The phone rang. With difficulty Felix held herself back from snatching it instantly. She let it ring once more before she replied.

'Felix?'

'Erol.' But there'd been something in his voice. Suddenly Felix was scared. 'Did your contact come back?'

'Only with a rumour.'

'Well, even a rumour can't be worse than nothing.' *Could it?*

Ersin cleared his throat. His deep voice sounded as if he was making some effort to keep it steady. 'There's no word on *Dragon Rapide*, but the rumour that's been passed on to me suggests that two Westerners, a man and a woman, have turned up at an Iranian air force base on the edge of Tehran.'

'*Iran?*' Felix was nonplussed.

'It may be them, it may not. I don't know which way to hope.'

Felix started to catch at what the rumour had told him. 'Erol, what is it?'

He told her.

*   *   *

Carefully, Erol Ersin replaced the receiver. The office bottle wasn't *raki*, the local aniseed spirit, it was good French brandy, and after delivering news – or even rumour – like that, Ersin reckoned he deserved one. *Poor Felix.* But there hadn't been another way to play it.

Tomorrow morning was the earliest she'd be able to get to the British embassy here with the request to contact the Tehran embassy to try and get confirmation. It wasn't going to be a pleasant night for Felix Wyer.

Ersin warmed the brandy in his palm and reflected on the briefing Kemal Koz had given him last time they'd met face to face.

What scared Turkey was the thought of a backlash by religious fundamentalists against the pragmatists in government in Iran. Not a few clerics there were muttering openly about the threat the pragmatists posed to the ideals of the 1979 revolution. That aside, the more particular cause of Turkish unease was the presence somewhere in Iran of anything up to fifty of Darvish Aksoy's *Yol* terrorists; men who'd escaped one round-up after another in Turkey and who'd found sanctuary in a country that was sympathetic to their aims.

Their aims, Koz knew, were to export terror and revolution, first to Turkey, then elsewhere. They could pretty well take it that Aksoy had found his way to join his fellow terrorists now; and the exiles must have had a tremendous morale boost to have him among them again.

This briefing, Ersin had come to understand, was one Koz had prepared originally for the Turkish government; but it was also for NATO consumption.

On Koz's reading, a fundamentalist backlash if properly timed and executed *could* unseat the pragmatists and put into power a government dedicated to a wider and much more rigidly interpreted introduction of *sharia* – Islamic law – throughout Iran, and committed to Islamic revolution in the countries that bordered on their own.

Interpretation was the key. So many religious extremists, Muslim, Christian, Jewish or anything else, Koz had told Ersin, made their own and others' lives difficult just because the only interpretation they would accept of Scripture was their own. They were *right*. Everybody else was wrong.

Koz reckoned there was going to be a revolution hit list. Iraq would be high on it; then Saudi Arabia; then Turkmenistan and Uzbekistan in the CIS. But top of the hit list would be Turkey.

Paranoia was an occupational hazard in a security officer, Ersin reflected, but he could see this scenario all too well. What Koz visualized was a 'holy' Tehran exercising the sort of influence over future religious 'satellites' that Moscow had once exercised over Cuba and the East European countries that had shared its religion of communism.

If Iran threw the pragmatists out, Aksoy and all his *Yol*

fanatics over there would see to it that the mischief spread to Turkey. A new domino effect. Turkey was possibly the Middle East's most modern, Western-oriented state after Israel, a US ally – the way Iran had once been – with a secular constitution. Turkey's army was pledged to defend that constitution and it would stick by its pledge; one of the horrors that Koz foresaw was the bloodbath that would engulf the country when the army took on the fanatics.

If Turkey went, it wouldn't be long before Saudi Arabia went, too. And then who was next . . . ?

That was the nightmare that Ersin and Koz were working to avert, the nightmare Dragon Jet had got itself inadvertently dragged into.

CHAPTER 14

Urgency got to Tamasin Masterson in a rush of adrenaline and she scrambled to her feet.

Rana Tezcan was straining at the bars of the cell door, in the pungent shadows and the body smells, trying to see through the bars; and there was shouting now, some way off, and more shots, another rumble that this time no-one mistook for thunder.

One of the Iranian women, a person about Tamasin's age with hollow cheeks and a cynical face and premature grey in her hair, was leaning up against the bars next to Rana. The other four had shrunk back.

There was screaming now, feminine voices ringing on the concrete walls, and running feet. As Tamasin picked her way over the prayer mat four of the guards went running past the door with no heed for the women in the cells.

Rana sensed or perhaps saw Tamasin at her shoulder, smaller than her but tougher. She flicked her eyes towards Tamasin.

'It's Darvish.' Rana's quivering voice was a low murmur, speaking English. 'He's coming for me.' Then she was pushing her face against the bars, yelling in Turkish, *'Buraya! Buraya! Ben buradam!'* She gripped the metal bars rigidly.

Then Tamasin smelt it, the nitrocellulose from the shooting, maybe explosives, too, and she tensed in fear. That smell brought Keith's face back to her mind; it brought back other faces, other horrors, it made her old bullet wound start to ache again.

Instinct took over, and, with her breathing shallow,

Tamasin crouched and put her shoes on and laced them tight.

Close by and just out of sight, one of the women guards screamed ringingly and Tamasin thought she'd been shot but instead she ran past and in that moment Tamasin heard the footsteps, pounding on the stairs.

'Rana! Rana! Rana!'

'Buradam! Buradam!'

Suddenly they were there.

* * *

At first Tamasin thought there must have been a dozen of them, big men in workers' overalls heavy with sweat and the gunsmoke clinging, crowding in the echoing corridor between the cells, most of them carrying old Kalashnikovs, some with butts folded. Then she realized there couldn't be more than five or so.

'Rana!' One of the men – it wasn't Darvish and Tamasin didn't know any of them – thrust his hand through the bars and gripped Rana's.

One man dived out of sight to the right to stand guard, another to the left. The man next to the one who'd greeted Rana talked suddenly in high, sharp Turkish.

Rana swung around, her eyes wide. She fired off a volley of Farsi and all the women scrambled towards the back of the cell. Tamasin figured that the second man was doing something with the door lock. Rana swung to her.

'Back! Quickly! The back of the cell!'

She grabbed Tamasin's arm and they cowered against the warm pile of shivering bodies with their moans of fear. Tamasin just had time to register *plastic* when it went off.

In the confined space the explosion seemed powerful enough to cave Tamasin's skull in. Her ears ached and the strong acid, metallic smell filled the cell. Through the thick deafness and the whitish smoke Tamasin started to hear the wails of the Iranian prisoners, and then Rana was gone, diving through the smoke.

Without another thought Tamasin dived after her.

*   *   *

Past the white, sightless curtain of the smoke Tamasin flew past the cell door as it swung uselessly. *Left*, because that was the way they'd taken her to see the embassy man and the lawyer and she came out of the swirling smoke and almost ran smack into Rana.

Rana had been cool before but now her highly strung nature was showing and she looked almost hysterical. She was yelling in Turkish and no-one was moving and suddenly she seemed to have a temper tantrum, beating with her fists. The man who'd greeted her grabbed both her wrists, his AK swinging from his shoulder. He wasn't much taller than Rana but his arms were brawny and his round pudding face, with its stony black eyes, was unmoved.

A man showed at the foot of the stairs and beckoned. They ran, Tamasin with them.

Adrenaline had helped her at first but now her fear was threatening to choke the breath in her throat. She was pounding up the narrow stairs with the others, aware that if the guards had rifles and caught them in this confined space they would slaughter every one of them.

Suddenly Rana realized Tamasin was on her heels. She flung over her shoulder: 'It's me they've come for, not you! You're not the faithful!' Her cry had equal parts in it of pride and panic.

Tamasin muttered, 'Don't you worry about me.' She knew what she was going to do now when she got out: break for the embassy and hole up there while the diplomats sorted it out. She'd abandoned her flight briefcase back in the cell, but too bad about that.

Then there was more smoke, black and brown — something burning in the admin offices as they reached the landing breathlessly.

Computer screens stood shattered on their desks,

chairs lay overturned, papers were everywhere. Tamasin couldn't see what was burning. It flashed across her mind to rummage for her passport but she dismissed the thought; too little time. She was piling through, following Rana, when suddenly she saw two bodies and the breath jammed in her throat.

They were curled into one another on the ground, one a mullah, white turban half unravelled as he lay gored and ripped open by the burst that had killed him, the other a tall Iranian in desert camouflage with no eyes, no top to his head; just blood everywhere and something greenish-greyish splattered against the wall that Tamasin, with the bile surging up in her throat, realized was brain. By his hand, a Heckler & Koch HK54 machine pistol, wooden butt sticky red. But the lobby and the outer door were at the end of that corridor and Tamasin ran on.

Just in front of her, Rana screamed and sprawled on her shoulder, clutching her forearm, and the five Turkish gunmen crouched, spreading out. Tamasin crouched instinctively, sweat prickling on her neck, eyes smarting in the smoke. Glass jangled, falling from a window to the left, and Tamasin's eyes were wide open.

Then another burst of automatic fire raked the lobby and they were pinned down, trapped inside the prison building.

CHAPTER 15

Roudabad, Friday, 12 June, 1120 local
Sunlight blazed down on the elegant Arabic script of the
Koran, and Azra Tabrizi sat a delicate distance apart
from Major Moussa Rezania, under the watchful gaze
of an elderly aunt in a chador as black as the one Azra
was wearing.

In his deep, persuasive voice Moussa said: 'Cousin,
I have the impression that you have reservations about
the things I show you in the Scriptures.'

Azra slipped Moussa a cautious glance over the top
of her veil. Moussa was virile and good-looking and
might have been desirable had he not been such a
fanatic.

'I'm sorry. Really I didn't mean to seem as if I had
reservations.' Azra needed no convincing of her Muslim faith; yet she distrusted extremes. 'But, well . . .'
she hesitated. 'How does one truly know the Will of
God?'

'When one submits, one knows.'

A whole gang of kids, some of them from the household, came shouting and scampering up the sloping drive
under the archway. The oldest of them couldn't have
been eight, a shaven-headed boy waving a stick as tall
as himself. High in the dazzle a red kite was swivelling
its forked tail to hold position.

'Yesterday,' Moussa said, 'Ali – you've met Ali?
Of course – Ali and I were scrambled in our F14s
to intercept an intruding aircraft.' Thinking back, the
thickset man screwed up his clear eyes into the bright
sky. 'There was cloud over the mountains but the
intruder was flying low. We had to climb above

the cloud to try and engage with our radars. Then we had to descend *through* the cloud to catch the intruder. That can be very dangerous when you're over mountain country.'

'Yes.' Azra clasped her hands in her lap attentively.

'We were blind as we descended and the mountains were all around. Ali was afraid.' It was true, and Moussa said it as if it was the insignificant thing it had been. 'I wasn't afraid. It was my submission to God's will that enabled me to make that descent. This time, God willed that Ali and I and our radar intercept officers with us should all live.' He shrugged. 'Yet, had God decided that it was time for me to die – in combat or in an accident in the air – it would have been wrong of me to subvert God's will by, say, breaking off the descent when we reached minimum safe altitude.'

'I do admire your faith,' Azra murmured.

Moussa was undoubtedly a courageous man as well as a skilled pilot, but he unsettled her. Quietly she felt that all religious fanatics – she'd met Christian fundamentalists who were equally extreme – were the same in their insistence that *they alone* had recognized the truth, *they alone* knew what God *meant* to say.

Faith was the crux. Yet, Azra reflected, the essence of a faith, whether in a religion or in a system – Marxism–Leninism, say – was that it took the believer *beyond* the limits of scientific testing, *beyond* the known and into the mystery of choice. And within the mystery of choice lay all the perils of self-deception.

'I don't ask for admiration,' Moussa said. 'I'm merely an instrument. I tell you that to show you how important it is to submit.'

*   *   *

120

Light had almost gone when Mansoureh called Azra to the larger of the two living rooms. Supper had been cleared away half an hour earlier and the spicy smells of cooking lingered. Akbar was there, the Iran–Iraq war veteran with the scar jagged and white on the dark tan of his face. Beside Akbar, on one of the divans, was the skinny man who'd arrived yesterday with all the Turks from Shahrud.

'This is Darvish Aksoy,' Mansoureh said. 'Darvish, my daughter Azra. Azra, Darvish is from Turkey and he'll be staying here in the house for some while.'

So this was it, the formal introduction.

In the dim yellow lighting of the big room, Azra took stock of Darvish as Darvish took stock of her. She was sitting on the divan opposite him, Mansoureh at her side, and she wondered fleetingly what he must see. Very little, she thought, in her chador with only her eyes showing.

He must have shaved that morning but already there was stubble darkening his cheeks, and his big black moustache was heavy. At first sight, Azra had thought him insignificant, far less attractive as a man than Moussa; yet suddenly she wondered. The intensity and energy about this little man were something almost sexual.

'How long did you live in England?'

The smile Darvish gave her with every question looked like one he had to practise. The conversation was formal and Azra felt uncomfortable.

Akbar sat at Darvish's side, saying nothing. There was an air of violence about the tough ex-infantryman with one eye permanently half-closed in the puckering of his scar. Hand-to-hand fighting with the Iraqis; that was how he'd acquired it.

The story went that Akbar had herded fifteen Iraqi prisoners into a small dugout and then tossed a grenade into the middle of them. Akbar's version was that they'd been moved to a hut hardly a kilometre from the

121

front when one of their own side's shells obliterated the dugout.

'More than twenty years,' Azra said.

'That is a very long time,' Darvish said thoughtfully, lips pursed. He held his hands in front of him, small but bony, the nails bitten, and he kept clasping and unclasping them. 'Is it true that the Muslim faith is repressed in England?'

'Oh, no – they have freedom of worship.' But she wanted to wriggle.

The sound of barking came from some distance away. Azra recognized it as that of the pack of wild dogs that ran around the town at night. The family had guard dogs of its own but the wild dogs were dangerous.

'Do you like being back in Iran?' Darvish asked.

'Well . . .' The answer to that was a complex one. 'Yes, I do, really.' Then she was annoyed with herself. That was the answer that all these people had *willed* from her. She let her gaze drop to the rich thickness of the carpet and said nothing.

'It is true, isn't it, Darvish,' Mansoureh said, endeavouring to get some momentum back into the conversation, 'that in your life before you formed *Yol* you had a good deal of material wealth?'

'My parents are very wealthy people from the upper levels of Istanbul society. They gave me a good, international education – the best that money could buy.' He spoke sneeringly when he mentioned *money*. Yet, Azra saw, he wasn't too proud to accept its benefits.

'Sadly, my parents are irreligious and in error,' Darvish said casually. 'They will have to pay the penalty when the time comes.' They were speaking Farsi, Darvish with hardly a trace of accent. A note of pride slipped into his voice. 'I myself have killed several of the government's servants of Satan in the course of our holy war against the Turkish secular state.'

Again his tone was casual, so that Azra wasn't even sure whether this was just bragging. Beyond the wooden window frame, evening had turned almost to night.

Half-teasing, she said: 'If you thought I was a servant of Satan, would you kill me?'

'If that was so,' Darvish said without batting an eyelid, 'it would sadly prove necessary.'

He meant it. Now Azra knew what it was about him that gave her the shivers.

Beyond the wall, boys were bringing a flock of goats down from the mountainside. You could hear the boys' shouts and the bleating of the goats.

'The *taghouti* in Tehran' – he used the Farsi hate-word for followers of Satan, meaning the pragmatists – 'are bent on turning Iran into a state as godless as Turkey. But the martyrs of *Yol* will rise against the *taghouti*.' His lips curled at the mention.

Azra watched him, one hand raised to her chador hood. The very notion that a country so permeated with religious observance might turn into a secular state was one of the most paranoid fantasies she'd ever heard.

'We shall win.' He sounded perfectly confident. 'The people will march behind the martyrs of *Yol*. The people will overthrow the state.'

To believe that, Azra realized, was to ignore reality. 'Are you sure about the people?' she asked cautiously. 'They've had Islamic revolution since 1979, and then years of war with Iraq – from what *I* can see, mostly what they want now is a bit of peace.'

Darvish sat back on the divan, dark eyes hardening. 'Are you telling me you support that attitude?'

'I merely report what I've seen.' Of course she supported it. So did anyone else with any sense.

'My sister, you are mistaken. Truly, what the people want is to live under the holy laws; they want a regime that will make no compromise with the forces of the

123

Devil.' He leaned forward in emphasis. 'You should know that *Yol* has strong support from elements of the army and the air force. We have armed, trained men who will rise up in support of our struggle.'

The more her fascination grew, the more she felt repelled. 'Armed, trained men?' she repeated. 'Who are they?'

Eyes gleaming, Darvish moistened his lips. He flicked a look at Mansoureh, but she was sitting back, hardly paying attention. Darvish leaned forward suddenly and clasped Azra's hand in both of his. 'My sister, are you willing to join us in our struggle?'

The question caught her off guard. For an instant, she was in danger; then she remembered what would happen if she said no. 'I am with you, Darvish, with you and with your struggle. I shall be always.' The clasp of his strong hands on hers was clammy. Mansoureh watched with pale approval.

As they locked eyes, Darvish smiled. He was wild and he was dangerous. It amazed her that Mansoureh couldn't see it.

He leaned closer to her, switching to English, his voice low. 'When I give the word to rise up, I shall have definite support from army officers in Tehran, Tabriz, Isfahan, Shiraz, Kermanshah and the oilfields of Khuzestan. All these are of colonel or even general rank, commanding many soldiers to bring to the struggle. I shall have definite support from eight major air force bases, including radar and missile batteries. Your cousin Moussa will be among my key military officers.' Again, Darvish showed his teeth in a grin. 'But the military will be far outnumbered by the people. With the army and the air force behind them, the people will rise up and march, and they will overthrow the Satan-serving pragmatists of this government as surely as they overthrew the Satan-serving Shah in 1979.'

Azra stared.

'And *then*,' Darvish insisted, '*then* we shall bring the purity of Islam to the godless state of Turkey, and to the America-worshippers of Saudi Arabia. Everywhere, the *people* will rise up.'

A chill was creeping up Azra's spine. Darvish meant it. 'You have *all* the army behind you?' She stuck to English, softly. '*All* the air force?'

Something furtive showed in his glinting eyes. 'All those of significance. Soon, anyway.'

Azra burst out: 'But surely, aren't you . . . aren't we risking civil war?'

'We shall wait until we are fully ready. Then there will be swift victory, there will be no civil war.' Proud of himself, Darvish started telling her how it would work.

* * *

When Azra tracked Ardeshir down, he was in the kitchen, telling silly stories to a couple of enthralled kids while he dried the supper dishes. Hardly any of the men took a turn at the housework. Confrontation had been in Azra's mind, but it was impossible to be angry with a man who was up to his arms in the washing-up. Azra waited impatiently while Ardeshir finished his yarn and shooed the kids off to bed.

'What can I do for you, Azra?' The kitchen light was even dimmer than the light in the living room, but the smile shone on Ardeshir's clean-shaven face.

'You can maybe tell me when I'm to be allowed to start training in Islamic law.'

'I've been thinking about that,' Ardeshir smiled. 'Don't worry – we need talents like yours; we would never let such gifts go to waste. Rest assured, you'll get your training . . .'

'. . . when the time's right,' Azra finished for him, heavy irony in her voice.

'Exactly.' Ardeshir grinned mischievously. 'We wouldn't want to act when the time was wrong, would we?'

There was no doubt about it, Azra fumed as she stumped through the starlit shadows of the courtyard, heading for her room: Ardeshir was fobbing her off, time after time.

It wasn't just the constant stalling that bothered her, either. Crafty old Ardeshir was up to something.

* * *

Roughly twenty-four hours later Azra got the call to the phone.

She was in her room, with the top light out and the spotlight showing just the bit she was working on, some sewing on the hem of a blouse, while the tubby Miriam grunted and moaned under the covers in ill-concealed protest. Akbar's raspy voice called her from outside in the yard. None of the men would ever enter the single women's wing.

'Azra! Telephone!'

Quickly, Azra tucked her work away under the bed-clothes; she didn't want Miriam getting interested. She turned out the light and dashed out into the courtyard. Even in the moonlight she flipped her *hejab* veil across her face.

When she got there, it was only Ardeshir. After all that. He was at the other end of Roudabad, visiting someone.

'Hello, Azra, can you give me Bibi's address and phone number in England?'

'What, you want to phone her now?'

'It isn't so late there. Anyway, the Bakhtiars want to write to her.'

Frowning, Azra glanced at the wall clock. Five past midnight. In a place that kept the hours Roudabad did, it wasn't that late to go visiting. 'All right,' she said with a bad grace, and told him what he wanted.

126

'Thank you, Azra.' You could almost see the smirk on his face.

'Why couldn't someone else have looked that up for you?'

Ardeshir chuckled down the line. 'I knew you'd have it in your head. Besides, you always stay up so late – I knew it would be less trouble for you than for some others I could name.'

That sounded loaded. Azra got off the line quickly and headed back for her room, wondering uneasily whether Ardeshir had understood the purpose of her busy sewing. Then as she shut the courtyard door after her, the heavy sound of a van or lorry engine came rumbling up the slope and into the courtyard.

Azra halted. She'd never heard a van around here at this time of night before.

The women's wing was in darkness. Azra moved stealthily to a window looking out on to the courtyard.

The van looked like quite a big one. It had backed into the courtyard and now in the meagre light Azra saw a couple of men walk around the back of it and open its doors. She recognized them: a couple of the Turks from down in Shahrud. They'd been up here that day Darvish had arrived.

Akbar came out. Azra couldn't hear what they said together. Akbar crossed the courtyard in his slow, strutting walk. He almost vanished into the shadows. When he turned back, he'd opened a door.

Azra strained her eyes through the darkness.

The courtyard was wedge-shaped, with a narrow end and a wide end. It had rooms on two sides, the wide end and its adjacent long side, plus a couple built over the entry ramp with its heavy gate. The other two sides were bounded by a wall about one storey high and wide enough to spread washing on, or to lounge on and sun yourself; from the courtyard you went up by an outside staircase. Into the wall were set a series of store chambers, mostly kept locked.

As Azra watched, the two Turks vanished inside the van, then reappeared toting a heavy box between them. Akbar supervised. The two Turks followed his thin torch beam, leading them into the store chamber by the outside stairs. They came out without the box and then fetched a second one from the van.

Azra's breathing was shallow.

Ardeshir was trying to catch her out over the sewing she did late at night, but now she'd caught *him* out instead. There was something secret about those boxes. She wasn't supposed to have seen them, she'd have put money on it.

*   *   *

It was almost an hour before the van left. Azra gave it another half an hour, keeping herself awake, to go exploring. One of the things she'd been doing systematically over quite a long time now was to get hold of as many spare keys as possible and keep them hidden.

She left Miriam snoring under her cover. In the darkness of the courtyard the big brindled mastiff guard dog raised his head ponderously with a half-hearted grunt as Azra moved softly into the open.

She gave one last glance around, then she went to the door by the steps to the flat-topped retaining wall. She started testing keys.

She'd almost expected the first one not to work. She hadn't expected it to take her all of six tries before she found the right one.

Again she looked carefully over her shoulder. The courtyard was still empty.

She slipped into the solid blackness of the store chamber. She pulled the door to behind her. She shone her torch.

The boxes were piled high and there was hardly room to move. On one of them a coil of thickish rope stood, and Azra noted it mentally: one day that might be handy. She tugged at the closest of the boxes, the topmost one on the pile.

It wouldn't move; it was too heavy for her. Her breathing was shallow, her ears straining for any sound from the courtyard. Stretching up on tiptoe, Azra fiddled the top of the box loose and shone the torch inside.

Ammunition. Jammed full of it, rifle bullets packed in metal clips. Azra didn't know much about guns and ammunition, but these weren't shotgun cartridges – she knew what they looked like – and they weren't the little .22 stuff she'd used herself on club target ranges – they were much bigger. Hardly breathing now, Azra quietly replaced the box lid.

Outside: still nothing. She let out her breath softly.

She lifted the coil of rope, stooped, and set it onto the floor. She opened the lid on the box where the rope had been.

This one held the rifles, Russian AK47s. These were weapons Azra did know, she'd seen so many pictures of them. Old, but difficult to break and highly effective.

She left the coil of rope on the box of rifles and slipped out of the store chamber. This was Ardeshir's secret, then. He and Darvish really were in on this together, plotting some crazy revolution. Moussa, too.

A revolution backed by an air force with F14s and MiG 29s would be a tough proposition to deal with, Azra reflected, crossing the courtyard quickly. She ought to warn someone. But who did she warn, where did she go?

No-one here, that was for sure. She wasn't going to be able to trust a soul. Heaven only knew what Ardeshir would do with her if he found out she knew. And Darvish. She'd promised Darvish she was with him in his struggle;

she'd promised never to repeat a word of the plans he'd so proudly told her.

If he caught her betraying him he would certainly kill her.

CHAPTER 16

Evin jail, Thursday, 18 June, 1443 local

Sharp silence rang inside Tamasin Masterson's skull and for a moment the gunfire had stopped. Rana was moaning, stirring, and with her heart in her mouth and crouching forward, Tamasin ran.

Blood was running freely over Rana's forearm and she was clutching the wound, her face harsh and pale under her tan.

'Let me see.' Tamasin was terrified it was going to be something really nasty like the wound that had killed Keith Cross.

The smells from the shooting and the burning were in her nostrils, her shirt clinging, wet. Gently, strongly, she prised Rana's hand away. She breathed again. A shard of glass had cut into the muscle, but it didn't look very deep.

'Keep still.' She eased the shard out of Rana's arm. 'Got a handkerchief, a tissue? Just hold it tight until it stops bleeding – it's not much more than a scratch.'

Rana didn't look grateful, her face still shocked.

Single shots were punching across the courtyard outside, unseen, with a *pok . . . pok-pok . . . pok*. They were still just as trapped, Tamasin realized with the sweat prickling on her neck and forehead. She lifted her head.

All the men had vanished. No, they hadn't, there was one still there. *One*. Something cold went down Tamasin's spine. They weren't going to make it.

In a flash of memory she saw Keith's face.

She wrenched around. 'Rana, get over there by the door!' It was where that last gunman was. 'Keep your head down!'

She didn't wait to see Rana do as she said; she dived back through the room to where the Iranian soldier lay with no top to his head but the HK54 by his hand. She avoided looking at the body, she just grabbed the gun.

She had to fumble for the safety. She'd never handled one of these. She remembered it was donkey's years since she'd handled *any* small arms; Sterling sub-machine-guns and Browning pistols in the UAS. She got her hand round the pistol grip and ran ducking to the window.

Most of the glass was shot out. At first she couldn't see where the opposition fire was coming from, and she knew as she looked up over the sill that this terrified her. She made herself do it; she got the short barrel of the HK up and steadied on the sill. Blood from the butt was sticking to her shoulder.

There were cars in the yard, a Peugeot, an old Peykan – the Iranian version of the British Hillman Hunter of the 1960s – and the asphalt was still wet from the thick rain. Nothing moving. Whoever had been shooting had been doing so from good cover. Breath was shallow in Tamasin's throat and she knew she had enough of her head showing over the sill for a single good shot to leave her looking like that poor bastard of an Iranian behind her. She glanced right, through the lobby and towards the door.

Rana was crouching, holding her forearm, shoulder propped on the wall in the warm, close afternoon. The Turk in the overalls had his Kalashnikov steadied against his shoulder. He glanced at Tamasin and their eyes met. The Turk looked thoroughly bemused, but an implicit understanding passed between him and Tamasin.

Pok, and the single Kalashnikov shot rapped back in echoes off the outer wall, breached now. *Tak, tak, tak*, and Tamasin saw the muzzle flashes big and bright underneath the old Peykan, so there was only one of them pinning them down in here and she let go with the HK54. She had the muzzle just below horizontal because she remembered the way the Sterling tracked up and right when you fired it and this one was the same, so she got the old Peykan, the way she'd meant to. She wanted to scare that man away from them, not blow his brains out.

He was still firing in a long burst under the car – didn't even know she was there.

Tamasin saw the Peykan rock on its springs as the big, blunt 9mm slugs slammed through the thin metal, close together, rear wing and wheel arch, at least one in the tyre and then the unexpected: the whole back end of the car vanished in red-yellow flame, blazing sprawling spreading and fireballing high in a *whoof* of raw energy. Tamasin stared, paralysed.

The Turk woke her, jumping to his feet, grabbing Rana, yelling aloud in his own language. He was beckoning Tamasin.

She dropped the weapon and ran for it.

As she approached him the Turk pushed Rana at the doorway and she vanished stumbling through it, and, as Tamasin caught up with him, he grabbed her arm. They tore through the courtyard and Tamasin felt the waves of heat from the burning Peykan, realizing what had happened; she'd blown the petrol tank open, while the guard under it had still been firing, with those big muzzle flames.

Then with the Turk still holding her arm she was over the dust-hazed rubble and outside, on the street with its tall eucalyptus, scrambling after Rana inside a big vehicle, an Isuzu 4×4.

*   *   *

He must have got out, Tamasin was thinking desperately, he couldn't have got caught in that fireball. Nothing she could do now if he had burned. Biting her lip, she looked round. There were six of them in the vehicle now: the Turk who'd got out last with Tamasin and Rana, two of the others she'd seen down by the cells, and the driver, a man she hadn't seen before. The one who'd been last was a lanky man with a strong chin and a bushy black moustache like Darvish's, and he turned to Tamasin now, the two of them bouncing around in the back of the Isuzu. Rana was in front of them, in the back seat, while Tamasin and the lanky Turk bounced around in the luggage bay, the top-hinged door bumping, not quite shut. Tamasin thought of the panic Rana had been in over that little scratch and realized of course she was genuinely highly strung; it had been pretty heroic of her even to run for it the way she had. The Turk grinned and said something in his own language.

He must have thought she was another terrorist. 'Sorry,' she said, grinning back, 'can't follow you.'

Rana went, '*A-a-achhh!*' and wrenched round, wide-eyed. 'My God, what are *you* doing here?'

Tamasin stared, open-mouthed, over her shoulder. The Isuzu hit a series of potholes and the motion flung Tamasin's shoulder against the lanky Turk's. Rana swung back and leaned over the front seat, voice shrill and spiteful in angry Turkish.

The driver answered monosyllabically without turning around, but Tamasin saw the way he tipped his head back. That meant *no* in much of the Middle East. The man beside the driver turned and spoke curtly to Rana. Then he looked past her at Tamasin, his eyes critical.

Rana turned back, tight-lipped. 'You don't belong with us, you're not even a Muslim! When we just get stopped, you're out!'

'Suits me fine — make it somewhere near the British embassy.' Tamasin realized she was going to stand out on the street — especially with fresh blood all over her captain's uniform.

Rana just sizzled at her.

The lanky man turned to Tamasin, the ghost of a grin on his thin lips. 'You are English?' His accent was thick.

'Yeah.' Tamasin grinned back, and then found she could hardly keep from laughing. It was years since she'd experienced a nervous reaction like this.

The Turk gripped her shoulder. 'You brave soldier. You make fire – poof!' He mimed the fireball with upturned palms. 'You want come with us, you come.' He shouted over his shoulder in Turkish. From the front, the driver answered briefly, and the lanky one laughed and grinned at Tamasin again. 'We no time stop. You come anyway.'

This time Tamasin let herself go; she yielded to the giggles.

* * *

For the first time, Tamasin started taking notice of where they were. The open hatch bumped up and down, but it was better like that, Tamasin thought. There was a second Isuzu a hundred yards in front of them; more *Yol* terrorists; her friends now, or at least her allies. They'd passed through a district of wide avenues and hedges, tall trees, big houses set back amid lawns and bougainvillea; north Tehran. Now it was industry and small shops and dusty vans and pickups parked at the kerbs, the 4×4 swerving around obstructions when it wasn't bouncing in the potholes.

'Where are we going?'

The lanky Turk grinned and pretended he didn't understand.

Tamasin thought of something else. 'What happened to the police? Why wasn't there anyone outside the jail?'

'Big march,' the Turk said. 'Many people want Islamic government. All police . . .'

It clicked. That demo, the one they'd told her about only that morning, that was where all the police had been.

In an avenue of cork oaks the industry fell behind and then, clustered and crowded up to the roadside, there was the shanty town, houses made from tin, houses made from packing cases, houses made from old, broken-down vehicles. Kids and cats, weary women with water containers. This was the human debris of Tehran,

135

Tamasin realized, the refugees from the 'war of the cities' way back in the mid-'80s. Some of them must have been here since the first Iraqi ballistic missiles started landing on Tabriz and Bahtaran, Isfahan and Tehran itself; and for all its promises of protection for the poorest, the regime still hadn't been able to house more than a handful of them.

They reached the start of a motorway.

*　　*　　*

From the front, someone passed round a pack of Marlboro. Everyone lit one except Tamasin. The motorway ran straight and the Isuzu was speeding. Tamasin ducked forward and peered out to try and gauge the direction by the sun, but the sky was still grey and threatening.

It didn't spoil the heady taste of freedom.

She looked at the motorway, wet patches still on the surface; lorries and buses, the occasional car; it wasn't busy. The two Isuzus were flat out, overtaking everything.

It wasn't possible to be sure, but Tamasin thought they must be heading north or east or something in between. She started wondering what she was going to do. She was pretty lost: what she knew about Iran you could write on the back of a postage stamp and still leave room for a verse of the Koran. To the right, a mountain skyline, farmland closer to, a scatter of low houses, a man far in the distance with a pair of yoked horses. To the left, grey and solid, a mountain range reaching right up to the cloudbase.

The Elburz was the big range that ran in a vast crescent north of Tehran, Tamasin remembered, cutting Tehran off from the Caspian coast. It *had* to be that range on the left. That put them heading east. Logical, Tamasin thought.

Then they reached the end of the motorway and turned sharply left, on to a road climbing up into the Elburz itself.

Tamasin's nervous reaction had evaporated now. She

felt weary, too weary to think what to do when she separated from these people. She'd be alone, on the run with nothing but the clothes she stood up in, not a word of the language.

Time to worry about that when it happened. She dozed.

When she opened her eyes again the engine was straining a bit in some intermediate gear, climbing. Only half-aware, she glimpsed a tanker truck as they overtook it. This was a good road, not as wide as the motorway but in good repair. Again Tamasin struggled to think where they might be heading, where she could make for and how. Maybe jump a ship to Russia, throw herself on the bureaucracy's mercy there.

They'd been through a village or two, she remembered, but now as she glanced either side of the speeding 4×4 the landscape was desolate, all rock and scrub and jagged mountain skyline under the overcast, not a habitation in sight.

Another pack of cigarettes arrived in the back, and the lanky Turk offered them to Tamasin. She shook her head with a smile, remembering immediately that she should have given him a backward nod for *no*. He grinned and lit up. The driver changed gear and the road swept into a tight S-bend, climbing amid scrub-covered banks. Tamasin braced herself in the turn.

Savage braking flung her into the seat backs and the 4×4 stopped in a howl of tyres. Rana screamed. Eyes wide, Tamasin twisted around and pulled herself up to see what had happened. In that moment she saw the lead Isuzu, stopped thirty yards in front of them, jolting on its springs as machine-gun fire poured into it from a police ambush.

CHAPTER 17

Ankara, Monday, 15 June, 1015 local
Breakfast was an hour and a half ago and Felix Wyer was starting to think it was almost time for the first coffee of the day from room service. Then the phone rang.

'Simkins here.' Felix recognized the plummy tones of the Second Secretary she'd spoken to on Friday. Something always made her deeply suspicious of embassy men. Even embassy women. 'Our counterparts in Tehran have managed to get in touch with the Interior Ministry over there. They confirm it, I'm afraid.'

'Confirm what?'

'Mr Cross is dead as a result of a bullet wound. Mrs Masterson has been formally charged with espionage and is being held on remand in Evin.' He waited. 'Mrs Wyer? Hello?'

'Yes,' Felix said in a dead voice. 'I understand.' Then she wasn't sure what it was that she understood.

Simkins said: 'I realize this is . . .'

'What's the Tehran embassy doing to get Captain Masterson released?'

'They were hoping to get someone in to speak to her tomorrow. What we don't know is what foundation there might be to any charges she's facing.'

'There's no foundation whatever!' Felix said angrily. 'It's nothing but Third World paranoia!'

She was bound to say that, Simkins reflected; and maybe she knew that herself. He gave her a few moments to cool down. 'The Iranian authorities have given us to understand that they are prepared to repatriate Mr Cross's body at an early stage,' Simkins said. 'What would you wish us to instruct them?'

138

'Well . . . they'd better fly him to Heathrow.' It crossed Felix's mind to send one of her own jets in, but, apart from the expense, she'd lost one aircraft already, presumed somewhere in Iran, and she didn't know how an application for landing clearance for a second might go down. 'Well . . . what have they *said* about this bullet wound? How did it happen? Have they launched an inquiry?'

Dragon Jet crew never carried weapons on a flight.

'We've been told nothing about any inquiry. The Iranian authorities seem to believe that the only other person in the case is Mrs Masterson – although I haven't heard that they've charged her in connection with the shooting.'

'I'd better get over there and talk to Tamasin.'

'What about Mr Cross's body?'

Damn, Felix thought. Receiving the body wasn't a job she could leave to someone else. 'Very well, I'll look after that. Mr Simkins, what have they said about my aircraft that the two of them were flying?'

'Again, we've been told nothing on that subject.'

'You mean no-one except the Iranians knows even where it is? Or whether it's damaged, or been force-landed, or . . . ?'

'I'm afraid we have no idea. Naturally our people in Tehran will make enquiries. Mrs Wyer, may I ask what your own plans are?'

Beyond the neutral, yellow-beige curtains it was a fine, sunny day over Ankara. Cars and buses were on the wide boulevard, with its central reservation shady with trees; people were out shopping; storks were flying.

'I'd like to go and talk to Tamasin in that jail. But . . . no, I'll have to get back to the UK. I'll get a flight today.'

Hanging up, Felix almost gave in to the tears. But tears wouldn't help, action would.

She dialled British Airways. She booked her seat. She hung up again.

She'd never seriously expected to have to claim on her crews' company-financed life assurance. And if Keith's death was down to some sort of act of war, would the insurers find some let-out clause? If they did, then Felix would feel morally obliged to find the money herself, through the company.

Dragon Jet was in danger. One member of staff dead, another jailed, untold expenses pending, and one valuable jet missing, unaccounted for. Why did it have to be that one? Her favourite aircraft out of the entire little fleet?

Felix didn't know how she was ever going to go back to Keith's parents now.

CHAPTER 18

Elburz mountains, Iran, Thursday, 18 June, 1556 local
Something in Tamasin Masterson's mind still hoped that she was imagining what she was seeing.

Gunfire pouring into the lead Isuzu must have killed the driver. As Tamasin gazed in horror, twisting to look ahead beyond the baggage area of the second Isuzu, the lead vehicle skewed slantwise across the road and jolted to a stop. One man tumbled out of the front nearside door and was diving for the herb-grown bank beside the road when several bullets caught him. They flung him right over onto his back, asprawl in the middle of the road, his whole torso flooded red.

Tamasin braced herself. The next burst had to hit her vehicle. There was nowhere to go.

The driver rammed the gear into reverse and went backwards down the road in a scream of rubber. The sky was overcast and Tamasin was aware of all the reds and browns and greens and yellows in the scrub landscape in this desolate place. Suddenly there were jeep-like vehicles coming up the steep slope behind them. No buses were in sight; no trucks – nothing.

Tamasin yelled: '*Police!*' The lean Turk beside her yelled something similar. He kicked the back hatch so it flew right up horizontal, and flicked the safety on his old AK47 as he brought the butt up into his shoulder.

They were trapped; police in front of them, police behind them – nowhere to go. And she'd shot at the prison guards herself; they'd prove it, from the gun she'd used and discarded.

Acts of espionage, now acts of terrorism. That was

141

two death sentences, supposing she survived what was happening here on the mountain pass now.

Well, she'd broken the rules before and got away with it . . . and she thought of the time in the B52 over Libya.

The Isuzu driver halted his wild reverse with a jolt that almost pitched Tamasin and the lanky Turk over the sill. Muzzle flame sparked sharp orange from the lead police jeep and Tamasin flinched away and felt the slap and snap as the shots passed through the interior and then from the front the man next to the driver screamed and flopped forward. There was blood sprayed on the windscreen and holes shot through the glass. The driver wrenched forward again and then hard around to the right, climbing the bank.

As they lurched over the top, Tamasin glimpsed the lead vehicle. There was a second body prone on the road behind it; no shooting came from the 4×4; and now suddenly a blaze of flame burst up inside the passenger compartment. Terror jammed the breath in Tamasin's throat as the fire swallowed up the whole of the vehicle.

Then it was out of her sight as her own Isuzu pitched into a hollow and stormed up and out of the other side.

There was no time for thinking, only for reacting. Choked with fear, Tamasin's mind wasn't working enough to start wondering what the driver thought he could do, simply crossing country at random like this.

Tamasin flung a look at the thin one beside her. He wasn't looking, his gaze directed out of the back of the vehicle, rifle muzzle lowered, ready to fire. The police jeeps hadn't appeared over the bank yet. How accurate his fire would be when they showed up was anyone's guess, the way the bouncing motion was throwing both of them about in the back.

It dawned on Tamasin that the driver didn't have a plan.

They'd put a hundred metres between them and the road but the 4×4 was now bucking and swaying worse than ever. The skinny Turk flung a look over his shoulder, worried, angry. Tamasin looked back the way they'd come. She could see the swathe they were crushing through the poppies and acacia, the wild rosemary, but she couldn't make out any sort of track that might have been there beforehand. Even an all-terrain vehicle needs a path to follow.

The lurching was getting worse, the Isuzu's engine straining in low gear. Still no sign of pursuit, but suddenly Tamasin wondered how soon it would be before the police called in helicopters. It amazed her how far they were actually getting from the road this way, two hundred metres now, two fifty.

They were just short of three hundred metres from the road when the Isuzu turned over.

* * *

Tamasin was lying on top of the lanky Turk and he was trying to shove her off him. She grabbed the seat back and pulled herself free and at once the man wriggled clear and out the open back hatch.

Tamasin was aware of moaning and yelling but she was too busy to take it in, lowering herself back to where the lanky Turk had been. She was on the point of squirming after him and out when she heard Rana's voice, piteous, wailing.

'Tamasin, Tamasin! Oh, please help me!'

Tamasin twisted around.

From her tone of voice, she'd thought Rana must be trapped somehow but she wasn't, she was just lying on top of the man who'd been next to her with no purchase anywhere to lever herself out. The Isuzu had gone over on its left side and the driver was pinned under the man who'd caught the police bullet.

The man under Rana grunted something in Turkish. Tamasin caught Rana by one arm and felt Rana's hand clutch at her as she pulled. She got both of Rana's shoulders, then she was free, lying in a tangle against the side of the vehicle.

The man who'd been under Rana levered himself loose. The driver was moaning.

Tamasin scrambled out into the scrub with its wild herb smells all lost now in the petrol stink from the Isuzu and crouched back to help Rana. This time she didn't need help, she just clambered out and accepted a hand from Tamasin to straighten up.

Slowly the first police jeep came over the bank from the road.

The lanky Turk was flat on his front on the edge of the dip that had ended the Isuzu's dash for sanctuary. He was half-inside a low juniper with his AK barrel steadied in a fork of the branches.

The man who'd been under Rana hauled himself out of the back of the vehicle. He said something in fierce, fast Turkish and Rana swung to Tamasin, her long dark hair falling loose.

'We've got to run!'

'Where?'

'Anywhere. To hide. They'll catch up with us when they've got the driver out, he's trapped.'

Tamasin looked around wildly. In this wilderness of rock and scrub and low trees, one place didn't look any better than any other place.

'All right, then, let's go!'

The AK let go with a short, angry burst behind them as Tamasin started leading the way at a run.

* * *

They must have made over a thousand metres through thorns and potholes when at last they flopped flat, panting, in the dubious cover of a little cluster of pistachio trees. Rana lay there, eyes shut, chest heaving. Tamasin turned and looked back.

She couldn't see what was happening. She'd heard the

AK firing a couple of times as they'd stumbled and run, and there'd been shots that she knew must have come from the police. Now as she looked back she could still hear shooting.

Then, slowly, as the heaving in her chest gradually lessened, the shots dwindled to single reports. They stopped altogether.

After a while, Tamasin noticed that Rana had levered herself up on her elbows beside her. Their breathing was shallow now, and they were straining their ears.

From back where they'd left the Isuzu they could hear occasional shouts of men's voices. The tension and alarm that had been present during the shooting had now disappeared.

Tamasin didn't like the implications of that.

Softly, Rana asked her: 'What's happening?'

'I don't know.' She wished she could just *see* something, but in the chaos of the mountain landscape she couldn't make out any sign of men or vehicles.

'*Allah, Allah*,' Rana breathed.

Tamasin moistened her lips. She glanced at her watch. But she hadn't checked it when they'd thrown themselves flat here, so she didn't know how long they'd been waiting.

It wasn't quite 1630. They *had* been here quite some time.

In a stronger voice, Rana said: 'We'll have to leave them. We'll have to go on, on our own.'

CHAPTER 19

Near Biggin Hill, Wednesday, 17 June, 1845 local

It had been the most harrowing day of Felix Wyer's life, far worse than the days immediately after Gerald's death. There was only one way to purge her system of it, and that was to run it out of herself.

It was a dry early evening with a touch of chill in the air and at this hour the lanes around the village of Downe, close to Biggin Hill airport, were busy with traffic; a runner had to keep a good lookout. As she ran, Felix thought back over the day.

Meeting Keith's parents had been every bit as bad as she'd feared. Their other son was with them, Keith's brother, and Felix thanked God that Keith hadn't been an only child. Emma, the girlfriend, was there, too, aristocratic and lean; red-eyed now. The father and brother had been tight-faced, stoical, but the mother hadn't been able to keep back the tears; nor had Emma.

Together the four of them had been at Heathrow to receive the coffin. There'd been a man from the Foreign Office, and a plainclothes police officer with him, to explain apologetically that there would have to be a *post mortem* as this might be the start of an official inquiry; but what office, Felix hadn't been able to grasp.

She edged close in towards the verge on the blind bend. Sure enough, there was a car coming too fast around it.

So the coffin hadn't gone home to Scarborough; it had gone to the police mortuary. No thoughts on when any summary of the findings might come out.

Felix swung off the road. Climbing the stile to the footpath broke her stride, but it was a relief to run where no cars drove.

She'd had the report from the Tehran embassy, Tamasin's explanation about a hijacker, which for some reason the Iranians wouldn't accept. She'd told them to get her the best possible lawyer; Dragon Jet would pay, for as long as the company stayed solvent.

Espionage, though. The thought terrified Felix. She didn't know a thing about the courts out there, she had no idea what Iranian justice was like; but she knew Tamasin was very much on her own.

Doggedly, Felix pounded the last three hundred metres down the lane to her home. She let herself in. The deep rise and fall of her chest was a welcome sensation; a good run always put an extra distance between her and the horrors of the day.

The house was empty. It had been empty for years now save for Felix, but she was comfortable now with the emptiness. Slowly, she went upstairs to the shower room, a hand on the banister rail. She was testing the water temperature, about to step under the shower, when the phone rang.

She answered it with a towel wrapped round her. 'Hello?'

'Felix, hi.' She knew that voice; it was one of her aircrew, Rob Pilgrim. 'How are you feeling?'

'Oh, I'm fine now, thanks, just been for a run.' Nice of him to ask, though. He'd never phoned her at home before. But then, he'd been flying all day and she'd been out of the office.

'I'm told we still don't know where *Rapide* is.'

'That's right.'

'Felix – would you have ten minutes to spare to have a chat about that? Tonight, maybe?'

She hesitated, surprised. 'Well . . . OK, then. Where are you, the airfield? Can we say half an hour's time?'

*   *   *

On the doorstep he gave her a smile, still dressed in his co-pilot's uniform.

'Come in.'

She'd never given this unassuming man any real thought before. She'd liked him, though, at the job interview; and his record looked good; even that Dominie that he'd aquaplaned off the runway could only marginally be held as his fault.

They sat down in the living room. Felix lifted an opened bottle of white wine from the cooler, but Rob shook his head.

'I'm driving.'

Felix poured herself a glass, her second that evening, but she sipped it very cautiously.

Rob said: 'Had you considered going to Iran at all to see if there's some way we can move things on a bit faster there?'

Over the rim of her slim glass Felix widened her eyes. 'Well . . . I had thought about going over to visit Tamasin. Why?'

His hair seemed tousled, shot with grey now. His eyes glinted; Felix had never noticed the determination about him before. 'If the company were to send someone over, there's at least two things you could do. For a start, this espionage thing is an obvious load of crap, so you could start getting on to people in the Interior Ministry, the Justice Ministry, I don't know what else . . . ginger things up, get it into their skulls that this charge doesn't hold water. The other thing is, you'd need to be over there, on the ground, as it were, to really look for *Rapide*. Which we presumably want back, if poss.'

'We certainly do.' Felix blinked at him, comfortably dressed in jeans and a loose top. 'Why, are you volunteering?'

His big grin would have won over a hanging judge. 'Basically – yes.'

'Why?'

*   *   *

He'd slung his jacket over the back of the armchair and was leaning forward, unaware that the knot of his tie had slipped down a little. He was explaining about Azra Tabrizi and her sister Bibi.

'So they worked out this code between them, sort of a letter within a letter. You know, sort of . . . every seventh word, then fifth, then seventh, then fifth, spells out a message. It worked. Azra got this message out to Bibi saying her relatives there were holding her against her will.'

Felix frowned. 'You mean they've got her chained up in this village?'

'No, nothing that crass. She's got freedom to roam around the village, and she can even go down the valley to this place Shahrud – provided she gets a male relative's permission. And this mullah of theirs is holding her passport.'

'Why would they be doing that?'

'Well, the way Bibi explains it, it's like a branch of Islam with particular fundamentalist ideas. According to their own way of thinking, this is their way of honouring and looking after their womenfolk. Theoretically, they've got equal rights – you know, rights to property, that kind of thing. In practice, it doesn't work out quite like that.'

Felix was still frowning. 'So what do you want to do about her?'

'I'd like to try and see her, to confirm whether it's true that she's keen to get out. If she is, then . . . well, I suppose we'll cross that bridge when we come to it. But in any case, I should've thought it was in Dragon Jet's interests to get someone in there with a view to making representations about Tamasin and finding and recovering *Rapide*.'

Felix pursed her lips. She took another sip of white wine, then gave Rob a direct look. 'What happens if we fail to get Tamasin released but we do find *Rapide*?'

'There are hundreds of legal moves to be made before, during and after any trial – even supposing she's found guilty. But you're right – we *might* find *Rapide* before we

149

get Tamasin freed to fly it. But suppose you and I went in there, Felix – I'm qualified to captain one of those jets. You've got your PPL and you've handled 125s in the air. Why not put yourself down as co-pilot?'

For a moment, Felix's hand froze on the stem of the wine glass. Then she began to smile. This was starting to sound at least as adventurous as the journey she'd made to collect *Rapide* from Las Vegas in the first place.

*　　*　　*

Next morning, Thursday, Felix rang the visa section of the Iranian embassy in London. Twenty minutes later she had a fax of the application form. She made a photocopy and passed that to Rob Pilgrim to fill in while she filled in the other. She faxed them back. Then waited.

*　　*　　*

It was Rob who rang her on the office internal phone next morning, Friday 19 June.

'Have you seen this morning's *Independent*?'

'No.' Felix took only the *Financial Times*; essential reading for a job like hers.

'I'd better come up, if you've got a sec.'

He was there in two minutes, hair more tousled than usual, an alert look on his terrier face. 'There.' He handed her the newspaper, opened to the foreign news pages.

Four prison officials died and nine were injured yesterday when terrorists attacked Evin jail, Tehran. The terrorists, who are believed to be members of an extreme fundamentalist Islamic sect, escaped after releasing several prisoners.

There was more, and Felix skimmed through it quickly. She looked up.

'There's no word about who the prisoners were who escaped.'

'It's the women's wing they attacked, though. Look.' Felix read it through again.

As soon as Rob left, she picked up the phone. The British embassy in Tehran didn't have any details or names, either; none had been released. Felix thought for a bit, then dialled the visa section at the Iranians' London embassy.

'Can you tell me what progress there is on my visa application and that of Mr Pilgrim? What's the waiting time likely to be?'

A pause. Then the accented voice told her: 'I am sorry, Mrs Wyer. A state of emergency was declared in parts of Iran this morning. No new visas are being issued.'

CHAPTER 20

Elburz mountains, Thursday, 18 June, 1632 local
This time Rana was right, Tamasin knew it.

She didn't like the silence from over where they'd left the men with the Isuzu. Slowly the certainty was growing within Tamasin that the men had been either killed or captured. They wouldn't be joining Rana and her now.

She thought aloud: 'They may not know who the *Yol* guys were but they must know by now that you and I are out. They'll be searching.' For the nth time she scanned the sky, straining her hearing. 'Why haven't they put helicopters up?'

'It's a badly organized, badly equipped police force,' Rana said. 'I thought of helicopters, too. But even if they've got helicopters, they might not all be in working condition.'

That thought was plausible, Tamasin realized. She looked at Rana, perhaps for the first time. Dislike the woman as she might, Tamasin could read the determination on her classically beautiful features.

The air over the wilderness of rock and scrub was still close, with hardly any wind. They grey sky hung threateningly.

'Which way is east?' Rana said.

Tamasin looked around. The road they'd been flushed from ran broadly north-south, following the line of the mountain pass, while the main line of the Elburz peaks lay in an immense, shallow crescent cutting off Tehran from the Caspian, pretty much east to west. They had no sun to guide them but Tamasin could read the lie of the peaks.

'It's this way.' She pointed in a direction roughly at right

152

angles to the way the road had led. It was the direction she and Rana had run when they'd left the men. 'Why?'

'Darvish was not with those men. That means he's at Roudabad. Roudabad is in the Elburz but it's east of here.'

Suddenly Tamasin remembered the flight; the way they'd followed that eastward road to the town; the way they'd doubled back to find the airfield Darvish had been so certain was there. She struggled to remember the name of the town.

'Is Roudabad anywhere near Shahrud?'

'Quite near.' Rana tossed her long, dark hair. Her impatience was starting to show.

The airstrip of Zedasht had also been quite near Shahrud. Now Tamasin understood what she hadn't understood before. Darvish had picked Zedasht because it was close to Roudabad and he had friends or allies there.

'We'd better go,' Rana said.

'Where to?'

'Roudabad.'

Tamasin stared. 'How are we going to get there?' There was something here she didn't quite grasp. Rana was talking for both of them, not just her on her own.

'Walk,' Rana said as if it was as obvious as the law of gravity.

'Do you know how far it is?'

'No. But we can walk it, we're strong.'

Quickly Tamasin calculated, her eyes on Rana. 'Listen, Rana. When they picked me up from Zedasht, it took 35 minutes by helicopter flying at about 250 km/h' – she cast her mind back; but that would have been it for that Bell Isfahan, the air had been pretty still – 'so, say that's 160 kilometres in a *direct* line. A hundred miles! Over the ground, I bet it'd be way more than that, probably as much as 300 k's. Do you *know* how long that would take us, crossing this sort of country?'

Rana looked at her sullenly and said nothing.

Tamasin said: 'We'd be lucky to make two k's an hour over stuff like this. That's at least 100 hours' walking, with, say, ten hours a day, max, not even counting what we're going to do about food and water and sleeping.' She glanced upwards. 'It's not raining at the moment and we haven't even got direct sun on us – but if that sun comes out, it'll be a killer, and the same goes if we get heavy rain. Soaked clothes can catch you death of exposure.'

Rana shrugged. 'Well, *I* can't see what else we can do. We'll *have* to walk it.'

Even though Rana's stubbornness annoyed her, Tamasin had to hand it to her for guts and determination. She wouldn't have thought Rana would have that much will-power in a situation like this.

'We'll have to walk to get out of here, sure. But where we walk to is another question.'

'What are you talking about?' Rana was rattled, testy.

Tamasin was thinking furiously and now she had it; she'd remembered enough to call up a mental portrait of the land she'd flown over in the few minutes before touching down at Zedasht. 'Train. There's a railway line runs from Tehran to Shahrud – I saw it from the air. It's the only sensible way. Jump a train – or even just buy a ticket, if we could only get hold of some different clothes. And we'd need chadors. Have you got any money on you?'

Rana blinked. 'Iranian rials, yes.'

'I've got . . . some US dollars.' Dragon Jet crews always carried dollars to cope with the unexpected. Tamasin had the best part of a thousand. 'Maybe we could actually buy some replacement clothes. And the rail fare.' For a moment Tamasin wasn't sure whether it was a safer bet to jump a train or to board legitimately and buy a ticket. But there'd be time enough to dwell on that question when they were within range of the line itself. 'Come on, then, we'd better get moving.'

Rana hesitated. 'Where do you want to go?'

'South. We're bound to strike the railway if we just head due south.' Tamasin set off striding through the brittle, scented scrub.

* * *

It wasn't that odd, Tamasin thought after half an hour pushing through the low brush, that Rana should be content to be together with her; and not even for the sake of simple human companionship. Rana needed Tamasin. She needed Tamasin's sense of direction; her sense for the terrain, a landscape half-familiar to her with its echoes of Arizona, where she'd lived before Edward died; her matter-of-fact confidence about what they could achieve and what they couldn't.

But Tamasin needed Rana, too. Rana was the one who could speak the language, the one who would have to talk their way out of any challenge they ran up against.

The landscape was tough. It was climbing now, up towards the ridgeline that separated this wild upland moor from the plain below where the farmland around Tehran turned gradually to desert, the further you went east. Sometimes Tamasin smelled wild herbs, crushed under her feet; sometimes the dry woodiness of the bald acacia as its spines clutched at her clothing.

Once she saw the tail of a long snake writhing away from her, in among the bushes, and she thought with a chill that if either of them got bitten, that one was doomed.

She clambered over a lichen-laden boulder and turned, looking for Rana, her chest heaving, her ribs running with sweat, her head pounding.

Rana was a hundred yards back and picking her way laboriously through the low growth. Watching her struggle up the slope, Tamasin spared a thought for how seriously the police might be hunting for them.

That lead Isuzu. It had burned pretty badly and there would undoubtedly have been bodies in there. Tamasin had a job to think back to that scene objectively. But she knew that if there were, say, only two bodies burnt beyond recognition – and in all probability it was more likely to have been three or four – the police were really rather likely to assume that she and Rana were among them. They couldn't have seen the two of them running off from the second 4×4; they'd have sent men after them if they had.

Rana laboured the last few yards and slumped on the rock where Tamasin was waiting. She propped her weight on one arm. She had tears in her eyes.

'Tamasin . . .' Her voice was a whisper. 'I'm sorry . . . I didn't know it was going to be like this.' She blinked, and two big tears got away. 'I . . . I can't manage any more.'

CHAPTER 21

Ankara, Monday, 22 June, 1430 local
It was the usual hotel, the characterless room, the plumbing that worked. For some reason, today's flight had left Felix Wyer feeling more tired than usual. She picked up the phone.

'Erol Ersin, please.'

With Iran freezing new entry visas, the closest Felix was going to get to Tamasin was Turkey. She'd sent Rob Pilgrim back to his usual job flying co-pilot to Melvin Trail aboard *Dragon Tempest* while, after a weekend kicking her heels, she got on the first available flight back to Ankara.

'Felix, my dear. How was your flight?' She could see the craggy Red Indian face the moment she heard his confident, deep voice.

'Tolerable, thank you. Have you heard anything more from . . .' That mysterious contact of his, that was what Felix meant.

'Nothing concrete. But I think he may have more to tell us later on today.'

Felix had never met Ersin's shadowy contact. Curiosity had been eating her up ever since she knew of the man's existence. 'How d'you mean, "us"?'

Ersin cleared his throat. 'Would you be in a position to join me at a meeting tonight at seven?' He named the hotel he had in mind.

*　　*　　*

It was even more impersonal than the one where Felix was staying; a sprawling two-storey complex on a hill on the edge of Ankara, apparently designed with the worst of

American motels for a model. Felix went by taxi. Ankara was far from being the worst city she knew for driving a car – even parking wasn't usually much problem – but unless she was planning a trip out of town she found self-drive hiring tended to be impractical.

In the car park she recognized Ersin's Lexus. He was waiting for her in the lobby, reading the daily *Hürriyet*, dressed in beige slacks, a navy sports jacket, a salmon shirt and a florid tie. Felix was wearing a white cardigan over a dress with a calf-length skirt of pine green. Ersin rose and smiled and shook her hand, and then led her to the stairs.

'Kemal knows which room number.'

'His name's Kemal?'

Ersin simply smiled affirmatively and unlocked the door for her.

Shadows were sprawling across the car park from the cypress and sycamore dotted around the edge of the motel complex. Inside, they needed the light. It was a twin-bed room but it had a sort of makeshift conference area with a low coffee table and four deep armchairs, and a fridge in the corner.

Evidently Ersin had stocked it up, ready. 'May I offer you a drink?'

'I say – that's very civilized. Have you got a G and T?'

Often when she visited Ankara Felix brought a bottle of Gordon's from London for Ersin. The bottle he fished out looked like one he'd been nibbling at home.

'Cheers!'

Ersin was drinking orange juice. Sneakily Felix got a look at him in profile and could see why.

A knuckle knocked softly at the door. Ersin turned his head quickly and said: '*Iceri, buyrunuz.*' Kemal Koz walked in.

He had a wary grin on his alert face and a slim briefcase under one arm. He was the same height and build as Ersin and had the sort of beer gut that Ersin was half-heartedly

158

trying to postpone. He'd dressed like a trendy in a denim suit with hipster trousers precariously held up with a hand-crafted Anatolian leatherwork belt too wide to be completely obscured by his belly. The open neck of his rust-red shirt showed thick hair, most of it white.

'Felix, this is Kemal. Kemal, Mrs Wyer.'

'Very pleased to meet you, Mrs Wyer.' The confident English had a faint American accent. The handshake alike was strong.

Now Felix didn't know whether *Kemal* was his first name or his last. He obviously knew exactly who she was, though.

They sat down around the table and Ersin bent over them. 'Felix, do you need refilling? No. Kemal, what can I get you?'

'Oh, beer, if you've got it.'

Felix slid Ersin a look as he stooped to the fridge. He'd obviously been expecting this.

He placed the glass in front of Kemal Koz and then sat at the narrow end of the table. Koz and Felix were looking at each other.

Koz gave Felix a quick grin, his little round eyes alert. 'Erol's told me a little bit about your company, Mrs Wyer. You are providing a vital training service to our armed forces here and I hope you're being adequately recompensed for that.'

'Oh, I think so,' Felix said. 'The naval contract is pretty important to Dragon Jet.'

Koz nodded, knees apart, his shoulders pushing a little forwards. 'Erol has also told me about some of the troubles you've been having.'

Felix tilted her head. 'It is very worrying – personally as well as in business terms. And with one of my staff murdered . . .'

'So it seems. Now, I gather another of your staff, the survivor, has been accused of espionage and remanded in custody in Iran.'

'That was before this incident . . .'

159

'Quite,' Koz said. 'The terrorist attack on Evin last Thursday – and today's Monday. Have the Iranian authorities said anything to you about it?'

'I've been unable to get any confirmation of whether Tamasin Masterson – my captain who was jailed – is still in custody. And with no visas being issued, I can't get into the country to find things out for myself.'

Koz watched Felix, just a couple of feet apart from her in the little dim room. A distant muezzin reminded them that Turkey was a Muslim country just as Iran was.

'And what plans have you,' Koz asked, 'for solving that problem?'

'None.' And if Koz thought he was getting anything more out of her than that, he could think again.

Koz opened his briefcase. He took out some papers. They had official-looking letter heading and were typed or wordprocessed in Turkish. Bureaucratic expressions can be difficult in a language as straightforward as English or French, but in Turkish, with its combinations of prefixes and suffixes and its idiosyncratic word order, it can be impenetrable. Koz frowned at the top page and took a slow swallow of beer as he read down.

He glanced up at Felix again. 'I have colleagues, you understand, who have access to certain . . . restricted information. They are confident that Tamasin Masterson *is* missing from Evin in the wake of that terrorist attack.'

Felix's eyes lit up. 'Do they know where she is?'

'Ah . . . no. That's something that we'd all like to know. However . . . ' he shuffled papers; he came up with a couple of photographs, 25cm by 20cm . . . 'I believe there was also a question as to where the plane Captain Masterson flew might be. Would you say this might be the plane?'

Felix took the first print. It was a big enlargement, judging by the grain on it, taken from above at not many degrees off vertical. There was some sort of van pulled up close to the jet's wingtip; there were men in overalls walking around it; there was a platform up to the tailplane. Felix looked up.

'This is *Dragon Rapide* all right. Where was this taken?'

'How can you be so sure?'

Felix tapped a pen top to the tail. 'This blister is the radar warning receiver housing. There's only one 125 in the world flying with one of these.' She met his gaze, hers challenging. 'Where was this taken?'

'This is a disused Iranian air force station called Zedasht. It's on the edge of the Dasht-e Kavir – the big desert in north central Iran. The nearest town of any size is a place called Shahrud.'

Satellite, Felix realized. They'd never have got a NATO reconnaissance aircraft way out over Iran like that, and it was obviously an overhead shot. 'How did you get hold of this?' She couldn't keep the curiosity out of her voice.

'These prints have been lent to me just until tomorrow morning,' Koz lied smoothly.

'When was it taken?' The date and time information she would have expected had been clipped off the corner.

'I don't know.' Another lie.

'And what's happening?' Felix frowned and tapped the print again. 'Who are these men and what are they doing?'

'Iranian air force technicians,' Koz said, truthfully for a change. 'They look as if they're preparing the plane for flight. My own private guess is that they're getting ready to fly it to some proper operational air base. How much longer it takes them is not something I can judge – although so far as we know the plane is still at Zedasht, and it hasn't been moved yet.'

Ersin watched the expression on Felix's face. He glanced at Koz, impressed. If the old spy chief's purpose this evening had been to put ideas into Felix's mind, he'd succeeded.

'Is this airfield guarded?' Felix asked.

161

'There are guards during the day. As far as one can make out, the technicians work only from about seven in the morning to eleven – after that, it is very hot in the desert. We don't know whether there are guards through the night – but Zedasht is a very remote base, with probably little of value there.'

Felix watched him a moment longer. 'Do your pictures tell us anything about, say, the runway at Zedasht?'

*   *   *

From her hotel she phoned Turkish Airlines to book to Antalya for the next day. Then she phoned Rob Pilgrim. He was flying, but she left the message with Zafar Rahim. She wanted Rob with her at Antalya ASAP.

*   *   *

Rob made it by five the next afternoon, Tuesday, 23 June. Antalya was a somewhat smaller airfield than Ankara, but its runway was big enough for the sort of jetliners the package tour groups put in there. Dragon Jet had part use of a hangar and full use of a suite of offices on the opposite side from the passenger terminal. Felix was there when Rob came through, beside her Walter Becker, who'd driven the open-top Suzuki round there.

Ginger moustache bristling, Walter drove out of the airport and back in on the other side. Chris Norton and Ron Harper were drinking English-style tea with milk in the briefing room Felix had asked them to reserve for her. They looked up as Felix led the men in, Norton lanky and blank-faced, with no idea what might be coming next; Harper shorter, wilier with his wealth of overseas experience, and his knowing grin.

The briefing room had a dais and a blackboard and a lot of chairs. There wasn't a table, so Felix got them arranged on chairs in a little circle. She spoke confidentially.

'How good *are* these Falcons of yours, exactly?'

Norton raised his eyebrows and gave Harper a baffled look. Harper's crafty grin widened a little.

'Pretty damn good,' Walter said. 'We can get past this lousy Turkish navy any time we choose.'

'Could you get past Iranian radar?'

* * *

After the pause, they were all talking at once, except Rob, who simply sat there and listened. Norton accused Walter hotly: 'You've been peddling those hare-brained ideas of yours again! One of these days your loony schemes are going to get all of us in shtuck.'

'Not me, my friend.' But Walter clearly enjoyed the turn the talk had taken.

'Well?' Felix prompted.

'I say yes,' Walter declared.

Felix looked at Harper. 'You're the electronics man, you're the one who would actually do the getting in and out. *Could* you do it?'

Harper deliberated a moment.

'No, we bloody couldn't,' Norton said. 'You're talking about an illegal intrusion . . .'

Harper's grin widened. 'Bullshit.' His voice was quiet. 'Of course we could do it.'

'We'd need to get down about first light,' Felix said. 'The runway is about 5,800 feet. You would then take off again immediately. Your passengers would remain behind, with a view to flying out in a different aircraft.' She paused. 'What about range? Walter? Could you make it to north central Iran and back on the tanks in those Falcons?'

Walter Becker raised his eyebrows and scratched the back of his neck. 'Could do,' he said, as if an illegal intrusion into a potentially trigger-happy neighbouring country was all part of a normal day's work. 'But if we want to do that, why don't we do it from Diyarbakir?'

Felix frowned. 'Diyarbakir?'

'Eastern Turkey,' Walter said. '*You* met Mahmut that time, Felix – Colonel Barka, from that F16 outfit. He was so pleased with that ride we gave him in the Falcon that time, he's invited us back to his base, any time we want.'

CHAPTER 22

Elburz mountains, Thursday, 18 June, 1750 local
Distress on Rana Tezcan's face was less self-pity than it was anger with herself at her weakness. She ground a knuckle into each eye in turn. She yanked at the tangles in her hair.

'Take your time, then,' Tamasin said coolly. 'Get some proper rest and we'll move when you're ready.'

'But *where?*' Rana's voice was almost a wail. 'This is awful terrain – there aren't even any paths through it.'

Tamasin resisted the urge to say *I told you so*. She considered. 'OK. We aren't even at the crestline going south, so I think there's probably no future in keeping ahead in this direction.' She took a slow look all around. 'I reckon we're less than a thousand metres east of that road we came up in the vehicles – although we must be quite a bit south of where . . . where it happened.'

Neither of them had wanted to refer to the carnage they'd escaped from back on the road.

'You want to go back to the *road?*' Rana stared. 'You're crazy! There'll be police all over it. What d'you want to go back there for?'

Tamasin had a think. She'd sat down on the rock, a little apart from Rana. Rana might well be right about police on the road, Tamasin reflected, but that road still looked like their likeliest bet. What Tamasin didn't like was the thunder she'd been hearing for a little while, rumbling uneasily off to the west of them. What wind there was, was in the west, and it would bring that thunder closer to them.

The first heavy drop of rain landed on her hand.

'What we want isn't the road, it's a village where we

165

can hide up and get shelter.' Tamasin looked upwards. 'This could turn out to be a bit of a storm, and I'm not keen on our chances if we get soaked through.' She turned to Rana. 'Your Farsi's pretty good – could you persuade someone to take us in and keep quiet about it? We've got those dollars . . .'

'I suppose so.' Then Rana broke off and surveyed the landscape, desperately. They were surrounded by nothing but wilderness. 'But how . . . how are we ever going to get to a village to . . . to try . . .'

Tamasin reached out and squeezed Rana's hand. She didn't much want to, but instinct told her that without reassurance Rana wouldn't move another inch; and Tamasin would be in trouble without Rana to do the talking.

'We'll manage,' Tamasin said. 'You're tougher than you think. You'll see!'

*　　*　　*

The shower was light and short-lived. Through it Tamasin and Rana headed doggedly west, ducking past the acacias and pushing through the poppies. Smells of lavender and oregano rose up from where the thick, slow raindrops fell, and Tamasin reflected wryly that in almost any other set of circumstances she'd have been only too delighted to enjoy the beauty of this landscape.

Yet the terrain was a potential killer and they had to get out of it fast.

*　　*　　*

This time when Tamasin saw a snake it was much closer. With cold sweat breaking out all over her she recognized it; a cobra. It was much smaller than an Indian cobra but it still had the hood and Tamasin was happy to give it the benefit of any doubt as to whether it was equally venomous. She stood stock still, hardly breathing; but in a moment the cobra slid gracefully away out of sight. Tamasin glanced back. Rana was thirty yards behind her and still moving slowly, wearily. Tamasin wondered whether to warn Rana of the snakes or whether that would panic her, freeze her up. In the end she didn't have breath for any comment.

'Wait for me!' Rana pleaded.

Tamasin waited, getting her breath back, letting the cobra get further away from them. She was much more cautious when she moved on.

* * *

Light was failing and the rain was starting to fall more steadily when they sighted the roofs and television aerials of the first village. They were slightly east of the road up to the pass; they'd been following a roughly parallel course for half an hour or so. Tamasin let Rana catch up with her and then they moved down the slope close together, using whatever cover there was.

Now and then a truck or bus would labour up the steep road, engine straining, headlamps probing the twilight.

Tamasin and Rana were barely in among the first of the shadowy houses when a woman came out from a back door to take the washing down and out of the rain.

Rana drew Tamasin back, behind an outhouse. Her uniform, let alone the state it was in, would be likely to startle people. Tamasin hid around the corner and Rana vanished; then Tamasin heard the voices.

She would simply have to trust Rana now not to betray her. She waited. The rain grew heavier.

Then abruptly Rana appeared again, her eyes wide in the darkness. 'Quick, Tamasin, come! They're supporters of the *Shohada*, the martyrs, the friends of *Yol*. We can hide here.'

* * *

167

The house was no more than a workers' cottage on the edge of the village where it clustered up to the road towards the pass. Sinking onto the chair she was offered, Tamasin realized that Rana wasn't the only one who was exhausted from the day.

The woman who'd called them indoors was plump, fortyish, wearing old, faded clothes and a headscarf. But her husband was the one who'd decided whether they were to come in or not; a brawny character with a cropped head and little dark eyes, wearing a stained and patched version of the blue boiler suit all the gunmen from *Yol* had worn. There was the daughter of the house, too, a slim girl in a headscarf like her mother's, about seventeen, Tamasin guessed; and a couple of shaven-headed boys of nine or ten.

With a lot of relief she accepted tea. Rana drew breath from her Farsi conversation with the mother and glanced at Tamasin. She was looking confident now that she was out of the wilderness. Tamasin glanced at the man in the overalls, watching her and Rana with frank curiosity but with a protective air as well. The two fugitives were still in the clothes they'd got wet in the rain.

'What are you telling her?' Tamasin asked.

'That you and I also support the *Shohada*, although we're not Iranians, and that the police may be looking for us. I knew we'd get help here. The *Shohada* get their support from the poorest people in the cities and the countryside alike.'

Tamasin could tell by now when she was hearing empty boasts from Rana, and that wasn't one.

Rana added: 'Also I've told them we need to get to the railway line to travel east. I didn't say where to.'

Tamasin nodded, thoughtfully. Evidently Rana had accepted the plan Tamasin had put forward out there on the mountain. Tamasin was beginning to think this partnership might work, after all.

'Did you say anything about this gear of mine? Or about chadors?'

Rana gave her a knowing grin and resumed her conversation. At one point the husband joined in. Rana broke off again and turned back to Tamasin. 'What about these dollars of yours?'

Tamasin slipped a hand inside her jacket. 'I've got them.'

Rana leaned closer. 'I've told her $100. It's quite a lot of money for them, but they are taking a terrible risk, after all. They say they can get us chadors and some different clothes. And for another $20 they can get us down the mountain to where the railway runs.'

Frowning, Tamasin carefully counted out six twenties. 'How are they going to do that?'

'He's a truck driver. He's got the truck parked outside.'

*   *   *

They were up the next day shortly before six. They'd eaten a hot meal with the family in the late evening, and then they'd slept on blankets on the living-room floor. When they woke up the mother gave them breakfast and sent them out with chewy bread rolls and plastic bottles of yoghurt. Tamasin kept her trousers but abandoned her uniform jacket in favour of a brightly coloured blouse with baggy sleeves. For once, she was glad of the chador. She hoped the family would have the sense to keep the promise she extracted from them to destroy the jacket. Gathering their chadors, Tamasin and Rana climbed up into the lorry cab.

It was six-thirty, the day bright and fine after yesterday's thunder and rain. Tamasin fought to keep herself relaxed, banishing any thought of police checkpoints. Too much worrying made you tired.

169

Beside her, in the middle, Rana seemed tense as she sat, wrapped in her chador. Then the cropped-headed Iranian in the overalls swung up to the wheel in a practised movement and started the engine.

CHAPTER 23

Diyarbakir, eastern Turkey, Wednesday, 24 June, 1600 local

Black mountains stood in a wall against the distant horizon and for as far as Walter Becker's eye reached the land beyond *Falcon Fang*'s sloping nose lay dusty brown. Far ahead, light glinted an instant, so tiny it took a pilot's training to recognize what it was; but an instant later Walter made out the blackish-brownish smoke trails.

'Diyarbakir, contact two ahead, *Falcon Fang*.'

'Roger, *Falcon Fang*, maintain speed one forty.'

Chris Norton, the lanky ex-Royal Navy helicopter pilot, glanced over his shoulder to Felix Wyer, enjoying herself on the jumpseat. 'That'll be those F4s.' Approach control at the big NATO station had put *Fang* number two to land after the pair of old Turkish air force Phantom fighters.

'*Ja*,' Walter said, and trimmed the nose gently higher, reining in the speed on his landing approach.

In the back, Rob Pilgrim tightened his harness. Ron Harper did the same. He had his EWO console switched off and was reading *The Lord of the Rings*, his second time through.

'Must be time to dangle the Dunlops,' Walter said, and reached to lower the undercarriage.

Drifting dust hazed the expanse of airfield but the runway was ample. Walter made a point of leaving his rubber scorches exactly on the threshold bars; precision flying had been his strong suit on the East German air force MiG 29s. With the turbofans hardly turning, he braked down the big runway.

Norton was doing the radio now, talking to ground control.

In the parking area as they rolled at fast walking

171

pace, Walter could see Turkish F16s and RF4Es, the reconnaissance variant of the Phantom; and USAF F15 fighters, dwarfed by a pair of KC10s, the air-to-air tanker model of the DC10 airliner. One of the NATO E3 Sentry radar platforms was parked close by the KC10s. There was supposed to be another of them, but Walter assumed it must be flying.

The helicopters were there, too; the newly acquired Russian Mi 8 Hip assault/transports, bulky and menacing with their rotor blades asplay. They were the aircraft Turkey was using in the Kurdish guerrilla war.

Colonel Mahmut Barka, lean, saturnine, the glare wrinkles at his narrowed eyes, waited in a minibus. Walter shut down *Fang*'s engines; by the time he followed the others out on to the heat shimmer off the ramp, Mahmut was clasping Felix's hand in both of his and then turning to greet the men.

'Good to see you again,' Mahmut smiled as he shook Walter's hand.

The prospect of recovering *Rapide* – and her captain, if they could find her in time – formed part of the reason for this visit; but the other part was the chance of further improving relations with the Turkish military.

Moustache bristling above his big grin, Walter clapped Mahmut on the shoulder. 'OK, then – I give you a ride in my ship when you come to us: how about me get a ride in one of your ships, now I'm here?'

'Had it in mind, Walter – we'll have an RF4E lined up for you tomorrow.'

'*Ach*, I thought you give me a ride in one of those F16s.'

It was only half a tease. The RF4E was a pretty ancient jet, even by Turkish air force standards; but the much more recent F16s were single-seaters, all but a single F16B trainer. Laughing, they climbed into Mahmut's minibus.

Flying was over for the day. In the officers' club bar they drank Efes lager; even Felix, who hardly ever drank beer. Mahmut and Walter alike wore air force flying suits. Walter's was the old Russian pattern and he had a garish MiG 29 logo emblazoned on the sleeve.

A young officer sidled up to Mahmut and spoke softly into the commander's ear.

Mahmut turned to Felix. 'There's a telephone call for you. Lieutenant Duzgunoglu will show you the way.'

Felix returned the young Turk's shy smile and followed him to a cubicle off the corridor outside.

'Hello?'

'Felix, my dear, how are you? How was your flight?' The smooth, deep voice was that of Erol Ersin.

'Super, thanks. How are things at your end?'

'I've heard from Kemal, whom you met . . .'

Felix reflected, intrigued: Kemal was a mystery – exactly the way he'd wanted to be. Her initial guess was that he was something fairly high up in MIT, and she'd discovered nothing to contradict that. 'What does he say?'

'His colleagues inform him that the airfield, Zedasht, is actually not guarded at night because it's too remote from any town or city and there's nothing there that's valuable enough to be worth guarding. *Rapide* was still on the airfield today – but there is a thought that it might not be there for a great deal longer.'

'Those were satellite pictures we saw,' Felix said, 'weren't they?'

'I assume so.'

Assume, Felix thought. He bloody well *knew* it. She was starting to get an inkling of why Turkish intelligence should want to get satellite shots of her jet, marooned in Iran. If Dragon Jet collapsed, so would the naval contract. 'What *is* the latest, then?'

'The aircraft was fully fuelled today. They sent a bowser.'

Mentally Felix cursed. That must be the final prelude to moving the jet to some proper, operational IRIAF base. 'Did Kemal say anything else?'

'Yes. He said to ask Colonel Barka about the radar intercepts from Tabriz Three.'

173

The club was a big room, cool after the dry heat deep inside Anatolia. There were aircrew and maintenance and air traffic people here from a dozen different nations. On the sound system someone had put a compact disc of Eric Clapton and it was playing *Lay Down Sally*. Felix paused a little inside the doorway and studied Mahmut Barka and Walter Becker with the eye of a woman who could have been charmed by the attentions of either of them. They were the same height as her, five ten, but whereas Mahmut had the build and grace of a dancer, Walter was built like a navvy.

She went over.

She came in halfway through the male bonding process; Walter teasing Mahmut, always something he was good at. 'Would *you* trust the Iranians?'

'Don't see why not,' Mahmut replied mock-innocently.

Norton and Harper were sharing a joke close by Mahmut's elbow, Rob watchful on the edge of both conversations. Darkly Walter said, 'I wouldn't trust them. What you ought to do, you ought to zap in there with a section of F16s. Then *Rapide* can get out while the Iranians are still wondering which day of the week it is. Get down low enough, they'll never intercept you in a million years.'

Mahmut smiled knowingly. Felix caught his eye.

'What about this base, Tabriz Three?' she asked.

'I'm glad you mentioned that,' Mahmut said slowly. 'Our E3 patrols have tracked some quite respectable intercepts lately. They've got some quite clever pilots in those F14s at Tabriz Three.'

A glint of mischief showed in Walter's wily face. 'I wonder. You'd be surprised, the tricks this ship of mine can get up to when we're really trying . . .'

CHAPTER 24

North central Iran, Friday, 19 June, 0755 local

The last leg of the journey down from the Elburz was the slowest, the old truck bumping cautiously along a track south from the main eastern highway. The track was mud and gravel, partly mud and grass, partly just mud, partly not even enough of that to tell you there was a track at all. When the driver pulled up, Tamasin Masterson couldn't see a thing that might tell them where they were.

Rana Tezcan did the goodbyes. Tamasin had said hardly a word the whole way. They clambered down from the high cab, clutching their chadors to keep them from catching in oily hinges or trailing in wet mud.

Then the truck rumbled away towards the distant mountains, and they were on their own again. Utterly.

Under the big sky, blue for once, the day was mild, but Tamasin hugged her arms around her for comfort. Slowly, she looked all round. The railway was a single line, a dozen metres further down the primitive track, with nothing to suggest a halt there.

North of them, a bluish haze softened the harsh jags of the Elburz. More yellow-grey hills formed the skyline to the south, and to the east and the west the plain stretched away, its brown blur the colour of the sun-beaten grass at their feet.

She turned. Rana was looking back to where the lorry had vanished. She glanced at Tamasin, worried.

'You don't think he'd sell us out . . . do you?'

'He's got a lot of dollars to explain away if he does.'

Rana looked down and bit her lips. 'I'm just worried.'

At times yesterday she'd been like this. It was an oddly

175

vulnerable side to a woman who was capable of some very determined action.

'How do we know this is the right place?' Tamasin asked.

'Oh, it's the right place.' Rana pointed roughly the way the lorry had departed. 'Look, there's the village. But it probably serves more than just that one.'

Tamasin made out the shallow roofs, now that she knew what she was looking for. In this clear air it looked a long way away for walking – a good couple of miles.

If more people came from there to wait, they'd know that a train could be expected. On the other hand, there would undoubtedly be more explaining to do. Tamasin started thinking up explanations.

Rana flopped to the ground, dry now in the morning sun. 'God, I'm tired! I slept worse last night than I did in that filthy jail.'

They were lucky, Tamasin thought, to have fine weather for their wait. She glanced down at Rana. Rana curled herself up on the rough grass and settled into a doze.

* * *

The quiet of the open plain worked itself deep into Tamasin's mind as she watched the buzzards soaring and the crickets jumping in the grass. With Rana dozing, it was a peaceful quiet.

An hour passed. Now and then Tamasin heard a vehicle engine from the village, but the main eastward road was too far away for her to hear anything. Sometimes a lark sang or a buzzard mewed; once she heard a jetliner and saw its contrail, high against the empty arch of blue.

There wasn't a sniff of a train.

Rana woke up, cramped, her mood fretful. 'Hasn't there been a single train?' She made it sound like Tamasin's fault. Throwing back her chador hood, she looked all around, as if expecting pursuers. 'We can't just sit here waiting forever.'

176

'It's the best option we've got,' Tamasin stated. Apart from being the only option she could see.

Rana drew her chador close around her shoulders, as if she felt cold. 'What if we get another storm while we're stuck out here?'

'Let's cross that bridge when we come to it.' The last thing Tamasin needed was someone pointing out all the dangers she was busy trying to ignore. The quiet was getting on her nerves and she knew they were horribly exposed.

Shortly after a second hour had passed, they heard a train coming.

* * *

By Tamasin's watch it was 1015. Rana scrambled to her feet, Tamasin was standing already. It was Tamasin who saw it first.

'Wrong way. This one's heading towards Tehran.'

Rana cursed softly. They stood side by side as the train – freight, not passenger – rolled slowly over the plain towards them. It trundled ponderously past them, two hissing locomotives and at least sixty clanking wagons. It didn't stop.

Nor did the eastbound freight train that came from the Tehran direction twenty minutes later.

* * *

It was gone 1130 when the third train of the day announced itself with a distant rumble. Heading east. Tamasin reached and helped Rana to her feet again. They watched.

'Huh,' Rana said. 'Another freight.'

Then as it approached, Tamasin realized that the squeaks and groans she could hear were coming from the brakes.

It still hadn't pulled up as it rolled querulously past

them, and they were half-walking, half-jogging in its wake when finally it halted, east down the line. This one had only a single locomotive; the driver, half-glimpsed, showing no interest in a couple of black-shrouded figures beside the rails. Tamasin had counted thirty-seven wagons, rusty and battered, some of them open, some of them flatcars, half a dozen cement or chemicals carriers, then a line of old wooden trucks with curved roofs and sliding doors in the sides. And she knew her moves now.

'This one!'

Rana was stumbling after her, cramped by sheer nerves, gasping aloud. Tamasin went past the last wagon in the train and picked the one just ahead of it. The base came chest-high on her and she couldn't reach the handle above.

'Rana, can you . . . ?'

Taller, she stretched up beside Tamasin, her lips parted, haunted by terrors of what might happen if she did this and what might happen if she didn't. She caught the handle on the sliding door. She hauled on it. It wouldn't budge.

'Tamasin!' Alarm in her voice.

Tamasin reached and caught Rana's forearm, as high up as she could. They strained.

When the door went, it went suddenly. Then it stuck again. Tamasin and Rana looked at each other.

A sound from down the line. The train was going to start moving.

'Quickly!' Tamasin muttered, and bent her elbow to give Rana a leg-up. Without thought Rana accepted it. Another moment, and she was on her knees in the van, twisting back quickly.

Tamasin got an elbow over the sill. The train jerked and began moving.

'*Tamasin!*' Then Rana had her by the shoulders and Tamasin's feet were swinging, the train slowly moving off, and she wriggled further and Rana grabbed her trouser waistband through the coarse cloth of the chador, pulling urgently.

She was up.

They grinned at each other, both breathing hard. Neither said thanks; it wasn't necessary.

* * *

Rana huddled herself into a rear corner of the van, empty, they discovered, of any goods. Tamasin went tentatively to the door and tried to close it. It was jammed. She left it alone: maybe it was no bad thing that there was enough gap there for them to jump through when the need arose. She went over and slumped beside Rana.

'What's that smell?' Rana said in a complaining voice.

Tamasin sniffed. There was dust on the floor and some fibres that might have come from sacking. There was a smell about the van all right, something pungent and lingering that Tamasin couldn't identify.

'God,' Rana said, 'what's this thing had in it?'

'Meal, I'd guess.'

'*Meal?* Meal doesn't smell like this. God, it's chemicals! God, it might be something poisonous!'

Tamasin was tired, she was edgy, she was in no mood for mothering. 'Well, if you know a better van . . .'

Rana fizzed at her and drew her chador nervously about her shoulders.

* * *

It was gone midday now. Aside from all the other things, Tamasin felt thirsty; and they'd used up their yoghurt hours ago. The train rolled slowly, stopping at times. Slow as it was, though, Tamasin could see that, apart from the halts, the speed was too great for them to be able to jump off without risking a limb.

Rana dozed.

After an hour and a half, the train clanked dolefully over a set of points and for a moment Tamasin was worried. Rana was still dozing and Tamasin couldn't

179

decide whether to wake her. She peered through the gap where the van door had jammed open.

The door faced north, she knew that; and the sun was out of sight the other side of the train. The track that ran off was in sight, swinging away at a fifty-degree angle. Either they were heading east and the other line ran off north-east, Tamasin thought, or that line ran east and they were heading south-east. She considered.

From the air, she'd seen only one line, and that had run pretty much east. To the south there was only desert. They would stay on, she decided; it was worth the gamble that they were going the right way.

Every now and then they went through a town. They didn't stop, as a rule. Tamasin couldn't read the names of the towns. Sometimes Rana woke up and read them off for her; most of the time she napped; fretting, when she woke, about whether she was going to see Darvish again.

Tamasin was struggling not to let Rana get on her nerves.

It was four, the afternoon cloudless, burning, when the train stopped again. Tamasin had lost count now of how many times it had halted. Rana woke and stirred. Tamasin poked a cautious eye round the van door frame.

The track formed a gentle lefthand curve. Enough to show her the driver climbing down from his cab and beginning a meticulous inspection of his train.

CHAPTER 25

Overhead northern Iraq, Thursday, 25 June, 0850 Turkey
At 42,000 feet the four Turkish F16s were above the simmering storm clouds and the morning was a vast, arching dazzle of flawless blue.

'Shark Tooth, on station, angels four two.' Colonel Mahmut Barka released the transmit button. He had the visor down on his bone dome.

'Medicine Man, copy.' *Medicine Man* was a NATO Boeing E3 Sentry AWACS – airborne warning and control system – co-altitude with the F16s and some miles to the north.

Mahmut switched to intercom and twisted against the ejector seat harness. 'Better view from this than you get in a Fulcrum.' *Fulcrum* was the NATO codename for the MiG 29.

'Ah, you sit up a little higher.' But Walter Becker, in the back seat of the F16B trainer, didn't like admitting it.

The other three aircraft making up Shark Tooth were F16Cs, single-seaters. The mission was a fighter CAP – combat air patrol – over the Kurdish region of northern Iraq. To Mahmut Barka it seemed incongruous for NATO to be keeping the Iraqi dictator from making war on his Kurds while a vicious little guerrilla war went on in Turkey between the government and its own Kurds.

Also he had only the flimsiest of excuses for carrying a man who was now a civilian in his back seat.

Mahmut bent over the tactical chart strapped to his knee. Overflying Iraq was part of the detail, but he didn't want to infringe Iranian airspace.

'Shark Tooth aircraft, right turn on to one zero five mag.'

Walter eased the little sidestick controller delicately to the right, flying the dual-control F16 from behind. The four wingtips dipped. The flight pulled clear of the border.

'Why you got to do all this nav, anyway?' Walter said. 'You're on radar.'

'NATO standard.'

The cloud flowed in heaps and bundles to every horizon. The sun made bluey silver glints and Mahmut hoped they wouldn't have to go down through it.

'Too much work for a busy pilot,' Walter said. 'Fighter pilot needs to concentrate on the main issues – finding the target and zonking it.'

Mahmut grinned behind his oxygen mask. All day yesterday Walter had been simultaneously badgering him for a fighter flight and trying to wind him up. 'You've had too much old-style Russian training.'

Warsaw Pact air forces in the '70s and '80s had based their tactics around tight control of air defence fighters from an all-powerful ground control. NATO philosophy placed the initiative with the pilots.

Iraqi pilots were Russian-trained, basically, Mahmut reflected as he once more checked the screen on his radar. The Iranians were a mixture. Only the older generation, the serious Muslims who'd escaped the bloody purges of the early '80s, still had their old US training. The senior men flying the F4s, F14s – such as remained – they were some of them.

Mahmut was Muslim, too, but he lived within the bounds of common sense. It was fanatics who caused wars, never mind which religion they proclaimed; people who were convinced that they alone were *right*.

'Yeah,' Walter agreed, 'but it worked!'

'Our airborne radar is better.'

That E3 could see several hundred kilometres into Iran and Iraq. Even Mahmut wasn't entirely sure how many targets it could track simultaneously.

'OK,' Walter needled, 'why doesn't it find us some contacts?'

'In that rubbish?' Down in Iraq there were thunderstorms. Never mind the added difficulty for the E3's radars, it wouldn't be worth Iraq's while putting aircraft up in foul weather.

Then as if to make nonsense of Mahmut's words, the radio fizzed back on.

'Medicine Man, Shark Tooth.'

Mahmut thumbed the transmit. 'Shark Tooth copies.'

'Say condition, Shark Tooth.'

'Shark Tooth is state tiger.' It was NATO codespeak to say the flight had enough fuel and ammunition left to complete its mission.

'Stand by, Shark Tooth.'

'Copy,' Mahmut said. He started getting a pleasant buzz of adrenaline.

For a moment, nothing. Only the rumpled cloudscape and the hard, brilliant blue; through the bone domes, the soft, ceaseless breathy sound of the single Pratt & Whitney F100 turbofan; the imperceptible tremble of power through the fighter's frame.

'Medicine Man, Shark Tooth. Bogeys, two, nine o'clock, range six five, closing. Looks like you upset someone in Iran.'

'Copy,' Mahmut said. 'Shark Tooth aircraft, left turn on to three six mag, weapons release checklist, go!'

Nine o'clock was directly left of the flight of fighters, out to the north, towards Iran. Shark Tooth would be staying inside Iraqi airspace unless something developed. If those Iranians locked radars on the F16s, it was tantamount to saying *come outside, Jimmy*.

'How often does this happen?' Walter asked cheerfully as he put the wingtip down almost vertically.

Mahmut was rubbernecking for his F16Cs. He caught one below in the ten o'clock position but the other two were hidden by his wing. It looked like a reasonably tidy formation turn.

'Not often,' he told Walter, then switched channels again as the ex-Fulcrum pilot rolled out smoothly on the new heading. 'Medicine Man, Shark Tooth.'

'Go ahead, Shark Tooth,' the fighter director aboard the big Boeing said.

'Shark Tooth. Any type information?'

A pause. Up here, only the compass and the sun gave them any clues as to which way they were flying; the cloudscape was the same, whichever direction you looked. Mahmut twisted round under the big, clear cockpit canopy until he'd picked out all three other fighters in the formation.

A fizz of static. The AWACS came back. 'Medicine Man, Shark Tooth. Flight profile suggests Foxtrot one four.'

'I know who they are,' Mahmut told Walter, back on intercom. 'They're those Tomcats out of Tabriz Three. Those boys are pretty good.'

Walter heard in Mahmut's tone that what he would like best would be for the F14s to have a go at them. Then they'd see who came out on top.

Again Mahmut checked the tactical chart. 'One minute twenty to that border.' He didn't like the idea of turning when he reached it, didn't like the thought of presenting a hot jetpipe to the risk of an infra-red shot.

Walter examined his radar scope. 'They're closing, Mahmut, they're Mach one plus . . .'

One minute to the border. Fifty seconds. Now Mahmut had the bogey aircraft on his own scope. Missiles *armed*. External tanks *negative*, none carried.

'Shark Tooth aircraft, stand by . . .'

Forty to the border and the bogeys still closing. If they didn't either turn or else switch off those radars, Mahmut was going head-to-head after them, border or no border. Thirty seconds. *He who blinked first* . . . Twenty. Fifteen.

'Medicine Man for Shark Tooth, bogeys . . .'

And he had it on his own radar. 'Shark Tooth aircraft,

bogeys breaking off. Hard turn right – one two zero mag, *go!*' Mahmut had hardly stopped his transmission when Walter put the starboard tip vertically down. 'Shark Tooth, resuming CAP.'

'Well, that was a disappointment,' Walter said.

'I'd have had a bit of explaining to do if I'd launched weapons with a civilian in the back.' Privately, though, Mahmut was disappointed, too. He started switching his missiles back to *safe*.

CHAPTER 26

North central Iran, Friday, 19 June, 1602 local
Sharply Tamasin Masterson turned her head. 'The driver's out. He's searching the train.'

Rana Tezcan blinked sleepily. 'He can't be looking for us. If he'd known we were here, he'd have stopped in a town and got help.'

'I don't know what he's searching for, but he'll find us if he comes down here!'

Rana didn't want to move. She was warm and sleepy from her doze. 'Look, we're on the train now, we're getting a ride . . . we're not at Shahrud yet . . .'

'We can't risk it! We've *got* to go!' Still Tamasin didn't seem to be getting through. 'Well, dammit, then *I'll* go!' She peeped around the door frame again.

'Tamasin, no!' Fright in her voice, Rana scrambled to her feet.

'Wait!' Tamasin hissed. Rana froze.

This train had thirty-seven wagons, and they were in the thirty-sixth along. The driver was still some way off yet. He seemed to be on his own.

Then as Tamasin watched, he vanished between two cement carriers, possibly checking couplings.

'Now!'

Vaulting down in a chador wasn't as easy as it might have been without one. Tamasin landed in a crouch, got her balance, then twisted back to look up at Rana. Rana dithered on the sill. Tamasin reached up with both arms. The driver still hadn't reappeared.

Rana grasped Tamasin's left arm in her right and levered herself down.

'Quickly!' Tamasin muttered. She set the pace, walking

briskly at right angles away from the train.

They covered 100 yards, stumbling in the coarse grass – there wasn't a path. When Tamasin looked back, the driver had almost reached the covered van they'd used. He turned. He saw them all right, but he didn't wave, didn't show any interest.

Anyway, Tamasin reflected, all he'd have seen was the backs of a couple of chadors. Maybe these things had their uses after all.

* * *

They'd covered fully 300 yards more when the train started up. It creaked and groaned its way slowly towards the east. Tamasin and Rana paused for breath while they watched it go.

'Where are we?' Rana said.

'Don't know,' Tamasin muttered. With a walking map or an aviation chart she was a good navigator, good enough to know pretty soon when she'd got off course. But there is a difference between being temporarily misplaced like that, and not having a clue where in Christendom or out of it you might be. Tamasin said: 'What was that last town we went through?'

'Duzahir.' Rana gazed at Tamasin with the dependency of a child.

Tamasin looked at her watch: 1616. 'Right, then, we went through there at five past three, say one hour and ten minutes ago. That train can't have been averaging more than about forty k's an hour. So we're forty-five k's or so east of Duzahir.' She considered. 'That's eleven or twelve hours' walking and it's the wrong direction, anyway. We'd be better off simply striking due north.'

'Why?'

'We know there's a road running east-west, and we know it's before we reach the foot of those mountains.' Tamasin gestured towards the Elburz. 'If we can follow even an approximate line due north, logically we can't

187

help but strike the road, eventually.'

'And then what?'

'Then we'll see.' Tamasin was fighting her irritation. 'Come on, let's move.'

*   *   *

After roughly an hour they rested. It was 1715. They got going again at 1730 and this time walked till 1820 before stopping again to rest. There were lizards on the low rocks, and Tamasin traced a harsh, cat-like screaming to a pair of golden orioles. She'd never seen orioles that close before but she was too tired to summon up much interest. At 1830 Tamasin made as if to leave, but Rana was too weary. They rested another ten minutes and then trudged off across the bleak, brown plain while the cirrus veining the approaching evening sank lower in the upper atmosphere, gathering into the thin sheet of cloud that is often the forerunner of a storm.

*   *   *

They rested again. It was 1930, the shadows lengthening visibly.

'There's just *nothing* here!' Rana wailed, her parched lips dry and cracked. 'Not a house, not a village . . .'

Tamasin, too, had felt they should have seen something before now. 'We've got to keep going. It's our only chance. If we keep heading north, we *must* strike that road, given time.'

'And how do you know we're not going round in circles?'

Tamasin pointed to the red and orange of the sunset. 'We keep that on our left side, we're going north all right.'

'But what about after dark?'

'We'll be at the road before then.' Tamasin made herself sound more certain than she felt. Getting caught out here

after dark was a prospect that worried her. They couldn't
risk moving over rough terrain like this; yet to stay put,
without a fire, would be potentially dangerous. Tamasin
had no idea what sort of wild beasts there might be about
here. Or snakes.

Rana's worries echoed her own, but if she told Rana
how she really felt, she'd have a panic on her hands.

*   *   *

For another three quarters of an hour they struggled across
the landscape.

It was 2015 when Tamasin, leading, spotted the
vestiges of a track, some farm animal prints, crushed
grass, wandering northwards. Following the track made
it easier going; but the day was dying quickly.

They'd been following the track for half an hour when
they saw the lights of a town.

*   *   *

Rana was almost asleep on her feet as they trudged down
the rutted dirt road of the first outskirts. Tamasin spotted the water standpipe, at a junction of two unpaved
roads, low houses all around, shallow-roofed amid the
shadowy cypress and bougainvillea. It was a life-saver.

Rana looked up at last wearing a bleak smile. She wiped
her face where the lukewarm water had run over it.

'What is this place?'

'I was hoping you might tell me that.' Tamasin managed
a grin that wasn't forced.

Rana shrugged. They set off walking again. They
reached the main road where it ran through the middle
of the town.

'It's Qushe,' Rana said. She'd read it off the sign-
board of a business on the main road, its frontage
hidden at this hour under a big metal roller shut-
ter.

Another Iranian place name Tamasin had never heard of. 'How far is it from Roudabad?'

'A long way.'

Tamasin had a think. Rana said, 'What are we going to do?'

Tamasin went on thinking. Rana muttered, 'I'm hungry.'

So was Tamasin. 'Do you think we can go into a restaurant or a coffee shop here? Two strange women with no escort?'

'Maybe not,' Rana sniffed dismally.

Tamasin pointed. A few yards from them stood a rough-surfaced vehicle park, deep-shadowed, a couple of big trucks there, a bus, some cars, and some vans.

'Let's see if we can find anything over there.' The vans and the lorries might have been carrying produce. The cars might contain someone's uneaten lunch.

They made for the vehicle park, their chadors gathered about them. The first van Tamasin came to was a newish Fiat Ducato, and, to her pleasant surprise, its door slid back easily when she tried it.

Then, in sheer disbelief, she saw the key still in the ignition lock.

CHAPTER 27

Diyarbakir, Thursday, 25 June, 1600 local
Out beyond the hangars, two of the old Turkish air force RF4E Phantoms were taking off in a lot of noise and smoke. The briefing room Colonel Mahmut Barka had promised Felix Wyer was empty as she and Rob Pilgrim walked in – the first two in the meeting.

Inside a few minutes Walter Becker strode in, wearing his flying suit with the MiG 29 logo. Ron Harper and Chris Norton followed him.

They sat down.

'First and foremost,' Felix said in her chief-executive voice, 'are we all entirely happy with what's being proposed?'

Rob looked blank. Walter's grin widened. Harper sat with his shoulders forward and an enigmatic smile on his face. Norton twitched a cigarette out of his pack.

'No, frankly, I'm not happy.'

Felix tilted her head and watched him with concerned understanding. 'I for one won't think less of you if you'd rather scratch.'

Walter would, though.

'All right, dammit.' Norton stuck the cigarette in his mouth and lit it in a nervous gesture. 'Don't worry, I'm not going to let colleagues and crewmates down. I'm content that we can probably get away with this. But I'm screwed if I'm going on record as saying I'm happy.'

'Right,' Felix said. 'Then the mission is to infiltrate two aircrew – namely Rob and myself – into Zedasht, where, according to the latest information, *Rapide* is sitting ready to be flown out to an operational Iranian air force base from which in all likelihood it will never return to us.'

191

Ersin had phoned her an hour earlier with that latest report. Felix didn't doubt he'd had that from the mysterious Kemal.

She leaned forward a little. 'That jet is my company's property and I mean to have it back.'

Rob was watching her. He knew the other element to that story. *Rapide*'s history.

'You get it,' Walter said confidently. 'Or at least you get every chance to get it. We get you in there OK.'

'Rob's been boning up on that runway at Zedasht.' Felix turned to him.

What Rob knew he'd gathered from Mahmut Barka's air force intelligence colleagues. 'It's 04/31,' he said. 'I understand it's 1,770 metres. It lies 1,590 metres above mean sea level. That's a length of 5,800 feet at 5,200 feet AMSL. Latest information tells us the aircraft now has full tanks, so we're talking about a max weight take-off at 23,300 pounds all up. Say we had a temperature of, oh . . . 22, 23 Celsius . . . we'd want the best part of 9,000 feet of runway – theoretically.'

An aircraft takes off whether it wants to or not when the air density under its wing exceeds that above. But air gets thinner, the higher up you go, and the hotter it gets, too.

Felix glanced at him. She didn't know whether to be worried yet. 'What are you threatening to do to my jet?'

'Those engines are watt-limited,' Rob told her. 'Too much throttle and you'll cook them. We could do it at maybe 21,500 pounds all up, using less than full throttle. We'd manage that.'

'On under 6,000 feet of runway?' Felix frowned.

'Don't forget,' Rob said, 'that 8,700 feet is the length you'd need to allow for in case you lost an engine on take-off. I've had Dominies up off a 4,000-foot runway at that sort of temperature and weight.'

Felix deliberated, her lower lip thrusting. She looked at Walter. 'What about *Falcon Fang*?'

'Can do!' Walter said confidently.

Norton tapped his cigarette but the ash wasn't ready to fall. 'What's the weather?'

'That's another reason to get in tonight,' Felix said. 'We're expecting clear weather overnight tonight but thunder moving in within the next twenty-four hours.'

'How are you going to get a take-off clearance?'

'Take off without, from Zedasht.'

'Yeah, but from here?'

'Night electronics test flight,' Walter said. 'Then when we vanish off radar, we come back and say it worked well, didn't it!'

Felix couldn't help liking Walter.

'What about timing?' Norton asked, and drew again on his cigarette.

Felix looked at Walter. 'Rob and I have been over that, and the ideal time to arrive at Zedasht would be between 0400 and 0415 local – which would give us light enough to get down, since there's no runway lighting – so that we can then take off in *Rapide* between 0415, and, say, 0445, before the day gets too warm.'

Walter went *humpff*. 'OK, Felix, I look at this already, and on the direct route the distance is 740 nautical miles, so if we average 380 knots groundspeed, that's one hour fifty-five minutes. But the way I see it, the direct route could be not the best route. Route I have in mind takes 850 nautical miles – that's two hours twelve minutes. Say two and a quarter. So we land Zedasht at 0415 local, that's 0245 Turkish time, so we want to take off midnight plus thirty. That OK with you?'

Felix looked round the little circle of flyers. She grinned. 'Let's do it.'

*　　*　　*

Rob picked up the receiver and slowly punched the keys for the international line. In Turkey it was 1640, in England 1440. The ward sister fetched Dr Bibi Tabrizi.

'Hello, Rob?' He recognized the tension in her voice.

'Bibi, it's a definite "go" tonight. Can you get through to you-know-who?'

'Rob, fantastic! You bet I'll let her know! And, Rob, there's one more thing . . .'

'What's that?'

'I spoke to you-know-who two nights ago. You know who else is there?'

Rob drew a breath. 'You don't mean . . .'

'The missing Dragon Jet captain.'

'Good lord! How did *she* get there?'

'I don't know the full story. It seems that she had a chance to get to Roudabad and she took it because that's close to where she left the plane.'

Rob thought for a second. 'Bibi, that's a fantastic bit of news. I need to let the Dragon Lady know about this.'

CHAPTER 28

Elburz mountains, Friday, 19 June, 2315 local
From the dim-lit streets of Shahrud the road climbed steeply, potholed and patched, jarring the steering wheel against Tamasin Masterson's hands. She'd had to wake Rana Tezcan to find her the road out to Roudabad but now Rana was nodding off again in the darkness. In her exhaustion Tamasin envied her.

Then around a shoulder of hill there were lights ahead.

'Where now, Rana?' They were in among the first low houses of Roudabad, dark bulks against the darker mass of the mountainside, the road still climbing, sharply cambered with the cobbles gleaming in the headlights.

'Keep straight.' At the edge of her right eye Tamasin saw Rana raise a hand to smooth her hair. 'It's right at the end.'

A T-junction, a left turn, the alleys narrowing suddenly in dense darkness, lights glimpsed dim yellow at little windows. In her headlights Tamasin saw a great fort of a house, steep walls and a stout courtyard door, flat-roofed defensive wall to the right, under it a hardstanding with half a dozen vehicles pulled up amid the weeds on the packed earth.

'Blow your horn,' Rana said. 'Let's get into the courtyard.'

The noise echoed off the maze of walls around and behind them, down through the little town. Tamasin waited. She was just about to sound the horn again when the great wooden door swung slowly back.

Outside lights flooded the cramped courtyard and there were six or seven people outside, one of them, Tamasin saw, a bearded man in a mullah's robes and a black turban.

Rana cried: '*Darvish!*' Then Tamasin saw him, too.

Her stomach tightened, her lips compressed in sheer reflex.

A stocky man beckoned her forward. He had a scar on his face, puckering one eye. Tamasin revved to get the van moving up the slope and then rolled it carefully uphill into the courtyard. Beside her she was conscious of Rana, lifting her hood back into place.

Tamasin cut the lights, cut the engine. Rana pitched out into the courtyard, crying out in shrill Farsi as the people swarmed round her. Nervous suddenly, Tamasin raised her chador hood, slid back the door, and climbed stiffly out into the throng.

For a moment it was all clamouring voices that she couldn't understand, and hands grasping her arms; friendly, but as much as she could cope with in her exhausted state.

'Sorry, I don't understand.'

She caught the eye of a young woman, slim and graceful in a chador, taller than her; more like Rana's height. There was a buzz going around and she heard something that sounded like *ingiliz.*

Then Darvish was there.

Fury flooded his face in the recognition. Rana was at his side, glowing with pride, and he turned and tore into her in Turkish. Tamasin couldn't follow it but she knew at once she was in trouble.

'In God's name, what did you bring *her* here for? Don't you know who this is?'

Rana's face changed. 'Of course I . . .'

'You must be mad! To bring this woman, this unbeliever, this *taghouti* into this place, at this time! Don't you understand the risk you've run us into?'

'Darvish, listen . . .'

'There are vitally important plans being worked on here and they need the utmost security. You call this security, to bring *this* unbeliever, of all unbelievers, into our most secret centre?' He paused.

'Without this woman I . . .'

'Listen to me, woman! *I* am the leader here and *I* say we dare not risk any danger to our holy plans! There is more than merely a country's future at stake here – what's at stake is nothing less than the survival of the Way of Faith and its purity!' He turned to Tamasin, venom in his face in the shadows and the harsh, high lighting. 'Take this woman away. She's a danger to security and she should be shot.'

* * *

Tamasin hadn't followed a word of it but she knew it wasn't good. What she wasn't prepared for was the sudden way Rana changed.

'All right, Darvish, I say this in English so we don't hide it from Tamasin, we don't hide it from the rest of the people. There's enough people speak English here!' Her eyes were sunken pools of darkness and the tension was tangible as her words rang off the tall stone walls. 'You say she's a security risk. You want her shot.' Tamasin gasped and Rana flung her a look. '*I* say she saved my life!' Rana was jabbing an index in towards herself. 'I say what I saw, what I know, and I can tell you, she blew up a car at Evin so that we could escape, and then she got me all the way here . . . from that place . . . using nothing, nothing . . .'

In her weariness and the release of tension Rana was growing inarticulate, but her meaning was clear. In a sudden movement, she stepped between Darvish and Tamasin, her left hand reaching back to grasp Tamasin's arm and shield her with her body.

'You want to shoot Tamasin? Shoot her now!'

* * *

This was the last thing Tamasin had expected, after the way Rana had fought with her, right from that first moment in the Isuzu.

The courtyard became silent.

In the warm night Tamasin could feel sweat on her rib cage. Insects were swarming in the lights shining down on the courtyard and something spicy hung in the air from the cooking. The Fiat's engine clanked as it cooled.

The bearded mullah with the black turban stepped forward, smiling, calm. Tamasin had an instinctive impression of a reasonable man – but one who might be hiding something.

He spoke in Farsi. Tamasin couldn't follow the words but she sensed the calming influence in them.

'Darvish, my brother, beware of allowing your zeal for God's ways to blind you to the elegance of His purposes. God has surely delivered this woman into our hands in order that His purposes shall be carried out. Behold, this woman speaks no word of our language and is a helpless guest in our midst. Truly, there is no danger to our cause as long as she remains our guest.'

Hojatoleslam Ardeshir Rezania turned, smiling at Tamasin. Rana relaxed a little and released Tamasin's arm. She moved slightly aside.

'My daughter,' Ardeshir said in clumsy English. 'You are our guest. Welcome. You not be afraid.'

'Well . . .' There was a lot here that Tamasin didn't understand, but at least for the moment she felt safe from Darvish's murderous anger. 'Thank you.' Then she was tongue-tied.

'Azra,' Ardeshir said.

The slim young woman stepped forward. She was intrigued, but the smile on her face was one of friendship.

Ardeshir put a chaste hand on Azra's shoulder and addressed Tamasin. 'My daughter . . . Azra, daughter of my sister. She speak best English. Your friend now.'

Azra stretched out a slim hand from under the chador.

Tamasin accepted it, the formality as odd as everything else about this whole situation.

'Hi,' Azra said.

'Hi. Er . . . my name's Tamasin.'

Ardeshir switched back to Farsi, speaking relaxedly to Azra. 'While this woman is with us as our guest, you can look after her. Let her take Miriam's bed in your room. She must stay a while, until . . . until the things that are being planned are put into practice. I know you support the Way of Faith and the *Shohada*. Look after her well.'

'I certainly shall.'

Azra's eyes met Tamasin's. Tamasin was too weary to think.

Azra wasn't, and the mystery uppermost in her mind was: *why me?*

CHAPTER 29

Diyarbakir, Friday, 26 June, 0010

Stars arched in the midnight sky and *Falcon Fang*'s APU moaned across the emptiness of the big NATO base. Felix Wyer turned in time to see the beam of the collision beacon sweep over Rob Pilgrim and turn his pale face red. The flight line at Diyarbakir was a lonely place to be.

She didn't like to raise her voice. 'Will Bibi have been through to Azra by now?'

'I'll trust her that far.'

'And Azra had some plan for getting out? With Tamasin?'

He nodded.

Felix stepped onto the little airstair door and ducked inside the slender tube of the cabin. This aircraft always had the feel of a fighter about it. So did the 125s when you flew them, but back in the cabin they felt like a flying boardroom.

The cabin was dark inside. The glow from the instrument panel was the only thing that lit up Walter Becker's and Chris Norton's faces, speaking softly across the throttle quadrant. Ron Harper poked his grin around from behind the ECM panel, aft.

'Here come the Paras. Welcome aboard – is that your grenades and Uzis in that satchel?'

Felix grinned back, stooping her way aft to the seat next to Harper's. 'No, silly,' she said, 'this is our picnic.' She sat down and strapped in as Rob closed and latched the cabin door.

There actually were some emergency rations in there, and a couple of bottles of water, just in case. What Felix was expecting to use were the four oxygen masks, each one with plug-in intercom. Rob and herself, plus two passengers.

She knew the jet had been holed by that bullet – she'd understood that from the copy the embassy in Tehran had sent through of its interview with Tamasin in Evin – she knew the bullet had holed the instrument panel. With the pressure hull penetrated, the aircraft couldn't generate artificial cabin altitude and circulate air; so you got your oxygen from the face masks. The standard emergency oxygen masks that *Rapide* carried in the cabin ceiling didn't have intercom; Felix had fetched these along specially. Felix also knew, because Kemal's satellite pictures had shown it, that at least one of the oxygen bottles stored in the nose cone had been damaged, because they had film of the Iranian air force technicians replacing one bottle.

Now they could fly *Rapide* out at whatever height they liked.

Rob moved stooping past her and strapped in opposite, across the gangway. He was dressed the same way as Felix: black Nike tracksuit with hood; running shoes; his own day-pack-sized rucksack.

Neither carried weapons.

In a deliberate action, Felix reset her watch. Iranian time: 0145.

Walter twisted and peered down the dark cabin. The collision beacon swept its red trail over the camber of the wing. Walter said gruffly: 'Have we got the self-loading cargo on board yet?'

'We're here and we're strapped in,' Felix called. 'Put a match to that gas, for God's sake.'

Walter turned round and muttered into the mike. The same old camel crap about electronics testing.

Then he was cranking up the first main engine.

* * *

Aft in the cabin and peering over Harper's shoulder, Felix could feel every joint in the concrete as Walter rolled *Fang* briskly over it. They weren't the only aircraft flying, she noticed; but the beacon she could see turning, way across the black vastness of the field, was on what looked like a KC10 tanker.

Tension had her by the gut and it was fear she was feeling, not the thrill of an afternoon out with some guaranteed safe ending. She glanced over at Rob and he grinned through the darkness, leaning back relaxedly in his seat. Felix wondered whether he'd been that laid-back that night in the Vulcan, 50,000 feet and weapons set to take out Chicago.

Walter pulled the nose tightly around and on to the runway. Felix peered forward but she couldn't properly see the amber lights of the centreline. A roller take-off, Walter wasn't stopping to rev against the brakes.

The jets wound up to a roar.

*　　*　　*

The cabin tilted gently towards the starboard wingtip. Felix looked out and could see the navigation light, steady green. Then she caught the gleam of starlight on a big body of water.

'Walter.' She was using intercom. 'Do I take it that's Lake Van?'

'Right,' Walter said. 'Now for the interesting bit.'

They were off airways, they were navigating, Felix knew from the briefing, by Global Positioning System satellites and by the accelerometers of the inertial nav, cross-checking with bearings off the range stations and other radio beacons on the way.

Walter's idea of a good route was to avoid all those radars in Iran and instead cut across the newly independent states of Armenia and Azerbaijan to the north. Then low down over the Caspian to sneak in under Iranian radar and pop up over the Elburz as low as possible in the starlight. There was a civil war going on in Azerbaijan and if they were lucky, any radars still working there wouldn't notice them.

If they weren't lucky, well, they still had tricks up their sleeve.

In the cabin, Felix heard the engine note drop as Walter throttled back and trimmed for a cautious descent.

* * *

It was Yerevan in Armenia that spotted them. Late, though; already the signals showed that they were past the beacon.

'Unidentified aircraft crossing Armenian airspace, track one one zero, groundspeed seven hundred kilometres . . .'

'Ron,' Walter said in the intercom.

'Stand by,' Harper murmured.

Over his shoulder Felix could see vertical lines of light on the display. She was intrigued but she was tense. Part of her couldn't believe it, but here she was, a respectable widowed lady of fifty-one, company chief executive, good standing at the bank, doing an illegal intrusion at dead of night into an ex-Soviet state.

But there were at least two good reasons why she was doing this, and she hoped within a few hours she'd be flying out with two of them.

'See that?' Harper half-turned. 'Right on his wavelength – spot noise. That should shut them up for a bit.'

'That's good,' Walter said. 'This time we get *right* down.'

* * *

Night descent over mountain country tensed Felix up again, even though she knew this had been in the briefing. She glanced at Rob, still relaxed where he sat.

'What were those heights, Rob?' She'd taken off the intercom headset, she was leaning across the narrow gangway.

'Around 12,000 feet here where we cut across Armenia. The really big peaks, 12,000-plus, are south of us. We're coming over Azerbaijan now, over the Kura river valley, and it drops right down to below sea level when you get to the Caspian coast.'

Felix peered out. Below them the land lay like an ocean of blackness and she hoped Walter's navigation was accurate. Still descending.

'Ah . . . radar,' Harper said. 'Painting us now. Just check on that PRF, it's . . . an area radar. Didn't think anyone'd have fighters up.'

'Where from?' Walter said gruffly.

They were losing height quickly now. Felix caught a gleam of starlight on water, a river, not much meander in it, heading roughly the way they were going.

'Kirovabad if it's anywhere,' Harper said. 'Fading out. We've got terrain masking, from the looks of it. What height are we now?'

Felix realized she was biting her lip.

'Two thousand four,' Walter said. 'Going through two thousand three . . . What about that one at Baku? That's the one that's going to be manned all round the clock.'

The city of Baku faces south from a promontory jutting eastwards into the Caspian. Close to the west of the city, the spine of the Caucasus starts the jagged rise that takes it to the Black Sea.

'Can you get their VOR?' Harper said. 'If you can't, they won't be seeing us on radar either.'

'Copy,' Walter said. 'Ah . . . negative on that VOR.'

Below them now Felix was glimpsing an occasional light, an occasional gleam of reflection in glossy dark water, tiny pools and reservoirs. She knew they were within hundreds of feet of the ground, no longer thousands. But just knowing that the Caspian was below mean sea level didn't make her any happier.

'This is good,' Walter laughed. 'I never seen zero metres before on my altimeter and be still flying.'

And then it was there, under them; the huge body of water spreading forever. Walter rolled briskly into a wide turn south.

'Next stop, Iran.'

*   *   *

The view down here reminded Felix of the height they'd been that day at Antalya. The stars were fading now but she could still sense, if not see, that glossy water streaking past below.

Down here barely above the crests, Walter would be hand-flying the jet, doing it all visually. Not for the first time, it crossed Felix's mind what any of them might look like if they clipped a wave at 380 knots.

'How do we look for position?' she said into the intercom.

'Ach,' Walter said, 'lost again!'

Norton said: 'We're getting weakish signals from two VORs on the Iranian north coast. We're fine for position, Felix.' He sounded much steadier than she'd feared he would be. 'We're still estimating touchdown at 0415 Iran time.'

Under an hour to go. Felix took a deep breath to calm herself and looked at Rob. He'd said hardly a word all the way. Now he smiled slowly through the darkness, still quiet, still unassuming, letting another captain get on with the work.

Walter put the throttles up. Coast ahead.

*   *   *

If they were going to show on Iranian radar, Felix realized, it would be now, up here over the Elburz. She checked her watch. 0354 local. First light must be very soon. She ducked her head and peered across Rob and out of the window his side, but it still looked as black as ever. Blacker, now there were no stars.

'Radar!' Harper said sharply. 'It's a military job this time. Let's see what . . .' He reached to the knobs down the lefthand side of the spectrum analyser display.

There'd been tension in Harper's voice but now Felix was rigid. They were right up over the mountains now, with nowhere to hide.

'False targets,' Harper mused, 'this should bamboozle him.'

The trick with the search pulse was to replicate the return. If you wanted, you could send back enough false targets to swamp the threat radar completely. This time Harper contented himself with sending a dozen or so.

'Now he'll think either the Russians are invading or he's got a bug in his radar.'

Clear. Felix breathed again.

Rob murmured: 'Looks like first light out my side.'

Again Felix peered across. The sky was shading to charcoal. 0402. Felix craned to see down to the cockpit.

She heard the engine note sink again.

Walter said: 'Right, that was the Elburz – now let's look out for this airfield.'

CHAPTER 30

Roudabad, Saturday, 20 June, 0045 local

There'd been hot tea and sticky pastries, there'd been small talk, there'd been prayers. The living room floor was thick with carpets. On the television set there was a picture of Ardeshir in his robes and turban and another of Moussa in his flying suit beside his F14. In her exhaustion Tamasin Masterson was hardly taking any of it in.

The young Iranian woman with the brown eyes, the one they'd evidently appointed as her chaperone, led her to the bedroom. Azra. Something in the back of Tamasin's mind told her that name ought to ring some sort of bell, but she was too tired to connect it.

The single women's wing even had a shower, a bit of a basic one but spotless. Tired as she was, Tamasin used it. She hadn't felt clean like this since she left the hotel where she'd stayed in Ankara with Keith in the next room. The thought brought Keith's face into her mind yet again, drawn, ashen, dying. Tamasin let her tears mingle with the shower flow.

Azra had found a nightdress for her to borrow. 'That one's yours.' She pointed to the bed that her cousin Miriam had hastily vacated.

Tamasin flopped onto it. Blindly she pulled the thin covering up to her shoulder, her head spinning in utter fatigue.

Then when she opened her eyes, Azra was sitting on the edge of the parallel bed, watching her with concern.

Tamasin mistook the look. 'Don't worry, I won't be running away anywhere, I'm too bloody tired.'

'I'm glad Ardeshir got me to look after you.' Azra's voice

was soft, her English confident, the delivery so Oxford it was almost aristocratic.

Tamasin knew who Ardeshir was: the mullah Rana had been dying to see; the spiritual leader behind Darvish and his campaign of terror. Tamasin grunted.

'Rana said you're a jet pilot.'

Grunt. She wanted to sleep.

'Do you know a man called Rob Pilgrim?'

Grunt. She must be dreaming already. But she wasn't. Tamasin jerked up her head.

*   *   *

'I thought that must be who you were,' Azra Tabrizi said softly. 'I'm . . . I'm sort of in touch with Rob still.'

Now Tamasin knew why she should have recognized Azra's name. Rana was here to be with Darvish and Darvish was here to gather his forces with old uncle Ardeshir's blessing. Tamasin was here because there was a sound chance *Rapide* was still down there on that desert airstrip, and if so it was the prospect of escape. Azra was here because she was family.

'How d'you mean?'

The light in the room, as it drew close around the two of them, came from a softly hissing butane lamp. The beautiful hand-woven rug on the floor gave the room a feeling of history and delicate sophistication.

'They won't let me write to him, so I write sort of in code to my sister Bibi,' Azra explained. 'Then sometimes Bibi phones me and now and then I'm able to get a message out, or she gets a message from Rob to me.' She watched Tamasin. 'Ardeshir wants to keep you here. They've got some plan, I think it involves an armed rising against the regime. They're afraid that if you leave here before it starts, you'll give the game away.'

Tamasin blinked sleepily. It seemed self-evident that she would do exactly that.

'Well . . .' Azra leaned closer. 'Don't you want to get out?'

It sounded like a trick question. 'Well, all right,' Tamasin mumbled. 'I'd better talk about it tomorrow – but if this priest of yours is prepared to accept assurances from me, I don't mind doing some sort of deal.'

Azra's voice was a near-whisper. 'Well, *I'm* getting out if I can. You can come with me or you can stop here, whichever you'd rather.'

*   *   *

Things were starting to make sense in Tamasin's mind. Except that they didn't make sense at all.

'This priest of yours must trust you pretty well.'

'Ardeshir.' That was what got Azra. She'd thought Ardeshir was too shrewd not to sense the way her mind must be working. 'Unless this is some sort of set-up,' she said.

Tamasin thought for a long time. When she stopped and tried to get her mind back on track, she knew she'd been sleeping.

Azra smiled at her, reached over and squeezed her hand. 'We'll talk some more tomorrow.'

*   *   *

It was bedtime the same evening, Saturday, 20 June, when Azra finally got her chance to tell Tamasin her story: redundancy from her post as company lawyer; selling up in England and moving out here; Mansoureh, content to be with her family and live the simple life again; while Azra, dying to get back to a life of her own, was simply trapped.

'And what's in this for Ardeshir, keeping you cooped up in the boonies like this?' Every so often, a word or a phrase from her life in Arizona would creep into Tamasin's dialogue.

209

That puzzled Azra, too. The answer she came back to every time was that it was simply part and parcel of the doctrinaire application of the Way of Faith.

'And if you can't even get your passport, how are you going to get out?'

Point one, Azra said: aim for a friendly country. It wouldn't be any use to her trying for Iraq or even Russia, and she wasn't that happy about trying Pakistan. But Turkey, with its NATO ties and its secular constitution, its Western-oriented economy, was a different matter. Get to Turkey, Azra said, and then talk her way out of it when she reached immigration.

'But how would you *get* to Turkey?'

It wasn't quite midnight. The big, rambling fortress of a house was asleep around them but still they were careful to keep their voices down. Out on the hillside they heard the baying of the wild dogs.

'If Rob could get in here,' Azra said, 'he could fly out in the jet that you came in on.'

'Dammit!' Tamasin said. For a moment she was angry, then the funny side of the situation came through in a grin. 'That's what I was going to do.' She watched Azra. 'Did Rob say how he's going to make sure the thing's fuelled up and airworthy?'

'Well, from what Bibi tells me of what Rob's told her, it seems that the Iranian air force is looking after that. They've obviously got plans for the jet.'

Azra turned out the light. Tamasin had spent much of the day catching up on sleep, and now in the dark and the quiet she found herself wakeful. There was more than one element in all of this that didn't fit, and she was distrustful.

What bothered her most was Hojatoleslam Ardeshir Rezania. There was no doubt about his commitment to his own special brand of Islam; yet his instincts, as Tamasin had seen for herself, were those of the sort of reasonable man that any plain, common sense Westerner could understand. It was odd to think of that simple common sense encouraging a revolution with the loaded rifles Azra had told her about; a revolution backed by army and air force units and almost certain to involve hideous bloodshed.

Darvish was actually easier to understand, she realized. Darvish was a fanatic with a one-track mind who would kill without hesitation if he bumped into someone who disagreed with him.

But she felt Ardeshir was complex; shrewd, too. Yet this complex, shrewd man with his undoubted understanding of human nature had without any obvious reason made Azra subject to a set of restrictions that were little short of house arrest. *Then*, having instilled thorough discontent into a brainy and resourceful member of the household, he put her side by side with a foreigner whose intention to get the hell out of there at the first opportunity had never been in doubt.

Tamasin turned over, exasperated. Maybe one day she'd work out what was going on, but not just yet.

Meanwhile, Azra was subtly playing games with this household and keeping quiet about her own agenda, and the obvious thing for Tamasin would be to follow suit.

*　　*　　*

The days seemed to alternate, one day fine, the next day thunder. Sometimes Azra had a word of encouragement for Tamasin, sometimes she had none. The days fell into a routine. Sometimes Tamasin took a part of the housework, often she didn't; but Azra faithfully ironed washing with the heavy old flat-iron, and then in the evenings sat in her room with her sewing.

It bothered Tamasin to think Azra might be keeping something back from her.

Sunday and Monday. Tuesday and Wednesday. Tamasin was getting edgy, fretting about what those air force technicians might be doing down there with her aircraft.

211

With an effort, she hid her impatience, playing the game the way Azra was.

Without Azra for moral support, she'd have gone out of her mind days ago.

Then the phone rang early Thursday evening, and Tamasin heard Azra speaking Farsi and English alternately; she couldn't piece it together to make out who was saying what on the other end.

In time to see Azra hang up, Tamasin wandered into the larger of the two living rooms, wearing her chador because this was a mixed area. Azra was in the chador, too. Turning from the phone, she caught Tamasin's eye, and Tamasin could see the excitement on Azra's face.

But Rana Tezcan was across the room, serving tea to a couple of the men, one of them Akbar, Tamasin noticed, with that great scar on his battle-seasoned face; Rana's antennae were quivering.

Azra vanished into the sunlit courtyard. Tamasin invented an errand for herself in the kitchen, then as soon as she could headed out into the courtyard. Azra was missing. Tamasin tried the bedroom and found her there, sure enough. No chador, just the light in her deep brown eyes.

'That was Bibi. It's a go, tonight!'

CHAPTER 31

Overhead north central Iran, Friday, 26 June, 0411 local
The colours were coming alive. Out of the charcoals
and greys of the dawn, browns and harsh yellows were
forming, sometimes even a speckling of dusty green. The
railway line was as straight on the ground as a contrail
in a morning sky.

Zedasht would be south of that railway line, Felix Wyer
thought. Almost there. Once again all the apprehensions
tightened up in her stomach.

'Got it!' It was Chris Norton's voice, not Walter
Becker's. 'Two o'clock!'

Felix's side, then. That was why it had been Norton
who'd spotted it. Peer as she might, though, Felix
couldn't make out anything in that long-shadowed brown
landscape.

A touch more throttle and Walter rolled steeply right. A
few seconds more, then steeply left again. Felix knew what
that meant, Walter had crossed the runway centreline —
or its imagined projection — to fly a lefthand circuit that
would put him, as handling pilot, in sight of the runway
all the way.

They would be busy up front but the hell with that. Felix
pressed the intercom button. 'Walter, how does it look?'

'Wincy little small runway.' For some reason, Walter
had never learned the English word *weeny*. 'Ah, we be
all right. I get you in there, Felix, if I run off the end
of the runway to do it, is too bad. Right, now, in a few
minutes we be landing at Zedasht International, please
extinguish all cigarettes and take your filthy hands off the
stewardesses.'

There was the double thump as the mainwheels came

213

down and immediately after that the clunk and rumble as the slats and flaps came out.

Felix flicked a glance at Rob Pilgrim. He'd been watching her, she discovered, and she recognized the concern there. He gave her a slow, knowing smile.

Walter pulled *Falcon Fang* tightly into its left turn, and for a moment all Felix could see was the early morning sky. Then he had the jets throttled right back, bringing *Fang* steeply down the final approach over the desert.

Light turbulence jogged them. Felix was gazing down as the ground rose up. There was the single hefty *thump* and then the howl of the thrust reversers.

For a moment she was almost scared Walter really would run off the end of the runway.

He didn't. He brought *Fang* almost to a halt and then turned very tightly on the ground. Felix was ducking and craning, peering to see where *Rapide* had been parked.

Rob snapped off his seat harness and went stooping quickly forward through the low cabin, the jet still on the roll. Felix unclipped her harness and went after him.

Rob was unlatching the door even as Walter pulled *Fang* to a halt. Her breathing tense, Felix crouched at Rob's shoulder. Warm, dry air flooded in as the airstair door came open.

Rob gave a thumbs-up to the pilots and dived down the airstairs.

Felix ducked into the cockpit. 'Fabulous! Well done!' Very swiftly she kissed Walter on the cheek, then Chris Norton, then she went after Rob. She didn't even look back to see which of them was closing the cabin door after her.

Her first impression was of yellow desolation stretching forever; the whine of *Fang*'s engines in her ear; the reek of burnt kerosene. Then she made out an ancient control tower, a hangar, a water tower that looked like hollow promises, a few low buildings – and *Rapide*, parked on the ramp in front of the hangar. It must have been a thousand metres across the airfield from them.

Rob caught Felix's eye and broke into a jog. His day pack bounced on his back. Felix loped after him. She didn't often run in a full tracksuit and this felt restrictive, especially in the warm morning, but they weren't running very far.

She was level with Rob in a moment. By the time they reached the aircraft, he was panting rather more than she was.

Walter had backtracked to the end of the runway where he'd landed. Now his jets wound up to a roar and howl as he held *Fang* on the brakes ready to go.

Felix fished in her pocket and came out with the spare key to the aircraft. She reached up, hand steady even after the run, and slotted it into the lock.

Rob looked all around, frowning, lips parted.

Felix glimpsed *Fang* starting its roll. She got *Rapide*'s cabin door open and then turned. Walter left it very late to rotate, but once the nose came up the Falcon left the ground very positively. Felix turned back.

Suddenly she realized what was wrong.

Rob was there ahead of her. 'Where the hell are they?'

*   *   *

Tamasin and Azra should have been out in the open by now, wherever they'd been hiding. They couldn't have missed hearing Walter's landing, let alone his take-off.

'D'you want to start searching?' Felix muttered, worried.

'First things first,' Rob said, voice tightly controlled. 'Let's do the walk-round.'

He scrambled up into the cabin. He'd been braced for seeing the bullet hole but it still shook him. On the captain's side he reached to unscrew the control lock. This flight was going to be his first for years as captain on a 125. Battery master: *on*. The right lights flashed and the right gyros whined up. Fuel contents *full*. Rob dashed back down the airstairs.

'Looking good,' he told Felix.

She thought: but not here. There was still no sign of Tamasin or Azra.

Moving quickly, Rob started on the external checks. Nose panels, undamaged. Pitots, aerials. He reached the starboard wing, and unscrewed the fuel filler cap. Visual inspection of contents: *full*. Starboard engine, lubricant level, torch on the sight glass. *Plenty*.

He went around the tail. He checked the port side, and the port wing.

Felix was by the airstairs, anguish on her face. 'They can't have made it. God knows what's happened to them! Now what do we do?'

Wait, and maybe watch the Iranians fly *Rapide* out of here? Or go themselves, leaving Tamasin and Azra to take their chances? The silent landscape brooded around them. Rob was worried about Felix, he'd never seen her dither like this before.

Felix scanned the view. She gasped, alarmed. 'What's that?'

Rob stared to where she was pointing. To the north, beyond the low crags at the end of the runway with their little tangle of tamarisk, yellow-brown dust moved and billowed. It was approaching.

'Well, if I had to guess,' he said, 'I'd say that was the Iranian air force.'

CHAPTER 32

Roudabad, Thursday, 25 June, 2355 local
Gradually the big house put itself to bed. The last of the sounds died away.

Tamasin Masterson was watching with just the thin blanket over her as Azra rolled briskly out of bed. Neither spoke. They knew all the drills in advance.

Under their blankets, both were dressed already. Azra wore jeans, Tamasin her uniform trousers, battered now. Tamasin wore the blouse she'd bought from the family that had sheltered her after the shooting. Azra wore the blouse she'd been working on, the hem heavy now at her hips.

'How much time have we got?' Tamasin murmured as she pulled on her chador.

'Bibi said take-off time was five,' Azra said. 'If we can get a car OK, we'll be down there in an hour, maybe a little more.'

Then Tamasin saw what she was putting on.

The mullah's robe was Ardeshir's, loose on her shoulders but not long on her legs. So was the black turban. Azra grinned through the dim lighting as she put it on laboriously.

'Doing the ironing has its compensations. He hasn't even missed this stuff.'

It wasn't quite midnight.

Tamasin said: 'What about a map?'

'Shouldn't need one.' She'd memorized the route. 'Anyway, in the dark we won't be able to read a map or anything else.'

'What if someone spots us getting out?'

'Don't!' It was one of the few things for which Azra had no fallback.

It was after midnight now. Azra laced her trainers tightly, slung her haversack onto her back with the things she couldn't bear to be without, and moved softly out of the room. Tamasin followed stealthily. The door creaked once, then creaked again as Tamasin closed it.

In its chiaroscuro of moon and starlight the courtyard was empty but for the big brindled mastiff on its chain. It sensed them the instant they moved into the courtyard and lifted its heavy head with a grumpy growl. As Azra stepped into the open the dog recognized her and let its head sink to its paws with a throaty mutter.

This isn't a bad disguise, superficially, Tamasin thought as she followed Azra over into the shadows, skirting the courtyard: mullah with dutiful wife in chador. Azra was even a bit taller than her, to make it more convincing.

As they reached the store chamber, the one with the rifles, Azra realized her hand was trembling. If Darvish caught them in here, he would kill them. Darvish terrified her. She fished under her cleric's robe. She had all those spare keys with her. She found the one for the store room.

'Watch the courtyard, Tamasin.' Her voice was a whisper.

'Roger.' Tamasin sidled just inside the doorway.

Azra risked the torch. She found the rope, drawing it towards her, heavy, awkward.

For a moment it wouldn't budge. Azra pulled harder.

It had snagged on something. As she pushed it the other way, the crate it had caught on fell with a crash. It sounded like war breaking out.

The breath jammed in Tamasin's throat. Azra froze. Someone was certain to have heard that. The big dog made another surly noise, its head raised suspiciously.

Silence. The dog lowered its head and waited peacefully.

'Let's move, Azra,' Tamasin whispered, 'no-one's coming.'

'OK.'

Unhurried now, Azra lifted the rope out. Then she

stooped to the crate that had fallen. She opened it. AK47s, the old sort.

Over her shoulder she murmured, 'Want one of these?'

'God, no!' Tamasin said. 'Someone's going to get killed if we start fooling around with rifles!'

Azra didn't hesitate, she picked out one of the AK47s. She fumbled a moment, then found the magazine release clip. She took out the magazine. Empty. The *clang* as she thrust the mag back made Tamasin jump. She propped the gun on its butt and opened another crate. Ammunition. She took out several clips and put them into her haversack, bulging already.

Then they eased themselves out of the doorway.

Azra closed the door. She locked it. Tamasin was keeping watch tensely. Still no-one looking. Azra looped the rope into the crook of her arm and went up the outer stairs to the flat roof.

They were exposed up here. They would have to be quick. Her ears straining for a challenge or for someone's approach, Azra fastened the rope round a protruding clothes-prop socket and lowered the end outside and down to the ground. Darvish. When he found them gone. With all those plans he'd bragged about, to impress her, the plans for the rising . . .

The retaining wall was barely a metre high. The street was in darkness. Starlight picked out the low curves of the roofs of the cars parked up against the wall, and ground level was no more than a dozen feet down.

Azra stooped and pulled hard on the rope. So far, so good. She hooked her haversack securely on her shoulders, clambered over the retaining wall, and trusted her fifty-five kilos to the rusty clothes-prop socket.

It held. A metre from the ground she could sense where the uneven surface lay and she dropped the short distance. Very tense, she looked about her. Then up.

'All clear, Tamasin!' It was difficult to make a whisper project far enough.

The shadows were dense and the silence of the street

was deep. No streetlamps, hardly a light in the houses. Tamasin shinned deftly down the rope.

Azra drew in the end of the rope, knotted it, then with all her strength threw it back up, over the retaining wall. That ought to delay anyone wondering who was on the other end. Azra turned to the cars.

Four vehicles stood nose-on to the house wall on a sloping patch of packed earth with weeds growing round the edge: a Mercedes saloon, an old Peykan, a Toyota pickup, an old Nissan saloon.

She ignored the Mercedes as she didn't have a key that would fit it. She tried the battery on the Nissan but its tank was almost empty. The Toyota pickup had petrol but wouldn't start. Now all they needed was for the Peykan to come out in sympathy.

Azra tried it. A touch over half a tank. She turned the key further. It started.

'I'll drive. Let's go.'

Tamasin scrambled into the passenger seat.

Reversing off the packed earth, Azra swung over the uneven cobbles. It had been a while since she'd driven a car.

The first couple of streets were slow going, narrow, twisty, almost unsurfaced apart from a few of the cobbles. Then they came out on to the main street of the little town.

This was the road that connected Roudabad with Shahrud and it followed a straight line downhill through the town; good tarmac on the top of its camber, cobbles and potholes along the edges. Headlights probing the darkness, Azra turned right and drove on to the road leading out.

On the very limit, where the houses became smaller and smaller and then gave out, the headlights caught a gleam of bumper on a car at the side of the road. Beside it, movement. Azra recognized one of the town's six policemen as he sauntered out over the crown of the road and into their path. Interestedly he looked towards them. *Blast.*

Azra changed gear and slowed the Peykan, face prickling as she wondered what to do.

'What's up?' Tamasin said.

'Bloody policeman. We'll have to stop if we go any further. They know me by sight, they know everybody in town . . .'

The policeman's car was parked on the left, facing into the town. For a dangerous moment Azra toyed with the idea of using the AK.

'No,' she told herself, tight-lipped; then, for Tamasin's benefit: 'Back to Plan B.'

She braked quickly and swung into the first available righthand turning. It took her around the back of the houses and out of the policeman's sight. There were a dozen old Peykans in Roudabad; she couldn't possibly have been close enough for the policeman to know which of them it was.

'Where are we heading?' Tamasin asked in alarm.

On the steep street, big stones jutted up amid the potholes, and the steering wrenched as Azra nosed the car cautiously uphill. She'd been scared from the very beginning but now in her fear there was an edge of despair.

'Got to ditch this car if we can't get out by road.'

By this time there might be a crowd of people outside Ardeshir's house. Azra dithered. Right, then, she thought, if there is a crowd, I'll just park somewhere else.

They were committed now. That was the terrifying thing. If Darvish caught her, heaven only knew which method he'd choose for killing her. Anxiously, Azra crept round the corner.

Tamasin let out her breath. No-one was there.

Quickly, nerves on edge, Azra swung the Peykan into where it had been parked before. They threw open the doors, and grabbed their haversacks. Azra slung the AK on her left shoulder. The webbing strap felt tough. Their ears were straining but this time even the dog didn't bark.

Azra checked her watch: 0020. They hadn't used up

221

much time. Just as well. They really were going to need all the time they could get.

'We'll have to walk it,' Azra said grimly. She'd have gone for a horse if she could have got one, but in all the time she'd been here she hadn't had the opportunity of getting acquainted with any of the horses of the town; she didn't even know where they were stabled. 'Are you fit?'

'Sure.' Tamasin stared. 'But are we going to have time enough?'

'Just – if we keep moving.' Azra slung the haversack onto her back and set off quickly through the shadows. Tamasin followed. In her chador, she was just another shadow in the night.

Through the trainer soles the street was hard, uneven. There was a real risk now that the jet might take off without them. What then, Azra Tabrizi? Rob, bless him, would do what he could, but Azra had no knowledge of what he might be up against. She didn't have another fall-back plan.

'Do you actually know the way?' Tamasin murmured.

'Up to the crestline, at least.' More than once in recent months Azra had walked up on to the mountain spine that separated Roudabad from the east-west road below. From the crest she'd been able to see far out over the desert. There were a dozen different tracks she could take to get up to that crest.

There were two snags. One was that she had no idea where the path went once it ran down the other side. The other was that walking it was all good and fine in daylight but a different matter altogether with the stars arching overhead and the ground nothing but murky guesswork underfoot.

She picked the path she knew best, a goat track running steeply up towards the spine. It was slow going. She could feel the weight of her haversack with the precious bottle of water, among other vital things. Pausing briefly, she switched the heavy rifle onto her other shoulder. When she glanced back, Tamasin was following doggedly. Night wind brushed softly on the sweat breaking out under the mullah's turban and on Azra's cheeks and forehead. She smelled crushed rosemary as she brushed through encroaching bushes. Far up on the hillside, an animal yapped. Wolves ran wild in some parts of Iran, Azra remembered; and even bears. And snakes; she didn't know whether snakes came out in the cool of the night. If she stepped on one, she'd never see it before it bit her. A worse thought was the wild dogs. Every little town had its pack of wild dogs living on the outskirts, and they were scrawny, mean and dangerous.

The bushes fell back. Starlight fell silver on the path amid the indigos and blacks, and Azra quickened the pace. The further they got away from the edge of the town, the less risk they faced from the wild dogs.

* * *

At the crestline Azra halted, her chest heaving. She checked her watch as Tamasin laboured up the path behind her. Five past two, and a lot more walking left to do.

'How are you doing?' Tamasin asked. Her breathing was level.

'Fine. You?'

Tamasin's feet were hurting in the leather shoes she'd worn to fly the aircraft, but she wasn't going to let it stop her. Also she'd twice turned an ankle in the dark and it was still aching. 'I'm OK.'

Azra looked around. 'I haven't heard the aircraft. They're still supposed to be coming in using that other jet, aren't they?'

'It's far too early,' Tamasin said. 'The runway's got no lighting, so it'll be dawn or thereabouts. How are we doing for time?'

'Hard to say.' Azra gestured. The terrain was a lake of blackness. 'As far as I can gather, the airfield's somewhere over there, but . . .'

Tamasin looked it over, her lower lip thrust out. She

223

couldn't see anything more than Azra could. 'Looks like more than two hours' walking to me.'

It did to Azra, too. 'You got any better ideas?'

'No,' Tamasin said, 'we'll just have to do the best we can.'

'Trouble is' – Azra switched the rifle from her right shoulder back to her left – 'I don't actually know the way from here.'

She moved the torch beam around slowly. They were standing amid more wild rosemary bushes, with old pomegranate trees just behind them. The night had grown cool and the stars were hard.

There were three or four openings in the bushes that looked as if they might mark a track. Azra picked the widest of them and began heading briskly down the slope.

With the bushes shoulder high around them the path was in dense shadow and even with help from the torch beam Azra's feet kept catching irregularities in the ground. Tamasin didn't have a torch. She couldn't help stumbling, and began to drop behind.

'Can we go a bit easier, Azra? I haven't got much light here.'

'Sorry.' Azra turned the torch on the path between them as the sturdy, graceful figure in the chador caught up.

They carried on.

Now the bushes crowded close together and for an awful moment Azra thought the path was petering out. Then she pushed her way through and found the track again in her torch beam, wandering left and right around gnarled little pines and outcrops of rock. She pressed forward, the hard stones shifting treacherously under her trainer soles. Behind her she heard a slip of leather on rock, and a muffled curse from Tamasin. This was trickier for Tamasin than for Azra. Then for a moment Azra couldn't make out what she had in the torch beam.

It didn't look like anything. In fact, it looked more like

nothing. Puzzled, Azra pushed through the curtain of pine needles.

And stopped, dead. At the point where the path ended she faced a vertical drop of what looked like going on a thousand metres.

CHAPTER 33

The pilots and groundcrews had just finished prayers and were heading in for breakfast when the young recruit with the shaving rash caught Major Moussa Rezania.

'Telephone, sir.'

Moussa turned and followed the youngster. In the F14 squadron crew room he picked up the receiver.

'Major Rezania.'

'Moussa, my brother.' He recognized Darvish Aksoy's voice.

He also recognized the tension there. 'What is it?'

Darvish said: 'The faithful shall follow the Way.'

Moussa drew a sharp breath. It was the code word for the rising they'd been planning. 'Have you contacted the others yet?'

'Assuredly.'

Mentally the thickset fighter pilot cursed. 'And what did they tell you?'

'They are the faithful. They are following the Way.'

Enigmas were all good and fine in a theology lecture, but the military mind needs precision. 'What does that mean?'

'The rising has begun!' Darvish's tone was a blend of anger and excitement. 'The downfall of the godless pragmatists cannot be halted.'

Moussa tightened his lips. 'Has no-one told you that we're nowhere near ready yet? Even the base commander here hasn't *promised* his support.'

'But you've been telling me for months that he is a sympathizer. Either get his support immediately or execute him!'

226

'Why have we got to go *now*?'

This time there was plain anger in Darvish's voice. 'Your cousin the speaker of English has been seduced into the ways of evil by that sister of Satan, the Englishwoman. I should have killed her myself when I had the chance, as I killed her co-pilot. My instincts were right when she appeared here at Roudabad – we had the chance to kill her then, but we ignored it.'

'What d'you mean? What's happened?'

'Azra and the Englishwoman have run away.'

Moussa was frowning, tense. 'Run away where?'

Darvish didn't answer directly. 'They have seized our plans for the rising and they must be making for Tehran. It's the only place they can go for – they have no passports. Ardeshir agrees with me. When we find them, we shall put them to death by stoning.'

Stoning was reserved as a punishment for the most serious crimes, like drug dealing, and prostitution. A man would be buried to his waist in earth to immobilize him, a woman to her neck. Then the judge who pronounced the sentence would cast the first of the stones by which the accused would die cruelly, slowly, and finally, horribly disfigured. Moussa said: 'How do you know where they've gone? How do you know they know our plans?'

'Tehran is the only logical place to go with what they know. They've gone to warn the *taghouti* in the present government.' Darvish didn't propose to tell Moussa that the way Azra and Tamasin knew the plans was that Darvish himself had bragged about them.

Moussa couldn't argue with that.

'You must join us, my brother,' Darvish said. 'Will you fulfil your assigned task in accordance with God's will?'

Submission to God's will was like obeying a military order. You just did it.

'Very well, my brother,' Moussa said.

227

They hung up.

Moussa took a deep breath and adjusted the waist of his flying suit. Then he headed for the base commander's office.

*   *   *

'How did he take it?' Ali asked Moussa three quarters of an hour later. They were heading into the briefing room with the two backseaters, Reza and Youssef, and the technical officer who would oversee the crew chief on the flight line.

'Took a bit of convincing,' Moussa said through thin lips. He hadn't enjoyed the interview.

'But he is with us?'

Moussa nodded curtly. He strode up to the blackboard and turned to face the aircrew.

'My brothers, the revolution has begun. The days of the godless in parliament are numbered. It is our honour to have been chosen to signal that fact to the *taghouti* and to our brothers and sisters on the streets of Tehran.'

Moussa surveyed the big room with the shafts of sunlight reaching down while the next storm threatened from the west. Conviction shone from their faces. Not a man doubted his role.

'Very well. Our mission today is a flight over Tehran – specifically, the *Majlis* – the parliament. We shall at all times run the risk that fellow officers of ours may side with the *taghouti* and may seek to intercept us as we approach Tehran or to attack us as we leave. We shall carry no bombs or other offensive armament, but we shall be fully armed with self-defence weapons, and our guns will be loaded. Armament will be one Phoenix, two Sparrow missiles and four Sidewinders.' Moussa started to go into the detail.

*   *   *

The thunder from the west was reaching out over Tabriz as the two crews left the minibus and went quickly over to the F14s. There were technicians and armourers and radar specialists all over the two Tomcats, missile trolleys under wings, compressors hissing. Reza and Youssef started up the ladders to their radar intercept stations. Moussa and Ali ran through the external checks rapidly.

Moussa climbed the crew ladder. As he swung his leg over the cockpit side he gave the silent metal a friendly slap. With these aircraft Moussa could outfly anything in the Iranian air force today, and anything the Iraqis or the Turks had.

He settled himself in at the controls. He pulled out the arming pin from the ejector seat, and started running through the checks.

* * *

'Defender Battle Flight, take-off clearance, over.' Moussa's F14 was nearing the end of the taxiway, the heat shimmer rippling from its two big jetpipes, ready to turn on to the runway threshold.

'Defender Battle Flight, cleared for immediate formation take-off. Guardian, over.'

Guardian was the fighter controller. *Defender* was short for Defenders of the Revolution. It was the name they'd chosen for the military wing of the Way of Faith movement.

Moussa looked out to the left as he turned the big fighter. Ali was close in his wake. Moussa made the turn a wide one. Ali turned tightly and brought his Tomcat up level with Moussa's. The two men's gloved left hands rested on the chunky throttle levers, both impatient.

'Defender Battle Flight, *go, go, go!*'

And then: brakes off, throttles smoothly forward, speed increasing, temperatures and pressures green, throttles through the reheat gates; smoothly all the way.

The two Tomcats punched hard up off the wide, grey runway and into the cloud as it edged over menacingly from the west.

* * *

At 38,000 feet they were way over the cloud tops and off airways, too, navigating by the inertial system. These aircraft had no receiver for the Global Positioning System satellites. They had the wings swept, tearing eastwards at Mach 0.95, barely subsonic.

'Guardian, Defender Battle Flight. Say weather information. Has this front reached Tehran?'

'Stand by, Defender Battle.'

Moussa waited. Then: 'Defender Battle Flight, Guardian. The front has *not*, I say again *not* reached Tehran. Tehran is clear.'

'Defender. Copy.' Moussa cut the radio. This was going to be good after all. He switched to intercom. 'Give me the countdown again, Reza.'

Reza was the formation lead navigator. 'Four minutes forty-one,' Reza said, disguising his tension under a mask of boredom. 'Four minutes forty.'

He got to one minute. Moussa opened up the radio.

'Defender Battle, stand by.'

Two. One. And zero.

As one, Moussa and Ali slid back the throttle levers in their tough metal slots on the left. They put the noses down. As one, they dived cleanly, their path ahead clear of cloud, and visibly clear of other traffic. When they went through Mach One there was nothing in the low engine note, nothing in the slipstream noise to tell the aircrew; just the needle on the Machmeter moving steadily round the dial.

People on the ground would know all about it, though.

* * *

They levelled out at 250 feet above ground, right of the motorway as it arrowed in towards central Tehran. Left of them, to the north beyond the motorway, the Elburz peaks towered all the way to 10,000 feet above sea level. The speed was exhilarating and they hadn't come all the way down yet. The rocky brown landscape of Iran swept up to them and poured away aft in a torrent of speed.

They were back down to Mach 0.95.

Ahead, the first roofs and minarets of Tehran. Moussa touched the transmit button.

'Defender Battle, combat approach speed, go!'

Combat approach speed had been agreed at the briefing: Mach 1.2. The order would serve also as the code word for when to get the height right off, down to 100 feet.

The *Majlis* was in session. The first the armed soldiers guarding the building knew about it was when the two dartlike shapes plunged near-soundlessly across the sky, wings fully swept, low enough to make them duck.

The twin double bangs of the two fighters' sonic booms sounded like the start of an artillery barrage. Then as the thunder of the four TF30 turbofans overwhelmed them they dived for their defensive positions and tried to work out where the attack was coming from.

It was adding insult to injury when the two Tomcats came round and did it again.

CHAPTER 34

Zedasht, Friday, 26 June, 0455

The dust trail was moving closer. Whether or not it was an Iranian air force vehicle, Felix Wyer and Rob Pilgrim were here illegally and they couldn't afford to get caught.

Walter Becker and his crew were long since gone. That was the way they'd planned it.

Rob caught Felix's eye. She looked close to panic. He'd never seen her like this.

'We've not got much time,' Rob said levelly. 'Can you nip up into the cockpit and screw that control lock in place, then lock up the airstairs? I've got a quick job to do down here.'

'Sure!' Given something to do, she recovered all her resolve immediately.

Rob left Felix dashing into the cabin. He ducked quickly under the nose, looking for the inspection hatch. He released it, and it swung down. He could feel the faint movement of the aircraft as Felix moved on board. Squinting upwards, Rob flashed his torch inside, the one he carried to check the engine oil by the sight glass.

Forward was the big, tough plate where they mounted the radar antenna. The oxygen bottles were above and aft; one of them definitely new, Rob noted. Directly above, piping. Rob reached up with his adjustable spanner. He set it on a joint in the piping. He started working the joint loose. This was the auxiliary reservoir, not the main one, but it ought to work all right.

Felix dashed down the airstairs.

The joint was stiff. Rob flicked a glance under the nose panels. The dust trail was coming closer quickly. He worked again at the joint.

The fuselage swayed slightly. Rob heard the thump as Felix reached up to shut the door. She locked it.

'Rob . . .'

The joint came loose and the sticky fluid poured, cascading, over his hands and his wrists.

His back stiff, Rob ducked quickly out from under the nose. He slammed the inspection hatch back into place and fastened it.

'Rob, what on earth . . .'

A thin thread of liquid ran from the edge of the hatch, viscous, catching the morning light as it fell. Another thin thread started at a different point on the hatch edge.

'Come on, Felix!' He ran for the buildings.

Felix ran after him, her movements fluid in the black track suit.

The hangar had a side door. Rob ran past it but Felix stopped and tried it. It was jammed, and she ran on after Rob. He swerved around the corner of the ancient control tower.

It was based on the standard Second World War Allied control tower, a two-storey concrete cube with an outside staircase up to the controller's glasshouse – a biggish, square room with great panes of outward-sloping, green-tinted glass. Rob ran up the stairs. Felix didn't like it – it looked too much like a trap – and she didn't know what Rob had in mind, but there was no time to argue the demerits of a hiding place now. She pushed through the tall weeds at the bottom of the staircase and ran up after Rob.

Behind the glasshouse, they were shielded from sight of the approaching vehicle. Even so Felix felt a need to cringe.

'Rob, what the hell are we doing up here?'

He was trying the door. 'There's been nobody up here since heaven knows when. D'you see those weeds down there?' The catch was rusty but it moved. Rob got it loose and then pushed hard on the door. It scraped slowly on the floor and then jammed, a foot open.

Easy. Rob slid inside, glanced back, and caught Felix's arm with his non-sticky hand as she sidled through. He shoved the door shut behind them.

Something black burst up from a corner and Felix cried out. A second black thing flew up from the same corner, shrieking harshly. Starlings. They shot through a big hole in one of the plate-glass windows and vanished.

Felix burst out with nervous laughter.

Rob stole forward around the bank of desks with the silent radar screens on them and peered cautiously from just short of the big green window.

'It's the airfield guards. We should have thought of that. The crews have been working from seven till eleven, but the guards must be here all through the day.'

'Will they come up here?'

'Doubt it. We can probably find a cupboard or something to hide in even if they do.'

In the desert silence Felix clearly heard the vehicle approach, turn in and park. They would have picked somewhere that had a bit of shade. She heard two doors slam, but the footfalls on the dusty concrete of the ramp were quiet.

Rob was looking around in between the front of the radar desks and the big windows where they looked out on to the airfield and gave a grandstand view of *Dragon Rapide*. Felix was looking around, too, and she saw now that there were birds' droppings everywhere, on the floor, on the inside of the sloping windows, on the desks, on the dead-looking radar screens. Rob poked around with his feet. A pile of what looked like rubbish in one corner turned out to be the starlings' nest. He found an old piece of newspaper on the floor, the script Arabic, and he stooped and started wiping the sticky fluid off his hand. He turned. Felix was watching.

'Rob, what did you do to *Rapide* back there?'

'Drained the hydraulics.'

'You did *what*?'

'At least, it'll take a bit of a while before all the fluid

runs out. Our ever vigilant two downstairs don't seem to have noticed. They haven't even bothered to take a look at the aircraft.' Rob gave Felix his slow, unassuming, surprisingly confident grin.

'Bloody hell, Rob!'

Next to avtur and lubricating oil, hydraulic fluid was the most precious thing on the jet. Hydraulics worked almost everything you needed to ease the workload of taking off and landing. They worked the nosewheel steering, the flaps, the wheel brakes, the anti-skid system, the parking brakes. They worked the airbrakes that slowed a slippery jet down in the air when traffic control warned you you were catching up too fast with the next aircraft ahead to land.

Felix was scared, angry. 'Where are we going to get spare fluid from? Now we can't fly out of here any more than the Iranians can!'

'We're not going to get it,' Rob said placidly, 'the Iranians are.' Felix stared. Rob said, 'They're planning to fly it over to an operational base, right? It's all ready to go today – except that when the pilots arrive, probably in half an hour or so if they want to get off this morning, they'll find there's a pipe come loose in that hydraulic system. So then they've got to send out for replacement fluid. They top it up, and by that time it's too hot to fly out. So it's all ready for us *tomorrow* morning.'

It was just too pat. 'For God's sake, Rob!' Felix burst out. 'What's to prevent them from taking off when the air cools down this evening?'

'Weather,' Rob said. 'You saw the forecast.' She had, too. 'It's been a moderately consistent pattern, judging by what we saw of it at Diyarbakir. It *might* do something uncharacteristic today, but it's worth gambling that it won't. By the time their early-evening take-off slot comes up, it'll be thunder and lightning all over the place. And don't forget this is an unfamiliar aircraft to those boys. They won't want to first-solo on a jet they don't know in the middle of a thunderhead.'

His audacity was breathtaking. Felix was staring, lips parted.

She said, 'They didn't put you on those Vulcans for nothing, did they?'

*　　*　　*

The pilots turned up later than Rob had reckoned, just before six. From the tower glasshouse Rob and Felix watched them, crouching behind the dusty old green tint. The pilots went to the aircraft. They found the pool of fluid. They pointed at it, argued about it, and finally got their car driver to do the dirty work for them; opening the inspection hatch to release the pool that had gathered on top of it.

It was half past six now. In the glasshouse it was growing hot, and outside Rob judged that it must have already been too hot for a take-off. The pilots trudged back indoors to phone for more fluid.

Waiting wasn't a job Felix found easy. She was still afraid the weather might not arrive in time. She sipped water from the bottle she'd brought, eking out the supplies. Rob seemed to manage the wait much more easily.

It was almost eleven when the van trundled down the track; almost too hot to continue working on *Rapide*. They did it, though, with Rob and Felix watching, unseen; they loaded the replacement fluid.

It was noon or thereabouts by the time the technicians finished, and the glasshouse was almost unbearably hot. Felix lay exhausted in the shade of the radar desks. Rob had chosen this place because it was too risky to be a likely hideout and because it gave them a view on what happened; he'd known it would be hot when the day warmed up.

Shortly after noon, the air force van and the air force car set off to the north along the airfield track, trailing their dust. But already the weather was co-operating.

Cloud covered the sky and the approaching storm was darkening the rocky landscape to the west.

It broke finally at five. By this time the glasshouse was sweltering in the sultry air, and Rob and Felix hadn't seen a sign of the guards for an hour or more – now sheltering in the office below, the one – Felix reflected – where presumably they'd brought Keith and Tamasin when they took them from the jet.

For an hour there was thunder and lightning; but despite the downpour the glasshouse remained warm. Felix's lips were parched and she didn't know how much longer the water was going to have to last out. Rain found its way inside the glasshouse through some crevice on the concrete roof. Rob and Felix sat in the middle, leaning against the desks, their shoulders just touching for moral support. The rain died away only slowly after the last of the storm cells had passed over. When it cleared up – it was getting on for seven now – the evening showed in red and gold and purple from patches of sky as the cloud began to break up.

The air force didn't return. Rob hadn't doubted that they would stay away and Felix found herself impressed by his confidence. Presently the guards got in their car and drove cautiously away to where the dust of the rocky track had turned to mud. Rob and Felix had the place to themselves.

The main snag was the same one they'd started with. There wasn't a sign of Tamasin or Azra.

'They're in trouble,' Felix said.

Rob couldn't argue with that. 'Question is, what we'd better do about it. We haven't got water to last out another day, and I can't go repeating that hydraulics trick.'

Felix nodded dismally. The corners of her lips turned down in the cooling shadows of the tower. 'I just *hate* to leave them.'

'I hate it just as much as you do,' Rob said levelly. 'Tamasin's a damn good captain and a damn good person, and, well . . . I care a lot about Azra.'

Felix glanced at him. That impressed her. Rob had risked a great deal for the sake of simple friendship, for a woman who wasn't even a lover.

'We've given them a decent chance,' Rob said. 'We're still giving them chances even now, 'cos *we* can't take off until dawn tomorrow anyway. But who knows where they are? If they're under lock and key, then there's nothing you or I can do about it. We've done all the irresponsible things – I wonder now whether the responsible thing might not be to get *ourselves* out so that Dragon Jet doesn't end up with *three* key personnel in an Iranian nick.'

Numbly, Felix nodded. Rob saw the glints of tears at her eyes, but he knew it was better to pretend he hadn't.

In the last of the light they went back down for another check over *Rapide*. Everything they could see indicated that the jet was flyable. They went back up to the glasshouse; it was beginning to seem almost like home. As the light went and the darkness came over them, they began planning how they would handle an illegal exfiltration.

'First light this morning was a bit before four,' Rob reminded Felix, 'but that was with nil cloud cover.' He looked up at the night sky with the stars showing patchily. 'We've got a bit of cloud now, and we've no means of knowing whether it's going to be the same six hours from now or different. I'm inclined to go for a take-off between 0430 and 0500, depending on what the weather looks like once we've got a bit of sun on it.'

'What if it's thunder?'

'Just have to go anyway.'

Felix supposed he was right. The anguish of leaving Tamasin to her fate overwhelmed her, and she curled up by the desks and tried to sleep.

Rob had dozed on and off through the day, as Felix had, but now as he tried to sleep he was restless. It was odd, he thought, how many sounds got through the quiet of the desert . . . An owl. A second owl. A patter inside the room that might have been a mouse. The harsh, dry bark of a fox over by the rocks with the tamarisk at the end of the runway. And something else . . . something that didn't belong in this natural world of kill or be killed.

Rob jacked himself up on an elbow. It was a car engine. He rolled over and went crouching to the window, the north side, overlooking the ramp.

Headlights. Some way off yet, but approaching down the track. At some speed . . .

'Felix!'

She came awake quickly, with a questioning grunt.

'There's a car heading our way.'

He caught her elbow as she scrambled to her feet. They went to the window.

'God, it's moving!' Felix muttered.

And it wasn't coming here by accident, Rob realized. Felix caught his arm and pointed.

'Hey, Rob, *look*!'

A second pair of headlights was closing visibly on the first.

CHAPTER 35

IRIAF Tabriz Three, Friday, 26 June, 1105 local
Blue smoke burst from the tyres as Major Moussa Rezania
touched his Tomcat fighter down on the big runway at
Tabriz Three. Ali was a metre off his port wingtip,
wings swept forward now, and touched down half a
second behind Moussa. Groundcrew and fellow pilots
were racing up to the F14s as Moussa and Ali taxied
into the dispersal and shut down the engines.

Getting off the bottom of the ladder was a fight, in all
the crowds. Another major in a flying suit had a mobile
phone and he was trying to reach Moussa. Moussa, still
in his bone dome, reached the man he wanted, the
groundcrew chief.

'Let's get these tanks topped up immediately! We don't
know when these aircraft might be needed next.'

The missiles were still on the racks and serviceable; the
two Sparrows, the two Sidewinders, the single Phoenix.

The major with the mobile phone struggled through
to Moussa's side. Close by, Reza, the radar man, was
laughing in triumph, shaking every hand he could see.

'Fantastic!' the major said. 'You really caused a scare
in Tehran – and the march there is going tremendously
well. There's a big march taking place in Tabriz, too, as
we speak – plenty of popular support. It's going well!'

It needed to, Moussa thought. They were committed
now.

'What about the others? Have the other stations joined
us?'

'Tabriz Two is with us, and we have the missile
batteries. Also Shiraz, Isfahan.'

Moussa stared. 'Is that all? What about the army?'

'There is no word yet on the army.'

Hiding his fears, Moussa unclipped his helmet strap and pulled off the big bone dome with its F14 Tomcat logo. 'Let's get to the crew room. I could do with some coffee.'

The whole crowd of them trooped off.

It was true, Moussa reflected, that the low-level, high-speed dash over the capital had had exactly the desired effect. But it bothered him a lot that they'd been forced to act before they were fully ready.

Darvish was openly fronting the rising now.

He'd planned to be in Tehran for the start of it, but that wasn't an option now. Ardeshir had persuaded him to stay in Roudabad; he'd convinced Darvish that it was the best place to co-ordinate their moves.

Frowning, strong legs a-straddle, Moussa sipped coffee. Something in all that left him a trace uneasy and he couldn't tell why.

Then the scrambler phone rang.

*   *   *

The groundcrews had barely finished fuelling the two F14s. The missiles were still on. Sweat ran down Moussa's forehead as he climbed the ladder but he was scarcely out of breath.

Reza dropped fast into the rear cockpit. Ali and Youssef were racing up the ladders to their aircraft. Moussa ran rapidly through the cockpit drills, setting up the inertial navigator, powering up the gyros.

All they knew so far was that they had threat aircraft approaching the base and coming in fast.

Moussa started his first main engine. He started the taxi on one, he could start up the second on the move. Twisting to peer around his ejector seat, he saw Ali start to roll. The two fighters moved quickly along the taxiway.

The pragmatists in Tehran would know by now which airfield had launched the aircraft that had buzzed the capital. Their riposte might take the form of a strafing attack on aircraft parked at Tabriz Three or more likely a pass with runway-cratering bombs.

Well, they weren't going to get their way.

'Defender Battle Flight rolling!'

With both engines running, Moussa steered around on to the runway centreline and pushed the throttles through the reheat gates.

*　　*　　*

In well under a minute the two F14s were climbing through 25,000 feet. They were still only on the leading edge of the storm, the thinnish layer of murky stratus around 8,000.

'Contact!' Reza said sharply from the back. 'Fulcrum, two, range one one zero, two o'clock low, bearing two nine zero!'

Two MiG 29s at 110 nautical miles heading a bit north of west. He'd identified the jets by the radars they were using. The Russian MiG 29 was the latest thing in Iran's air force inventory: a capable dogfighter, an aircraft that could also carry bombs.

'Escort?' Moussa said.

'Negative.' Wherever they'd come up from, the base must have had only two they could arm up in time. Tehran had wanted a rapid response to the buzzing.

Moussa radioed. 'Defender Battle Two from One. Let's get these two before they get near the base.'

The two Tomcats had levelled out at 28,000. Now they cracked into full afterburner and went supersonic.

Moussa's Machmeter steadied on 1.9, close on double the speed of sound. They were rapidly closing the gap with the Fulcrums. Moussa glanced out. Ali was half a mile off through the frozen air, silver contrail streaming.

'Reza, how's the radar?'

'Perfect.'

The Hughes AWG9 was probably the best airborne

radar in Iran. Fleetingly it crossed Moussa's mind how much he preferred fighter flying to the morass of intrigue down there on the ground; decisions were so much simpler up here. The unease he'd felt over Ardeshir's moves still hadn't left him but it wasn't foremost in his thinking any more.

He made the call on Guard. 'Bogey aircraft approaching Tabriz Three base, be warned: the Defenders of the Revolution are intercepting you. Show your peaceful intent by turning back at once!'

The Fulcrums were down at 5,000 feet above ground, hiding under the cloud and too low anyway to make contrails. On the radar the gap showed as closing terrifically fast. Moussa tested his conscience to see whether to engage with that precious Phoenix, then selected his Sparrows. The range was right.

'Bogey aircraft, acknowledge the Defenders of the Revolution immediately or you will come under attack.'

No response.

'Defender Battle Two from One. Let's go!'

The gap was fifteen nautical miles, closing fast.

Moussa pulled back the throttles, rolled the Tomcat inverted and drew the stick, studded with triggers and control buttons, back into his stomach. The red-brown earth of Iran filled his screen and the harness held him as the gravity rammed him into his seat and the g-suit inflated. His head was heavy but he swivelled his eyes right. Ali was diving in parallel.

'Crossover,' Reza reported, cool as the aircraft plummeted. 'In his six now.'

The half-roll and the huge, supersonic half-loop had put Moussa and Ali where they needed to be, directly astern of the Fulcrums as they streaked in menacingly for the base. Now the F14s were closing from the six o'clock position they needed to give them an easy shot at the MiGs.

They punched through the layer of stratus.

'Radar missile lock,' Reza reported.

243

An instant later, Ali reported the same, courtesy of Youssef.

They would need to be closer in to fire their infra-red-guided Sidewinders.

The Fulcrums broke into the attack in a wrenching, climbing turn.

'Bombs gone!' Reza shouted, wide-eyed at the radar scope as the half-loop flattened out and the Tomcats closed the gap savagely with the MiGs. 'They've jettisoned!' He could see the tiny traces as the bombs that had been meant for Tabriz Three separated from the Fulcrums' undersides.

Bombs or fuel tanks underneath an aircraft cut down speed and manoeuvrability. To dogfight, a fighter sheds anything it doesn't need.

They were levelling out of the half-loop, the Fulcrums still climbing hard, burning their fuel at a horrendous rate.

Moussa's Machmeter was showing 1.2. He was going to have to kill speed pretty soon. 'Bogey aircraft from the Defenders of the Revolution! Save yourselves now and go home! This is your final warning!' He didn't want to kill fellow Iranians.

Suddenly it was all happening breathtakingly fast.

Both Tomcats overshot the MiG 29s, below and beyond, too close for the Sparrows now and they pulled up steeply, in unison, into the speed-killing zoom-climb manoeuvre they call the high yo-yo. Gravity piled on to Moussa, his bone dome a colossal weight, as he strained his powerful shoulders to look out through the top of the big, clear canopy.

The Fulcrums rolled beyond vertical, breaking again into the Tomcats' attack. Moussa pulled through the top of the yo-yo in a rolling, pitching turn. Cloud almost smothered him, then it was brown earth, then grey cloud, all streaming past in a whirling blur.

Flame blazed out from under the MiG wingman and Moussa caught the smoke of a missile trail.

Nowhere near his parameters yet, Moussa realized. That was to frighten us. But it took more than that to frighten the two best F14 pilots in Iran. The missile soared harmlessly away.

The yo-yo had burnt off all Moussa's excess energy and now he was on a wingtip, angling in for the Fulcrum wingman's tail. The Fulcrum pilots were trying the same, all four fighters tightening in on one another. But Ali's yo-yo hadn't seen off enough energy and he slid wide, out and down towards the edge of the spinning globe of combat.

Underneath a MiG 29 was an unhealthy place to be.

The lead Fulcrum did what Moussa had known it would do. It used the fighter's superb aerodynamic control to rear up near-vertically and come almost to a halt in mid-air.

Ali slid under it, helpless with too much speed to kill off. The MiG started nosing over and now with the look-down missiles the Russian fighter carried Ali was in danger.

Moussa wrenched away from his rolling and looping contest with the MiG wingman. He caught the leader at the critical moment, the MiG virtually motionless in the air, and his thumb hit the gun button.

'Fox Three!'

For an instant he thought he was going to collide with the Fulcrum even as his blaze of cannon struck all over it. Rolling into the break-turn away from it, gravity piling down on him, he almost missed what happened.

Fuel showered from the Fulcrum's ruptured tanks and some of it caught when the rest of Moussa's burst hit, some of it caught on the jetpipe, and the whole aircraft vanished in a dazzle of flame and smoke.

But Moussa had given away a position advantage now to the Fulcrum wingman.

For an instant the two pilots were practically looking at each other, canopy to canopy as each stood on a wingtip, hardly forty metres apart. Then they'd slashed past each other and rolled back in.

The scissors, they called this, each fighter parallel with

the other and criss-crossing each other constantly as each pilot strove to get into the other one's six. This time it was Moussa who was in trouble.

Of the two aircraft, the MiG 29 was the better angles fighter and it had started the scissors from maybe a metre astern of the F14. Earth and sky spun left, spun right, spun left again and Moussa's head was growing heavier as the gravity piled on; he was sweating hard under the g-suit. Slowly but surely the MiG started widening its advantage and Moussa knew that before much more of this the fighter would be on his tail. A man who'd just seen his leader destroyed, a man bent on revenge.

But a less experienced fighter than Moussa. Ali was still in this, and Moussa had remembered it but the MiG pilot hadn't.

Saved as Moussa destroyed that first Fulcrum, Ali had powered his Tomcat back up to 8,000 feet where the cloud started and then turned, searching for Moussa and the MiG. He found them and he dived, and in his headset the growling tone told him he had infra-red lock for his Sidewinders.

'Defender Battle One, stand by for Fox Two, stand by . . .'

Moussa yanked out of the scissors and cracked the throttles through the reheat gates.

Ali yelled: 'Fox Two, Fox Two!' and launched.

Gleefully the MiG pilot hauled round after Moussa and realized only in the next split-second that the infra-red missile was coming at him. He wrenched away and down but the Sidewinder was closing fast viciously and the MiG was diving as Ali's F14 braked out of its dive and the Sidewinder blazed down after the MiG and it hit. It drove straight up the Fulcrum's port jetpipe. Secondary explosions shattered the pilot's ejector seat and broke both engine mountings and with its throttle still wide open the starboard engine wrenched itself clear out of the fuselage.

*　　*　　*

In radio silence and with fuel critically low, Moussa and Ali headed for base. It angered and saddened Moussa that he'd had to kill fellow Iranian pilots; but it was what they'd asked for, they'd had chance enough to turn back and they'd ignored it.

The trouble was that this fight had raised the stakes, so soon into the rising. It had made this whole affair immensely serious.

CHAPTER 36

Elburz, Friday, 26 June, 0105 local

Groping her way through the thick dark bushes, Tamasin collided with Azra coming the other way.

'What's up?'

'It's a sheer cliff. I can't see a way down.' Despair quivered in Azra's voice.

Tamasin stopped short. 'Let me look.'

'For God's sake be careful!' Azra gave her the torch.

Delicately Tamasin peered over the edge. The size of the drop took her breath away. She looked right, looked left. Not the trace of a path anywhere, and the cliff seemed to run for hundreds of metres either side.

She took the couple of paces back to Azra. She kept her voice steady. 'Well, I think that kills any idea of getting down to the airfield for daybreak.' She paused. 'What the hell, we wouldn't have made it anyway. Let's head back up the track and find somewhere to wait for morning. It's too risky to keep blundering around in the night like this.'

'But . . .' Azra stared. 'What are we supposed to wait for?'

Tamasin was thinking rapidly. 'We're expecting Rob and another pilot to fly in there about daybreak. They're expecting us to be there, ready to go. It's a question of what they do when they find we're not there.'

'How do we know what they'll do?'

'We can't know, we can only gamble. But I'm ready to gamble that they'll give us another chance to get down there.' Tamasin paused. 'If they don't, then we'll just have to take whatever chances come our way.'

She took the lead, and started heading doggedly back up the mountain path through the dense bushes.

* * *

A hundred metres or so below the crestline Tamasin found a place that looked comfortable enough for them to wait it out. Azra flashed the torch over the crevices to see if there was anything there that might take exception to them. No sign. They sat down and propped their backs against the rocks.

They rested. After a while, they dozed.

It was just gone four when Tamasin jolted out of her doze with jet noise in her ears. The daylight was bright with the sun not yet up, driving its rays over the crests to their left as they looked out over the plain.

'Azra!'

She grasped Azra's arm. Azra came awake at once.

They saw it, the Falcon, coming from behind them, low over the crags and hunting; they saw Walter Becker's S-turn bringing him back west of the runway at Zedasht. The pale grey paint scheme the Falcon wore made it hard to follow as it rolled in on finals, flaps and gear down. They almost lost sight of it as it landed.

Almost at once, it seemed, the jet noise increased and the Falcon came up. They watched it as it climbed quickly and vanished over the mountains to the north.

After that, the wait was nerve-racking.

* * *

It was six, the sun pleasantly hot on their bodies, when Tamasin turned to Azra.

'That's it. I can't believe they'll be taking off now, with the temperature as it is. It must be even hotter down there.'

'What's going to happen, then?'

Tamasin considered. 'Rob and whoever the other pilot

249

is must be stuck down there.' She checked that mentally, but she couldn't find a way round it. The aircrew couldn't surely have disliked what they saw at Zedasht and simply flown out again on the Falcon. 'They should have two chances of getting out – one at dusk today, the other at dawn tomorrow. What about us? Have we got two chances or only one?'

Azra considered, frowning, fiddling once more, thoughtfully, with the magazine on the old AK. She'd loaded the clip, unloaded it, loaded it again, rammed it back in place. She'd have liked to test it, but she didn't want the noise.

'We can't walk down there,' she concluded. 'We can't find a way round that precipice. We'd have to go back to Roudabad.'

'Back to Plan A.'

Azra nodded, sliding her fingers contemplatively up and down the smooth wooden stock with the groove in it, meant for fingertips when you fired. She fondled the pistol grip.

'It's got to be,' she said. She was still wearing Ardeshir's black turban and her head felt sticky under it. 'We're simply going to have to go for the road. We'll have to get a car, and the best bet for that really is from Ardeshir's house. And we can't go now, during daylight, the place'll be far too busy. It's got to be after dark tonight, so our only hope is if they don't take off at dusk but at dawn.'

*   *   *

Birds called in the trees and bushes. While Azra took the first turn sleeping, Tamasin saw what she thought was a bee-eater flitting among the branches. She sipped water cautiously, unsure how long it might have to last. It seemed a long time before her own turn came for sleeping.

When she woke, Azra had discovered how to strip the AK and was finding out how to put it back together. Tamasin watched sleepily as Azra worked, totally absorbed in what she was doing.

'Have you fired one of those?'

Azra glanced over. 'No, have you?'

Tamasin's memory was vivid, but what she saw wasn't the AK47 assault rifle, it was the HK54 machine pistol that she'd fired at that car, a lifetime ago in Evin jail.

'Not that one. But I've fired . . . a thing called a Sterling sub-machine-gun. I was training. It was a sort of advanced cadet corps.'

'I've fired .22 rifles,' Azra said. 'I went to a range a few times when I was living in England. This weighs ever such a lot compared with those. And I suppose, if you're firing automatic . . .'

Then she took her turn for sleeping again.

*   *   *

They were way out in the open when the thunder broke.

'Can we get to any shelter?' Tamasin asked.

The rain had gone within instants from a few slow, heavy drops to a steady downpour. Lightning flashed and they were badly exposed.

'The only shelter's down in Roudabad,' Azra said.

'We'll have to get down there sooner or later. May as well make it now.'

Tamasin trudged off up the short distance to the crest, her chador starting to cling around her as the rain soaked into it. Azra hurried after her. Both were frightened, as the thunderclaps and the lightning came again and again, closer together than ever.

Lightning strikes at the highest object. Again and again on exposed sections of the path, it could have been either of them.

In the shelter of a little cluster of pistachio trees Tamasin waited for Azra to catch up, looking bedraggled, her black turban starting to sag.

'There's one consolation,' Tamasin said.

'What's that?'

'They're never going to take off into stuff like this!'

*　　*　　*

Before they came within sight of Roudabad, the storm was passing; even the rain had eased off. The day was still warm yet, but the soaked clothing felt cold on Azra and Tamasin and they were shivering. Tamasin fought to ignore it. Her own body heat would turn cold wetness to warm damp, given time.

Underfoot, the dust had turned to mud, slippery in places. Tamasin realized the brisk walk through the downpour had left her thirsty. She still had a swallow of water left but she wasn't sure whether she ought to leave it for a time when she was really desperate.

Ahead they saw the single minaret on the mosque of Roudabad.

Azra caught up with Tamasin. She stopped her, a hand on Tamasin's arm. 'There'll be far too many people about here. We'd better just wait in cover until things settle down.'

Tamasin looked around. Shadows were long and deep under the ragged remnants of the cloud and a big clump of bushes looked like cover of sorts. Azra followed her over to it.

'How long d'you think we'll have to wait?'

Azra considered. 'I'd rather leave it until after midnight.'

They crouched on the drying ground and waited, their clothes clammy on them. Big insects buzzed around them as the night came on. Then there was barking.

Under her breath Azra cursed. 'That's the wild dogs.'

Tamasin had heard about those wild dogs. Running in a pack as they did they would have less hesitation to attack humans than one dog would on its own. And she and Azra were exactly the right distance out of Roudabad to be on the circuit where the dogs ran.

They waited. Neither spoke. The barking grew nearer,

faded further, grew nearer again. It was full night now, the stars hard bright in the gaps and tatters of the cloud. Moths blundered about.

Tamasin looked at her watch. 'Azra, it's eleven. What d'you think?'

'Let's wait. There'll still be plenty of people about.'

Slowly the air was growing chilly. Tamasin fought a shiver, her clothes going from warm damp on her body to cold damp. She couldn't hear the dogs at all now.

She waited. Eleven-twenty. Eleven-forty. Eleven-fifty.

The dogs gave tongue again, startlingly close. Tamasin and Azra both jerked upright.

'Azra, let's get going.' Tamasin's voice was soft. 'It's nearly midnight. Don't let's make those dogs find us!'

Azra hesitated. She wanted to wait, but the dogs scared her, too. Heaven alone knew what they might catch if the creatures bit them.

'All right,' she murmured, and rose, stiffly. She slung her haversack on her back and hefted the rifle.

Tamasin followed her in the dark.

A gap in the bushes. Tamasin saw domes and the minaret, square-built houses, walls, only a couple of hundred yards from them now, down the hill slope. But Azra had been right, there were lights still showing.

A soft sound behind her, another. Fear choked her throat and in that same instant she heard the snuffling, a low growl, at her very heel.

'Azra!'

Azra whirled around, the big rifle balanced in her hands. Tamasin had the torch and she swung it around behind her. There were dozens of them, eyes a-glitter in the torchlight, fangs, and Tamasin screamed. She was between the dogs and Azra and she flung herself backwards into the bushes with the torch still trained on the dogs as Azra fired.

Out here in the open the burst was loud but not skull-shattering the way it could be inside a building. Tamasin heard the shots echo off the thick walls of

Roudabad in the same instant that she realized Azra had fired high, she'd gone over the vicious creatures' heads. Now the dogs were barking in rage tinged with fear.

Azra got the butt in her shoulder and the muzzle down where Tamasin had the torch playing on their bright eyes and hungry fangs. Before the burst even ended there were the unearthly screams of dogs ripped to pieces in the hail of 7.62mm slugs.

Azra and Tamasin ran for it, but they weren't going to be followed.

*   *   *

More lights were showing as they dashed down the hill and into the shadows of the alleys. Tamasin's chador was hindering her but Azra in Ardeshir's robe wasn't doing any better. Everyone in the village would have heard those two bursts.

No-one was about in the alley as they ran down, Azra leading despite the encumbrance of the big rifle. They came under the walls they'd left not quite this time yesterday.

A light showed over the great wooden courtyard doorway but, to their relief, no-one was in sight. The vehicles on the steep old hardstanding were a different mixture from yesterday. The old Peykan was missing but another car was in its place, a newish Peugeot 305.

Azra ignored the Mercedes and the Toyota that had refused to start. She pulled open the Peugeot's door, stuck her head inside eagerly.

No keys.

She was panting. 'Tamasin, get in the other side! Here, take this!' She thrust the rifle at her.

Tamasin grabbed it in plain reflex. 'God, what are you doing?'

'Have to hot-wire it.' She was craning under the control column. 'Don't worry, I used to do this all the time with my old MG Midget.'

Tamasin ran round the front of the Peugeot. It had been reversed up the hardstanding. She grabbed the passenger's door open and then stood in a half-crouch, the AK in her hands. Thirty rounds in a clip, she remembered from some age-old lecture in her UAS days, but how many had Azra fired?

Dexterous despite the darkness, Azra felt quickly for the wires leading into the ignition switch. She'd loved that old Midget. Technique; tried and trusted . . .

Two wires, three. *Which was which?* Carefully she touched two of them together, gritting her teeth in case one of them was the starter-motor cable.

It wasn't. But she'd got a live circuit now with the power cable that led into the switch linked into the ignition circuit cable. They were split-seconds from disaster but Azra strove to ignore it.

Cautiously she tried releasing the wires. They came apart. Fighting the shakes, Azra ripped off Ardeshir's damp turban and grabbed into her hair for a hairgrip. She slid it out.

A chador-shrouded figure came out of the courtyard gate. The woman turned, caught sight of another figure, similar to her own only carrying a Kalashnikov.

She gasped. '*Tamasin!*'

Recognition was immediate, the response as fast. 'Rana, get out of here! I don't want to shoot you!'

Biting into her lip, Azra jammed the hairgrip on to the two wires. They held.

Rana vanished inside the courtyard but Tamasin heard her voice. '*Darvish! Ardeshir! Darvish, come quickly!*' She was shouting in Farsi but Tamasin got the drift all right.

The big mastiff started barking fiercely.

Azra touched the starter-motor cable to the live circuit. The engine burst into life.

'Tamasin!'

Azra threw her haversack into the back and swung behind the wheel. With the rifle in one hand Tamasin yanked off her haversack with the other and tossed it after Azra's.

A man appeared in the courtyard gateway. Akbar.

Tamasin knew he wouldn't understand English. It was easy enough to find a language he would. She pulled the AK muzzle high and blasted a squirt into the wall over Akbar's head.

Echoes thundered and back-echoed off the close-set walls, masonry dust burst out, catching the light amid the shadows, and Akbar vanished.

Tamasin swung back into her seat, panting. Azra wrenched away to the right in a howl of revs.

She swung left, heading for the main road. There wouldn't be any stopping for policemen this time. Tamasin twisted around, heart in her mouth, terrified that Akbar would shoot after them.

She saw Akbar in the gateway light, gleam of car keys in his hand, Darvish beside him, running, and amid the throng of people and small boys behind them Rana, her hood thrown back recklessly. She seemed to be struggling with a man; Tamasin recognized Ardeshir.

She twisted forward. 'I think we might have to boot it a bit.'

CHAPTER 37

If that little warthog Darvish Aksoy was in Roudabad, Kemal Koz thought, it was a sound bet that the *Yol* terrorists who'd vanished earlier into Iran weren't far away.

On the wall in his office Koz had a map of Turkey, but there wasn't room for one showing Iran. He spread out the road map on his desk and frowned over it.

Koz had rushed into the office without making time for breakfast and his ample stomach was rumbling. He was wearing the clothes he preferred for an office day when he wasn't expecting visitors: the American designer jeans, the leatherwork belt, a black shirt open at the neck.

It was Shahrud all right. They knew from the satellite pictures that Shahrud was the biggest town close to Zedasht, where Mrs Wyer's jet had landed. They'd considered Roudabad, further up the hill, but the satellite shots again showed that Roudabad wasn't big enough to house fifty-odd Turkish terrorists. Shahrud had been on the list of possibilities from the start, because this obscure little provincial town was one of the places where Hojatoleslam Ardeshir Rezania most often preached.

For Darvish Aksoy, Roudabad was another matter.

Koz had his agent in place now in Shahrud. Moved in yesterday, in fact, using the same cover he used all the time in Tehran: computer salesman. Pretty soon now Koz could count on getting locations and probably IDs for the *Yol* members who'd taken refuge in the town.

What bothered him was Mrs Wyer herself. He'd known what she was doing when she set out from Diyarbakir with those crewmen of hers, and now the Falcon was back in Kurdistan without La Wyer. It was worrying to think that La Wyer ought to have been back herself by this time.

That NATO E3 patrol ought to have some info, if anything did.

The airconditioning in Koz's office wasn't working properly.

The phone rang and Koz grabbed it. '*Evet?*'

'Communications, sir. The one you were waiting for.'

'Bring it straight down.'

The phone call had been to see if Koz had anyone with him who wasn't to be disturbed.

The young clerk knocked and came in briskly with the signal slip. It had the right message preamble for the man in Shahrud. Koz raised his eyebrows. The coded preamble indicated a burst transmission relayed off a comsat; he hadn't expected anything urgent out of there.

The young clerk shut the door after him and Koz ran the decrypt.

It was a demo in Shahrud, a hundred-odd people marching, with that bunch from *Yol* leading them. They were calling for the overthrow of the 'apostate' government in Tehran.

Frowning, Koz lumbered across to the window. Television aerials sprouted from every red-tiled, shallow-pitched roof in Ankara, and there were white storks circling.

Koz didn't know what to make of this.

A hundred people didn't amount to much, even in a town the size of Shahrud. But if there were other demos, other marches . . .

He would need to know the scale of this before he got on to the Defence Ministry with a suggestion of putting Turkish forces on alert. Lips pursed under his straggly moustache, Koz sat ponderously at his desk and filled out a signal slip.

This one was in clear, he could leave this to comms to encrypt into a standard cipher. One copy to the Ministry of the Interior, one to the Foreign Ministry, just a brief line to report the demo. He wrote out a second signal, this time enciphering it himself into one of the special ones. This one would go to the computer salesman in Shahrud, asking him to keep sending the signals; in particular, to give Koz an idea of how much popular support the demo was getting.

Popular support for *Yol* all over Iran was a worrying proposition.

Koz called comms and fetched someone down to collect the two signals. Then he sent for a messenger to take the original signal to the Iran desk and see what they made of it. After that, he sent for his assistant, the one with the American MBA and the smirk.

'There's a demo in Shahrud – I'd like to establish whether there are marches in other Iranian towns as well. Keep an eye on the Reuter news wire, will you?' Merkezi Istihbarat Teskilati took the international agency's news service as a matter of course. Sometimes Reuter got the news before MIT's own people did.

Koz phoned the base at Diyarbakir. He spoke to the same intelligence office as before, when he'd been trying to trace Aksoy on his flight to Iran. 'We're getting reports of marches in Iran.' It was only one march so far, but inflating it to plural improved the effect. 'Indications suggest that there's a possibility of unrest. Have you got radar in position yet with any capability of looking into Iran?'

'We've got an E3 standing patrol up there now,' Diyarbakir told him. 'I'll pass on what you say to the requisition conference.'

'What's that?'

'Part of the planning for the flight. Everyone who needs particular information gets an opportunity to state their needs, and, if they can be accommodated, the flight is planned around them.'

Koz hung up. Five minutes later, communications were back with another cipher squirt from Shahrud.

Koz decrypted it.

Not much support for the march, the agent reported. Police moving in to break it up.

Disappointed, Koz filed the report. This thing was going to fizzle out before it even got interesting. Never mind. He still wanted whatever he could get off the radar on that E3.

A sharp rap on the door, and his assistant rushed in. Koz sat up; it took quite a bit to shake the arrogance out of that youngster's attitude.

'What have you got?'

'Reuter.' The young man in the snappy suit and tie passed over the printout. 'They're reporting marches in Tehran, Tabriz and Isfahan. There could be others, too, from the look of it – how many towns over there does Reuter actually have a correspondent in?'

Koz didn't know. He ran a quick but careful eye over the news printout. It was the same pattern in all three marches: five or six hundred people each time, led by local – Iranian – fundamentalist dissidents.

This was bigger than Shahrud, but in places that size it would need to be. Five or six hundred people still didn't add up to a lot, but it all depended upon what kind of support they got, who else there might be backing them.

The scrambler phone rang.

'That'll do, then,' Koz said with a curt nod, and his assistant vanished. Koz picked up the phone.

It was Diyarbakir. 'I don't know whether this is connected, but we've just had a signal from the E3 to say that Iranian air force jets are buzzing Tehran – they're up there right now!'

'What base are they from?'

'We don't know yet. The E3 crew are hoping to trace them back to where they land.'

With a grim smile, Koz hung up. This was shaping up into something nice and serious.

He began drafting a new report for the minister; this would keep the man's mind off any risk of an inquiry into how and in what fashion Aksoy had managed to get out of Turkey in the first place. He'd heard nothing yet from the interpreters on the Iran desk, and he dialled them impatiently.

He was just as impatient to know what was happening about Felix Wyer, but he couldn't yet quite think how to get a handle on that.

CHAPTER 38

Roudabad, Saturday, 27 June, 0006 local

The stolen Peugeot's tail lights disappeared.

In the sharp shadows of the sloping courtyard gateway Hojatoleslam Ardeshir Rezania had a strong hand on Rana Tezcan's shoulder but she was trying to dislodge him.

'*Please!* Let me go with Darvish!'

Half the household was huddled behind them in a mutter of tense Farsi. Akbar, the old soldier, was opening the driver's door on the Mercedes 300 as Darvish dashed round to the passenger side.

'Someone is going to die tonight.' Ardeshir's voice was soft with deadly meaning.

'I must go!'

'No-one can answer for your safety if you go with them.'

Akbar's door slammed. Then Darvish's. The engine started.

'I've been in danger before, I've been in battle. Darvish needs me.' It was more than that, though. Rana herself didn't know why this should be, but her instincts were telling her she had to be there.

'Rana, I implore you one last time . . .'

She would never have thought of herself as ready to go against the word of a *hojatoleslam*. 'Please, I need to be there!'

The big car swung backwards down off the hard-standing. As it surged forward, Rana broke free of Ardeshir's grasp. Akbar was at the wheel, a skilful driver, Rana remembered. He saw her. He paused at the corner but didn't quite come to a halt.

Rana dived forward, grabbed open a rear door, and tumbled in as Akbar accelerated down the sloping alley with its ruts and its potholed cobbles.

Rana reached for her seatbelt. In the front, Darvish was checking his pistol, the Beretta, working the slide, testing the magazine release.

Rana said: 'Where have they gone?'

Akbar said: 'There's only one road. In this car, we'll soon catch them.'

Darvish slammed the loaded magazine back into the grip feed on the Beretta.

*   *   *

Ragged starlight showed the steep camber of the road down to Shahrud and Azra Tabrizi was keeping to the middle where the dilapidation was least. Tamasin Masterson twisted against the seatbelt.

'Nothing coming yet.'

'They will, though,' Azra said. She felt tense, yet confident. She was good with a car.

The road followed a steady descent above the little river that had formed this valley. The river ran fairly straight and so did the road. Every now and then there was an S-bend where the road ran round some shoulder of hill or some side gully. Sometimes the bends were tight enough to make Azra slow down.

Groping in the dark, Tamasin found the magazine release on the AK. She pulled out the mag, slid out the clip. Four bullets were left. She discarded the almost empty clip, reached into the back for Azra's haversack, and fished out one of the fully loaded clips. She got it into the magazine and rammed the magazine back into place.

They had 140 km/h on the clock, almost 90mph. This was a narrow country road, badly kept, badly cambered.

'Here they come,' Azra said above the engine noise and the roar and thump of the tyres. Tamasin twisted round.

The headlights were on main beam and were dazzling, even that far back. The car had a spotlight, scouring the road.

'Which one d'you think it is?' Tamasin said.

'They'll take the Mercedes. It's easily fastest.' But that Mercedes was a bigger, heavier car than the Peugeot. And Azra was leading, Azra held the initiative. Azra knew that the place to exploit her car's advantages was the back alleys of Shahrud.

On a patch on the asphalt the Peugeot bounced, almost airborne, and for a moment Azra wasn't sure she could hold it. In the mirror, the Mercedes was closing the gap.

She had her foot on the floor. She was using the added energy of the descent as well as all the horses that Peugeot's smallish engine had, and still she couldn't get the speed up beyond 160 km/h, 100mph. Tamasin had one hand to the dashboard, the other propping the AK. Except for that time in the bomber, she'd hardly ever done anything she rated riskier than this.

Little, scattered lights showed, down ahead in the blackness. Shahrud.

*   *   *

Azra cut all her lights the moment she came in under the sparse streetlighting. They were still doing 100 km/h. Tamasin braced herself. Then Azra saw a pit of blackness to the right, a side alley, and she braked in a screech of tyres.

She didn't have a hand free now to get the lights back on. They were overshooting the alley, and with the wheels all locked up Azra tweaked the steering and grabbed up the handbrake. The back end screamed sideways around and she released the handbrake, spun on the steering again, and flicked up the lights as the engine noise poured back on them from the narrow-set walls of the alley.

'God,' Tamasin said over the noise, 'have you driven rallies?'

'Only a couple of times.' Azra was fighting the steering

as the front tyres jolted in all the holes and ramps of the ancient asphalt. 'Oh, *shit*!'

Tamasin twisted round. Akbar's Mercedes was nosing warily into the alley.

A crossroads. Azra took the right. It was frighteningly narrow and with a *bang* she caught the offside front wing on a house wall. She accelerated into the alley, testing the steering, but there was nothing there to suggest that the wing was fouling.

'Maybe this'll be too narrow for him.'

But they both knew that was wishful thinking; the best they could hope for was that the big car would take longer getting round the tight turn.

Tamasin said suspiciously: 'Any idea which way we're heading?'

'Er, well . . . sort of . . .'

Tamasin's voice sharpened. ''Cos I think we're heading back the way we've just come!'

Azra didn't answer. The headlight beams poured over the close-set house walls and then reached out to nothingness. They tore away out from the buildings on to a dirt road across the countryside.

'We're going uphill!' Tamasin said warningly. 'This *must* be the wrong way.'

But it was the only way they had. Tight-lipped, Azra floored the accelerator again. This surface was packed earth, moist still after the rain, and they were sliding. *Nice*, Azra thought. No sign of lights behind them, though, and she was just starting to hope when the Merc's headlight beams probed out from the alley.

The wide, chunky tyres on the big car's wheels would bite into the surface better than the Peugeot's were doing. The Peugeot was struggling, straining to take the rise, but with that three-litre, six-cylinder engine, the Mercedes wouldn't even notice the climb.

The track ran on to the north side of the field, heading west. Tamasin said: 'If you see one to the left . . .'

'OK.' Azra had the car flat out in third, engine straining.

No sign of the Merc yet.

A left turn appeared. Azra slammed the gear down, wrenched the wheel over and hit the brake. Gravity slammed Tamasin into the door. As the Peugeot slid sideways through the turn Azra spun the wheel back and caught the accelerator before the car had even stopped sliding, and she wrenched it free and on to the uneven dirt road.

The Mercedes came over the brow, heads and spot lunging up into the night.

Tamasin braced herself again, the Peugeot bouncing and swaying along the dirt track. For an instant she thought back to that Isuzu, up in the Elburz. Maybe that man had just had bad luck, but she could see this time Azra knew what she was doing.

The Peugeot's headlights picked out a plank bridge. It crossed some sort of culvert, maybe an irrigation ditch. Tamasin was hardly breathing. If they caught a wheel there, between the planks . . .

Azra didn't slow down but instead belted the car straight on to the bridge.

Braced on the dashboard, Tamasin felt the planks flex under the car's weight and thought for one awful moment that they were going to collapse. But they got over. And found themselves heading straight for a two metre rock outcrop.

This time Azra had to brake, and in the headlights she saw the track ran left and she spun the wheel again. They slid through it sideways, rally fashion, but they were sliding wide, Tamasin crying out in anticipation, and they hit.

The *spang* rang through the inside of the car and they bounced off, slewing wildly. Azra caught it again, fought to regain control, and drove hard down the long, gentle curve of the track.

Tamasin twisted round. She saw the Mercedes follow

them, but very cautiously. The gap was pulling out and for the first time since she'd seen Akbar coming after them Tamasin dared to think they might actually make it. Azra slowed sharply for the main road.

'What . . .'

Azra said: 'It's the main road.'

Tamasin couldn't believe how busy it was – it was all lorries, hardly any cars, no buses. The turn they wanted was to the right, and Azra picked her gap and then scorched out into it.

They were four kilometres up the road when they saw the Mercedes' lights behind.

*   *   *

They were in trouble now, there was no getting around it. The Merc would inevitably catch up with them, given time. The fuel wouldn't last forever, it was well down below half now, and from the feel of the steering Azra was starting to fear that the tracking was out on both front wheels. Then, ahead in the light beams, a signpost. Arabic lettering but an air force flag logo.

'Azra, we're there!'

Azra cursed, the words lost in the noise as she slammed down the brakes. A lorry was coming the other way, too close, but Azra went for the turn anyway, wrenching across the carriageway perilously. Tamasin cried out. Headlights swamped the car and the oncoming lorry's horn blared. Azra powered the Peugeot hard on to the airfield track but not quite hard enough.

The lorry hit them. It was a glancing blow to the rear near side but it jarred right through Tamasin's body and knocked the car off its track. Azra fought the wheel again. She won. She usually did.

*   *   *

'How far down here?' Azra said. There was tension in her voice that Tamasin hadn't heard before.

'Five or six kilometres.' Tamasin watched Azra worriedly in the highlighting from the dashboard.

'Should make it, then.'

Azra was swinging the wheel around on the slippery ruts of the track, mud viscous after the rain, the exhaust loose and rasping.

'Why wouldn't we make it?' Tamasin said.

'That Merc's still there. It's not gaining on us any longer but it's there.'

'Why wouldn't we make it?'

Azra tightened her lips. 'This steering's not right and I'm not happy about the engine, it's running hot.'

Tamasin glimpsed the bright, stabbing headlight beams from the Mercedes. A thousand metres behind them. She felt the track dip sharply under them and she swung forward.

'Oh, God!' Azra said, almost a prayer.

The dip took the track into the bottom of an old watercourse – a muddy torrent laced with white.

Tamasin braced herself for a crash stop. She'd started thinking what they might do about Akbar and Darvish when she realized Azra wasn't stopping – she was accelerating full-tilt into it.

'Jesus!'

In the headlights the wash poured from right to left of them and with her eyes on the track where it came out of the far side, Azra tweaked the steering right to compensate. They hit the wash with a *bang* like a bad crash. Tamasin felt the huge jolt of the water on the car and the torrent swept them left. In her ears there was the roar and hiss as the water fountained up either side of them and steam spewed.

They were through. Tamasin didn't believe it.

*   *   *

Fifteen hundred metres on and they still couldn't see the airfield, or see the telltale curve of starlight on *Rapide*'s fuselage. Yet the aircraft must be there, they would certainly have heard it had it left.

What Tamasin was hearing now was the hiccuping of misfires in that engine.

She caught Azra's eye.

'Water in the electrics,' Azra said. Tamasin turned to look for the Mercedes.

Through the wash already and coming closer.

'Hey, Tamasin!'

She twisted forward. In the dim starlight they could see geometric shapes, buildings, a gleam of glass. Still two thousand metres off – but there all right.

The Peugeot was lurching, staggering. Two cylinders out completely, one missing half the time, only one firing properly. They wouldn't get far on one cylinder.

They didn't. They'd made no more than another five hundred metres with the Merc gaining steadily when the Peugeot's engine gave out altogether.

CHAPTER 39

Ankara, Friday, 26 June, 1545 local

Even all these hours at work hadn't put a wrinkle into Kemal Koz's assistant's coffee-coloured suit. He gave Koz the usual self-satisfied smirk and handed him the latest from sigint: signals intelligence, radio and telephone eavesdropping.

Koz read it through eagerly.

They'd been monitoring police phone and radio in Iran. This report was to say that the march by *Yol* supporters in Isfahan had been broken up with little violence and only a handful of arrests; Koz had received similar stories within the past hour from Tehran and Tabriz.

Shahrud looked like a different story. Koz compared his latest from there, another burst signal from the computer salesman that reported vicious street fighting between police and *Yol* supporters. Much of the resistance was coming from the hard core of Turks – Koz's old friends – but there seemed to be plenty of Iranians who'd been infected with *Yol*'s ideas.

No word on Darvish Aksoy, Koz noted thoughtfully; and no word on Hojatoleslam Ardeshir Rezania. One or other or maybe both of them were up to something.

No word on Felix Wyer, either. That was potentially just as worrying.

The assistant came in again. Afternoon was fading over the rooftops of Ankara but the golden light had something harsh and parched about it. Koz felt parched, too, and in need of a beer.

'Thanks,' he muttered, and took the report.

It was from Diyarbakir, the intelligence digest of data from the E3 radar platform patrolling only the Turkish side of the Iranian border with four Turkish F16s flying escort. They had two E3s at Diyarbakir and right now they were keeping one of them in the air around the clock.

The army hadn't rebelled. What the E3 had picked up was radar returns showing that loyal army vehicles had surrounded the rebel air bases, Tehran, Shiraz, Isfahan and two at Tabriz. No more loyal aircraft were flying, but they were pretty sure two aircraft had been destroyed in combat with the rebels.

It wasn't going to fizzle out quite so quickly after all.

It was stalemate at the surrounded rebel bases, and the only reason for that was that the regime was doing its best to let tempers cool and wanted to avoid bloodshed. Of course the army could blast its way in there if it wanted, but right now there were people from the regime trying to get negotiations started with the rebels.

Koz sat back and had a think. It was time to get over to Diyarbakir.

He called his assistant.

*　　*　　*

An air force Cessna Citation twin-jet executive was waiting with its APU running when the car delivered Koz to Ankara airport. Koz trudged across the ramp, leather jacket slung over his shoulder, white hair showing in the open neck of his black shirt. They had the runway lit. It made late afternoon seem like evening already.

Koz crouched to squeeze inside the aircraft. Cabins the size of the early-model Citation's hadn't been designed with men his shape in mind. The jet carried two pilots and an air force steward in an immaculate uniform who took a dim view of carrying passengers who didn't wear ties.

'If you've got a beer in that fridge, I'll have one.' That wouldn't endear him to the steward, either.

The Citation took off. It occurred to Koz, finishing his Efes as the jet climbed out – he called for another one – that he might almost as easily have been put on board a chartered Dragon Jet aircraft instead of this one.

Something had gone wrong with the rising in Iran; it had gone off early and at half-cock. There was a reason for that, and Dragon Jet, Koz was prepared to bet, was somewhere there in the works.

Stars were showing in the early night as the Citation floated down the big runway at Diyarbakir, touching down with half the space left to go and needing rather less than that.

A man with a major's badges was waiting in the back of a minibus on the ramp where the Citation parked. Not far off Koz was aware vaguely of another executive jet, a Falcon; he was pretty sure it was one of Felix Wyer's flight from Antalya. He wondered briefly what the aircraft was doing still here. The major's name badge said *BARAN*. 'Very pleased to meet you, Mr Koz. I'm second-in-command of the intelligence section here and they've assigned me as your liaison while you're here.' Baran was mid-thirties, a stringy man with glasses and an academic's stoop; not a man you could spend an evening with drinking beer.

The minibus took them to the intelligence wing. It was a low brick building in a maze of low brick buildings, streetlamps on now in the gloaming; well away from the flying areas.

'This is your office, Mr Koz.' Baran waved a hand. The office was big enough, functional like a motel room. 'I'm just a few steps down the corridor here in case you need me. Is there anything I can get you right away?'

Koz sauntered into the middle of the office and looked around critically. Phone, scrambler phone, satcom phone, telex, fax, desk, neatly made up camp bed, no fridge.

'A case of Efes, then,' Koz said, 'and a coolbox, if you can't get me a fridge.' He'd been sober on the job too long.

If he hadn't had his back to Major Baran, he'd have seen the stringy man's jaw drop.

Koz sat down at the desk and started settling in.

An airman came in with a coolbox. Another came in with the Efes. Baran came back in and gave him the latest off sigint; the Farsi interpreters on the base were working their butts off.

There was a flurry of telephone calls going into Tabriz Three air base and the man they were all asking for was Moussa Rezania. Koz knew who that was. Darvish Aksoy was a murderous young hothead, Ardeshir Rezania was a crafty old mullah with a bias towards fanaticism, but Moussa Rezania was a level-headed – yet no less fanatical – professional who'd been trained all his life to kill. All three were bloody dangerous, but, of the three of them, Koz reckoned Major Moussa Rezania was the one he would most like taken out.

The way things were shaping up, Turkey wasn't going to be called upon to do that, officially or surreptitiously. Moussa Rezania had made a rope for his own neck and unless something altered dramatically within the next few hours, the pragmatists in Tehran were going to hang him with it.

The Iranian army could have cut those phone lines to Tabriz Three any time they wanted to, Koz reflected. As well they might. Most of the calls coming in to the man of the moment were from air force rebels who'd suddenly discovered that hardly anyone had joined them in their rising and were wondering what to do next. It was, Koz considered, rather in the army's and the government pragmatists' interests to let the rebels carry on winding one another up.

Koz wished he knew what had possessed the *Yol* supporters to go off at half-cock like this. He wished he could think of a way to find out where Felix Wyer was.

He left his office. In the officers' club he ordered supper and another beer. He sat at a table with his back to the wall while it dawned on him what the simplest way was of finding out La Wyer's whereabouts.

At the bar there were three men in civvies drinking what

looked like mineral water. Men drinking mineral water at this hour of the night could be legitimately suspected of attempted clearheadedness for tomorrow morning. Koz signalled the air force steward.

'Would you please order another round for those men at the bar and find out for me if one of them is a Captain Walter Becker?'

Walter lumbered over, bristling with suspicion, and sat opposite Koz. They spoke English.

'Captain Becker, my name is Kemal. I can't claim to be a colleague of your boss, Mrs Wyer, but I have met her and she has my friendship and my greatest respect. There is one problem. I have been trying to contact her by phone at your base in England, your office in Ankara and your field station in Antalya, but I am told she is not in any of those places. Can you shed any light?'

Walter sized him up. He grinned and spread his hands.

'I'm very sorry, Mr Kemal. Chief executives don't consult us humble jet crew about what they do and where they go. Wish I could help you.'

Koz had sized Walter up long since and he knew when he was being lied to. Yet the lie as good as confirmed to him what he suspected. 'Well, thanks, anyway. Ah . . . is that your plane, the Falcon out there on the flight line?'

'Yeah.' Walter frowned. 'Why?'

Koz fished out a card. He had several different sorts, but this one named him as Brigadier General Kemal, army staff, Ankara. 'If you have any difficulty while you're here at Diyarbakir in getting the support you need; spares, say; services – get in touch with me. I'd be glad to help, for the sake of my friendship for Mrs Wyer.'

Walter looked at the card. He tucked it into his shirt pocket and looked back at Koz. It surprised him to realize this big man actually meant it.

*   *   *

It was late when Koz got back, but Baran, who'd explained that his shift had started at 1600 and was meant to run late into the night, was in his office. He gave Koz the latest off sigint, more phone calls for Major R.

'What are the times of these E3 patrols of yours?' Koz asked.

Baran checked his wrist-watch. 'The next one's due to take off at 0330, taking over the patrol at 0345.'

'Get me on it, will you?'

It was more than just instinct that told Koz things weren't going to happen overnight. All the indications were that the Iranian government wanted negotiations, not conflict, with the rebels and they wouldn't be sending special forces into the air bases under cover of night until they'd exhausted all chance of talking.

He dozed fitfully with the spotlight switched on over the desk. More sigint kept him waking up constantly, but it all pointed one way: the rebels were getting cold feet.

Koz was glad now that his name wasn't Moussa Rezania.

At 0310 sigint got a phone call to Moussa from the air base at Isfahan. Isfahan was quitting. They were starting talks immediately with the army to negotiate a surrender.

By that time, Koz was most of the way through getting up.

*   *   *

Koz hadn't had time to fetch spare clothes from home but he'd managed to get an airman to find him some clean underwear. He showered, towelled down, dressed, and ate breakfast in the officers' club. An NCO called for him. There was a minibus waiting. Koz left Baran minding the shop and slouched in the back of the minibus on the way out to where things were whining thinly aboard the NATO E3.

The E3 is built by Boeing and is basically a 707 airliner

with a huge, saucer-shaped dish atop the fuselage housing a Westinghouse radar scanner wired into equipment that, from a cruise height of 30,000 feet, can monitor almost anything mechanical that moves in an area of 312,000 square kilometres from the scanner.

Armed guards at the foot of the airstairs checked Koz's pass. The stairs creaked as he climbed, and the big jet's red collision beacon was turning steadily. Koz ducked inside the cabin.

Men – no women – in flying suits were testing things on consoles with screens and knobs and keys. A man appeared, wearing an RAF Wing Commander's three blue-and-black bands and the name tag *PRICE*.

'Good morning – Mr Kemal? Good to have you on board. I'm tactical director today – that's about equivalent to boss of the show, for me sins. Come this way. I believe you speak pretty good English, don't you? We're a mixed bunch aboard this bird – fighter allocator's Danish, we've got surveillance operators from Canada, Norway and Italy, and I'm Brit.' He was leading Koz along a corridor down the side of the aircraft, both men stooping. They were passing rank after rank of equipment consoles. 'You probably know we've standardized on French and English as common languages, and in fact English is the one we use mostly on this crew. Ah, here we are, the observer station.'

It was obviously another equipment console, but the gear was switched off. It had three seats side by side and in one of them a lean, saturnine, youngish Turk with a colonel's badges was looking up. Koz stopped stock still and stared.

'*Allah, Allah!* Mahmut Barka – what the hell are you doing on board this flight?'

Once, years ago, Kemal Koz had had a run-in with Mahmut Barka as a captain flying F5s, and it had been a knife-edge decision whether Koz broke Mahmut's career. He'd given Mahmut a chance then and seen no cause to regret it.

'Just the same as you, sir, sitting in as observer.' Mahmut delivered his slow, knowing smile.

'And if I believed that' – Koz slumped into the seat next to Mahmut – 'I'd believe anything.'

CHAPTER 40

Zedasht, Saturday, 27 June, 0132 local
Light flooded the inside of the disabled Peugeot from the
Mercedes' heads and spot. Azra cut the ignition. Tamasin
threw open her door and got a hand on the Kalashnikov
as the Mercedes hit them.

It got them fair and square on the back bumper and
shoved the whole scene two metres forward.

The impact jolted Azra upright in her seat. Tamasin
was half out of the door. With a cry of fright she pitched
out, on her shoulder, asprawl on the moist earth, rolling.
She'd lost hold of the AK – it was still in the car.

Azra grabbed the rifle and dived out through her
door. She came up kneeling, the rifle in her shoulder,
dangerously, elbow steadied on her knee. Akbar saw her
and crouched right down under the wheel.

Already both doors on the passenger side were open.

Tamasin flung out an arm and stopped herself rolling.
She got mud all over her chador sleeve. She was panting,
winded; she propped herself up on her arm.

Darvish had sprung out of the front passenger seat and
was running at her, a gleam of teeth bared in the headlight
beams, a monstrous shape, oversized by the light effect.
Behind him, Tamasin was aware of the other door coming
open, a robed figure dashing after Darvish, she couldn't
tell who.

She was halfway to her feet when Darvish reached her.
He flung up his right arm, cursing her steadily in Turkish.
Tamasin hardly had time to raise her arm to defend herself
when the heel of his hand smashed down on to her head.
In it he had the pistol butt, the magazine retaining clip
jutting down.

278

Azra didn't know where Akbar had gone but she didn't have a target on her side any more.

With her hair tumbling loose she rose to a half-crouch, turban gone but still wearing the robes, damp from the rain, smelly now, the AK butt still in her shoulder. On the far side of the cars she saw Darvish. There was someone in a chador running after him but Azra wasn't paying much attention to her. The car obstructed her field of fire. Tamasin obstructed her, half-rising.

Azra was running round the front of the car to get a clear field when Darvish hit Tamasin hard and Tamasin just folded up in a heap on the dark earth.

Akbar jumped out from the driver's door. He was the far side from Azra now and she couldn't tell whether he was armed but even if he was he would have the same trouble as her finding a clear field.

He was a distraction, even so. For an instant Azra's field was clear and she swung up the rifle but she was dithering over Akbar and the figure in the chador ran up to Darvish and now Azra wasn't going to shoot without knowing who she was shooting.

She yelled: 'Darvish!'

He ignored her. In utter horror Azra saw him cock the pistol and point it down at Tamasin as she stirred faintly, struggling.

The woman in the chador flung herself at Darvish and the shot went wide. She grappled with him, grabbing for the Beretta. Azra heard Rana Tezcan's voice, high, desperate.

'*Hayir, hayir, hayir!* No! No! No!'

Tamasin had saved Rana's life once.

Darvish flung Rana away from him and swung towards her. Azra braced her legs and held the rifle in her shoulder but she couldn't take the shot because of Rana. Even now she hadn't fully understood what Rana's purpose was.

Rana had known Darvish would kill Tamasin on the spot if he caught her. Azra, too. She had no obligation towards Azra, but she had towards Tamasin.

Rana got her balance back. In Turkish she flung at Darvish: 'We want them alive! We must have both of them alive!'

Through bared teeth Darvish yelled: '*Taghouti!*' Rana had said this herself but forgotten it; anyone who obstructed Darvish was by definition a follower of Satan and must be removed.

Darvish shot her.

The two hard, flat reports rang in the emptiness and Rana screamed and doubled up, both hands clutching her abdomen as she stumbled back – leaving Azra's field clear at last.

Dimly, Azra was aware of another shot, coming from somewhere else. She wasn't very interested. She let Darvish have the long burst she'd been saving up for him. She would rather that he'd been facing her when she squeezed the trigger, but you couldn't have everything. The 7.62mm slugs caught him in the small of the back and then tracked upwards across his spine and rib cage as he buckled forwards, head thrown back, arms out and the pistol falling.

Azra just stood there. In about a second she heard the echoes of her burst off the airfield buildings.

Darvish was just a shape in the blackness, like the others. Azra lowered the rifle muzzle. She wasn't sorry.

A throaty, masculine voice called in Farsi through the darkness: 'Don't shoot! Don't shoot!'

'OK!' Azra called back, and then saw the quick movements as Akbar ran round the back of the Mercedes and went towards the bodies. His infantryman's survival instincts once again hadn't let him down.

Azra realized where that other shot had come from; Akbar himself. She slung the rifle on her shoulder and sprinted to Tamasin's side.

*   *   *

Moist earth was like shifting sand as Tamasin strove to prop herself up. The whole world was black and she was blinded, a huge pain spreading, pulsing through her head. She was dizzy, the black world spinning round as the pain filled her whole being and began wrenching on her abdomen. All strength had gone out of her and she hung her head helplessly. Someone was calling her name; Azra's voice; a hand now warm on her shoulder. Tamasin tried to lift her head but it wouldn't come up, so she part-opened her eyes. She saw faint, reflected light and the harsh grasses on the desert floor. She tried to turn her head but again it wouldn't go, so she swivelled her eyes right, the side where she could feel the hand on her shoulder.

Azra was there, eyes wide, hair all over the place. 'Tamasin, are you all right? Are you hurt badly?'

Her stomach was surging and with the pain pounding in her head it felt a bit like the worst stage of being drunk. Then she discovered what had reminded her of being drunk.

Her gut heaved without warning and she vomited violently. She was doubled over, abject. She could hear Azra as if through water, trying to reassure her. The retching came again and again and it smelled foul.

She unbent a little, the slime and acid taste down her throat.

A big figure squatted down, half shown up by the light from the cars. Tamasin recognized Akbar and gave a start of fright.

But his voice as he spoke to Azra in Farsi was level, without tension.

Azra translated for Tamasin. Her own voice sounded deadpan, too. 'Darvish is dead. He was . . .' she glanced at Akbar. 'Akbar says he was a mad dog. Rana's been hit. The bullet . . .'

'Oh, God! Rana . . .'

'It looks as if only one bullet hit her, low down the rib cage, in the lung. Akbar reckons she'll be fine if he can just get her to the hospital.'

With difficulty, Tamasin raised her head. She looked at Akbar through the darkness and he looked back at her. 'What does he want, then?'

'He was going to try and catch us alive to bring back to Roudabad, but obviously he can't do that now.' For the first time, Azra's voice trembled a little. 'He just wants to take Rana to the hospital to try and save her.'

Tamasin's mind was working but her voice was still slow, with the foul taste in her mouth. 'If he . . . gets to the hospital . . . he's going to tell . . . people where we are.'

Azra fired off a stream of Farsi. Akbar answered. Azra said: 'If they ask him, he'll say he doesn't know where we are – we ran off. They won't start a search before daybreak, and that's when we've got to take off, anyway.'

'OK.'

Azra helped Tamasin to her feet. She supported her over to the Peugeot and sat her on the passenger side, facing outside. As she did so, Akbar dragged what was left of Darvish over to the Mercedes.

He went back to Rana. Azra helped him get her into the big car. Then Akbar was reversing away, and driving rather more carefully than he'd been before.

Azra went back to the Peugeot. She was kneeling down at Tamasin's side, Tamasin swallowing water, recovering, when Felix Wyer loped up out of the shadows to them, Rob Pilgrim at her shoulder.

CHAPTER 41

Zedasht, Saturday, 27 June, 0302 local
In the darkness they stood by the port wing, Tamasin propping herself on the leading edge, while Felix unlocked the cabin door. Tamasin still felt weak, but the two thousand metres' walk over here from the abandoned Peugeot really had cleared her head.

'What do you think, then, Tamasin?' Felix said as she lowered the airstairs. 'If you feel up to flying, you're the one who's qualified on this jet – I could handle it, but you'll be better.'

Of them all, Tamasin realized she was the most experienced 125 captain. She dithered, she couldn't help it. She looked at Rob in the last of the starlight. Azra was close by him, wanting to hold his hand but not daring to in the context, the Kalashnikov still slung on her shoulder beside her haversack.

'Were you going to fly P1?' P1 is air shorthand for captain.

He nodded. He was picking up the sensitivities of what he'd got himself into. Felix was prickling a bit and Rob didn't want to look like the big male hero rescuing the helpless maidens. For a start, they were anything but helpless.

'What d'you reckon, then, Felix? I'm happy to fly P2 if . . .'

'Well, yes, actually,' Felix said. 'I would quite like to have Tamasin as captain, provided you're up to it, Tamzie.'

Propped on the wing leading edge, she said: 'I'll manage.'

'Good for you,' Felix said. 'Now, do you want to have a look at this flight plan?'

*　　*　　*

Stars were going out. It was just short of half past three. Tamasin should have been tired but wasn't. To her delight, Buster, the fluffy rabbit, was still in his place, swinging gently from the headset hook.

None of the four of them had been anywhere near any news sources all day yesterday. None of them knew that the man they'd killed was the leader of a fundamentalist rising.

Rob said, 'I was going to do it all on airways. Pick up Whisky One east of the Dehnamak NDB and get the highest level they'll clear us to.' His side was where Keith had been, but from what he could see all the blood had been cleared up. It was still sobering to him to see the bullethole in the panel, the damage petals.

Tamasin glanced at him, very pale in the thin light from the instrument panel as he leaned to her over the throttles, the APU humming thinly in the night aft of them. Tamasin had shed her chador and in the patterned blouse she felt chilly.

'How were you going to get on to the airway in the first place?'

Felix and Azra were in the cabin, Felix showing Azra how to plug in and use the intercom oxygen mask. Felix was pleased at her foresight in bringing four of them out. She'd strapped herself in at the EWO station that had got them into so much trouble, a bit aft of the door.

'Bluff on to it,' Rob said. 'Fake callsign, fake type – call us a Lear 55. The IAI Astra's probably closer to us in terms of radar return, but if they'd allowed an Israeli-built jet into their airspace, everyone here'd know about it. When they moan about not having our flight plan, say some prat must have lost it. Once we're up there, chances are they'll just give in and let us have a slot. There won't be much else up there at this hour of the day.'

'Hm.' Tamasin considered dubiously. 'Sounds all right.'

'I tell you what else.'

'What?'

'I do the radio.'

Tamasin gave a short laugh. 'Right enough – they just might put two and two together if they heard *me* over the air as captain!'

She peered forward and up into the pre-dawn air. No stars, no moon, no daylight. 'What was the last you heard about weather?'

'May still be some thunder about over that border region. We'll be over it anyway if they give us FL 400. We can expect a westerly jetstream at that height at around 120 knots.'

'Hm,' Tamasin said again. *Dragon Rapide* could manage a true airspeed of 400 knots, but against the jetstream that would be 280 at best over the ground.

'We can check on the jetstream easily if we use GPS,' Rob said.

'Sure,' Tamasin agreed, and peered at the sky again.

First light. She caught Rob's eye; he'd seen it, too.

Rob found where he'd written down the co-ordinates. 'OK, we're 54,45 east and 36,20 north.'

Both INS were running. In the cockpit, Tamasin dialled in the co-ordinates. She said: 'OK, GPS.' She set the satellite navigation system running and reset the dashboard clock, taking the time from the satellite reading. 'Right, let's start those engines.'

Rob watched the interstage turbine temperatures rise as the engines spooled up. Tamasin pulled on her oxygen mask. Rob did the same. They plugged in the sockets. They weren't going to need oxygen until they got above ten or twelve thousand feet but they needed the intercom.

'Fifty-five per cent on both,' Rob said, looking at the N1 gauges. 'Let's roll.'

Tamasin released the parking brake.

* * *

'Wind's still in the north,' Rob said. 'Pretty light, three knots max.' At a couple of minutes short of four, daylight was as good as complete.

'Roger.' Left hand down to the wheel, Tamasin brought the nose round and headed for the southern end of the runway.

In the cabin, Felix gazed bemused at the controls and screen at the EWO station. She'd watched Ron Harper working one of these; what she didn't know was whether she could make it work herself, at whatever elementary level. She plugged in her intercom and oxygen mask. She pulled the mask over her face and twinkled her eyes at Azra over the top.

'Intercom test,' she said. 'This is the EWO.'

Tamasin grinned and put her mask to her face. 'Copy.'

Rob said the same. He was testing the airbrakes, checking the hydraulic system. Everything worked.

'Azra,' Tamasin said, 'how's your intercom, clear enough?'

'It's fine.'

Tamasin reached the hold and glanced up automatically to check the approach, out to her left. The whole big sky was empty.

'We won't have room for a roller take-off,' Rob reminded her with a trace of tension.

'Roger.'

She steered slowly on to the faded threshold bars. *Dragon Rapide* pivoted about its starboard mainwheel as Tamasin held it on one brake and pulled the nose round to the runway centreline. The sky dazzled her, a piercing pain in her eyes, and she could still taste the vomit. Yet in the endless dull landscape with the warmth reaching through to her and the faint, keen aroma of kerosene trailing in the cockpit, she held no doubts. She glanced measuredly at the dark outcrops at the end of the runway with their sprinkling of tamarisk, but already her hand was pushing the power levers up to the stops.

The scream of the Garretts filled the aircraft. Tamasin was standing on the brakes but *Rapide* was inching forward.

'We're there,' Rob said in her headset, 'that's all the power. Don't let's cook those exhausts.'

Tamasin released the brakes.

CHAPTER 42

Diyarbakir, Saturday, 27 June, 0330 Turkey, 0500 Iran
Distant whining from a jet they were running on one
of the reconnaissance squadrons served only to empha-
size the quiet of the big NATO airfield at daybreak. Low
over the horizon towards Iran the sun fell smooth and
golden on the shadowy ranks of aircraft.

Tough and bulky in his flying suit, Walter Becker
strode ahead of Chris Norton's lanky build. Ron Harper,
the EWO, tagged along with a grin that looked like
mischief.

This was the fallback plan Walter's crew had developed
in case anything had gone wrong yesterday, Friday. And
they'd known it had, before they'd even got out of
Iranian airspace, known it because Felix and Rob were
off the air.

Short of getting any word earlier, the drill was to go
back in, twenty-four hours later. Wild weasel. If Iran
tracked *Dragon Rapide*, it would use radar to do it, and
the wild weasel mission is radar suppression.

They'd even managed to get a man into position to tell
them when *Rapide* got airborne.

The Oberleutnant reached up to the door lever and
Falcon Fang's door swung up. Last night when 'Kemal'
called him over he'd been pretty sure they'd been rumbled;
even now he wasn't convinced they hadn't. He climbed
into the cockpit, released the control lock that held
rudder, tailplane and ailerons in position to prevent
damage from gusts of wind, and picked up a checklist
and a torch from the pocket where he'd left them. Ron
was climbing inside the cabin as Walter and Chris set off
for the pre-flight.

Daylight was spreading slowly as they bent and peered and pried. The jet that had been running its engine taxied to the runway, an RF4E Phantom, its strobe lights and collision beacon bright against the shadows.

Walter ducked inside and took the captain's seat. Chris eased himself down into the righthand position. They put on their headsets.

'Ron?' Walter said.

The battery master was on and the thin whine of gyro instruments made a metallic counterpoint as Walter started his cockpit checks.

'Loud and clear,' Harper said in the headset.

'How's it looking?'

'Fine.' That battery was on at present mainly for Harper to test his electronics.

Wordlessly Norton reached to the radio panel. He set it to Guard. He started the inputs for the inertial navigator. Nav was going to be mainly his job on this flight, while Walter, who knew Falcons inside out, handled the flying and Harper handled the electronics. Walter reached for the APU panel, set the unit running, then brought back the power to a low setting.

Norton went on listening-out on Guard. Either they would get the word or they wouldn't. Right now the only thing to do was to wait.

*   *   *

Fine cirrus veined the dawn sky at 30,000 feet and the rugged black landscape of the Kurdish mountains stretched below forever like a stormy sea. There was thunder to the south and east but the NATO E3 was clear of it so far. Kemal Koz tested the coffee one of the airmen had just brought him. It wasn't Turkish coffee, it was standard NATO – plenty of milk and sugar – but above all it was hot.

'Excuse me,' Colonel Mahmut Barka murmured smoothly

through the drilling hissing of the pressurization, and in a graceful movement stood up and eased out behind Koz's seat.

Koz looked up suspiciously. 'Where are you going?'

'Just checking the displays.'

The E3 was flying a racetrack pattern just west of the Turkey–Iran border. Suave in his flying suit with the pilot's wings, Mahmut Barka moved into the gangway that ran the length of the big Boeing. Koz could see a light glowing on the console where Mahmut had been sitting. It hadn't been there before.

Koz parked his coffee in the ring holder and threw off his seatbelt. That light was some sort of signal. He'd known from the minute he saw the crafty young colonel's face aboard this flight that something was getting past him.

Koz dealt wholesale in conspiracy theories. It was an occupational hazard of being a security agent.

Prising himself out of the seat, he lumbered along the gangway after Mahmut. The E3 was flying steadily at height but the floor underfoot seemed to tremble slightly. Koz found Mahmut stooped over one of the radar displays. The surveillance operator was a man of about twenty-five with Royal Canadian Air Force badges, looking up and speaking softly to Mahmut. Koz caught 'Lear 55, callsign Lima Golf', then the operator noticed him arriving. Koz frowned at the display. It showed the letters TBZ and TRN. Tabriz and Tehran; and the thing that looked like a squashed doughnut must be Lake Urmia, just west of Tabriz.

Koz said in gruff English: 'Operator, what's your range setting?'

The operator flicked Koz a glance and went on adjusting the brightness.

Koz said: 'Is that the 520 kilometre range setting?'

'Yes, sir,' the Canadian said. So they were looking way into Iran.

Out on the righthand – eastern – rim of the scope, the sweep lit up a trace crawling very slowly northwest.

At this range setting, Koz recalled, the E3 could pick up medium-altitude targets but not low-flying targets.

Ignoring Koz, Mahmut Barka plugged in a headset to a socket on the Canadian's console. The operator seemed to have been expecting it. Mahmut reached to the tuner and set 243.0 megahertz.

He said: 'Frodo, this is Samwise calling *Gandalf, Gandalf, Gandalf.*'

*   *   *

On *Falcon Fang*'s intercom Chris Norton said: 'That's it, gentlemen, *Gandalf.*' He reached to the tuner and reset to Diyarbakir Control.

The Oberleutnant turned up the power on the APU. He selected right main engine, starter, high-pressure cock. Norton listened a moment on the radio, but at 0352 Turkish time it was quiet.

'Diyarbakir, good morning, this is Falcon 20 callsign *Fang* outbound, electronics test flight, local area northeast. Could you very kindly give us a take-off clearance, please?'

CHAPTER 43

Zedasht, Saturday, 27 June, 0403 local

Full tanks, Rob was thinking as *Dragon Rapide* started its take-off roll. Not many passengers, though. Then his eye was on the rock outcrops and the jet wasn't accelerating nearly quickly enough. What the hell was that temperature outside?

On the airspeed indicator the needle was off the stop and showing eighty knots. Tamasin moved her left hand from the handwheel and cradled the ram's-horn yoke that always reminded her of bicycle handlebars. Accelerating nicely now, the deep throaty noise flooding the cockpit, but this still wasn't a C130.

On the dial 121 knots came up and Rob called: 'That's V1.'

Decision speed. But with hardly any runway left they weren't going to be cancelling this take-off. 'Vr,' Tamasin called in the same instant, and eased gently back on the yoke.

Dragon Rapide lifted its nose towards where it belonged.

One hundred and thirty knots. 'V2,' Rob said, and the tamarisks on the rock outcrop slashed past below as the jet rose powerfully.

Tamasin grinned at Rob as he reached to raise the undercarriage. But as Rob grinned back at her he saw she was disturbingly pale.

*　　*　　*

With 250 knots on the airspeed indicator they climbed strongly through 9,000 feet above sea level, high ground still beneath them. Tamasin had the jet trimmed into the climb, her palm resting lightly on the yoke as she tried to convince herself she was feeling better. She bent and reached behind the seat for her sunglasses from her bag. The whole sky was an angry glare of sun.

Rob was methodically checking the GPS readout, marking the times on the upper-air chart.

In the cabin, Felix found the *on* switches for the radar warning receiver and the spectrum analyser screen. She switched them on and waited while the equipment warmed up. How much of this she'd actually be able to use she didn't know yet. One of the knobs to the left of the screen said RGPO; she'd seen Ron Harper use that one. There were triggers below the screen; one said CHF, one said FLR. She could follow that much, chaff and flares. Then there was another knob, marked with figures, and she realized it was the chaff cutter control. This switch was manual instead of automatic and you had to set the control each time to cut the aluminized plastic chaff to the right half-wavelength. When he set this thing up Jerry Yeaver had taped a strip of paper down the right-hand side of the screen, giving the likeliest suspects.

Now as the set warmed up in soft luminescence the captions were showing: sensitivity level; centre frequency; memory; signal power in decibels.

Pretty soon it was going to start telling her things. That left only the question of how far she was going to understand it.

The aircraft climbed through 10,000 feet, closing on airway Whisky One.

Tamasin said: 'Oxygen test. Felix, would you make sure Azra's getting oxygen OK?'

'Rog.' It was coming through fine.

Tamasin blinked at the chart. Her vision wasn't really that blurry, she told herself. A/c overflying Tehran to contact KARAJ RADAR 123.7. Well, why weren't they getting any response from Karaj? 'Rob, would you . . . ?'

Another try. 'Karaj Radar, this is Golf Papa India Lima Golf.' Out of devilment, he'd been tempted to say Golf Foxtrot Uniform Charlie Kilo, but realized in time that the controllers would know exactly what that meant when they entered the initials on their forms.

No answer.

It was because of the emergency, but the jet crew didn't know that yet.

'Better try Tehran Control,' Tamasin muttered, and reached right to reset the radio. Rob pressed the mike button on his yoke. 'Tehran Control, good morning, Golf Papa India Lima Golf.' Actually it was the first four letters of his surname.

A pause. Then the thickish accent. 'Go ahead, Lima Golf.'

'Tehran Control, Lima Golf is a Learjet 55 out of Delhi for Ankara. Clearance for overflight and en route. Can you give us FL four zero zero?'

Flight Level 400 was 40,000 feet with the altimeter set to 1013.2.

A pause. They went through 14,000 feet. A beeping started in Felix's headset and she gave a start. The set was actually working. It was giving her a vertical line in the middle of the scope, the wavelength for Tehran's waves, picked up on the RWR as they painted *Rapide*. The beeping was in time to Tehran's pulse repetition frequency.

Tehran came back. 'Lima Golf, you have no flight plan.'

'Affirmative on flight plan,' Rob radioed back. 'Our route is via Tehran, Tabriz, Van and Diyarbakir to Ankara.'

Tamasin was glad it was Rob doing the radio. He sounded so confident. Tamasin was getting twinges again in her stomach. The blurring vision wasn't grease patches on her shades, she'd wiped them twice now.

She didn't like to let Rob know about this.

'Lima Golf, Tehran Control. Who cleared you on to Whisky One?'

'Tehran, Lima Golf. Cleared through by Masshad Radar.' And disprove that if you can.

'Lima Golf, we have no sign here of your flight plan.'

'Somebody must have lost it, then,' Rob radioed bluntly. 'We're here now. Do we get overflight clearance or don't we? – over.'

Another pause. Rob looked at Tamasin but she was scanning the instruments as they climbed through 19,000 feet.

'Lima Golf, be advised there is heavy military activity west of Tehran and in the Turkish border area. Airspace west of Tehran is closed. Stand by to copy new clearance.'

'Roger.' Rob threw a glance at Tamasin. She was as baffled as he was.

'Lima Golf, you are cleared to Tehran on Whisky One westbound at FL four zero zero, report Tehran VOR. From Tehran, Whisky Seven to Saven NDB; Bravo Five One to Malayer VOR; then report Baghdad Radar for routing via Siirt into Turkey.'

Rob read back the clearance. 'Thank you very much, Tehran Control, and a very good day to you. Out.'

* * *

At 40,000 they levelled out. Rob put the radar in mapping mode and checked the drift. He checked the GPS readouts.

'We're over the jetstream but we've got about 12 knots headwind component. It's around 125 degrees.' They were flying west.

The cloud was a layer of stratus around 8,000 feet reaching south from the Caspian towards Tehran, then some scattered puffs of cumulus around 20,000 feet. The airconditioning wasn't working well and Tamasin felt cold. She disliked the feel of the oxygen mask, disliked the idea that she was probably going to be wearing it for another three hours or more.

'What's our true?'

'Four hundred knots,' Rob said. At this height and temperature, in the thin air, the pressure reading off the ASI showed only 230 knots. They were crossing Iran at roughly 385 knots. It was 0434 local, 0304 Turkish time.

'Lima Golf, Tehran Control.'

Tamasin and Rob swapped a glance. This wasn't expected.

'Lima Golf.' The acknowledgement was a short way of saying: *go ahead.*

'Lima Golf, you are instructed to land immediately at Tehran International. Lima Golf, do you copy?'

Tamasin jerked her head round, liquid eyes wide behind the shades. Rob was tight-lipped under the oxygen mask. He said: 'Someone's been to Zedasht. Nice to know they miss you.' He played for time. 'Tehran Control, Lima Golf. Say again your last transmission.'

Tamasin leaned haggardly across the quadrant to Rob, stretching her oxygen pipe across her. 'Well, do we land or what?'

It alarmed him to see her normal decisiveness desert her; that, more than anything, alerted him to the certainty that something was wrong. 'How the hell can we land? This flight is illegal squared.'

Tehran had finished repeating its message. Now it wanted a response.

Tamasin was the captain and she was running out of ideas.

Again Rob stalled. 'Lima Golf, Tehran Control. Say again – your transmission is garbled.'

The controller was getting impatient. 'Lima Golf, you are ordered to land immediately at Tehran International. Unless you comply immediately, I say again immediately, you will be intercepted by the Islamic Revolutionary Iranian Air Force and escorted by fighters to a military base. Lima Golf, confirm you copy.'

Rob told Tamasin: 'They've got to find us first.'

He radioed, 'Roger, Tehran Radar, Lima Golf copies. Understand cleared at FL four zero zero as per flight plan, thank you very much.'

Already Tamasin was on the intercom, sounding shaky. 'Felix, are you having any luck with that ECM?'

'Yes, er . . . sort of,' Felix said uncertainly. 'Are we just going blithely ahead at this height?'

Rob knew, as Tamasin knew, what Felix meant. Up here they would stand out to a brace of fighter radars like a lame rat on a snowfield, even given the Iranian air force's pathetic record of fighter intercepts against Iraqis.

Tamasin said: 'We'll have to stay up here. We're flying at 400 knots – we should make it.' She didn't want any sudden moves. But Felix didn't need to know that any more than Rob did. She wasn't sure she was getting oxygen properly through that tube.

0436.

'Lima Golf, Tehran Control. Be advised there are air force fighters airborne to provide you with escort to a military air base. You will comply with instructions from the air force fighters. Lima Golf, do you copy?'

Tamasin dithered. She was feeling worse than she'd realized.

Rob turned to her, eyes urgent over his oxygen mask. 'Tamasin, really – we do need to get down while we've still got time. We'll never outrun those fighters now!'

Maybe if she refused to listen, the threatening calls would go away. She'd been in combat before, she knew what it was like when the missiles started firing off at you from the ground. It hadn't been fun.

'Felix, do you think you can do chaff on this frequency?'

'Er . . . I think so.' Hesitantly Felix started setting the cutter.

Rob caught Tamasin's eye, the question unspoken. Do you really want to do this?

Aluminized plastic strips are very light. From 40,000 feet they can take well over an hour to drift down to ground level. Tehran Control would be out of action for all that time once Felix fired that chaff. A civilian facility.

'Can we have some chaff now, then, please?'

'Roger.' She launched.

Bundles of foil became bursts as they sprang from the launcher in the extended keel straight into the jet wake howling through the frozen air. They went everywhere, spreading out, whirling, hanging aloft in the thin atmosphere before they began to sink. Good grief, we did it, Rob thought, sobered rigid, we just took out Tehran Radar for at least one hour. Then he realized Tehran would be far too busy to be able to hunt through the morass on its screens to track *Dragon Rapide* masquerading as Lima Golf. Maybe Tamasin had been cleverer than he'd thought.

It was 0439. Rob checked the readout on the GPS. Still on course, still on target, still at FL 400 but no longer showing on radar now any more than anything else apart from chaff.

Tamasin glanced at him. 'You didn't hear tell of any traffic in our area?'

'Negative.'

'Let's get out over the Caspian, then,' Tamasin said, 'at least we know what height it is, and it's flat.'

She rolled smoothly into a medium level turn to starboard, unwilling to tilt the wing too steeply in this thin air. She watched 360 degrees come up on the direction indicator. She rolled them out heading due north. Then she throttled back and put the nose assertively down. She started trimming out. The fastest she'd yet managed to come down in a 125 was at 8,000 feet a minute and she trimmed out for that now.

CHAPTER 44

Overhead Turkey–Iran border area, Saturday, 27 June, 0352 local, 0522 Iran

The NATO E3 was riding in hard little jogs like a car going over cobbles. Precision flying, Mahmut Barka thought as he hung the headset back on its peg: probably the aircraft had run into its own wake turbulence from the last racetrack pattern it had flown.

At Mahmut's shoulder, Kemal Koz was bulky and dishevelled, annoyed at being left out of the fun.

Koz said: 'What's going on?'

Mahmut gave him a big smile and nodded his attention to the radar display.

*　　*　　*

Thunderclouds stood in a wall ahead of *Falcon Fang* as the jet climbed hard eastwards. It was clear of airways, clear of anywhere its crew knew might be in use for military flying.

'Ron, how's that stuff of yours?'

'Warmed up ready to go, Walter.'

Chris Norton didn't hear that, he was listening-out on Guard. What Walter Becker knew now was that Ron Harper had his electronic countermeasures gear standing by for action.

Walter had taken back the navigation while Norton listened out. The chart was on a clipboard attached to Walter's knee. They were on the 258-degree radial signal from the VHF range station at Van and Walter was waiting for the distance-measuring equipment – a radar-based device co-located with the VOR – to come in; they were too far out yet, but closing.

The DME was the system that would tell Walter when to break off this leg and head flat out for the Iranian border.

*   *   *

Daybreak at Tabriz Three found Moussa Rezania sleepless and tormented. The phone calls were still coming in.

Tabriz Three was surrounded by army units still obeying the orders of the pragmatists in Tehran but there'd been no shooting yet. It would be tragic, Moussa thought, if that was what it came to: yet more bloodshed between brothers.

Things were looking grim for the rising.

The people had failed them. They hadn't rallied to the banners the way Ardeshir and Darvish had been so certain they would. The marches had been a fiasco, too few of them, too few people supporting them, too easily broken up by police on the orders of that crew in Tehran.

Moussa was feeling very angry with the pragmatists but, as always, he held his anger down.

He was bitter but he was still determined, still convinced that everything he'd done was God's will. Now, he resolved, if it was God's will that he should be a martyr, he would accept his fate in brave submission.

It puzzled him a lot that he couldn't get through on the phone to Ardeshir.

He'd tried several times over recent hours and each time the result was what he got now: one of the womenfolk at Roudabad answered, and insisted that Ardeshir wasn't there and that she didn't know where he was. For all his courage, for all his conviction of being right, Moussa still felt the need of Ardeshir's religious guidance and moral stiffening.

Ali came wearily into Moussa's office as he hung up. Like Moussa, the thin pilot was wearing his flying suit. In the early light Ali looked pale, dark bags under his eyes.

'Isfahan has surrendered to the army.'

Moussa slapped a big palm flat on the desk and cursed. 'Any word from the others?'

Ali tipped back his head, gesturing the negative. 'We still have all the others – Tehran, Shiraz, Tabriz Two and ourselves.'

Pitifully few, Moussa realized. But here at Tabriz Three there was solid support for the revolution to unseat the pragmatists; they'd even got the base commander on their side, convinced by Moussa's personal zeal and religious arguments.

Face set, Moussa pushed himself upright, thick neck thrusting his round, balding head forward. Ali leaned tiredly on the door frame and watched as Moussa paced.

'All right!' Moussa said over his shoulder. 'Losing Isfahan is a blow, but it isn't the end of our rising. We may yet inspire our brothers in the army and the rest of the air force to seek the truth of the Way of Faith. If not, our martyrdom will shine like a beacon to those who come after us.'

Ali watched him. Ali was as convinced as Moussa that their way was right, but he couldn't make himself believe that the rising could succeed, at a stage like this. If only those hotheads at Roudabad had waited till the time was right . . .

'What worries me is what happens if the government mounts another air attack.' Ali gestured at the wooden window frame. Daylight was growing, the prime time for an attack.

Moussa frowned through the window. Ali had good reason for his fears. Moussa turned, decisive, and put a big hand on Ali's thin shoulder.

'Very well. It's time for you and me to mount today's first combat sortie. We'll show the world that the men of Tabriz Three mean business – we'll set an

example and encourage the brave men who've supported us.'

After a moment, a wan smile flickered on Ali's lips.
'Good enough. Reza and Youssef are in the crew
room.'

CHAPTER 45

*Overhead north central Iran, Saturday, 27 June, 0446
local, 0316 Turkey*

With the icy air whistling around the airframe, the descent
looked steep. That suited Rob Pilgrim, listening-out on the
Tehran Control frequency as the vertical speed indicator
jammed on the stop and the hundreds needle on the
altimeter became a blur.

Tamasin said: 'How about if I listen out on Guard
and you on 121.5?' The military and civil emergency
frequencies respectively.

'Roger.' Rob reached to retune.

She was hand-flying the jet, nosing down fast towards
that scatter of puffy cumulus at 20,000 feet. The thousands
needle on the altimeter went through 35,000. Slippery,
Dragon Rapide plunged through the empty air.

Rob was thinking quickly, coolly, and he realized
that even at 8,000 feet a minute it would take them
fully five minutes to get down to surface level over
the Caspian. He wasn't sure any longer how much
forward speed they had. As if experimentally, Tamasin
pried the nose gently left, then right. She was craning
over the coaming and so was Rob. They were dropping now through 33,000 and this was the height
band at which they were most likely to encounter
conflicting traffic. Something uneven in the air jarred
the jet from stem to stern, maybe wake turbulence.
The wing swung but Tamasin caught it and headed on
down. Thirty thousand. That cumulus was still 10,000
feet below them.

Rob kept up a good lookout.

All this time Tamasin's head had been aching in pulses

of pain and now without warning it became indescribably worse. In the dive she was suddenly dizzy, disoriented, stomach surging again.

In his headset Rob heard a weak, plaintive voice: 'Plea . . . please, Rob, get me a sick bag . . .'

They didn't have sick bags in the front.

'Azra! Get down here with a sick bag, fast!'

Then Rob twisted round against the pull of the oxygen pipe. Through his headset he was aware of slipstream and engine noise, the jets throttled back to sixty per cent N1, and he was conscious dimly of something going *beep . . . beep . . . beep . . .*

Azra's eyes widened and she snatched off her mask and grabbed for the seat pocket in front of her. Clutching at whatever she could, she half-climbed, half-slid down to the cockpit. She braced herself in the doorway, and pushed the bag at Rob.

. . . Beep . . . beep . . . beep . . .

Tamasin whipped off her mask and pulled the bag to her face and filled it immediately in helpless retching. Azra was gazing at her, starting to gulp for air herself in this thin atmosphere, and Rob was watching Tamasin, not registering the *beep . . . beep . . .* just wondering what he could do for Tamasin.

Then he felt the wing shudder. It shuddered again, harder.

No-one was controlling the jet. That beeping. The overspeed warning – the two orange lights were flashing alternately on the top of the coaming. Because no-one was controlling the jet, it had accelerated to the speed where the guarantees don't apply if the wings tear off.

Horrified, Rob knew that what he'd just felt was Mach buffet, the shock wave forces you felt on the wing profile at the point just before you went supersonic.

'I have control!' *He hoped.*

Tamasin, dry-retching, couldn't answer. Rob eased

the yoke back to flatten the dive, and as he did so he saw the altimeter showing 16,000 feet and he saw that cumulus was above them now. He checked the direction indicator, he checked the N1 gauges. Both engines were still running, both still showing sixty per cent, but the direction indicator showed 015 degrees. They'd wandered way off course to the east. The VSI needle was starting to ease up off the stop and Rob glimpsed 6,000 feet a minute. Still easing out of the dive, he rolled the wing gently and the heading came back to due north. Azra was gripping the cockpit door frame, anxiously waiting by Tamasin, and Tamasin was still bent over, nauseous. The floor level was flattening out and Azra wasn't gulping air any more, they were down to 10,000 feet above sea level.

Then they punched into the stratus layer and Rob was blind.

He put out the airbrakes and left the throttles where they were. On the ASI he saw 380 knots and he realized true airspeed would be well over that. It dawned on him that by the time he caught the jet, they'd been coming down like a streamlined brick at over 10,000 feet a minute. He started a blind-flying instrument scan.

They came through the cloudbase into clear air with 7,800 feet showing on the pressure altimeter and the radar instrument still warming up. The Caspian Sea lies 92 feet below sea level but it has mountains all around it.

It made Rob a lot happier being able to see. His eyes met Tamasin's.

'You'd better stick with the control,' she said shakily. Her face was pasty and her sunglasses had gone askew.

Felix came through on the intercom, 'Can I do anything?'

'Thanks a lot, Felix, but we're coping,' Rob told her. To Tamasin he said: 'Can you manage?'

She tried to grin. 'Maybe I can navigate for you.'

'Right!' Rob smiled back and said, 'Now hold tight, Azra, 'cos I want to get low down over that sea surface.' He put the nose down again and let the VSI needle swing down to the big number Six. Then he trimmed out for the final stage of the dive.

*   *   *

Rob levelled out still flying north with 600 feet showing on the radar altimeter and 460 on the pressure instrument. He'd co-piloted Vulcans at a lot less than this height, but seldom over water.

Tamasin was ill and haggard, and Rob knew he had the whole flight to himself. 'Felix, you getting anything off that RWR?'

'Er . . . no, I don't think so.' What worried Felix was that she might not recognize a fighter radar if she saw one. She didn't doubt that Tehran had meant what it said when it told them there were interceptors up.

Overhead, the stratus had big breaks in it. Rob tilted *Rapide* tightly left, avoiding Russia, and let the heading come round to 270 as he levelled out. He reached to the radio panel and switched output channels. He got the one that had been tuned to Guard.

He got voice but the language sounded like Farsi.

He looked quickly ahead over the high coaming of the instrument panel. The mountains looked blue-black and threatening and the cloud came right down over the tops. It was 0511; 0341 in Turkey.

On the intercom, Felix said: 'Rob, where are we headed?'

'West.' He hadn't a hand free for the charts.

Tamasin shook her head hard and then reached across the quadrant for the charts. She studied them. 'That's Nagorno-Karabakh – you realize that's a prohibited zone?' Then she remembered. 'Oh, what the hell, everywhere in Iran's prohibited except airways.'

306

'We got over there OK to get in here with Walter,' Rob said. 'Felix, what d'you reckon?'

The air low down over the Caspian was choppy. *Rapide* bounced and rocked.

'I vote we retrace Walter's route,' Felix said into the intercom. 'That way we can probably steer clear of any Iranian fighters.'

It was 0516.

Again Rob glanced at Tamasin, again she was too ill to help. 'OK,' Rob said, 'let's go for the most direct route to Nagorno-Karabakh.' He rolled right and levelled out heading north-west.

*   *   *

Azra turned to the galley, forward of Felix's ECM controls. Rob felt the aircraft's faint movement in pitch as Azra moved. She drew a beaker of water and brought it to Tamasin. Tamasin rinsed her mouth and swallowed.

'More?'

'No, thanks,' Tamasin said. She focused on the charts.

Rob had opened the throttles now. They were flying at ninety per cent. He grinned at Tamasin, relieved that her spirit was coming back.

Sharp beeping came across Felix's headset, the rapid PRFs of a couple of interceptor radars. She struggled to make sense of the vertical lines on the scope.

'Oh God! I've got radars! Fighter radars, I'm sure of it!'

*   *   *

'Yeah?' Rob prompted, his laid-back tone belying his fear that Felix might really panic. The blue-black mountains of the disputed region were coming closer but only slowly.

The shiver in Felix's voice betrayed her tension as well as the effort she was putting into reading the screen. 'Judging by Jerry's list here, it must be . . . Fulcrums. It's two Fulcrums, that's MiG 29, isn't it? Range looks like, er . . . six zero, getting closer, bearing, er . . . two zero . . . two one . . . They're really getting stronger fast!'

Rob brought the throttles back to sixty per cent and trimmed the nose high. *Rapide* sank gently towards the sun's gleam on the water surface. The Caspian was bigger than he'd imagined it.

'Levelling out.'

Felix said tautly: 'Coming up on the nose. They're about to cross over us. Oh, God!'

'Calm down, crew,' Tamasin said, 'those Fulcrums run out of fuel after the first few seconds in the air.' She'd heard all the inside stories from Walter Becker.

Wherever they were, the MiGs wouldn't be scraping through the spume off this sea surface.

In a gap in the stratus, two tiny shapes gleamed briefly silver in the sun, highish, but not yet contrail height. 'Contact, two, one o'clock high!'

Hesitantly Felix said, 'They've gone . . . I mean, I'm not picking up their radars any more . . .'

'They've overshot, lost us!' Rob said. He leaned forward and peered up again but the tiny shapes had gone. A gabble of Farsi came over the Guard channel.

'Tamasin, can Azra have your headset for a mo?'

Tamasin pulled the headset off immediately, the oxygen mask still swinging. This low down, Rob had turned off the oxygen.

Azra clamped the headset over her ears. She frowned as she listened, trying to make sense of it.

'Here's those fighter radars again.' Felix sounded more confident than before. Rob glanced at Azra, impatient as he grew more worried, but Azra was still struggling to follow the radio chat. Felix said: 'Ah . . . they're fading out. Is this . . . ?'

Azra understood in the same moment. 'I think they're circling! That's it!'

Rob recognized it: an orbital pattern. Felix, still hesitant, confirmed it.

'I think they may be just clear of Nagorno-Karabakh airspace.'

Azra said: 'They're waiting for us.'

CHAPTER 46

Overhead Turkey–Iran border area, Saturday, 27 June, 0422 Turkey, 0552 Iran

Piled heaps of threatening vapour rose from the boiling mass of thunder below and Walter Becker eased *Falcon Fang* on to the starboard wing to pick a course between them.

Chris Norton said nervously: 'This is it, the Iranian border. We're into that closed airspace now.'

Walter said: 'If this beauty can't do it, nothing can.'

Tension prickled on Chris's neck. What Walter said was absolutely true and he knew it.

Walter snapped: 'Getting anyone, Ron?'

Ron Harper said: 'Neg . . . correction, yes, we've got a ground radar from way out to the east.'

The challenge came almost immediately on 121.5. 'Tehran Radar, unidentified aircraft speed three eight zero, bearing zero eight, be advised you are entering airspace that has been closed to civilian traffic. Unidentified aircraft, confirm you copy!'

If they muffed this tackle, it wasn't just them stuck, it was Tamasin, it was Felix, it was Rob. Three very sound reasons for sticking their necks out.

'This'll be easy,' Harper said. He turned the knob on the console that said RGPO.

He waited. Inside a minute he had the ground radar responding to his signals instead of its own return wave.

This was what they were trained for, this was what they were good at. This was the same mission as the ones they flew training the Turkish navy. Wild weasel, radar suppression.

In a shooting war, Walter reflected as he bored deeper

310

into Iranian airspace, you would go for the hard kill; but *Fang* didn't carry anti-radiation missiles, *Fang*'s special trick was the soft kill.

In Vietnam, wild weasel missions had carried the deadly AGM45A Shrike missile. You flew high, you deliberately got yourself caught on enemy radar. Then you tuned the radar seeker head in the Shrike to the length of the wave painting you and launched, leaving the Shrike to ride the beam of the radar's transmissions, right the way down to the hostile antenna. Hard kill.

These days there were better missiles around than that old Shrike. But you didn't carry live missiles on the sort of training mission that *Fang* flew. *Fang*'s soft kills – they were tactically just as effective, either deceiving the threat radar into thinking you were somewhere you weren't – as Harper had just done – or else simply swamping its transmissions.

This is the real thing, Walter thought, as more kilometers of illegal airspace piled up behind him.

CHAPTER 47

Overhead Caspian Sea, Saturday, 27 June, 0539 Iran,
0409 Turkey

Rob could see it now: the MiGs had moved into position to cut off the executive's escape route.

'Tamasin' – she was the one with Walter Becker's inside knowledge – 'how long can they keep up that orbit?'

'Not long,' Tamasin said. 'Those are As.' *Fulcrum A* was the NATO codename for the early-model MiG 29 that had been around since the start of the '80s. It had two big Tumansky turbofan engines and the small internal fuel capacity of a dedicated point-defence fighter.

Rob started a slow orbit, low over the Caspian. 'Maybe we could wait this out.' The MiGs would run out of fuel long before *Rapide* would.

0541.

Felix said: 'Er . . . Rob – I'm getting signals on the scope here, I'm sure it's radar off the MiGs.'

Tamasin's eyes met Rob's. 'They've got pretty good lookdown radar. If they lock us in . . . and with downward-firing missiles . . .'

Waiting it out wasn't an option, then. Whichever route Rob picked, he would very shortly be in high mountain country. To keep his aircraft separated from the terrain, he would have to climb, and then those MiGs' radars would have him. Surface clutter was the only thing hiding him from them as it was.

He decided.

'Felix, would you please stand by with some chaff for us, on the Fulcrums' half-wavelength? Tamasin, I'm heading west. We'll go for that Tabriz route.'

Tamasin's heart sank. She remembered the Tabriz

route from this level. 'What about this "heavy military activity"?'

'Probably means lots of nice, empty airspace, if it's true.' Rob held *Rapide* in the level turn, watching for due west to come up on the DI. Felix reset the chaff cutter.

'Ready, Felix?'

'Standing by.' She'd started to sound as if she was enjoying this.

'Chaff *now*, please!'

Felix keyed the dispenser button. Chaff cut to half the MiGs' radars' wavelength – as shown on Jerry Yeaver's list – burst out into the slipstream as Rob levelled out and went hard to the west, pushing the throttles back up to ninety per cent. 0544. Rob pulled back the yoke and trimmed into the steep climb he needed.

'I'm going over this cloud. It's the only sure way to get clear of these mountains.'

Tamasin bent over the chart again and checked the nav plot. Power flooded the aircraft and it climbed strongly due west and the air became calmer as it rose. She checked the fuel: still plenty, and the burn was only a bit more than they'd allowed for. She reset the VOR navaid receiver to 115.3 for the range station at Tehran and she got them crossing the signals, the way they should be. The GPS readout checked. She glanced up. They were coming up to that cloudbase now.

She blinked and blinked but still her eyes were swimming. The headache and the nausea wouldn't leave her.

'I make it 330 nautical miles to the closest point on the Turkish border.'

'Roger,' Rob said. He thought, *shit*. It would probably take them a whole hour just to reach that border.

*   *   *

Tamasin had the headset back. 'I make it a groundspeed of 305 knots.'

Rob cursed in his head: *over* the hour to get to Turkey.

They came out of the top of the cloud and Tamasin parked her shades quickly on her nose.

Azra took back the headset. *Rapide* was through 13,000 feet and still climbing. They were well off controlled airspace but still this mountain country was a worry, even back into clear air. Rob still had the radar altimeter on and he kept giving it a check. Here and there he could see black peaks poking through the cloud.

'I think that's the MiGs.' Azra frowned, hands clasped over her ears. They were at 18,000 feet but she was still there in the cockpit doorway, managing without oxygen. 'I think they're returning to base.'

'That must be right,' Felix agreed. 'My signals here are all sort of fading out.'

0556.

The altimeter needle came up to 20,000 feet and Rob levelled out. Tamasin was using her own mask intermittently and sometimes Azra took a gasp of oxygen from Tamasin's.

Tamasin rechecked the GPS reading and equated it with the map.

She was relating their height, FL 200, to that of the terrain below. 'Rob, we have some spot heights. East of and around Tabriz, we have, ah . . . 12,200 feet . . . 15,800 feet . . . 9,320 feet. It looks like sort of table land at the base, sea level altitude, ah . . . 4,900 to 6,600 feet. It gets flatter as we approach the Turkish border and then we cross Lake Urmia.' She remembered Lake Urmia from when she'd crossed it with Darvish. 'The lake lies about 4,000 above sea level. Then we get to a big line of mountains running pretty much north-south, with the border running down the middle of them.'

'Is that where those anvil heads are?'

Tamasin jerked her head up and resettled her sunglasses, blinking in the dazzle. Far to the west she could see the ugly heads of the big thunderclouds rearing. It had been thundery for days over that border region. She didn't like thunderheads. No sane pilot did.

0603.

Voice came off Guard. 'Defenders of the Revolution Tabriz Three, unidentified aircraft, track two seven five, speed three zero five knots, identify yourself, identify yourself.'

*　　*　　*

Skin prickling, Tamasin turned to Rob. Lonely as they were in that dazzle of sun, they were in full radar view. 'Keep ahead at this altitude until you're forced to do otherwise.' The thought of getting into that cloud terrified her.

'What's Defenders of the Revolution?'

'Allah only knows.'

Thoughtfully Rob reached down to the radar; it was in weather mode. He reset the range to fifty nautical miles and checked what traffic he could see.

Nothing, not a single airliner. They really had closed this airspace. This was an air force killing zone. Defenders of what bloody revolution, anyway? Closed airspace, diversions in place. There really was something going on.

'Tabriz Three, unidentified aircraft.' The controller's voice on Guard was impatient.

Rob looked left to where Azra was crouching in the doorway. 'Tabriz Three – do you know anything about that?'

'It's Moussa's base.'

Rob groaned. 'Just what we needed.'

The controller came back, definitely annoyed now. 'Tabriz Three, unidentified aircraft, track two seven five, speed three zero five knots, you are ordered to land immediately at Tabriz. Intruder aircraft, confirm you copy.'

On the other hand, it might be fun to test skills once more against Moussa Rezania.

'How far to the border?'

Tamasin had gone pale again. 'Ah . . . 276 . . . 275

315

nautical miles. Bloody hell, that headwind component's growing!' She ran the calculations. 'About 35 knots. TAS must be . . .' she checked. 'I make it 360.' So they were making a groundspeed of 325 knots: each minute they were covering not quite five and a half nautical miles. *Would it be enough?*

0606.

Mentally Rob was back in that Vulcan. He didn't know how precise Tamasin's position fix was; this was the first time he'd flown with her and he was supposed to have been doing the navigating . . . They hadn't had GPS that night in the Vulcan. They'd actually taken cross-references off Aldebaran and Betelgeuse; it had been a damn good night for stars.

Moussa Rezania would undoubtedly scramble fighters. Quite likely including his own. Well, then we'd see.

'You still want us up here, Tamasin?'

'Let's use the height while we can.'

She frowned at the chart, studying the spot heights, studying what little contour information she had. She was still weak, still feeling ill, but she knew now she could conquer the physical handicaps. A plan was forming in her mind and she didn't like it; she remembered how terrifying the flight with Darvish had been. She didn't want to get down in the weeds again.

But she'd made military-flying decisions before.

'Looking good for position,' she told Rob. 'GPS and INS confirm the radio readings.' The last check she'd done, she'd actually had five satellites in line of sight from the aircraft. How many satellites would she get when she was down in that cloud? Shouldn't make any difference, but her instincts rebelled.

'Roger.'

Tamasin reached a hand out to Azra. Azra gulped oxygen, then pulled off the headset and gave it back. Tamasin pulled it over her ears and put the mask to her face. 'Rob, I'll have to leave you listening to Guard – I may need this one for nav.'

'Rog.'

The air at FL 200 was smooth the way it seldom was on the airways, with other traffic constantly churning up the atmosphere.

Tamasin remembered about those F14s – their first-class radar. It was bad enough when you had radars down on the ground hunting you.

*　　*　　*

Tamasin said deliberately: 'Rob, I want you to stand by for a descent.'

That was her captain's voice. It was good to hear it but she was talking seriously risky flying now. Everywhere ahead of them the cloud hid the high ground.

But it was as bad staying up here, exposed to radar.

'Right now?' He had his right hand resting on the yoke and the autopilot switched off.

'Wait till I say.' Tamasin studied her charts, timing the distances. Ground speed, 325 knots now with the throttles on this setting.

Rapide had been 212 nautical miles short of the border when Tabriz Three had given its final warning. Already it was closer but it had a long way to go yet.

Going down through the cloud would mean some very precise positioning.

'Keep holding this height,' Tamasin told Rob. 'When we go for the descent, I want it steep, with a low forward speed. I'll tell you when.'

'Rog.'

Tamasin took the GPS readout again.

Rob kept listening on the other headset. That last challenge from Tabriz had used English and he was pretty sure any call from the fighters would use English, too.

Voice on the Guard frequency, a crisp rattle of Farsi.

'Azra, what are they saying?'

Azra clamped the headset to her ears, straining to follow the jargon. 'They're saying . . . Warrior One, entering . . .

317

Delta Five North. Warrior Two . . . that's him, responding. Is Warrior One the leader? What's Delta Five North?'

'Some zone on their charts. We've got no way of knowing where.' All this was taking so long.

'Damn,' Tamasin muttered, and reached to the instrument panel. 'Can't get that VOR at Tabriz. Maybe it's been taken out.'

Felix was watching that spectrum analyser like a cat at a mousehole, constantly worrying in case the mouse came out somewhere else. She gave a gasp. 'Now there's another radar! It's . . . it must be another fighter.' Anxiously she scanned Jerry's list. 'Oh God, it is, it's an F14!'

Tamasin said, scared: 'What do they carry?'

'Built to carry the Phoenix missile,' Rob said. 'But I can't see them using something that's got a kill range of 120 nautical miles. We must be well inside that now. They'll more likely be using Sparrows for radar and Sidewinders for close-in infra-red stuff.'

'We don't know that they're actually carrying Phoenix,' Tamasin said, fighting nerves. 'We don't know whether the things are serviceable even if they are carrying them.'

They'd covered two more minutes at the 325-knot groundspeed They still had 201 nautical miles to the Turkish border.

'Felix,' Rob said on the intercom, 'can you do us any range and bearing info?'

'Er . . . oh God, how d'you work this thing? Looks like, ah . . . forty miles' range, at, umm . . . zero eight? Does that sound right?'

'Well done, Felix,' Rob said. But he wasn't sure how far he could trust her readings.

Tamasin reached with her right hand to the radar but it was already on max forward sweep. Azra crouched wide-eyed in the cockpit doorway, breathing in long gulps, gradually starting to go dizzy. Far at the edge of the radar scope Tamasin picked out the two traces. Rob saw them, too. Fear shot through him as he saw the speed at which they were closing. Then a voice came through on Guard.

It was cultured, with excellent English that had implacable hardness in it. 'Unidentified aircraft, this is Warrior One of the Defenders of the Revolution. Stand by to await fighter intercept on your present course and altitude. You will be escorted to land at a military air base. If you attempt to resist your escort you will be destroyed.'

*   *   *

Slicing through the frozen air, *Falcon Fang* still had the ground radar looking for it everywhere except where it was. Chris Norton had the yoke. Walter Becker had the charts and he was fretting over them.

'Wind on the tail . . . can't see *Rapide* on that lousy radar . . . we *must* be coming up to the crossover point. Eighteen minutes I make it.'

Norton had his headset tuned to Guard. He heard: *You will be escorted to land at a military air base. If you attempt to resist your escort you will be destroyed.* He swapped a sharp look with Walter.

'Must be Gandalf,' Walter said, 'there's nothing else flying apart from military.'

None of them was quite sure why they'd turned to Ron's copy of *The Lord of the Rings* for their codenames. Still tuned to Guard, Walter keyed the mike.

'Tamzie, Tamzie – how do you read, *Rapide*?'

A moment's pause. Silence on the airwaves.

Walter keyed the mike again, tension in the grin on his chunky face. 'Tamzie, this is Wild Weasel Support on call-sign Frodo. Be advised you are going to make it!'

CHAPTER 48

Overhead north-west Iran, Saturday, 27 June, 0612 Iran, 0442 Turkey

Across *Dragon Rapide*'s cockpit Tamasin's eyes met Rob's. In hers there was plain disbelief. Rob grinned.

'Well, I hardly think it's worth keeping things a secret any longer.'

'Roger that.' Tamasin switched her mike from intercom to transmit. 'Hi, Frodo, good to hear you! This is *Rapide* and I'm afraid we have a little bother on our hands here. Carry on with the wild weasel – we may have to do a spot of bobbing and weaving.' The colour was actually starting to return to Tamasin's cheeks.

'Frodo, roger.'

She released the button, and looked across the cockpit with the grin spreading across her face. Azra looked up wonderingly but Rob was watching Tamasin with some concern.

'Er . . . don't you think it's time to get some of this height off?'

And risk the peaks.

'Dead right,' Tamasin said. 'Let me count you down.' She bent back over the chart, flicked a look at her watch, and a look at the dashboard clock. 'OK, Rob, it's eight seconds, then I want you to give me a steep descent. Seven seconds. Set forward speed 220 knots, descent rate 7,000. Six seconds. Azra, you might want to get back and strap in. Five . . .'

Azra knew what she meant. She ignored Tamasin.

'Four . . . three . . .'

Rob reached left and grasped the throttle levers.

'Two . . . one . . . *now*!'

Throttles back, they plunged into the white fog of cloud. *Rapide* kicked about as it sank.

Rob said: 'What's our MSA?'

'Sixteen five,' Tamasin said.

Felix said, 'Umm . . . this radar still seems to be getting us. D'you think I should have a go with some more chaff?'

'Yeah, go for it, Felix!' Rob said. He was amazed at her, a respectable middle-aged lady, dicing with an F14 and she didn't turn an iron-grey hair.

Studiously Felix adjusted the chaff cutter. She keyed the trigger. More bundles of aluminized foil sprang out into the slipstream.

Walter's wild weasel had put the ground radar out of action already, Rob realized; now Felix had blinded the airborne radar.

In the murk, *Rapide* dropped sickeningly and Rob had to fight to get the wing level.

Moussa Rezania's voice came again, angry. 'Intruder aircraft, your actions are leaving me very little alternative but to destroy you.'

He could do it, too, Rob thought, but only if he followed them down through this cloud. He would need to get inside range for his infra-red missiles – assuming Felix wasn't too quick for them with the flares – and he still had the gun. For the gun, though, he would definitely have to be visual.

Azra said grimly: 'How do I transmit?'

*   *   *

The mike switches were on the yokes. 'Talk to him, then,' Tamasin said, not knowing what was going to happen, and pressed the tiny button.

Into the mike Azra said: 'Moussa! This is your cousin Azra and I'm aboard the plane you're chasing. All we want to do is to leave Iran. We're unarmed and we mean you no harm – let us through.'

Turbulence forced the nose up and now, despite all Rob's efforts, the airspeed was tailing off dangerously. He couldn't get the height off.

'Azra!' Rage strained through Moussa's voice; this wasn't what they'd expected. 'You were sent by Satan but now God has delivered you into my hands for due punishment.'

It had the mercilessness and the certain rectitude of an Old Testament prophet's denunciation, Rob thought, and now *Rapide* suddenly sank like a stone.

'What do you mean, Moussa?' Azra's knuckles were white. She hadn't thought it would be like this.

'You were the one who forced our hand! You were the one who betrayed the Way of Faith and the Defenders of the Revolution!'

Tamasin said, 'Bring that heading back to the right, Rob, we need two six five.'

'Rog.'

Easier said than done as they sank deeper amid real danger. Already the altimeter was unwinding past 16,500 feet, MSA.

In scared protest, Azra said: 'But I had nothing to do with the Way of Faith!' Maybe that was the trouble.

The aircraft jolted so hard Rob thought they'd hit ground. The wing swayed almost vertical before he could catch it.

'You deceived us into believing you were faithful,' Moussa radioed, 'then you ran to the servants of Satan with all your knowledge of us. Now you must die!'

Dimly, Rob realized that the man in the fighter behind them was a leader in a revolution that was petering out. A desperate position to be in.

'No-one's betrayed you but yourselves,' Azra said. She sounded amazingly calm about it as the wing rocked around and the jet dropped sickeningly and the nose fought up and away from the heading. Rob didn't feel calm. He had better things to do than die. Azra said, 'You have no right to impose your ideas upon other people.'

322

Rob rammed the nose back on to 265 degrees. Azra's arguments were more like those of the Anglican Church than those of a mullah with a bee in his bonnet; and it was no good expecting Moussa to understand any of that.

Moussa's voice came through, metallic, harsh. 'Those who oppose our ideas are *taghouti* and must die.' Suddenly he was shouting. '*Taghouti!*' the voice came in the headsets. '*Taghouti!*'

Braced on one knee in the doorway, Azra pulled off the headset, her face grim, bright-eyed. 'He's calling us followers of Satan. That must mean he's going to attack.'

*   *   *

'Seven thousand for the cutoff,' Tamasin said. They were going through 12,000 feet. 'If we clear 7,000 and we're still in cloud, we'll have to break off and just keep going with the chaff and flares.'

'Rog.' But even 7,000 gave them a scant 400 feet clearance over the top of the table land.

Tamasin was an expert navigator but Rob had never done anything this risky, even on Vulcans. It's very difficult to break a 125. But fly it into a mountainside and it'll break all right. A flood of rising air caught them by the nose and Rob forced it back on to his heading but he couldn't get the height off and now the speed was tailing down again.

Ten thousand feet. The peaks were all around them. Rob fought to nail his correct forward speed.

More voice came on Guard but the words were in Farsi.

Nine thousand feet. Cloud barged *Rapide* around so hard Rob thought again for an instant that it was ground impact. He pulled the nose back round.

'Tamasin . . .' Despite himself, he heard his voice cracking. 'When d'you want me to break off this descent?'

'Not until we absolutely have to.'

Rob glanced at her and saw her casually take off her shades and park them on top of the coaming, then blink out into the murk. *Tamasin Masterson, I don't believe this. You don't exist.* Fear was rising, his breath quivering, his heart racing. Inside the next two minutes they were going to smash themselves apart against a mountainside, Rob just *knew* it. And now the captain was a crazy little lady with her cheeks pale and her face battered who was taking them into the Valley of Death and not batting an eyelid.

'We're clear, Rob,' she said almost nannyingly. 'We've got miles of clearance laterally from that 15,800 spot height, and the next one.'

Yet even as she said it she felt the nausea start to surge in her gut, she felt the pain pulse spearing through her head again. She needed all her faculties for this game, why couldn't she have them back?

0618.

Felix said: 'I've got . . . would this be search pulses? On a different frequency? And still the same two F14s?'

'Could be.' Rob tried to keep his voice steady. 'If they get close enough to us, they can burn through the chaff.'

Tamasin forced her hand steady as she studied the chart. So little room here in a 125 with that big yoke in the way. That last GPS readout had shown them flying into a north-westerly wind and it was pushing them south and that put them . . .

Dead on track for that 9,320 foot spot height.

'Rob, stand by . . . turn right, heading two nine four mag. Turn *now*!'

He'd been watching the radar altimeter and now suddenly he saw the way the height readings were coming down, *racing* down. 'Two nine four mag.' Blinking sweat out of his eyes, he rolled the jet steeply into the turn.

They broke cloudbase.

*　　*　　*

In shock, Rob saw the grey hardness of the mountainside, 250 feet out to the left at most. Tamasin had told him the exact right heading at the exact right time.

'OK, Tam, going visual now!' Impressed was an understatement for the way he felt.

'Roger, you have it!'

He eased the jet away from the peril of the mountainside, conscious suddenly of the sheer speed the rock was slicing past his windscreen.

It dawned on Tamasin that she was suffering from vertigo. The jet felt level to her; what she saw was the dark, rocky horizon, all tilted down to the left.

On Felix's scope the F14s' radar signals were growing stronger.

'Moussa . . . he *must* have burnt through, these signals really are awfully strong now!'

'He wants a visual on us,' Rob said.

He hoped he was right. If Moussa got close enough to identify them visually, he would be too close to fire those radar missiles. Rob rolled *Rapide* level and watched the mountainsides, all too close below. He was starting to get pretty scared himself now. Once Moussa burned through that chaff, *Rapide* was defenceless.

A ridgeline swept towards them and Rob lifted *Rapide* over it and then let them sink beyond. An updraught caught them and for a moment the aircraft wouldn't lose height. Rob remembered there could be downdraughts as well.

If Moussa actually fired, if he actually hit them, could they survive?

0623.

Back in 1987 it had actually happened. President Quett Masire of Botswana had been aboard a BAE 125 that had actually been hit by a surface-to-air missile, heat-seeking its way into one of the engines. The 125 had survived, had come down safely and under control on the remaining engine. But that hadn't been in mountain country. A gust

325

rocked the wing, the aircraft jarring in wooden jolts from the turbulence.

For an instant Rob lost vision. Rain splattered on the windscreen and streamed and Rob started to reach for the wipers but then it cleared. A valley ahead. Rob eased them down into it.

Tamasin was clutching the charts but she was starting to lose track of the navigation. Her sunglasses slid on the coaming.

'Is this what you did on Vulcans?'

They were burrowing hard down into the valley, following the ripples of the contour.

'Sort of,' Rob said absently.

Another low crest rose up and Rob aimed beyond it and the crest slashed below in a grey-green blur. The valley was still leading them lower. Yes, this *was* what he'd done in Vulcans.

The Vulcan looked and sounded frightening, coming at you, high turbine whine and a monster of a delta wing that spanned 111 feet, over twice *Rapide*'s 47 feet. It had been designed for high-altitude bombing, not for flying down in the weeds like this. *Rapide* hadn't been designed for this sort of flying, either. Size came into it, though. *Rapide* was pretty responsive, down here.

The terrain flattened out and Rob flattened out with it, with the radar altimeter showing 190 feet. Yellow-brown landscape flowed away around them and Rob brought the heading back to due west.

'Felix, what's happened to Moussa?'

A pause.

'Looks as if they've lost us.' She sounded puzzled. She was praying that the reason she couldn't see them wasn't her own incompetence as an EWO.

'Both of them?'

'So it seems,' Felix said with wonder in her voice. 'They must . . . d'you think they might have had *orders* to break off?'

Tamasin got a creepy feeling. Something was wrong about this.

*   *   *

Fang speared through the frozen upper air with the contrail dazzling behind it.

Aft, Harper frowned at his spectrum analyser screen, working out what was going on. He got it. He'd been working out which way the Iranians were playing this and the answer was: doing it from the base in a ground-controlled intercept and saving the fighters' radar for the latter stages. Simple spot jamming wouldn't do: the radar down there on the ground was frequency-agile and would be hopping between channels to keep *Rapide* in radar view faster than Harper could retune. He could try swept spot noise, running sequentially through all the possible channels, or he could try barrage noise. Maybe it was time for the barrage. He keyed the command.

Energy lashed down on the ground station on all the channels it had. In their darkened room, the controllers saw their colour radar scopes turn to a mass of orange as the jammer swamped the returns from the other aircraft.

Harper wasn't relaxed enough to grin to himself yet. He didn't know what tricks the ground station had up its sleeve.

Walter checked the nav. Norton pulled back the throttles and held the nose steady on the horizon and the speed came back through 300 knots, slowing.

'Bet we've upset them now,' Norton said.

He had them flying towards Tabriz on the 260 degrees radial signal from Urmia VOR. They crossed the radio beacon.

The Oberleutnant craned over the nose a moment. If they came in sight of *Rapide* at this speed all they'd see would be a fleeting flash.

'Don't like getting too far into here in an unarmed

plane,' Walter muttered, betraying a trace of *angst*. 'Chris, what the hell's happening on that radio?'

'Not entirely sure.' Norton was frowning. He was getting voice off Guard, some of it in Farsi, some in English, but he wasn't making much sense of any of it.

'Tamzie. Come in, Tamzie.'

But other voices on the frequency kept cutting across him, jamming his transmission.

'Tamzie. Come in, Tamzie.' Same result.

The cloud swept forever and there wasn't another aircraft in sight. Norton had the autopilot doing the work but he kept a palm placed lightly on *Fang*'s control yoke.

A smooth voice with urgency in it came on the frequency. 'Frodo, this is Samwise. Frodo from Samwise.'

Norton said: 'Go ahead, Samwise.'

Mahmut Barka aboard the E3, invisible and miles away, said: 'Gandalf's gone into what looks like a missile box, and we think it's under rebel control. We're showing missile guidance radar up and tracking them now.'

CHAPTER 49

Overhead north-west Iran, Saturday, 27 June, 0626 Iran, 0456 Turkey

Something was definitely wrong if Moussa and his wingman had broken off at the very moment when they'd burnt through the chaff and locked on. Hairs at the back of Tamasin's neck were rising.

Walter Becker came through on Guard, accent thick in his alarm. 'Tamzie, this is Frodo – be advised you're in a SAM missile box! Get out of it any way you can, but fast!'

*   *   *

Under the ragged grey cloudbase, Rob could see the detailed features of the landscape – even cattle on some scruffy pasture.

Shrill with alarm, Felix cried out, 'Missiles! Oh God, now what do I do?'

'Chaff if you can,' Rob said crisply. 'Same as the others.'

Terror drained the strength out of Tamasin but Azra hadn't fully grasped it yet. When it happened, it happened so fast no-one had time to do anything.

In Felix's headset the steady beeping went to very rapid beeping. There were vertical lines all over the scope and the captions were changing too fast to follow but she'd started to get the hang of reading the scope and with her fingers beginning to shake she turned the chaff cutter. The missiles had launched.

In shock, Rob saw the blaze of the boosters, far out to the right. Three, no, four. *He'd never had live missiles fired at him.*

Felix started punching out chaff, simply hoping.

Rob rolled right and kicked off the height, slipping *Rapide* down towards the farmland. Tamasin reached up behind her and squeezed Buster: *bring me luck*. Terror got through to Azra as she realized what was happening.

One missile lost lock. Then the ground guidance radar burnt through Felix's chaff. The three other missiles headed straight for the jet.

* * *

Frozen air lay untroubled at 25,000 feet but in *Falcon Fang*'s cockpit Walter Becker and Chris Norton were tense, Walter still listening-out on the Guard channel. Norton was minding the flying. He'd tried looking for traces on the weather radar but it looked ahead, not down.

It was Ron Harper, back in the cabin, who was doing the real work here and he cut across, tension in his voice on the intercom.

'They've launched missiles! Confirm SAM launch!'

Silence. Walter watched out left. Norton held *Fang* straight and level, glancing at the instrument panel when not gazing out into the burning sky, and both pilots could picture Harper, desperately working to find out what sort of missile this was, how it was being guided.

'Yeah?' Walter prompted.

'Guidelines,' Harper said. 'Old SA2 Guidelines, four. They're chaffing, they're . . . there goes one, gone ballistic.'

The old SA2 Guideline was still a potent means of knocking aircraft out of the sky. NATO's codename for its fire control radar was Fan Song, a system that guided the missiles by means of a UHF link. The trouble was, Harper remembered, Fan Song could operate in the A/B or the D/E bands and his job now was to find out which band this one was using.

Unless he found out fast, *Rapide*'s life could be measured in seconds.

He found it. D/E band, 1–3 gigahertz. Instantly he retuned and gave the fire control all the power he'd got in spot noise.

'Walter, can we get them manoeuvring?'

If they weren't manoeuvring already, Walter thought, something was wrong. 'Tamzie, this is Frodo – we're jamming the guidance. Can we have some manoeuvring, please?'

He watched the compass. Pretty soon *Rapide* would be west of him. If it stayed in one piece.

A man's voice came over Guard: 'Roger, Frodo, am doing.' Rob Pilgrim, Walter realized.

The biggest thing *Fang* was missing was any radar picture of what was happening; all it was picking up was a few storm cells.

Walter radioed: 'Samwise, this is Frodo. Any activity?'

*   *   *

Little lumpy jolts made the NATO E3's ride faintly uneven as it cruised straight and level at 30,000 feet and kept carefully inside Turkish airspace. The four-ship F16 escort kept position, close off the port wingtip.

'Stand by, Frodo,' Mahmut Barka said into the mike.

Kemal Koz was craning over his shoulder and the Canadian surveillance operator was alert, constantly fine-tuning the brightness as the scanner swept round. Koz couldn't entirely make out what was happening. Mahmut could, and to judge by the young colonel's shallow breath he was almost petrified.

Mahmut thumbed the mike. He avoided looking over his shoulder at Koz. 'Samwise, Frodo. It's right on the edge of the scan and there's a lot of ground clutter, but . . . Gandalf is manoeuvring. Missiles tracking . . . ah, one SAM lost! One gone!'

'Rog,' Walter said in Mahmut's headphones.

331

Koz stifled a burp. He could taste coffee, standard NATO. He preferred Turkish. His eyes felt hot and he could sense the drama that was being played out on the big round screen with the thin orange triangle sweeping round and round.

'Two missiles, three missiles! Three gone!' Mahmut couldn't keep the excitement out of his voice.

'Shit,' the Canadian muttered, impressed, 'that's the Fan Song gone down. Someone zapped the guidance.'

'Four!' Mahmut radioed. 'All four lost guidance!'

Relief washed over them. Koz shared it.

'And what do I take it is the significance of "Gandalf"?' Koz said with heavy irony.

A shadow of a grin flitted across Mahmut's lips as he pulled the mike boom down. 'As if you couldn't guess – sir.'

'The English executive jet,' Koz rumbled. '*Tamam*.' He made his eyes round and piggy; you couldn't have told the calibre of brain behind them. 'What are we doing and what is the English jet doing?'

Mahmut threw him a critical look. He spelt it out. 'We're acting as a flying observation platform, using radar as our "eye". *Gandalf* is, as you say, the English jet – *Frodo* is a wild weasel.'

'*Tamam*.' Koz knew what that meant.

It was just what he needed. If that jet failed to get out, the resulting inquiry would undoubtedly trace back the events that had led to the jet's being hijacked in the first place. What Koz was looking at was his chance of getting out of this mess unscathed.

Soberly Mahmut pointed to the Canadian's display. 'You see these traces, Mr Koz? It's two of the rebels' fighters.'

'What are they doing?' Koz asked edgily.

Walter came through on Guard before Mahmut could reply. Mahmut pushed the mike back to his lips, listening to Walter. 'Samwise, any idea of Gandalf's position right now?'

Mahmut turned to the scope. 'East of Lake Urmia, coming up on the lake now. Possibly on a radial for the Urmia VOR.' He heard *roger* in his headphones, but he was frowning now, studying the display. He covered the mike. 'What those rebel fighters are doing,' he said, 'is going after *Dragon Rapide* – they're the ones that broke off when they came to the missile box. If those are F14s, which we think they are, their radar can get them if the intercept officers are up to the job.'

*   *   *

Above cloud, Walter swapped glances with Norton.

'Well, where are we in relation to Lake Urmia?' Norton said.

Walter dithered uncharacteristically, peering at his charts. It was 0503 Turkish time, 0633 in Iran.

'Listen, we *must* have crossed over *Rapide*,' Norton said urgently. 'They *must* be west of us now!'

Jerkily Walter nodded. 'OK – time to go.'

Norton rolled into the turn. He watched the vertical indicator on the VOR receiver slide slowly out to the middle of the dial and then stabilize. They were on the 100 degrees radial for Urmia VOR. Norton nudged the nose slightly to the right, into the north-westerly airstream.

A black speck showed on the horizon. A split instant later it materialized into a loyalist MiG 29 Fulcrum, rolling smoothly on to a wingtip to haul hard round towards Walter's six o'clock.

*   *   *

If the two Turks were crowding the Canadian, he gave no sign of it. Mahmut still had the headset, Koz was craning over Mahmut's shoulder again.

'And the fighters are . . . ?'

'To the right on the scope.'

All three traces seemed to be about the same size. They

were crawling very slowly from the righthand perimeter towards the centre of the scope.

Koz said: 'What are the fighters doing now?'

'Closing in on *Rapide*.'

*   *   *

Walter rasped: '*I have control!*'

He shot the charts and clipboard at Norton and cracked the throttles open as he stood *Fang* on a wingtip. Engine power alone kept the line true in the savage turn; with the aerofoil perpendicular to the flight path, the wing wasn't producing any lift whatever. Walter whistled softly through his teeth, cranked his neck and looked out through the top of the cockpit.

'Where is he?' Norton called tensely. His view was blocked by the canopy.

'Eightish,' Walter said, unperturbed.

'Well, for God's sake . . .'

'It's OK, I know what he's doing. I used to do the same thing myself with Fulcrums.'

'Walter . . .'

Walter rolled *Fang* level, trimmed nose-high, and watched the altitude start to slip off. The Iranian pilot levelled out, squarely in the six o'clock and a thousand feet higher.

Close to panic, Norton yelled, 'Jesus Christ, break, break! Hold on this path and he'll . . .'

The Fulcrum was overtaking the Falcon quickly, but the Iranian pilot was wise to that one. The MiG 29's speciality was the pendulum manoeuvre that swung the fighter's nose sharply down, and the Iranian played that card now.

CHAPTER 50

Overhead north-west Iran, Saturday, 27 June, 0634 Iran, 0504 Turkey

For a brief moment Moussa Rezania had lost trace of the executive jet. Reza in the back was adjusting his radar to regain contact. It had shaken both of them to see the way the hostile came through the missile box.

'Warrior, Eagle's Nest.' The controller at Tabriz Three.

'Go ahead, Eagle's Nest.'

'Single bogey approaching from the east, Mach 1.2. In your wide six, height ten thousand, range one two zero, closing.' That meant 10,000 metres at 120 kilometres.

It was pretty obvious what that was; a loyalist fighter. And they didn't need two F14s, with all those missiles, to go after a single exec jet.

'Warrior One, roger,' Moussa said. 'Ah, Warrior Two, defensive standoff.'

'Copy,' Ali said. He peeled off steeply on the port wingtip and started climbing hard.

* * *

Storm cells flashed up, distant on the edge of *Dragon Rapide*'s radar screen. They began to creep closer as the aircraft streaked towards the west.

Tamasin said: 'Two minutes to Lake Urmia.'

Crouched in the cockpit doorway, Azra was subdued. They all were. There'd been a point when none of them had expected to survive the SAM attack.

Rob caught the distant gleam on the water, sun filtering through the cloud. He could see the dark wall of mountain rising up beyond to block their path, the summits mist-shrouded. *Rapide* was getting a lot of bouncing and jolting, down here 200 feet above ground.

Sharply Felix said: 'There's radar again! It's that F14, I'm sure of it!'

'One aircraft or two?' Rob snapped.

Felix dithered. 'I can't tell.'

0546.

Tamasin faltered: 'Rob . . .' Scared half out of her wits with what she'd got them into, she hadn't time to wonder what the other F14 might be up to.

'Must be guns range by now,' Rob said casually. 'He won't shoot, he's got to catch us first.' He eased back the throttles and bent steeply left with the yoke pressed back to hold his height.

A guns kill held the mystique of the primitive, Tamasin realized vividly, the nakedness of close-quarters combat. She remembered the old fighter-pilot adage: *there's no kill like a guns kill*. Rob hauled up, crested a rise, and rolled hard right beyond.

Terrain dropped away below them into a sheer-sided valley winding and dropping towards the lake. Azra was having a job to hang on.

'Umm . . . I think the F14 seems to have lost radar lock,' Felix said, excited despite her uncertainty.

Manoeuvring had done that, Rob reflected, and then as he started to let *Rapide* drop down towards the valley floor something had gone terrifyingly wrong because it didn't drop down, it plunged bodily, nose high and falling fast. Rob rammed the throttles fully open and hauled hard back on the yoke. They were sinking, airspeed teetering down towards the stall, and Rob couldn't understand it but he knew they were in trouble. Hail burst around the aircraft, crashing on the cabin roof, bouncing off the windscreen and then an instant later with the same suddenness *Rapide* was ballooning upwards. Rob pushed forward, grabbed the throttles back, grabbed for the trim. He was breathing quickly. They flew clear of the hail.

'What the hell was that?' Tamasin sounded shocked.

Rob realized. 'Microburst. Just what you need at this height.'

Microbursts happen in thundery cloud conditions. Thunderclouds hold ferocious up and down draughts and when the downdraught happens close to the ground it punches vertically down and spreads out as it hits the terrain. The resulting 'microburst' can be powerful enough to smash an airliner into the ground if it's low down at slow speed approaching an airport.

He settled the speed back at 220 knots and concentrated on the contour lines. His mouth was dry again.

* * *

Tamasin had faced death before, on that B52 mission. What she'd found was that, having once accepted death as a risk, she could more easily relax her mind's hold on life. Now Azra, clinging doggedly in the cockpit doorway, was showing the same courage.

The contours were dropping gradually towards the lake. Rob let *Rapide* drop with them with the radar altimeter flickering between 230 feet and 190 feet. If they ran into another microburst . . .

Glancing at Rob, Tamasin realized she was impressed. High speed and low level scared the wits out of her, she was feeling ill again, but Rob was hand-flying the jet as if he'd done nothing else but this all his flying career.

'Tamasin,' Felix said, addressing the captain, 'do you think we want chaff or flares yet?' Toys like these could be fun to play with.

'Wait!' Rob replied, and ducked the nose left then right as the valley snaked away below him. They'd used a lot of chaff so far, and they needed to conserve supplies.

The valley was broadening, flattening out, and Rob could see the lake, ahead to the right. They had the sun behind them, above cloud, and under the overcast the vis was better than Rob had expected, clear for a mile or more except in the rain squalls. They ran into one now as Rob rolled on to the starboard tip to bring them out heading for the lake and, for a fraction, all vision went. Turbulence rocked *Rapide* and they flew out over the lake. 0635. Rob ducked his head and peered up through the cockpit side window. Nothing. He rolled level – over the lake and heading north now – and glimpsed it: the F14, lunging down the valley with its wings swept forward to cope with the low speed.

They were dealing with a man who was prepared to kill you just for disagreeing with him.

'Bloody hell,' he thought aloud, 'he's almost too close for his Sidewinders!'

He rolled out and let the height slip off to show 100 feet on the radar altimeter. There were islands in the lake, ugly chunks of rock and foliage jutting up from the still, steely water. Felix could see that no ground radars were getting them down here, only that single AWG9 off the F14. If they went down in the lake they would never be found.

Time for a little manoeuvring. Rob put the throttles up a touch. He pressed back the yoke and then rolled left, ruddering hard into a turn perilously low over the shining surface of the lake. One second . . . two seconds . . .

Shockingly, Moussa's voice came over Guard. '*Taghouti! Taghouti!*'

Three seconds. Roll level, resume count. One second . . .

'He's going to die anyway when he gets back down,' Azra said, her bottom lip trembling. This man had terrified her but now her tears were for him.

. . . and three. Rob racked *Rapide* back into a vicious turn starboard with the lake surface racing past its nose.

Felix felt the g-force shoving her out towards the gangway, dragging on her headset so she thought it would come down around her ears. She ducked her shoulders and craned at the window on her right. She had one brief glimpse of the F14, rolling right to hold the six o'clock position, then the *g*-force shoved her against the window as Rob rolled hard back to port.

The spectrum analyser showed the fighter's radar locking them in, yet, Felix realized slowly, Moussa was too close for his radar missiles. Not for guns, though. Felix was deeply afraid; yet, she discovered, it exhilarated her.

The steep port bank put Tamasin's window closest to where Moussa was hauling the F14 into the turn across their path. She forced herself against the *g*-force, her vision clearing and receding in waves, her head pounding.

'Felix.' Her voice was strained. 'Stand by with those flares!'

They hadn't tested their infra-red flare launcher, Felix remembered; but they hadn't tested the chaff dispenser, either.

'Will do.'

The F14 had its wings swept and now under the belly a flame blazed, bright orange. Tamasin yelled in the intercom mike: 'Missile launch! Second missile!'

Felix hit the launcher. '*Flares away!*'

Azra's knuckles were white as she clung on with the jet tilting and pitching under her. Dying was a distant idea; yet she wasn't going to die, she sensed it.

0636.

Felix was craning and bobbing, trying to see whether her flares had distracted the Sidewinders. If she hadn't turned them away, this crew had fractions of a second left to live.

Something caught the lower rear fuselage quarter with a huge *thump* and the tail kicked up hard.

*　　*　　*

As the E3 orbited just west of the border, the high definition on its scope gave a clear reading for the shoreline of Lake Urmia. Even Kemal Koz could see it. He could see why everyone was holding their breath.

'What's happening?' His voice was a whisper above the grinding steady jet noise.

Mahmut Barka wasn't sure.

The Canadian surveillance operator said, deadpan: 'We have one missile going way astray.' He indicated a tiny trace, gone off the lake shore now and heading west for the mountains, unguided. 'Looks like one missile detonated. But we still have our customer' – he glanced up suspiciously at Mahmut – 'Gandalf? – clearly flying.'

Koz said incredulously: 'It took a *missile hit*?'

With his lips drawn thin in his tension, Mahmut said: 'A single Sidewinder, an aircraft like that BAe 125 could probably keep flying. They won't be getting a comfortable ride, but . . .' He jabbed a finger at the screen. 'There's the real worry, that F14. It's still after Gandalf.'

CHAPTER 51

Overhead north-west Iran, Saturday, 27 June, 0636 Iran, 0506 Turkey

The pendulum manoeuvre flown by the MiG 29 is potential death to any airman ahead of and below the fighter.

Under faultless control, the Iranian Fulcrum reared up its nose and slowed sharply in mid-air.

Walter Becker yanked *Fang* level out of the rolling turn. Chris Norton didn't understand why but he used the opportunity to grab the clipboard with the chart on.

The MiG was coming smoothly to a halt in mid-air, above and behind *Falcon Fang*. Walter knew this one, though, it was the manoeuvre he'd flown time and again in practice with Czech and Hungarian and Russian stablemates. Walter hauled *Fang*'s yoke squarely back into his stomach, his right hand down to the twin throttle levers as the nose lunged up and blocked the cloudscape of high altitude.

Norton was craning around, trying for a sight outside.

The Iranian Fulcrum nosed slowly over, still under total control. Walter had *Fang* standing on its tail and now he cracked the power levers right to the stops. The two mini-turbofans howled but the jet was moving upwards . . .

. . . as the Fulcrum plunged.

Norton muttered something incoherent.

Walter had *Fang* climbing steeply and now the whole sky went dark as the Fulcrum slashed across their vision and then Walter had the height and the Fulcrum was below and ahead. With an executive jet under his hands, not a fighter, there was only one way to play it.

Walter half-rolled inverted and dragged the yoke back

to get the *g*-force acting towards where the top of the aircraft usually was. The amount of negative *g* in a pendulum would have had *Fang* reduced rapidly to a kit of parts in mid-air. Half-rolling erect, Walter could see the Fulcrum wrenching out of its dive and he had the height of it, he had it for position and his jet was unarmed but that didn't matter. No fighter pilot will tolerate so much as a moulting magpie in his six o'clock and this Iranian was no exception. The moves so far looked like the start of a scissors in the vertical plane.

'F14 two o'clock low!' Norton yelled.

They weren't to know it, but it was Ali's aircraft, sent to hold the Fulcrum off while Moussa killed *Dragon Rapide*.

Walter hadn't bargained for that. *Fang* was plunging suddenly steeply but the Fulcrum was break-turning left, the natural direction, in a blaze of reheat that looked like nerves.

'Where's the other one?' Walter growled. He'd done what no fighter pilot could resist doing, he'd swung left, hanging on to the Fulcrum's six.

'Only one. Coming in pretty fast – confirm only one!'

'Padlock the bastard, then.' *Don't let him out of your sight.*

Distant against the cloudscape, Norton saw the F14 as a dart-like shape rolling in towards both other aircraft as the Fulcrum pilot cut his afterburner while he still had some fuel left, and rolled right steeply, back towards Walter.

Walter's idea had been to give the Fulcrum driver a fright, then bolt for home. The F14 added an inconvenient new dimension. Then Walter spotted something else.

'*Scheisse!* That's the wingman – the lead fighter's gone after Gandalf, this one's just up here to keep the Fulcrum off the leader's back.' He hard-turned right. It meant breaking out of the scissors, but he thought he knew the next few moves.

A Sidewinder leaped from under the F14, slicing away

through the thin, cold air with its bright trail of white smoke.

'Silly sod,' Ron Harper muttered into the intercom, and fired his flares. 'He's way outside parameters.'

But for the missile, the Fulcrum pilot might not have realised about the F14 for several seconds more. The other thing the Fulcrum knew was that Walter had just presented him with a gift of a tailchase.

Walter levelled out heading north of west and then rolled into a shallow turn to pick up due west and meanwhile get back in sight of the Fulcrum.

The F14 had vanished, way higher than *Fang* and east of both other aircraft. Walter reasoned: as long as that Fulcrum was still around, it was still a threat to the other F14. This one would *have* to deal with it.

The Fulcrum pilot was greedy. He wanted to hit *Fang* first and the F14 afterwards and he closed the gap with *Fang* in another hefty wallop of afterburner. Walter broke into the attack with the silken smoothness of long practice. They were canopy to canopy, inside fifty yards apart, rolling aggressively into another scissors, lateral this time.

It wasn't looking good for Walter. The Falcon was a handy aircraft, tight, manoeuvrable with its warplane pedigree, but the Fulcrum was built 100 per cent for combat.

Walter was muttering violently as he yanked right, yanked left, yanked right again with every loose speck of dust floating in the Falcon's cabin. The Fulcrum was gaining angles on him and he hadn't thought this through to the point of what to do when he found an Alamo missile from the Fulcrum heading for his jetpipes.

Norton called: '*F14 coming back in!*'

Walter fought to look outside but the *g*-forces were too much.

'Jesus!' Harper sang out. 'F14's locked radar on the Fulcrum!' He'd read it off his spectrum analyser.

A loose headset hurtled down the middle of *Fang*'s cabin.

With the F14 in its wide six, the Fulcrum was in potential trouble and it ripped out of the scissors but not before loosing off a long burst from its 30mm GSh301 cannon – slap across Walter's path as he rolled and turned.

Walter broke right in a turn that bled his energy perilously. Too late.

Impact jarred the Falcon nose to tail as a belt of the cannon burst caught it. Big holes punched all down the port wing and something wrenched away with a cruel *graunch* of noise.

Norton said: 'Christ, what . . .'

Walter screamed: 'Keep that fucker padlocked, I said!' Suddenly *Fang* had its own ideas about where it wanted to go.

Face like parchment, Norton craned over the instrument panel. 'He's gone . . .'

Fang was wrenching, twisting and bobbing against Walter's hands on the yoke. Walter rolled roughly level and got it stabilized heading west. He flung a look back over his left shoulder.

Two foot of structure was missing off the port wingtip, including the aileron. Jet fuel was fanning and feathering out into the frozen air from the ruptured tank.

CHAPTER 52

Overhead north-west Iran, Saturday, 27 June, 0637 Iran, 0507 Turkey

Bright lake water filled Rob Pilgrim's windscreen and for a moment he didn't think he could hold the jet. Then as the airspeed tailed off towards aerodynamic stall he got the yoke back to level out and trimmed fast nose high to get them sinking back towards the big lake.

Moussa overshot with a huge thump of noise, misled by the unexpected deceleration. Rob glimpsed the F14 pulling sharply up to kill speed, wheeling left steeply to block their path to the west.

A side valley opened out to the east. It was the wrong direction but Rob rolled sharply towards it anyway.

Tamasin in a strained voice said: 'Are we hit?'

'Felt like it,' Rob said grimly, and rolled level, tearing across the lake. He wasn't sure what had happened but that impact had been heavy. Quickly he checked the engine instruments but nothing showed as faulty; the turbines were running, the interstage temperatures were normal. The elevator and rudder were answering to all control inputs.

'Oh God!' Felix wailed. 'What's this red light? It's a . . . it's the flare launcher! It's a fault light on the flare launcher!'

They crossed the lake shore and the valley walls closed round them.

Cold horror filled Tamasin as she realized with the flare launcher out they had no defence against the Sidewinders. He'd fired two, and they could carry up to four. She pulled the chart towards her as Rob steered low through the valley. There'd been a couple of houses down by

345

the lake shore but below now there wasn't even a road. Tamasin shot a look at the fuel gauges, wondering how long they could afford to fly in the wrong direction.

Turbulence bounced *Rapide* down and then up, tipping that wing, and Azra was having a job to keep braced in position, yet she knew as long as Rob was flying like this she had no chance of getting back to her seat. Rob held the wing steady as the jet punched through the grey-black spume of another squall tracking down the valley and then put more airspace under the keel. That microburst had scared him more than he cared to admit.

Felix sat there helplessly, the fault light a steady red. Green-shrouded rocks blurred past the window. 0639.

Rob started to get an uneasy feeling that time was running out.

*   *   *

In the shallow turn, *Falcon Fang* seemed to be bouncing and jolting over unevennesses in the air at altitude. Walter Becker had the yoke canted over to hold the wing where he wanted it.

'Any sign?'

Chris Norton was craning his neck out the cockpit window, hunting for the Fulcrum that had done the damage. 'Negative, Walter, the sky's empty.'

Ron Harper said: 'That F14 and the Fulcrum must be taking care of each other.'

'Check,' Walter said, and rolled *Fang* the other way. Norton adjusted his body into a different demonic contortion.

Never in his flying career had Walter had real battle damage to bring home; but he wasn't going to tell the others that.

'Not a trace,' Norton reported, 'they've both gone.'

'Time to go home, then,' Walter grunted.

Norton put his head down. He had the ME1 aviation chart on his knee. 'Steer three hundred for Van VOR.'

Walter watched the heading come round on the direction indicator as the fiercely pointed nose tracked lumpily across the horizon. He had the yoke on the tilt, as he steadied up, to keep the wing level. Against his palm he could feel the jolting, cobblestone effect as the airflow tore and flurried around the damage petals where the 30mm cannon shells had smashed through the metal skin of Felix Wyer's aeroplane.

At the corner of his eye as he held the damaged executive jet unevenly on course he could sense Norton staring at him, scared. He damped out another roll. To anyone else it would have been alarming, the lopsided way *Fang* was flying.

Sharply Norton said: 'Are we going to make it?'

'Sure we make it.'

Norton bent forward, his young face set in harsh lines. 'Walter, we've lost the whole of that tip and aileron! And look at that fuel . . . ' The fuel was fanning out thin and brown in the air. 'Screw the heroics, Walter, we'd better just get down where we can!'

The look Walter slid him left no doubts as to his obduracy. 'I spend most of my life to date in one prison camp,' he said dourly, 'you don't get me walking through a jail door at this stage.'

More shreds of metal flicked off the damaged surfaces. Lurching, bumping, *Fang* limped gamely towards the Turkish frontier.

*　　*　　*

Pulses from the AWG9 radar washed over *Dragon Rapide* and Felix saw them on the spectrum analyser, locking the executive jet in. She was trying the chaff cutter, but that seemed to be damaged, too.

'He's back in the six o'clock.'

Tamasin braced herself. This could be it, a guns attack, and this time there would be no scope for doubt about the outcome. She didn't look at Rob.

347

Even Azra knew *Rapide* was a sitting duck for the F14.

For a moment, nothing.

Tamasin said: 'He's still got two 'Winders left, hasn't he?'

'Quite likely,' Rob said.

Still nothing.

Voice trembling, Tamasin said: 'Jesus, why doesn't he shoot?' She could picture the Tomcat in her mind's eye, closing in comfortably until Moussa had *Rapide* square in the middle of his gunsight.

Breath shallow, Rob eased them round another twist of the valley, climbing more steeply now. 'If he *has* got 'Winders left, they must've hung up – he'd have fired long ago if he could have.'

Hope jumped in Tamasin's chest, then she got scared again. If this was just some shaky electrical connection, the fault might right itself. Even if it didn't, Moussa was a dangerous adversary with that gun alone.

0641.

More rain reached down, splattering on the windscreen and streaming off, and far ahead the valley ended in a steep rock wall.

Rob said: 'Tamasin, how you doing with that nav?'

'I've got us, I've got us fixed. You have control.'

'OK, hold tight, everyone!' He ducked a look down to his left to Azra; she'd heard his warning, she was hanging on grimly.

Rob thrust the power levers up to the stops and the Garretts wound up, screaming, as he pulled up the nose to block the whole horizon and ruddered left. The nose tracked round. Out of the steep lefthand climb, Rob ruddered hard the other way. And now for the interesting bit.

He chopped back the righthand throttle and banged the yoke over, up to the aileron stops. The jet was on a knife-edge and in the instant that Rob remembered Azra, with no seatbelt, Tamasin grabbed down and caught Azra's arm, a stifled cry from Felix, and the nose plunged back down and he was ruddering it level into the dive, bringing back the other throttle.

Tamasin said through her teeth: '*Jesus*, Rob!' No-one to her knowledge had ever done a Zurakowski turn in a BAe 125 before.

He wanted to be back in that side valley again because that was the direction he could see.

Tracers blazed past the cockpit.

Rob had known Moussa would shoot, he'd known the fighter pilot couldn't resist a target shown suddenly in plan view, but the sight of those tracers shook him nevertheless. *Rapide* slid down on the starboard wingtip, wing vertical and no longer making lift, and Rob let it go and brought the port tip back down and then kicked off the slide with the rudder. Azra almost lost grip. The cloud trailed tendrils and Rob punched through one and it jarred the jet. When he could see again, Moussa was coming at him, closing horrifically fast.

In that instant, Rob saw clearly that Moussa was fully prepared to turn this into a kamikaze; to destroy his own aircraft, forfeit his life, if it meant the promise of destroying *Rapide*. This was Moussa's last chance to make a success of something in this life, and he was giving it everything he had.

Rob crossed the controls, right aileron and left rudder, and sideslipped *Rapide* right, down towards the valley floor. He'd never sideslipped a jet before, it was an ancient technique from the days of tailwheel prop-powered aircraft, but it worked, it slid them down out of harm's way. Tamasin – in a mixture of admiration for Rob's flying style and terror at the F14 as it grew swelling lunging shark-like at them – saw the big bright blaze at the fighter's underside.

The tracers screamed over *Rapide*'s canopy and a moment later the F14 followed them with a bellow of tearing jet noise. It missed them by no more than three metres. *Rapide* bucked savagely in the F14's wake.

Rob had this jet by the scruff of its neck now and he wrenched them through the ruthless turbulence and got the wing level again and steered back down the valley for the west.

'He *has* still got 'Winders!' Tamasin called into the intercom. 'They must have hung up; he'd surely have used them by now instead of that gun.'

Valley walls streaked past *Rapide*'s wingtips and Rob was thinking quickly, working out what Moussa would do.

He would have to go for the same sort of reversal Rob had thrown. Probably, though, he'd need more room. In the glimpse Rob had managed to have of the F14 he'd seen its wings extended for low-speed manoeuvring; at 64 feet, extended, that took up more room but Moussa would want full afterburner to get clear of the valley walls before he reversed his turn, and that would bring his wings back automatically as the fighter accelerated straight up, but would also put him back in the cloud and blind him. *Rapide* was still in this with a chance.

Rob straightened out as the valley straightened. He eased forward on the throttles. This time they were heading west.

Hunched over the EWO console, Felix was shocked-pale as she clung on, trying to pretend this wasn't happening.

Azra raised her head as the swaying and bouncing eased off.

Tamasin was scared. She knew Rob was handling the flying far better than she'd dared hope, but she knew too well what the dangers were. A rain squall reached down like a grasping hand and Rob punched them through with the yoke pressed back and then the valley bent left and Rob bent *Rapide* into the turn with it.

'Contact!' Tamasin yelled.

She caught Moussa as he eased down out of the cloud and into the valley behind them, catching up quickly, wings fully back. Suddenly she had a clear preview of coming events.

'*Slow down!*'

Rob didn't know why but he knew to trust Tamasin. He raised *Rapide*'s nose, in the same moment pulling back the throttles and pushing the flap lever to the take-off position.

0644.

The flaps came out but for some reason didn't seem to want to.

Tracers blazed over the canopy and Moussa thumped past in a wallop of noise and they saw the missiles lurking spiteful against his underside with the little steering vanes sticking out and a sudden orange blaze in his jetpipes. Suckered, Rob thought, well done, Tamasin. Then as the reheat plumes stretched out dazzling towards *Rapide* Rob realized in shock that Moussa was actually trying to catch the executive in the flame.

It was the jet wake that was worse.

The nose wrenched up and left and the wing swung, the whole fuselage jolting. Rob rolled level and again the aircraft jarred bodily and then he was out.

Fiercely Moussa hauled into the turn port to come back, furious at the way *Rapide*'s deceleration had lost him his shot.

Rob reached to retract the flaps. He brought the jet out over the lake surface, low down with the radar altimeter showing 80 feet and reducing. Moussa was a hard dark shape way to the south, his wings sweeping forward. Rob peeled off starboard. An island jutted up from the surface and he banked shallowly round it.

'Felix, are you OK?'

'I . . . I'll manage!'

Azra took a deep breath. Rob grabbed the half-second's opportunity to look down inside.

Hydraulic pressure. It was into the red, the little

needle still dropping. Of course. The main reservoir was back in that tailcone and it must have had chunks of missile through it. Now they really were going to see what it was like to land manually. Of all the things . . .

When Moussa came back out of that cloud, Rob realized, he would have a lot less energy and a lot more manoeuvrability. He would have the measure of the executive jet, he'd be able to match his speed to Rob's. Rob was running out of ideas.

'Turn port, Rob!' Tamasin cried out. 'There's a side valley!' And it was running west, towards Turkey.

It was the narrowest one yet, its sides steep with the trees and bushes heaped down them, deserted like the last one, and Rob lifted the nose and increased throttle, wary of being too close to the valley floor.

'Where's Moussa, Tamasin?'

'Can't see him!' The F14 must be still coming down out of that cloud.

Angry air caught *Rapide* as it entered the valley.

Rob saw the VSI needle flick down, felt the floor sink under him, and he rammed the throttles hard to the stops as his last few precious feet of height started draining away. Full flap. The chart tumbled aside on to Azra's knees as Tamasin grabbed the yoke and hauled back, the way Rob was hauling.

The whole aircraft lurched upwards as they broke clear of the rain squall.

'Another bloody microburst!' Tamasin said, and let go the yoke.

Rob pulled in the flaps and eased back the throttles and the speed picked up again.

The contours swung them right, then left. Rob glanced upwards but they were still right down there, the tops of the valley half-seen in the murk. Wary of more microbursts, Rob lifted them higher. They reached 250 feet.

He'd done this in Vulcans but not within the confines

of a narrow valley with its top lurking dangerously in cloud.

Sickness was getting to Tamasin again in waves. She ignored it, reaching down with her righthand. 'Azra . . .'

Azra handed her the chart on its clipboard.

'He's in the six,' Felix said tautly. It was the best she could do with equipment she'd never been trained on.

It dawned on her that the valley had become a trap.

Rob had two choices: follow the contour or get up into that cloud. But if he kept along the contour, Moussa would catch him with the guns and if he tried upwards, Moussa would find him on the radar, stick with him right through the cloud and get him when he came out. He thought of the saddle, thought of that M61 20mm cannon.

The valley floor climbed and the walls bent sharply right. Rob rolled into the turn with *Rapide* bouncing around in the weather, and, as he did so, ducked a searching look back.

Moussa was rolling in to follow him, wings fully forward. Rob rounded the hillside.

A grey tentacle of rain squall groped menacingly from the cloudbase and he felt the jet sink. There wasn't enough room below and Rob firewalled the throttles with the fog of the squall blinding him and the swirling wind currents bouncing his wing, tugging on the nose, throwing the cabin around. Rob fought his way clear.

The saddle was coming up. Rob increased the ground clearance but he was in as much danger from Moussa's gun as he was from the rocks of Iran. Grey ground streaked below.

'Er . . . Rob.' Felix sounded mystified. 'I'm not getting any radar any more from the F14. Has the set gone . . . ?'

Rob took his eyes off the flying to look at Tamasin. Her gaze met his; her beautiful eyes bloodshot, her cheeks pasty. They both got a creepy feeling.

The saddle slid away under them. As Rob pulled back the throttles, Tamasin said suddenly, 'No! Climb, Rob, straight ahead!'

As he pushed the throttles open, he knew she'd understood something he hadn't.

Cloud swallowed them. Tamasin said: 'Come to 8,000, we'll be safe at that height. Felix, let me know if you get any more radar.'

Then Rob knew it, too.

* * *

At 8,000 feet Rob circled slowly back. They were still in cloud but Tamasin took a new satellite reading. She brought Rob back over Lake Urmia. He let down cautiously.

'Right there!' Tamasin said. She'd found their side valley again.

They went into it higher this time, the speed down to 150 knots; it still looked fast. They found it where they'd thought it would be, on the final righthand bend.

Debris lay sprawled in the long, angry scar it had carved along the flank of the valley. Rob made out one of the twin fins, on its side in a clump of twisted pine; and there was black smoke gusting in the wind off what must have been the engine bay. Tamasin and Azra craned over, breath shallow at their lips. Rob after the first glance kept his eyes on the flying. He'd seen that happen to too many men he'd flown with, years ago.

'They can't have got out of that,' Tamasin breathed.

Felix was crying silently, and she didn't care.

Rob lifted the nose and put the throttles forward. Power surged through *Rapide* and he brought the nose around until due west came up. Fog surrounded them and he glanced over at Tamasin.

'OK, you're the captain – care to take it?'

Tamasin smiled bleakly. She was fighting the shudders. 'No, thanks, Rob, you have control.'

EPILOGUE

Over the rocky brown landscape of eastern Turkey the storm had passed. Rob got the flaps and gear down for the long approach, but with the hydraulics out he had to hand-crank them.

Azra was back in the cabin and strapped in but she was leaning across to Felix, talking softly. The Dragon Lady's tears were sheer nervous reaction, and she accepted Azra's words of comfort gratefully.

As Rob greased the wheels on to the big runway at Diyarbakir he saw the big radar dish atop the E3, parked now with the other NATO forces' heavies. He wondered. But he was too tired to do much more, after he rolled *Dragon Rapide* past the parked jets, than turn on to the taxiway and follow ground control's directions to his own parking ramp.

'God,' Tamasin said disgustedly, 'who are this lot?'

There seemed to be half a dozen people waiting at the parking bay. One of them at least wore a flying suit, and another was a big man with white shot through his rumpled hair, dressed in blue jeans, a black shirt and a battered brown leather jacket.

'No idea,' Rob muttered, and ignored them, concentrating instead on shutting everything down.

Felix, patched up and back in control, strode down the gangway and unlatched the door. She gave a gasp as she stepped down the airstairs.

'Why, it's Mahmut! And Mr Kemal!'

Tamasin levered herself wearily out of the captain's seat. Despite her white face and red eyes, she moved gracefully through the cabin and down the airstairs. Rob released his seatbelt, parked his oxygen mask on the coaming and looked aft. Azra was hesitating nervously. Rob gave her a battered smile and reached out his hand.

In the dry warmth of the ramp, Azra clung close to Rob's shoulder. It was still early. In the clear air the jagged brown outlines of the mountains to the north stood out crisply.

She heard Felix saying: 'What about *Fang*? What's happening in Iran?'

'We're in radio contact with *Fang*,' Mahmut Barka answered smoothly. 'There may be some combat damage, but they're certainly flying and they should report pretty soon on the approach.' Dapper in his flying suit with the colonel's badges on it, he turned to Koz.

'Iran has declared a national state of emergency,' Koz rumbled, 'but the rising is over. Tabriz Three was the last base to hold out, but they surrendered twenty minutes ago. It seems they may have lost one of their key officers.'

Poor Moussa, Felix thought. He wouldn't be the last; it wouldn't be long before leaders of the *Shohada* and the Way of Faith would be stood against various walls in various prisons throughout Iran.

'What sort of combat damage did they say?'

A man with a mobile phone spoke to Mahmut before he could answer Felix. Mahmut turned back to Felix with his usual saturnine smile.

'We should see any moment now.' He pointed to the approach.

It was there, flaps and gear down, distant against the backdrop of the retreating storm. As she watched it, Felix felt a lump in her throat.

The bay next to *Rapide* was empty. The group of waiting people saw the damage to *Fang*'s wing as the jet taxied in. The repair would be expensive; but the expense in materials wasn't uppermost in Felix's mind as she joined the others, crowding up to the airstairs as Ron Harper let them down.

No-one had been hurt. Felix hardly believed it. She hugged every one of them. But it was Walter who gave Tamasin the biggest hug.

The big Turk with the white in his hair looked them over. 'OK, well, sooner or later you're going to have to answer this one – what's your position, all of you, with papers?'

Tamasin and Azra swapped baggy-eyed glances.

'My passport was taken off me in Evin jail,' Tamasin said with a hint of truculence.

'Mine's been taken from me, too,' Azra said. Her crisp English reminded Rob of their first days together.

Koz narrowed his little round eyes. 'So you need travel documents? Well, that need be no problem. Let me look into that. Colonel Barka, can you find a briefing room where we can all sit down and maybe have a bite of breakfast?'

*   *   *

At Mahmut's fighter wing they'd given over a small lecture theatre to the Dragon Jet crews. The light was bluish, muted from the half-closed venetian blinds. Everyone sat down while Mahmut went to organize coffee.

'All *right*!' Tamasin snapped; Walter was fussing. 'I'll get a check-up, but not *now*!'

'I think,' Felix said, 'we'd better all get a check-up before we go on to England – and then some rest.' She'd sat down with one arm around Tamasin's shoulders and the other round Walter's.

Two airmen came in with trays of coffee, cold drinks, and bread rolls. They handed them out. Norton and Harper were joking together but Rob and Azra sat wordlessly, close together.

Mahmut came back. A few moments later, Koz lumbered in with a sly grin on his face and a couple of sheets of paper with official-looking letter heading and lots of stamps.

'One for Captain Masterson. One for Ms Tabrizi.'

Tamasin looked at hers and her jaw dropped. 'Hey, what's going on? What's *Yüzbaşi*?'

'Captain,' Koz said. 'You're a captain, aren't you?'

'But mine's got *Yüzbaşi*, too,' Azra said suspiciously.

'It's got it in English at the bottom,' Koz said, and jabbed a thick finger at the forms.

'I'm not a bloody *Turkish air force* captain,' Tamasin protested.

'Well, just for the sake of argument,' Koz said with an ingenuous look that he didn't do very well. 'Just till you can get that passport replaced properly. Think of it as a safeguard.'

'For who?' Azra said shrewdly.

Koz turned to her with a big smile. 'Us. We won't regard you as being under military orders while you're commissioned temporarily as Turkish forces officers, but it may help to ensure that you are able to help us in . . . let's call it a debrief, about your experiences in Iran. You both undoubtedly have important information.'

'About what, for instance?' Tamasin said.

'Well, for instance, Hojatoleslam Rezania.'

'What's happened to him?' Azra asked. For all her antipathy to him, she dreaded the thought of him being arrested, jailed, maybe shot.

Koz grinned. He'd had more than one highly interesting report from his computer salesman in Shahrud. 'Would it surprise you to learn that Hojatoleslam Rezania called in the police to investigate an arms cache within the grounds of his house in Roudabad?'

Azra stared. She'd been toying with her blouse hem. 'He did *what*?'

'Or that a tape he had prepared has been broadcast within the past hour on national radio, saying that the *Shohada* and the Way of Faith are in error, and appealing for those involved in the rising to lay down their arms?'

Tamasin and Azra locked eyes. On Tamasin's face there was only incomprehension. On Azra's, with her wily way of thinking, understanding dawned.

'What a total *rat*! Tamasin, he's been playing with us.'

'Playing with us?' It still hadn't clicked.

Azra leaned forward. 'He took my passport deliberately! He knew that the more I felt trapped, the more effort I'd put into getting out of there. That was the whole point of those restrictions he made me stick to. And the washing I was stealing, I bet he knew all about it. Then when *you* turned up, it was a godsend to him – that made *two* of us desperate to get out. I thought it was extraordinary that he should have got *me* to keep an eye on you, when he must have sensed that I was already making plans of my own – that question of me being an English speaker was nothing but a red herring.'

'I don't understand.' Tamasin blinked blearily. 'Why?'

'What I hadn't realized was that Ardeshir never invited the *Yol* people – they just turned up. They'd constructed their beliefs around Ardeshir's preaching, but they'd taken their actions to a point way beyond what Ardeshir could agree with. But can't you see? Why Ardeshir could never come out openly against them?'

'He'd have been . . .' Tamasin tailed off.

'Right! A *taghouti* himself! And we've already seen how Darvish deals – dealt – with people who obstructed him.'

'God,' Tamasin breathed, 'Darvish would have killed him.'

'Exactly! So he got *us two* to get him off the hook.' Azra paused, triumphant. 'When we made our move, Ardeshir convinced Darvish – not that he took much convincing – that we were on our way to Tehran to warn the authorities. So Darvish reacted too soon and the whole of the rising went off at half-cock.' Azra bit her lip. She remembered some of the lives it had cost when the rising went wrong.

Tamasin turned to Koz. 'I suppose you wouldn't have any word on a woman called Rana Tezcan, who got shot?'

'Well, as it happens, I do.' The computer salesman had made a point of establishing a contact in the hospital. It was a good vantage point for finding out what damage was being done to the opposing sides' strengths. 'Seems she arrived there a few hours ago with a lung wound, but they were able to operate, and they think she'll be OK.' He saw Tamasin's sigh of relief. 'Friend of yours?'

'I'll tell you all about her at the debrief.'

Then another airman came in, this time calling Koz away to a secure phone.

* * *

'There are rooms here,' Mahmut said, 'anyone who needs to catch up on sleep.'

'Come on, Kept'n,' Walter said, and put a hand on Tamasin's shoulder again.

'I'm not sleeping with *you*.'

'No, you come with me to the repair shop.'

'Yes, come on, Tamzie,' Felix insisted, 'it's high time. I'm going, too.'

Hand on Tamasin's shoulder, the Oberleutnant steered her away towards medical. The Dragon Lady followed them.

Norton and Harper headed off for a beer and a sleep.

Rob turned to Azra. She avoided his eye. He studied her, wondering what she would do, and it worried him: in leaving Iran the way she'd done, she'd abandoned her family, abandoned her possessions. She was free, but what she had was what she stood up in. He moistened his lips, unsure how to express himself.

Mahmut was talking to a couple of his airmen who'd come in to clear the breakfast debris.

'It's going to be damn difficult for you,' Rob said softly, 'to make a fresh start with nothing. But you may have to recognize that now and then you'll have to grit your teeth and accept help when you need it. I know that won't come easy for you – but you can maybe start by being ready to accept help from friends.' He smiled, trying to catch her eye.

She raised her eyes to his, deep and dark and knowing. 'I know what you're thinking,' she said. 'All I have is what I stand up in.'

Rob was between her and Mahmut and Mahmut had his back to them, supervising the airmen. Azra snapped a couple of threads of her blouse hem. The ruby was the biggest Rob had ever seen; he hadn't the faintest idea how much it was worth.

'Family heirloom,' Azra murmured. 'It's legitimately mine. This piece alone is worth maybe a quarter of a million dollars.' She ran her fingertips along the hem. 'Altogether – well, I'd have to get a valuation . . .'

Rob stared. 'I only ever loved you for your money.'

THE END

FINAL FLIGHT
by Stephen Coonts

Tension in the Mediterranean. The fate of the world hangs by a thread as master terrorist Colonel Qazi plots to steal six nuclear warheads from the heavily guarded arsenal aboard the American supercarrier *U.S.S. United States*.

Jake Grafton, hero of the bestselling **Flight of the Intruder**, is back as commander of an air wing on the *United States*. While the ship is in port in Naples, it is stormed by a terrorist commando group. And Jake, past forty and recently grounded by night blindness, is the only man who can stop Qazi – in one last confrontation in the skies above the Mediterranean – one final flight.

'**This may be the best thriller of the year.**' *Tom Clancy*

A Bantam Paperback

0 553 17674 9

STOLEN THUNDER
by David Axton

You can push only so far before someone decides to act . . .

B52 Bombers, the kind that attacked North Vietnam from 40,000 feet, now stand obsolete in endless lines on the dry desert floor in Arizona.

Six ex-USAF personnel, including a woman pilot, hijack one of the B52s and set out on a 12,000-mile flight to Libya. The mission: to bomb a terrorist training camp outside Tripoli and avenge the murder of a young pilot whose father and widow are in the B52 crew.

In a desperate attempt to frustrate their mission, the air-forces of NATO, the Soviets, and Libya come to collision point over the Mediterranean. Will the B52 make it through to it's target and, if so, will its crew survive to tell the tale?

'Unputdownable . . . the story moves with an exciting pace to a sensational climax.' *The Log Magazine*

A Bantam Paperback

0 553 40616 7

PATRIOTS
by Steve Sohmer

Gorbachev declares the Cold War over. Germany is unified. Peace breaks out in Europe – and the President of the United States announces massive cuts of American troops in NATO. The Soviets, French and Germans rejoice – only Britain stands opposed.

But within the highest echelons of the American military, there is no joy – only outrage and a sense of betrayal . . . until a small group of veteran officers sets in motion a series of violent events calculated to bring the world to the brink of nuclear war.

In Washington, a young Air Force Intelligence officer – Lieutenant Christy Russoff – stumbles across the key to the conspiracy . . . and finds herself in a desperate race against time as the awesome strategic forces of NATO and the Soviet Union rise toward battle.

'A miracle of suspense, a mined labyrinth of electrifying politics, terror, and philosophy which will rank with the classics . . . a memorable and masterful novel.'
Richard Condon, author of *Prizzi's Honor*

A Bantam Paperback

0 553 17690 0